A Fantasy Novel-Type Thing by Jason A. Plott

Thank You

For Valliant & Tallman:
Cool people, cooler LARP names.

For Ma & Pa:
This is all your fault.

For Rachel:
All my love.

For You, the Reader:
Your faith and/ or unbelievably poor
judgment is appreciated.

Table of Contents

ONE	Disappointing the Furniture	5
TWO	Chain Mail Bikini	9
THREE	Making New Friends	15
FOUR	Sourire	21
FIVE	Something That Almost Resembles a Plot	29
SIX	The Garden	38
SEVEN	The Fixer	47
EIGHT	Comfort within the Chaos	61
NINE	The Sisterhood	78
TEN	The Boy Who Exists But Only Just	87
ELEVEN	Dirty Thoughts	95
TWELVE	The Quiet One Who Says Everything	111
THIRTEEN	Freedom	117
FOURTEEN	Lost in Familiarity	126
FIFTEEN	Crash	134
SIXTEEN	Darkness Personified	146
SEVENTEEN	Mistakes Might Have Been Made	158
EIGHTEEN	Smattering	168
NINETEEN	Glass Wishes	174
TWENTY	Wings of Hope & Sorrow	182
TWENTY ONE	The Girl Who Listens to Rain Inside Her Head	196
TWENTY TWO	An Idiot Unbound	207
TWENTY THREE	Three of a Kind	217
TWENTY FOUR	Success & Failure	228
TWENTY FIVE	Love's Lost	241
TWENTY SIX	Demolition	254
TWENTY SEVEN	Hooks	264
TWENTY EIGHT	A Matter of Forced Perspective	272
TWENTY NINE	Fortune Favors	281
THIRTY	Leaf Blower	293
THIRTY ONE	Keeping Promises	304
THIRTY TWO	All That Is Lost	313
THIRTY THREE	Heartbroken	321
THIRTY FOUR	Loose Threads	327
THIRTY FIVE	Daybreak	336

Ends.

ONE
Disappointing the Furniture

First came misery. Misery was followed by discomfort. Discomfort preceded resentment and misery, discomfort, and resentment led to terrifying rage.

What will you do?

Lree had dreamt this dream before. It was the only dream she had ever dreamt. Scenes changed and actors varied but the feeling was familiar and the question was always the same.

What will you do?

What did that even mean? What would she do? What could she do? And about what? The dream had begun to fade and the more she tried to remember it the less she actually could. Soon she was left with little more than a general sense of unease which only made her feel that much more miserable. She couldn't even remember why she had originally felt miserable—perhaps she was feeling miserable now only because she thought she had been miserable before.

Eventually she'd awaken from this disconcerting cycle of self-doubt feeling not only miserable but uncomfortable, resentful, and quite, quite angry. This time, though, it was different. She awoke shrieking.

Lree sat straight up and almost immediately slumped forward, catching half of her face in the palm of her hand. The fight had not gone well and it achieved nothing save for a swollen cheek, split lip, and a bit of crude otoplasty. Generally speaking, the entirety of her face ached and, upon looking at her hand, oozed. She wiped much of the alarmingly colored discharge on the rock she called a bed and in doing so spotted her needlessly aggressive wakeup call. A small, sharp, and evidently malicious blade of grass had managed to navigate a system of minute cracks in the giant stone that acted as her pillow. Snatching it from its tiny exit she glared at the bastard weed in contempt. Though her sight was still a little blurry and the lighting was less than ideal she noticed a bit of red liquid dripping down its tip.

What will you do?

Dropping the malignant sprout Lree stumbled to her feet and staggered out of her room into the sweet-smelling night air. The sky was filled with the sound of bristling leaves and the sight of twinkling lights and she hated all of it. She would tear the heart from this wretched darkness and watch it whither in the shining. If she could.

She set her misery aside and did her best to pass off her aches and pains as nothing more than inconveniences. With a heavy sigh she shuffled over to a particularly flat rock just outside the entrance to her room. Unlike other rocks that typically feature a bit of moss or additional rocks on top of them this one carried a change of clothes and several rolls of leather bandages. She hated that.

She tended her wounds first, resulting in the bulk of her small, deeply dark ochre frame being wrapped in thick bandages. She then turned her attention to the clothes, converting what had only moments ago been a rather festive party dress into a significantly less festive pile of ribbons. Lree continued to wrap herself in the remains of the dress until she felt only just uncomfortable. She hated that, too.

For brevity's sake, let's just assume she hates everything.

A vast field brimming with wild grass lay before the great bramble walls that surrounded the inner complex. This made it difficult, if not impossible, for Lree to go anywhere outside of a stone path that had been laid between her rocky home and a rough trestle that created an exceedingly small hole in the thorny wall. Beyond the wall she could clearly hear activity—a horrible chorus of laughter, music, and frivolity that caused her to shiver. It had to be coming from the courtyard far beyond the massive hedges that bound her to this dreadful place. Or that were supposed to bind her, that is.

It had taken her a long time and was excruciating work but it was now complete. Again. A narrow path had been carefully cut from behind her home to another hole in the hedge wall: a secret hole. She used this route to escape the confines of her cold, little cave and explore both her benighted prison and the shining beyond.

Unfortunately, her surreptitious excursions never lasted too long because the field that surrounded her home grew quickly. Lingering gave the passageway time to repair itself. Once the grass was high enough she would be trapped outside the wall. Horrible as it was, her cave was safe. Safer, really.

What will you do?

Lree ran her hand through her hair, an activity that proved to be quite the challenging obstacle course for her four frail fingers. She was sick of this place. Sick of the night—the oppressive and never-ending night. Mostly, she was sick of herself. Each and every resentment left a stinging scar on her psyche. It was her feelings of hope, however, that left the deepest, most painful scars.

It was by no coincidence one such scar that would inspire Lree to come to a particular decision, the quality of which would have to be determined at a later time. It is safe to say, however, that it wasn't a well thought out decision. Of course, this had never stopped her before.

Somewhere not terribly far from Lree's little stone house was a much larger, more important house almost bereft of stones. Within this house, which really was more of a grand lodge, up many flights of stairs and past countless rooms, we find ourselves in a gallery of sorts. Abstract sculptures stand like sentries before the portrait-laden walls. Said portraits are just as abstract as the sculptures, depicting scenes, landscapes, and possibly people in the most unusual fashions using mediums that may or may not be actual paint. At present, the most conspicuous object in the gallery is an enormous coat rack rocking back and forth anxiously.

"She's not there," said the soft-spoken coat rack. "She's not anywhere."

A chair at the head of the gallery cackled. "Where or where has our little flower gone, I wonder."

"I don't think she's here. Inside, I mean. She probably escaped through the, uh...maybe..."

"Don't strain yourself, dear—It was a rhetorical question. It doesn't matter. She'll be back. Our little flower is bound to me, after all."

The coat rack wasn't so sure. Not this time, not after the incident— but the chair didn't need to know about that. "Yes, mam," it said weakly. "Maybe I should check things out anyway. I can go find her, bring her back, and..."

"You will do no such thing," said the chair with sudden authority.

The coat rack stiffened—not an altogether unusual thing for a coat rack to do—and would have apologized had it not been interrupted. "Leave. Go about your duties. I will deal with our little flower myself when she returns."

The coat rack gave an awkward curtsy and floated out of the room, closing the massive door behind it. Moments later, the massive door opened again.

"You sent for me?" a new voice said. It was much different from that of the coat rack's. It was prim, proper, and quite deliberately seductive.

"You are aware of the situation," said the chair as more of a matter of fact than a general inquiry.

"I am."

"Fine," said the chair and with that the door closed once more. The chair was alone with its weird sculptures and weirder paintings. "Little flower," it sighed, "you disappoint me."

TWO
Chain Mail Bikini

There was something unusual about his new surroundings other than the fact that they were no longer his old surroundings. He was standing in, as far as he could tell, an endless field of uncomfortably tall, unnaturally green grass. The curious height of the grass allowed him to study it in a greater detail than he typically ever would have. It wasn't particularly exciting as far as grass was concerned but it was unsettling. For instance, as oppose to gently waving in the breeze the way proper grass tends to do, this grass leaned as if it was being pulled by a horizon-spanning vacuum cleaner. It did so without any breeze worth speaking of.

His interest in the grass and the breeze—or lack thereof—waned as the realization of his current situation slowly found its way to the vast portion of his brain reserved for panic and pants wetting. Wherever he was, it was not where he wanted to be. He wanted to be pretending to enjoy inexplicably named coffee at a local roasters, meeting new, local roasters friends while discussing important matters of the day that bore little relevance to those discussing them. He wanted to be at the big game cheering on whoever his school's team was. They were probably named after some kind of obscure animal, he thought, and they would have to be fighting—like the Fighting Tamarins or the Fighting Dholes. He wanted to be creating a new life, a real one this time, filled with acquaintances, small talk, and frequent casual sex. There was a very strong possibility that none of that would happen now though to be fair his current location had very little to do with this.

It was the sound of a crashing wave that broke him out of his regret-filled stupor. This was a surprising sound because, try as he might, he saw no sign of water or indeed anything else other than strange grass for miles around him. Well, except for that guy over there. Where'd he come from?

This was the first person he'd seen since finding himself in this rhinitic nightmare. Maybe he was lost, too. Maybe he was a she. He pondered for a bit on that idea—and what an idea it was—and began to walk towards her with foolish optimism. Oh yeah, it was definitely a her, he decided. Perhaps they were the last two humans alive. At first they wouldn't get along but then he'd rescue her from, I don't know, an especially nasty case of rhinorrhea and her feelings for him would slowly change. She wouldn't tell him this because, being the first person she'd ever loved, she wouldn't even realize it was happening.

Suddenly and dramatically he'd fall ill—probably as a result of her dangerous rescue from all that pollen. His fever would worsen during the night. He'd twist and turn, babbling incoherently and annoying her until she hears him call out her name. In a delusional state, rasping, he says, "I'm so glad I met you," and then falls silent, his lips forming a peaceful and satisfied smile.

Her steel heart, tempered by a traumatic past that found her tormented by a number of cruel grasses, like saw grass because damn that plant's sharp and evil, would begin to crack. She'd sigh and slip off her chain mail bikini as if it were silk. I probably should have mentioned that she had been wearing a chain mail bikini but now that she was naked—very, very naked and wearing nothing but nudity—the point's rather moot, isn't it? Anyway, she'd lay next to him and use the heat from her incredibly nude and naked body to keep him warm. Though still quite delirious, he'd feel her sweet breath upon his ear as she whispered, "Jesus Christ!"

The smell hit him hard and fast, knocking him to his knees as a wave of rotting everything washed over his entire existence. He covered all of his tasting and smelling orifices to no avail. It was horrible—as if stench itself was decomposing in a whale carcass stuffed with bad cheese and rotting fruit. And it was getting worse.

Through waterfalls of uncontrollable tears he noticed that the unvaried plant life surrounding him was trying desperately to regain his attention by dying, creating a path of decay that seemed to end with him. A small yet violent civil war had erupted in his head as panic attempted to prevent his body from getting up. He could see his presumably chain mail bikini-clad companion standing off in the distance. No. He would not allow a little funk to get in the way of a romantic interlude. This, sadly, had less to do with his immediate situation and was more of a personal mantra he had sworn to some time before.

Pulling both his jacket and his shirt over the majority of his face and taking in a huge breath of sweaty young man, he continued his journey towards the mysterious and doubtlessly beautiful woman by crawling along the path that had opened up before him. As he got closer his excitement brought him to his feet in order to greet his beloved with at least a little bit of decorum.

"Disappointed" fails to fully capture his true feelings upon reaching his goal. Instead, something like "horrified" or "wanting to run away screaming" would be far more appropriate. It wasn't a woman—at least, it wasn't obvious if it ever was one. It was most definitely dead.

"Hello…thing?" he said with a fair amount of hesitation. Though a bit vague, thing was an appropriate enough description of the monstrosity that stood before him: a massive, skeletal statue made almost entirely out of trash. There was an old wooden plank standing in place of its left leg and its arms seemed to have been crudely fashioned out of a mess of steel, bone, and rope. Even more disconcerting, they appeared to be inconveniently forced into opposing clavicles with a crude axe and giant railroad spikes, respectively. As if to preserve its dignity, it wore a ragged cloth around its waist, covering whatever naughty bits it hopefully no longer had.

Its jaw hung eerily to one side, held in place with what appeared to be the remains of a large insect. The rest of its skull looked as though it had been used as a piñata at a birthday party for a child who received a gift of striped socks instead of the puppy they'd always wanted, save for the eyes. The skeleton's eyes, that is. Had the analogous child received the puppy's eyes for their birthday it's doubtful they would have had time for any piñata fun, what with the police arriving to arrest mom and dad. Ah, what a birthday that was!

No, the skeleton's eyes—or, at least, its eye sockets—seemed to have been painstakingly hammered into a permanent malicious glare. They were filled with a black void that didn't quite feel natural. It was a wicked and cruel emptiness that served only one purpose: to crush souls. Or maybe it was just poor lighting.

At the center of this controversial work of shock art was a large, rusty metal plate. Held by industrial-strength chains, it hung atilt in front of what was supposed to be the statue's chest. The plaque was covered in deep scratches and gouges, however, its inscription—IN—was clear, if not necessarily decipherable.

Peering inside the weird statue, beyond the plate and what he had assumed had at one point been a ribcage, he found nothing particularly noteworthy. Just more precariously placed junk and a penetrating feeling of despair.

The short burst of energy and ensuing adrenaline rush caught up with him, making demands that his body simply could not agree to. He collapsed into an uncomfortable seated position before the macabre sculpture and began to feel a little ill. There would be no chain mail bikini-clad warrior woman ready to strip down and nurse him back to health through the power of nudity, just this idol of death. Though it had obviously been stripped down it was unlikely that it would be able to make him feel any better.

Again, the sound of a crashing wave. The disconcerting noise sent him to his feet with an amusing lack of grace. It still wasn't clear where the sound was coming from. Fields of grass to the left, fields of grass to the right, fields of grass before him, and whatever the hell that pile of skeletal garbage was behind him. He turned to look at the towering terror again and received much more than an eyeful as what was left of its face was now less than an inch away from his own rightfully disturbed visage.

It had started off as a normal, boring day. Avery woke up, rolled his slightly dumpy physique out of bed, and fell onto the floor where he promised no one in particular that he would definitely wake up again in five minutes. He kept his word, though twenty-seven minutes and twelve seconds later. Wrapped in a comforter that appeared to have been used to clean up a toxic spill, he staggered to the bathroom and gave the toilet a concerned stare. Though his digestive tract was in the middle of a number two emergency and desperately needed the toilet's assistance, this would mean that the comforter would have to come off and it was very, very cold. Eventually he compromised; he'd utilize the remarkable capabilities of the toilet to resolve the emergency provided he could wrap the comforter completely around it.

Minutes later, he emerged from the world's most awful tent refreshed but only in the figurative sense. This could be one of the many reasons why he didn't get invited out much or why he didn't have any real friends or why people in general tended to give him an extraordinarily wide girth. Today, all of that was going to change. He had been invited out and by a real friend. It was too soon to tell whether or not his presence would physically repel others but the odds were not in his favor.

Still, two out of three wasn't bad and today was definitely going to be a good day. Today was going to be the beginning of a new life. He just had to wait for it.

"What are you?" was what Avery fully intended on saying were it not for the overwhelming sense of panic taking complete control of his body. Instead, all he could say was "What?!" followed by a series of incomprehensible sounds that may or may not have involved some form of swearing. As he stumbled over his words his feet followed suit, returning him to the ground with a harsh thud. The bizarre idol shambled towards him with as much grace as a heaping pile of bone and refuse could, which is to say none. Losing its balance, too, it fell on Avery like a dead redwood falling onto a squirrel that just wet itself.

For reference, the average adult human skeleton weighs just under twenty pounds. A particularly large frame will weigh a little more but even if spread over an equally large area the effect of having one fall on you from a minimal height would feel like being hit with one of grandma's old goose down feather pillows. This was a particularly large skeleton and it did feel like being hit by one of grandma's old goose down feather pillows provided all of the goose feathers were removed and replaced with jagged rocks, sharp knives, and grandma herself. It landed with a hard crunch, violently pushing the air out of Avery's lungs and crushing parts of his body he had either ignored or simply forgotten he had. The pain was real. It really, really hurt and whatever hopes he had that this was all some deeply troubling dream were crushed by the remnants of what had to have once been one giant fat ass of a person.

As his thoughts turned to freeing himself, the grisly abomination lifted the bulk of its weight off of him. With a great deal of luck it managed to move its ruined face back in front of Avery's without causing further distress. Physical distress, that is. Psychologically the damage was irreversible. As he stared death in the face he instinctively thought of happier, more peaceful times. And since his life was an utter bore he chose to borrow thoughts of other people, mostly fictional. He thought of that time he faced off with a giant dinosaur on a rickety drawbridge above a moat of lava. He managed to outmaneuver the beast and cut down the bridge, sending his reptilian adversary to what must have been a slow, excruciating death. Exhausted but elated, he rushed into the next room to rescue the princess of the land only to discover that she was apparently being held in another castle.

He was just about to move on to World 2-1 when he was forced back into his new, awful reality by an overwhelming sensation of terror. He stared deeply into the monster's eyes—or where its eyes should have been—and his brain screamed and screamed and screamed. For the first time in his life, he saw nothing.

Unable to escape the nightmare's gaze he remained still as the skeleton picked itself back up. It then bent over ever so slightly to grasp him by the front of his jacket. This was it, Avery thought. This was how he was going to die. Far less spectacular than he personally would have chosen but now that he was resigned to it the idea of death seemed sublime.

It should be noted that this isn't really how Avery felt as he didn't know what sublime actually meant. He found the idea of dying at the hand of the elephant man's recycled skeleton horrifying in every sense of the word. And the worst was yet to come. The reanimated terror lifted Avery to his feet, let go of his jacket, and proceeded to dust him off. Satisfied that he was now clean (or clean enough), it smacked him on the side of the arm, nodded, and returned to its eerie, inanimate state.

After a series of involuntary eye twitches Avery realized he was standing. How this came to be just didn't make any sense to him so his body decided to simply turn itself off. Time seemed to dramatically slow down as he fell back to the ground, listening to the sound of crashing waves and drifting off into a safe darkness.

"Sublime," Avery thought to himself.

THREE
Making New Friends

While he wasn't a particularly attractive young man Avery Hall, to his credit, wasn't all that unattractive, either. Sure, he had the physique of a retired golf professional and when he sweat his fluorescent-tanned skin would take on an oily, iridescent glimmer but at least his hair was immaculate. Despite being an ordinary dark brown affair, every strand had been given a very deliberate part to play in drawing attention away from his pockmarked face and poor fashion sense—a truly mesmerizing performance of misdirection.

He had always found the task of matching clothing at best tedious and at worst devastatingly difficult, however, today he had managed to cobble together an ensemble that would hold up well enough for public scrutiny. He had found a relatively clean pair of cargo pants that had been sealed in his dirty laundry hamper, protecting it from some of the dirtier, more predatory articles of clothing that littered his apartment. Choosing a top proved more of a challenge than he anticipated, settling on t-shirt with the least offensive phrase he could find ("Lick Me").

Impossibly neat hair, clean-ish, unassuming clothing, and now no longer smelling like a truck stop restroom, he was ready. He checked his phone for the umpteenth time—no new messages. That's okay, he'll text soon.

A few days ago, before class, he had struck up a conversation with Avery that was completely uninvited. It wasn't a riveting discussion—at least, one not worth remembering—but it was a discussion nonetheless. As class started, he said, "Cool blah blah hey blah drinks blah blah blah," or something. The details were hazy but the message was clear enough: it was an invitation to real social interaction. They exchanged numbers and everything.

Avery was so nervous he walked around his tiny little apartment looking for things to avoid doing. Anything that involved effort was right out, so studying and emptying the trash were not viable options (not that they ever were, really). He could play a game for a while but then he'd have to get out the controller, turn the system on, choose a game—ugh, just the thought of it was stressing him out.

Evening fell and Avery's optimism grew into worry. What if he gave him the wrong number? Should he text him instead? No way. That's not going to work. He couldn't even remember the guy's name. He's sure he mentioned it but at the time it just didn't seem very important. John? Ron? Byron? Brian? Better play it safe. Just find something to do for another couple of hours and then turn in. It's no big deal.

Maybe he'll text tomorrow.

Despite his body's sensible protests, Avery picked himself up in an attempt to reestablish his situation. In front of him was the Ghost of Christmas Yet to Come, to his left was a field of grass, to the right was a field of grass, and behind him were rolling hills of grass. Literally rolling hills of grass. They seemed to swell and crash like waves on a beach. He was suddenly stung by an idea. Then another idea stung him. And another, and another, and another. Now overwhelmed with ideas—and no small amount of blood—he tried not to think as it simply hurt too much. Eventually, he realized that it wasn't his rarely fired synapses causing the pain but the grass. More precisely, the many blades of grass being ripped from the field all around him and sucked into the oncoming waves of greenery. Very quickly, they merged into a single gigantic torrent of monocotyledonous daggers that, naturally, was looming ever closer to him.

Panic and adrenaline returned with a vengeance, encouraging Avery to race past the deathly idol and down the corridor of decay as fast as he could. Later, much, much, much, much later, he would look back on this event as a major turning point in his life. First, only the grass that made up the corridor's walls was being pulled into the torrent. The trail itself remained undisturbed which was rather nice as it allowed him to continue living. Second, the corridor would also lead him to his first true friend.

He slowed down a little, looking back briefly to see the wave of graminoids begin to crest. He also saw that the skeleton was sprinting right behind him. This was enough incentive to run faster. At least, until he saw another wave form in front of him. What he didn't see was the large pile of hair running along the path towards him. Its existence didn't even register until it collided with Avery. The two barreled backwards, stopping only when crashing into the skeleton.

The sound of the waves was deafening. Avery lifted his head just enough to see the oncoming wave pass over him without slicing him into a horrific deli tray. The wave had been split in two by the corridor—any stray blades of grass that crossed into the corridor withered instantly into dust. The dueling waves collided into each other in a spectacular explosion of lawn trimmings—not that Avery saw any of this. He had been otherwise preoccupied by a blurry fist approaching his face.

It had started off as another normal, boring day. Avery woke up, rolled his not-quite svelte physique out of bed, and fell onto the floor where he promised no one in particular that he would definitely wake up again in five minutes. He kept his word, though thirty-one minutes and twenty-two seconds later. Wrapped in a comforter that appeared to have been used to clean out the interior of a dead rhino, Avery staggered to the bathroom and gave the toilet a scornful stare. Though his digestive tract didn't seem to care one way or another, here he was. Standing in the bathroom wrapped in an increasingly disgusting comforter. For the first time in as long as he could remember, he wondered to himself, "Why?"

"Stopstopstopstop!" Avery pleaded, pathetically fending off the flurry of tiny, four-fingered fists. Quite by accident, he managed to grab both of his attacker's wrists, temporarily ending the adorable onslaught. This allowed him to finally get a good look at his assailant—a small, frangible creature whose head appeared to have thrown up a family of charred raccoons. Its tendril-like hair seemed to be moving entirely on its own. No, not move. Intumesce. Look it up. It was the second worst thing he had seen recently and he feared it was setting a terrible precedent for the rest of the day.

At the risk of being repulsed further, he tried to locate the creature's face. Only one of its massive, yellow eyes was visible from behind a mask of rags that ranged in colors from I-hope-that's-just-mud-on-my-shoe brown to week-old-vomit-bag green. The disgusting assortment of cloth and leather scraps covered the hairball's entire body like a mummified treasure troll.

A muffled but distinctively girlish "Let go!" startled Avery, forcing him to immediately oblige with the request and surrender his face to another round of forced fist shiatsu. The pummeling continued long enough to make the transition from "this is really annoying" to "this is really starting to hurt" and was well on its way to "seriously, I'm bleeding" when the pummeler suddenly stopped. She—we're going to assume that pronoun is accurate—sniffed the air gently, at first, then took in a large enough whiff to make her spasm. Her sickly golden eye stared down at Avery in obvious judgment.

"It wasn't me!" Avery protested.

The creature jerked her head upward, bringing Avery's nightmarish follower into her line of sight. Without taking her sights off the skeleton, she pushed herself away from her pudgy punching bag and onto her feet. Her pudgy punching bag, failing to regain what he felt was his composure, politely asked, "What the hell's your deal?!"

She seemed to totally ignore him, refusing to remove her attention off the skeletal sentinel. It didn't seem terribly interested in her, though. It did seem terribly dead.

"Well?" asked Avery, struggling to his feet.

She hissed in his general direction without moving her head, completely locked down by the skeleton. The skeleton, too, didn't seem to move but that's really a more natural thing for a skeleton to be doing having been separated from its body. This uncomfortable standoff presented an opportunity that was obvious even to Avery. He crept carefully by the hair-thing until he was behind her then burst into a full sprint.

"H-hey, hey," she quietly yelled back at him. "Y'can't leave me here with...!" The sudden sound of bones cracking reset her attention on the skeleton, now lumbering towards her. She spun around and bolted after Avery.

"Wait!"

That wasn't going to happen. Avery looked over his shoulder and saw both the girl and skeleton chasing after him. And they were gaining. Curse this retired golfer's body!

Speaking of which, the abuse his body had been subjected to recently—being knocked to the ground, having a pile of desiccated garbage dropped on his person, and all of this horribly healthy jogging—had taken its toll. The girl overtook him, but not before thrusting her bony little elbow into his doughy midsection. Avery sputtered something quite crude and not at all appropriate for a high-class novel such as this. In an effort to protect the more sensitive readers and establish a foundation of dignity for the story, Avery's words will be replaced with something a little more "approved for children's television."

"You wicked little scamp! I greatly disapprove of your actions. Come back here this instant so that I may give you a good talking to," he raged between clenched teeth.

That wasn't going to happen either. Going back would mean having to face that monster. Everything about them—from the awkward way they shambled to their catastrophically offensive odor—violated her sensibilities. Just thinking about them overwhelmed her with a loathsome rage. She didn't just want to get away from them, she wanted to destroy them—to wipe out their very existence and even any memories of their existence.

Enough. She'd deal with them later. Right now she had deal with the voice inside her head.

"Come back," it said.

"Too dangerous," it said.

"Going to die," it said.

In truth there wasn't much she could actually do about the voice because it was absolutely right. Maybe she shouldn't have left the Garden. Maybe she shouldn't have even left the complex. Maybe maybe maybe.

Now what? Would she would return to huddle away in her cave until the fear subsided and the resentment returned? Would she forge onward, overcoming nature's ire and escaping the deadly valley? She had taken so many precautions—at least, she thought she had. Her route had been carefully planned, she wore multiple layers of clothing for additional protection, and, well, that was about it. Still, it was enough. Right?

Her layered armor had long since been reduced to rags. Presently, the only thing protecting her dignity and her life was the path. Surely it led somewhere, preferably out.

It didn't. The further she ran, the higher, more alive, and more aggressive the grass within the corridor became. If this was how it was going to end, she tried to console herself, at least it would be beneath the warmth of the eternal sun. It would be agonizing, of course, and absolutely terrifying but warm nonetheless.

She closed her eyes and tried to clear her mind. The voice returned, louder, angrier, and more ominous than ever.

"Cursed!"

"Coward!"

"Disappointment!"

Energized by a combination of anger and overwhelming shame, she gave up on giving up and quickly developed a new plan. She'd go back along the path, kill the fat guy, and wear his blubbery carcass as armor against the ceaseless, grassy onslaught.

It wasn't the best plan.

She had made it as far as pulling out an adorable knife from somewhere on her person before realizing that were she to carry out this ghoulish task she'd inevitably have to face the, ah, ghoul or whatever they were. They seemed to stick closely to the boy. Could he be some kind of sorcerer? Perhaps a really stupid one? And large?

How would she rather die: shredded into small pile of gore by a hurricane of razor-sharp grass or torn apart and devoured by an undead creature controlled by a tubby idiot? This depressing train of thought was temporarily delayed as the grass beneath her feet began to wither, restoring the path. Any elation she felt was quickly squelched by an unbearable stench—like a tidal wave of abandoned pet shops. This was followed by the sound of clanking metal and unintelligible cursing. She put her knife away—somewhere—turned around, and walked towards the stink and the noise.

She pulled the knife back out, though this time it featured an extremely faint but no less noticeable dark cloud about its blade. Worst best case scenario, she thought.

Reluctantly, the knife was then returned to whence it came. Wherever the hell that was.

FOUR
Sourire

Today was going to be a good day. Today he'd go to places he'd never been. Today he'd talk to people he didn't know. Today he'd open the front door and walk out of his apartment a new man.

Dear god this was exciting!

Avery grabbed a light jacket, stuffed his wallet and phone in whichever pocket was least sticky, put on his quote stylish unquote shades, swung open the door, and walked into an oddly placed wall. He took a step back and, thankfully, removed his questionably stylish sunglasses so that he could better appreciate whatever it was that had successfully managed to destroy nearly every trace of his enthusiasm. The wall—which was less of a wall and more of a large, person-like object—was completely covered in a garbage bag made out of a material clearly not meant to be woven. It was also very, very tall, easily surpassing the height of the doorway.

This wasn't fair. Everything was...today was...he couldn't remember. Gone were the visions of sitting around a smoky, uncomfortable cafe in a poorly lit art house sipping a bean-based drink he couldn't pronounce and discussing the merits of a Klimt over a Popova with like-minded intellectuals with fluffy berets and striped scarves. He wouldn't be catching the final game of the playoffs at his new favorite sports bar, either, and buying a house beer on tap for his best mate when his team scores a point or wins a goal or whatever is supposed to happen in sports. Oddly enough, the one ludicrous expectation that remained was that of bumping into a beautiful, mysterious woman. Together they'd embark upon a wondrous journey that would open their eyes to entirely new outlooks on life. Over the course of their many adventures they'd become good friends until one day...

"Oh, Avery, this wondrous journey has been so eye-opening. I wish it would never end."

"It doesn't have to, beautiful mysterious woman showing just the right amount of cleavage," he'd say, curling his mustache ever so slightly. Oh yeah, he has a mustache in this vision.

"It doesn't?" she'd asked excitedly.

"No," he'd purr. "I know of another wondrous journey we can

embark on. Upon. Up on?"

"Oh, please, oh please do tell!" she'd exclaim, now sounding like a character from a Jane Austin novel for reasons that aren't altogether clear.

Curling the other side of his increasingly suave mustache, he'd release a slight grin and ask, "Shall I...kiss you?"

"Oui! Ce sera merveilleux!" because it would be awesome if she was French or at least spoke French via Internet translation.

Slowly, Avery would lean forward so that she might be blessed to partake in the sweet taste of his soft yet oh-so passionate lips.

"Avery," she said with an accent from somewhere entirely else than France.

"Yes?" he whispered, eyes shut and taking a particular liking to this unexpected new voice.

"Your hair looks ridiculous."

"What?"

"Your hair. It..." the human wall paused mid-sentence to sigh. "It's really you, isn't it?"

Before he could respond an enormous hand emerged from the massive object and placed itself upon Avery's chest. The hand, despite resembling the size, shape, and texture of a catcher's mitt, was warm and surprisingly gentle. For a moment he was content. Then that same warm, gentle catcher's mitt of a hand shoved him to the floor.

Clumsily returning to his feet, he mustered up as much anger as he could to sputter out a weak, "Hey, man, what gives?!"

"There's no time," said the wall. The ragged material covering it fell, revealing a woman that doubled as a small storage unit.

Today was important and no one—especially She-Hulk here—was going to stop him from doing whatever it was that he was so determined to do. That's right, he would just look her in the eyes and order her to step aside. If he could, that is.

Looking people in the eyes was an activity he wasn't particularly fond of nor one that he was he any good at. His eyes scrambled for somewhere to focus on, awkwardly settling on her partially exposed chest and all of the surrounding areas. Whatever she was or at least had been wearing was shredded, torn, ripped, and cut, revealing a most perplexing build similar to that of an unfinished marble statue. Her body was covered in jagged muscles and her skin seemed to consist almost entirely of scar tissue. It was evident that were he to try to push his way out of the apartment she had it within her ability to break him in two then four then eight and so on. Two would have been enough however his imagination took a perverse pleasure in presenting him with horrific images of personal pain and suffering.

By now his gaze had lingered far too long on her body to look her directly in the eyes. He knew that she knew he was staring at her chest. The only choice he figured he had was to play it off as some sort of daze. His jaw was already hanging loose so he had that going for him. He'd just have to shake his head, look her in the eyes, and tell her to move.

Avery shook his head, looked her in the chest, and said, "Bwa."

"Avery," she said in such a tone that brought him to immediate attention. Finally he was able to look the muscle-bound blockade in the eyes. Though haggard, her countenance had been carefully sculpted into something rather handsome. Her eyes were colorless and sorrowful, her glare disappointed and frustrated.

"Look, I don't...I don't have anything. I mean, I've only got like a couple of bucks and there's nothin' in my house worth anything. Apartment. Not a house. It's not a house. I've got nothing. I don't know why I called it a house. I live here, yeah, but alone. Except for a big angry dog. I have a dog. You can't hear him right now. Or see him. He's asleep. And big. I...don't hurt me."

Nothing.

"I don't really have a dog, but I have to...can I...I need to go. Now. Can I just...can I get you anything? I mean, before I leave. I need to leave."

Again, nothing.

"Okay," he said, unnecessarily stretching out the O for several seconds, "so, I'm just going to go and I'll see you later?"

At this point he wasn't really concerned with hiding just how uneasy he felt. He picked up his minute market sunglasses and began, once again, to head towards the door. He'd just politely squeeze his way by the human skyscraper and that would be it—off to a new tomorrow or whatever. All he had to do was make it out of his apartment. He'd just have to pick up his exceedingly slick and not at all lame sunglasses first.

"I was the last one," she said, as if carrying on a conversation with someone else in the room—not that Avery was listening. He was too busy not picking up his sunglasses. Every time he felt he had a grip on them his fingers would pass right through the cheap, plastic frames. And then each other. He began to shake and, in doing so, sink slowly into the floor. Hard as it may be to believe, this sent him into a bit of a panic.

"So why...?" she began to ask before quickly stopping herself. As she watched Avery flailing wildly about and slowly fading away, she took a breath and steeled herself.

"Avery," she said again in the same commanding voice as before. "Look at...focus. Look at me."

Avery complied, though wild-eyed and crying.

"This is what you wanted, right?"

"What are you...what are you saying? I don't—why am I drowning in shag carpeting!?"

While she didn't respond in actual words, her expression clearly stated that she did not share his concerns.

"Help me!" he screamed, stumbling towards the towering woman.

"This is," she said, following Avery as he fell into and through her. "No. This...please. Go...all...quickly..."

Avery looked up at her in justified confusion. What was she talking about? Wait, was she still talking? Her words were breaking up—as was the world around her. If the incident with the carpet caused a bit of a panic, it's conceivable that this caused a rather violent freak out.

"Avery," he heard her say.

"...trust..." he believed he heard her say, though it might have also been lust, rust, or crust. It's not like any of this was making any sense to him anyway.

"...don't..." he might have heard her say.

His world disassembled itself into millions and millions of tiny fragments, all of which seemed to be dragged away in random directions until they were no longer in view. Though his mind was in chaos and his vision was fading fast, he realized that he had actually made it outside of his apartment. Feeling a small sense of satisfaction, he smiled a satisfied smile and then he was no more.

"...say hello," he didn't hear her say.

According to his watch—a cheap, solar-powered accessory won from a prize catcher that stole money from naive children and imprudent adults—nearly an entire day had gone by yet he hadn't seen any sign of night or indeed any change in his surroundings whatsoever. The sun never seemed to move from its position, causing his shadow to permanently cower beneath him. Avery had opted to walk the corridor of dead grass as the rest of the field was still committed to maiming him. As if to reinforce the idea that the universe was out to get him, he was haunted by two ghastly companions: one was a violent, ugly little tumbleweed with a bad attitude and the other would typically be dropped out of a tree to frighten kids during Halloween or other holidays if you were a truly cynical person. His fatigue and hunger only added to his irritability.

"Stop followin' me!" a voice exclaimed that was not his own.

Avery could feel the individual blood vessels in his temple bursting. "Stop fo—you're behind me!"

"But you're goin' the same way Ah'm'!"

Turning around to confront his accuser, he said with much frustration, "Look, you probably haven't noticed because of that avalanche of so-called hair in your face, but there are only two possible ways we can go: that way and this way." He pointed to and fro for effect.

"Then go that way!" she said, pointing fro.

Avery paused thoughtfully and looked at the skeleton beyond the girl. Quietly and with a new sense of calm he simply said, "No." He then straightened his jacket, turned back around, and continued walking down the endless corridor of stench and death.

This odd procession went on for quite a while with no change. Avery was now well beyond hungry and entering the parched realm of thirsty. If he ever got back, he thought, he'd never again open a can of soda just for one sip. He'd never again agree to a refill that he had no intention of finishing. And he'd never again use a public drinking fountain to wash his feet when they began to stick to his sandals. He'd drink like a freshman attending an out-of-state college, except he wouldn't limit himself to the least expensive canned beer the older students provided. Soda, energy drinks, sports drinks—even water.

Actually, maybe. He'd always hated the tastelessness of water. There was just something so sterile about it. Sure, you could dress it up as tea or some such concoction but then all you had was a tasteless liquid mixed with dirty leaves, like drinking from an open swimming pool in the fall. Still, he thought, a sip of water right now would taste like heaven.

"Paaaah!"

The sudden exclamation of quenched thirst caused Avery to stop and look over his shoulder. Several paces behind him the girl had unwrapped her swarthy face and was wiping a precious, life-giving stream of what he assumed was water from the corner of her odd, toothy mouth in what seemed to be slow motion. In her hand was something that looked very much like an old-time water skin.

"What are you lookin' at?" she asked in a tone that was equally annoyed and angry. Also—and it could have just been because he was exhausted—her words seemed, well, out of sync. As if she was being dubbed in English by an Italian production company. Whatever, it wasn't going to dissuade Avery. He needed that water skin. Just a quick swig would suffice. But he had to be delicate. Smooth. Charming.

"You know, I...I think we got off to a bad start."

"So?"

"I," he began. He still couldn't shake the feeling that something was off about the way she spoke. Beyond sounding like a made-for-TV street punk, that is. "I...would like to be your friend?"

Though the majority of her face was hidden by what might be considered her hair, Avery could feel the disdain and disgust emanating from beneath. In all fairness, he wasn't exactly trying his hardest to mask his own misgivings. She was young, maybe ten or twelve, and armed with a smarter mouth than his, fueling his resentment. This wasn't working. "What's your name?"

"Huh?" she grunted.

"I don't know your name."

"That's 'cause Ah hadn't told you."

Patience. "Okay, right. Could you tell me your name?"

"Why?"

It was a damn fine question and he knew it. There was no reason for him to learn her name as he was perfectly content referring to her as hey you, little bastard, or any other colorful insults that came to him. Time for a different approach, he thought.

"My name's Avery..."

"Avery?!" she yelled in what appeared to be actual shock. This was not the reaction he was expecting and wasn't quite sure where to take the conversation from here. His eyes wandered down to the water skin by the girl's side. Focus on the goal, Avery. Focus focus focus.

"Yes," he said in confidence but still with no idea where this was leading. In a condescending tone that would have insulted a toddler, he said, "My name is Avery and..."

"Avery what?"

"What?"

"Just Avery?" she insisted.

"No, of course not. Avery Hall. That's my…"

"That's a girl's name," she interrupted rather matter-of-factly.

"Excuse me?"

"That's a girl's name. You've got a girl's name. That's weird."

Avery snorted. "It's not a girl's name. Lots of guys are named Avery. My grandfather was called Avery."

"You mean your grandmother?"

"Yes. No. No! It's a guy's name, alright?"

Without looking at Avery, the girl whispered, "Lree."

"We what?"

"Lah-ree," she said again, stressing each syllable. "You wanted t'know."

"That's a dumb name," said Avery, quite noticeably chagrinned and completely missing the girl's sudden change in demeanor. "I'm going to call you Lee."

"You can't do that. That's not my name. It's Lree. Lree!"

"I don't care. I'm not going to call you by that weird little pixie name. Lee's a fine name for a boy."

"Ah'm not a boy!" she retorted.

"What are you then, like, oh, what are those things? Urchins. You an urchin? You know, like one of those spiky ones?"

"Shut up!"

"Urchin."

"Shut! Up!"

The urchin and the boy with a girl's name glared at one another with such intensity that were this a story written by a particularly rabid fan, they'd be mashing lips by the next paragraph. Fortunately, this story has no fans so there's no chance of such a thing happening.

The two were locked in mental combat, almost daring the other to make the first move. It wouldn't take much—clenching a fist or even blinking would signal the beginning of a battle in which there would be no survivors.

"Can I have some water?"

"No."

"Please?"

"No."

"It's hot."

"Take off your jacket."

"I don't want to."

"Not my problem."

This was hopeless. Then again, so was Avery.

"Please can I have some water?"

"No."

"Please?"

"Ah said no."

"Pleeeeeease?"

"Fine." Lree threw the water skin to Avery who had a terrible time catching it. Once confident it was no longer at risk of slipping out of his hilariously inept hands he excitedly uncorked the stopper. "Only a sip, got it?" she ordered.

Avery peered into the water skin. "You didn't backwash, did you?"

"If ya' don't want it, give it back."

"I want it, I want it." And with that, he took a swig. It wasn't exactly as heavenly as he had hoped, unless heaven tasted like a sweaty sock. If it did, he thought, a lot of people were in for a major disappointment. What if heaven was like a locker room for souls? That would make Earth a sort of gym and all of its inhabitants were simply filling the role of the out-of-shape, middle-aged office jockey trying to regain his 20-something body. This was getting too deep for Avery. He shook off any extraneous thoughts and took another swig of holy sock sweat.

"Okay, enough. Give it back!"

Avery returned the pouch to Lree via a lazy toss and sans stopper. Naturally, this caused its contents to spill out every which way. "Oh, right," he said, and tossed the stopper to her, as well. Not being very much of an athlete or, indeed, having any sort of coordination whatsoever, his aim was off by a couple of yards and the cap was immediately lost within the potentially deadly sea of grass.

"Idiot!" is what Lree thought. What she said, however, was, "S'okay." If there was any bitterness or frustration in her voice it would have gone unnoticed. Avery had already turned around and continued down the path. He had no idea where he was going and the lingering aftertaste of tinea pedis haunted his mouth, but he wasn't thirsty, no one was hitting him, and he hadn't fallen on his face in at least a half hour. The terrible tagalongs were still around, sure, but once they got out of this field they'd be able to go their separate ways.

He smiled. Maybe today really was going to be good day, after all.

FIVE
Something That Almost Resembles a Plot

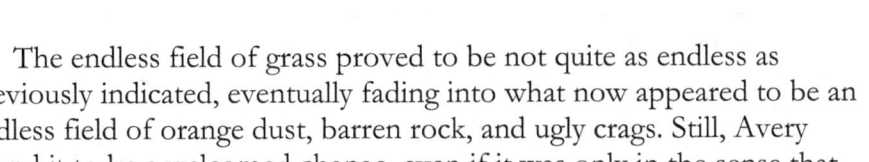

The endless field of grass proved to be not quite as endless as previously indicated, eventually fading into what now appeared to be an endless field of orange dust, barren rock, and ugly crags. Still, Avery found it to be a welcomed change, even if it was only in the sense that the environment was no longer actively trying to assault him. Now all he had to do was ditch these losers and go...to...place? Where the hell would he go? Where the hell was he now?

Aw, man.

"Y'okay?" Lree asked as Avery came to a sudden stop. She had genuinely attempted to emulate sympathy but the result was much closer to something akin to sarcasm.

"I just need a moment. I've got a lot of stuff on my plate right now and if I can just take the time to sort it all out I'll be fine," is what Avery thought he said. Instead, he just whimpered.

Lree came around from behind the strange boy and looked up at him. He was trembling slightly and wore a confusing expression that was crumbling quickly. "Are you...cryin'?"

"I am not crying. I am a little stressed out. I don't know where I am, where I'm going, or why I'm being followed by a couple of horrible monsters," again is what he thought he said. Instead, he cried.

"Listen," she began, reaching out to console him. Standing on the tips of her toes, she placed her shaking hand not that gently upon his shoulder and smiled a thin-lipped smile. Then she laughed and laughed and laughed.

"Shut up! Shut up, I swear just...shut up!" he blurted out through a steady stream of snot and tears. Avery jerked his shoulder loose and continued. "I'm lost, okay? I'm not supposed to be here—I don't even know where here is! I don't have a plan, I don't know what I'm doing, and I certainly...I don't...gah!"

Avery did actually have a plan, though it was only now that he realized its one glaring flaw. Originally, he was going to exit the field, ditch the two terrible tagalongs, and be on his way. He hadn't considered that the main reason he had any sense of direction before was because he didn't have much of a choice—the path only went two ways. Now that narrow path was gone and he could go anywhere. It's just...which anywhere would actually lead him to "on his way?"

He looked at his two companions with utter contempt. There was the skeleton, the ugly, creepy, useless bastard. That thing was really obnoxious—the way its bones popped as it walked and how pieces of it kept falling off. The way its skull hung to one side, making it look like it was constantly wondering if it should buy the four pack of toilet paper or the money-saving twelve pack. The four pack was cheaper, however, the twelve pack cost less per individual sheet, resulting in a nice savings compared to buying three four packs, none of which mattered because the only reason this thing would ever purchase toilet paper would be to wrap itself back up and return to its cursed sarcophagus. And let's not forget about that smell—that soul-crushing, mind-melting, downright aggressive smell that could easily be mistaken as an declaration of war.

Yet despite all that, the kid—the guffawing ragamuffin before him—was far, far worse. Children in general made him uncomfortable—always screaming, always laughing, always judging— but this one! This one just stared at him with her giant, jaundiced eyeball. A sedulously hateful, accusing glare made worse by the fact that he didn't know what sedulous meant. The other eye was also probably up to no good, however, the dense layer of black foliage that acted as her hair obscured many of her undoubtedly unpleasant facial features. Her smartass mouth was, unfortunately, highly visible and the stuff of nightmares. Resembling an ivory bear trap, it was unusually large and full of viciously pointed teeth. The fact that it couldn't seem to keep up with her own words was just loathful icing on a crap cake.

"This," he muttered, "*is* crap."

Wiping a tear from her eye, Lree mostly regained her composure and asked, "What?"

A bit louder and certainly more agitated, Avery replied, "This. Is a load. Of crap."

Lree was rightfully confused. "Here. You can have some," she said, handing the water skin over to Avery. "Ah think the heat's getting to..."

"Craaaap!" Avery suddenly sang aloud and horribly off key. "This is a loooooooad of crap!"

"You," he continued, knocking the water skin away from a rather startled Lree "that thing, this place, all of it. It's all a load of crap and you know what? I just don't care anymore. I. Don't. Care. Excuse me."

Avery's anger and bitterness and despair and abrupt musical inspiration subsided into an all-consuming fatigue. He was so very tired.

The only rest he'd had recently was that one time he fainted. His body simply couldn't take it anymore—and it wouldn't. It had had enough and, without consulting Avery, shut itself down. The staff was quickly ushered out of the building, the blinds were closed, the doors were locked, and the lights were turned off. There would be absolutely no overtime.

As his vision faded and his body fell, he was struck by a rather odd memory: the encounter with the strange woman back at his apartment. What was it she said? Something about…something. It didn't matter. Nothing mattered—not anymore. His old life was over and all of his carefully laid out plans for his new life had been rendered null. This—whatever this was—was his life now. This was his home. Avery slumped awkwardly to the ground, curled up into a ball, and fell fast asleep.

"H-hey," Lree called to him. If Avery replied, she wasn't able to hear him. He did scratch his posterior but it's likely that this was an involuntary response and not an act of communication. She stared at him for a while thinking about what had just happened. He cried, he yelled, he sang, and finally he passed out.

Tiny, crafty gears began to spin deep within Lree's impish skull. Slowly. "You 'wake?" she asked Avery, tapping him on the side of the head with her foot. Still, there was no response.

The gears spun faster and faster and faster until the friction threatened to set the forest of hair atop her head on fire. She had a plan—a scheme, really—and she derided herself for not realizing it earlier.

Lree grinned then almost immediately frowned. There was one fatal flaw in her otherwise fantastic idea. Truth be told, there were many flaws in her decreasingly fantastic idea ranging wildly in degree of severity but she wouldn't or simply couldn't recognize them. The one real issue, she thought, was that the idiot on the ground currently lacked the awareness necessary to either be tricked or forced into her scheme. Not that she knew how to do either which incensed her ever more.

"Get up, dummy," she finally said, opting to ignore the problem for now.

Unsurprisingly, the dummy did not get up. He just laid there, wrapped snuggly in his jacket, asleep. Lree poked him a few times with one of her bony fingers but he completely failed to respond. She took this as an invitation to carefully—and quite skillfully—remove his jacket and claim it as her own. It didn't fit quite right and it was far too warm for the shining but it was nice. Too nice for this Avery person, at least.

The jacket had a couple of pockets that Lree wasted no time digging into. The untrustworthy cur had layered one of the pockets with some sort of sticky trap, making it very difficult to retrieve her hand. The other pocket was a touch less sticky, however, and bore a curious bounty: a small, shiny tablet of sorts and a bit of folded fabric secured tightly by black patches of what appeared to be matted neck hair. Clearly these strange objects held value to him otherwise he wouldn't have bothered setting the traps, which is why she ultimately decided to toss them into a large, nearby crag.

Her thoughts returned to her grand scheme. She had to get the jerk up and onto his feet and clearly the "gentle" nudges and pokes weren't working. Lree was about to enhance her wakeup tactics with punches and kicks when a loud series of cracks, pops, and clangs prevented her from doing any serious damage to the unconscious load. Quickly, she jumped over Avery's fat, boring carcass and spun around to see the skeleton shamble near.

Her entire body began to tremble. "Stupid," she thought to herself. She had been so focused on the boy that...of course he would have had his guardian looking after him! Maybe he wasn't such an idiot, after all.

The creature drew closer. Too close for Lree. All thoughts of scheming and doubting and self-loathing came to an unexpected end, replaced by an irrepressible urge to maim and destroy. Now completely at the mercy of her instincts, she leapt at the unholy behemoth with her ominous, enchanted blade ready to strike. It's not clear where she pulled the diminutive dagger from and it's not really something worth worrying about right now. I mean, it's not like it's going to be used as a surprise plot device much, much later in the story so just drop it, okay? Jeez.

Lree was not altogether unfamiliar with irrationality. It was pretty much her forte and as such she had developed a unique ability to respond quickly to almost any precarious situation she faced. She'd separate herself from the crisis at hand, carefully evaluating the situation to determine the best course of action to take. Unfortunately, she was only able to do this after having already taken an action. Usually the least advisable action.

Her wild attack put her at a significant disadvantage. She realized this mid-air as she drew ever closer to her target. It's not like she'd actually be able to cut them and even if she could, how much damage did she really think she could do? She was almost certain they were already dead so killing them was out of the question.

It had been a dumb decision, yes. Absolutely. In retrospect, however, it would turn out to be rather fortuitous. She closed her eyes just before her blade made contact. The creature let out an ear-piercing scream and began making all sorts of unintelligible noises that sounded not at all pleasant.

Lree hit the ground hard—the result of her airborne momentum and voluntary blindness—but managed to quickly pop back up onto her feet without so much as an "oof" or "Christ, my leg's broken." The skeleton was still screaming which was odd in any number of ways. It was shrill and dreadful and becoming extraordinarily annoying. Cautiously, she circled around the shrieking terror to discover that the terror wasn't the one shrieking, it was their shield. A funny, potato-shaped shield that looked a lot like Avery, only much, much paler. Also, it was bleeding.

"What? How? How?!" Lree gasped, bordering on the territory of denial.

Avery screamed louder. His eyes were wide with terror yet he didn't appear to be conscious, making the whole scene even more unsettling. The skeleton released their grip, dropping its clamorous load to the ground where it promptly fell silent.

This wasn't good. Her plan. What about her plan?! What did that idiot do?!

Lree removed her brand-new jacket and cut off one of its arms using her petite though evidentially dangerous knife. Being all too familiar with dressing wounds she had Avery's arm wrapped up in a flash. The cut was superficial at best, which means either her aim was off (which it most certainly was not, thank you very much) or the skeleton had some astonishing reflexes and foresight (which was even more preposterous). There was an awful lot of blood, though, and a slight, shadowy aura seemed to enveloping his upper arm, both of which drew some concern.

"Stupid. Damn. Stupid, stupid," she spat. It's as if he deliberately allowed himself to get injured to mess up her plan *and* her new jacket! To be so vindictive even when unconscious—what a jerk!

The bleeding hadn't stopped and the description of the aura could safely be upgraded from slight to dense. "Jerk," she said aloud, now sitting back and staring at the pale lump before her. The word—jerk—bounced around inside Lree's head for a while, occasionally coalescing with thoughts of additional violence against Avery. Her gaze lazily fell upon him. He didn't appear to be mortally wounded yet he was certainly in significant distress. Even she had to admit to that it was pretty bad.

Lree, still fixated on Avery, punched the ground beside her as the tiny gears once again began to turn. It was pretty bad, yes, but it was also pretty good. In his current state he couldn't argue with her. He couldn't even speak! She could take him back to the complex in peaceful silence.

And this is where the reason for the qualifier "pretty" in "pretty good" becomes evident. There were a number of rather large flaws in her otherwise flawless plan. For starters, Avery was a gigantic load. Dragging the beached whale back to the complex wasn't going to happen. And even if it was the odds of him surviving the journey were bleak.

The most glaring fault, however, was standing right in front of her: Avery's animated abomination. Lree looked up at the manifestation of all that's offensive nervously and just in time to witness a small centipede skitter out of an eye socket and into another. The creature repulsed her very core. It wasn't that they were hideous, frightening, or foul-smelling—which, of course, they were all three of these things and oh so much more—but that they were malevolent, foreboding, and cryptic. She didn't fully understand it herself, but the monster had an aesthesis about them that both frightened and angered her. Simply staring at them too long caused her to break out in a heavy sweat.

She could always...no. Never mind. What was she even thinking? Lree returned her attention to Avery in order to recollect herself. He wasn't looking well. Not that he looked well to begin with but what little color he did have had faded into an unflattering shade of corpse and he seemed to be shivering.

She stood up and paced a very short distance back and forth. At this rate, she'd never be able to get him back to the complex. Not alive, at least, and unfortunately that was a rather important part of her plan. She needed help and that would mean returning to the Garden. Fine, she thought, but it wasn't an insignificant distance away and Avery would be probably be exploring the later stages of decomposition by the time she made it there.

Lree frowned. This boy, this fat sack of idiocy and annoyances ignited a tiny yet no less potent spark of hope from deep within her. He presented her with an opportunity she had never expected and would never see again. She couldn't let that opportunity die. Not just yet.

Now, whether or not Avery is actually dying isn't important, at least to you. Avery might be a little more concerned about his fate but he's in no condition to say anything about it at the moment so, you know, screw him. What is important is that the thought of losing Avery forces Lree to do something so reckless, so drastic, and so terribly irrational that describing it may be too much for readers with sensitive constitutions. So we'll just skip ahead to the part where Avery wakes up staring at the ground.

Avery woke up staring at the ground. It was still filled with rust-colored dirt and rocks, the latter of which appeared to be moving away from him. After a while he determined that it wasn't the rocks that were moving but he himself. Backwards.

Funny. He didn't feel like he was moving. He didn't feel much of anything, really, except for a throbbing pain in his arm.

"You fell," said a familiar voice rather unconvincingly.

"What?" Avery replied. He couldn't quite tell where the voice was coming from but found no immediate reason to care.

"It was a rock," continued the voice, a voice that now almost certainly belonged to the human hairball that represented at least fifty percent of his ire. As if to confirm his suspicions (or possibly fears), Lree walked into his field of vision. It was odd, though. She was short, yeah, but was she always this short? He felt like he was towering above her. Indeed, she was craning her neck just to look him in the eye.

"You started singin' and dancin' and...fell. Onto the rock," Lree persisted. It was unclear who exactly she was trying to convince. "A sharp rock. You got cut there."

Avery still couldn't get over how short she was. She looked like an angry ball of lint—a mental image Avery found hilarious. He started giggling to himself and simply said, "Okay." Then he drooled a little.

For a while they walked in silence—well, aside from the occasional creaking of metal and snapping of bone. It was on one such occasion that Avery became a little bit more aware of his situation: he was being carried like a sack of discarded body parts over the axe-less shoulder of the undead miscreation that made up the remaining fifty percent of his ire. It was cold, hard, and jagged but he was too tired and too weak to raise any valid objections. He could always panic, he thought, but found it much easier to pass out again.

Sometime later he awoke with what could best be described as a semblance of cognizant awareness. Lree was still walking below and behind him, but there was something else. Something in the corner of his eye that seemed out of place.

Flowers.

He moved his head to the right ever so slightly to get a better view. There were flowers of every color growing sporadically throughout the wastes, as if spring was showing the first signs of male pattern baldness. There were yellow ones, red ones, blue ones, yellow ones that looked slightly different than the other yellow ones, red ones that were nothing like the other red ones but kind of looked like the blue ones, and whatever the hell that one was over there. It was spotted with a sort of leopard print and that was just bizarre.

It's safe to assume that the scene before him was reflected on his far left, however, since he couldn't be bothered to turn his head to verify this, it could have been filled with pink, pygmy elephants and a talented troupe of dancing bovine for all we know.

Once again, Avery closed his eyes and drifted into unconsciousness. Sometimes he'd wake up screaming or cursing or whimpering but these episodes were becoming shorter and more infrequent—a fact that hadn't escaped Lree's attention.

It was during one of his quieter episodes of semi-consciousness that she said, unprovoked, "Ah' can get help. Thas where we're goin' now. To the Garden to get help. So...hold on, okay?"

"Yeeeeeah," slurred Avery, unabashedly delirious.

"Ah know this guy there. He's kind'a...he's fine. He can rejuvilate your arm for sure."

It was unclear if Avery was able to comprehend anything Lree had said, though one word in particular stood out.

"Thas' not a word," he said. "Rejuve-a-late. Re. Juve. A. Late." He snickered then giggled then laughed aloud. Just as quickly as his raucous outburst had begun it ended. He rolled his head around as if his neck was broken, stopping to look at Lree.

"Thas a cool jacket, man," he said with more than a little inebriation. "I've got a...I knew that. Hey!" His head dropped but he continued giggling softly to himself.

Lree shut her eyes and released a small, annoyed snarl. At this rate he wouldn't even make it to the Garden. Her plan—her tremendous plan—was in jeopardy.

What will you do?

The words haunted Lree as they had done for so long. This boy—this horrible, obnoxious kid—meant both everything and nothing to her. She absolutely needed him and hated him because of that. His skeletal guardian, too, despite the near-overwhelming desire to either run from them or destroy them, had become a vital part of her plan.

Carefully—extremely carefully and not without a visible expression of distrust and fear—Lree ran in front of Avery's guardian and held out her hand to stop them. Frighteningly enough, they did just that.

"He's not go'n make it," she said, now pointing at Avery. Y'know that. He needs help fast, so we gotta run 'cuz he—"

Avery groaned, shouted something that sounded like "battling cucumbers," then fainted.

"He ain't got much longer," Lree finished. "Follow me. Can you do that? Run with me straight to the Garden?"

The creature didn't reply or give any indication that they understood a word of what she had said. Lree was undeterred. She turned around, took a deep breath, and yelled over her shoulder, "Try ta' keep up!" And with that, she was off.

To both her relief and slight disappointment the creature started running and was soon in close pursuit. This encouraged her to run even faster, jumping over small crags, weaving around the larger boulders, and plowing right through the ever-growing patches of flora that weren't quick enough to do any permanent damage to her.

And it felt good—to run again and let the wind blow her hair back. The cool air brushing against her face seemed to soothe her to the point that she didn't care if anyone saw her. Not that anyone was around—or at least anyone worth mentioning. Avery was out cold and his guardian was, well, dead. And about to overtake her.

To say that this caught Lree by surprise would be a bit of an understatement. She glared at the undead minion as they shot past her, leaving a path of barren earth in their wake. For a moment, all of her fear and hatred and anxiety and deep, deep resentment temporarily found themselves impotent.

What will you do?

She pushed herself onward, hard, and eventually reclaimed her lead. Barreling through the painted wasteland, loosened flower petals filling the air with each carefully placed step, Lree smiled. Try as she may, she couldn't stop smiling. For the first time in as long as she could remember, she had an answer. Only, she had forgotten the question.

SIX
The Garden

Just as the grassy valley had slowly given way to a craggy wasteland, so too did the craggy wasteland yield to an altogether new terrain. This one was riddled with deep fissures, many bursting with orchids, lilacs, carnations, daffodils, irises, and other striking flora. Eventually the field grew so dense with flowers that Lree was forced to retreat behind Avery's macabre manservant—a position she was not overly fond of. Nothing seemed to escape the creature's evil aura and it disturbed the young girl to no end knowing that the desolation and ruin they wrought ultimately secured her safety.

Not that she felt particularly safe. The skeleton was still running at a startling speed and it took almost everything she had to keep up with them. Worse still, she had no idea how much further they had to go.

Now the cynical and, coincidentally, friendless reader might find fault with that statement. "Clearly Miss Mary Sue's been this way before," says the cynical, friendless reader whom will hereinafter be referred to as TheRealFan13 in lieu of his or her given name because they are most likely lauding their inspired insights anonymously on a message board no one even remembers . "She should definetly known how long it takes."

"It's rediculous! Does she have amnesia?! Is she stupid!?" they continue because no one is responding. "And another thing, how did she even make it thru the flowers to begin with? It makes nocents! Let's not forget that she would have died in the field of grass at the very beginning of the book were it not for the goofy skeleton thing. Seriously, the plot has more holes than a Wiffle ball." Swiss cheese, the ozone layer, a porcupine's inflatable girlfriend, or some other unrelated item distinct for its perforation can also be used to complete the analogy.

Well, TheRealFan13, despite your extraordinary impatience and obvious learning deficiencies, I'll tell you exactly why Lree doesn't know how long it will take to cross the field and even how she made it as far as she did. Just as soon as I stop crying.

Where were we? Worse still blah blah blah. Right. It wasn't that Lree was stupid or suffered from amnesia, it's simply that she never actually crossed the field to begin with. Her original route had taken her around the vast majority of the foliage. It was much safer but tremendously longer. With her bargaining chip bleeding out she had neither the time nor the patience to play it safe. Her priority was to get Avery to the Garden alive.

Satisfied? Well, tough.

It was later—well after Lree had lost all feeling in her legs—that the horrid sentinel began to slow down. "Finally," Lree gasped, embarrassed at her own exhaustion. Thankfully, neither the skeleton or their heavy load seemed to notice. Since entering the offensively colorful valley Avery spent much of his time moaning or sleeping or occasionally cheering on an imaginary team as they fought vigorously to take the championship. It wasn't clear what the championship was for as his cheers were filled with an ignorant cocktail of sports jargon—not that Lree would have picked up on any of this.

To their credit, Avery's bizarre creation appeared to be preoccupied with carefully navigating the increasingly treacherous terrain. The many small cracks and clefts that littered the landscape still grew both in number and size, forcing the creature (and Lree close behind) to detour on multiple occasions.

One such detour around a particularly deep ravine took them up an impressively tall hill. Reaching its windy apex—and her limit—Lree noticed something far off along the horizon. It was small, blurry, peculiar, and familiar.

The sight of that unfocused object simultaneously filled her with despair and rejuvenated her drive. For better or worse, they were close now. Soon they'd be upon the outskirts of the Garden and her plan would continue as, well, planned.

Of course, this was a matter of perspective. Avery, were he not preoccupied with nailing that seven-ten split with a man on first and third, would most likely disagree with Lree's assertion. Close, he'd argue, meant "right around the corner" or "just downstairs," not "in another time zone" or "need to update my passport."

But Avery was in no condition to argue. What little color once barely made up his spotty complexion had been lost. His incoherent commentating waned into total silence. He wasn't moaning, he wasn't drooling, and it wasn't clear if he was even breathing. Things certainly looked bleak. The fact that he was being carried over the shoulder of one of the Grim Reaper's long dead grandparents made said things look that much bleaker.

Lree remained steadfast. Mostly. She was concerned but not about Avery's condition. At least, not any more.

"So close," she thought. She watched the creature shuffle dangerously down the hill, leaving a safe passageway behind them. Lree figured she'd better hurry before the trail repaired itself.

It never did. Looking behind her, she saw that it never had.

Standing alone on the hill, Lree struggled to come to a decision that she thought had already been decided. It wasn't too late. There might be another way—maybe the old florist was wrong. He had to be wrong. Probably.

She looked at that strange, unfocused object again. It was so bright. It was so dark. Don't make me go back. Don't—

"Ah!" Lree shouted, swinging her arms about wildly. A small but no less dangerous armada of flower petals, propelled by a strong breeze, swarmed about her. Still swatting at the pullulating perianth, she stumbled off the path and fell backwards into a large patch of flowers. It wasn't long before her furious thrashing about sent her tumbling down the hill like an angry, cursing bowling ball of pain and regret.

Thick brambles, thorny vines, sticky petals—nothing slowed her down. Indeed, had she not collided with a conveniently placed boulder she might have kept rolling right into the ravine.

Disoriented, enraged, and in a considerable amount of discomfort, Lree found it impossible to think. All of her actions were now being driven entirely by instinct and adrenaline. She tore at the plants, kicked at their roots, and bit their stems—none of which did any good. She was quickly overwhelmed and entangled. It was becoming difficult to breathe and she suddenly felt very, very tired. Still, she struggled.

Calm yourself. Rest. Be free.

"Free," she thought, thrashing about less and less. That *is* what she wanted, right? To be free? Sure, it would have been better had she achieved freedom in a far less terrifying and painful way but it wasn't at all surprising.

The vines wrapped around her tiny frame tighter and tighter, slicing her flesh as they pinned her to the ground. It hurt. It hurt so much and yet no tears accompanied her anguish. Soon it would be over and she would be free.

Free.

But also dead.

Hold on, that's dumb. This is dumb. No...

Lree's body jerked upward from its center and she screamed a horrible, guttural scream as the roots and stems and vines tried their damndest to hold her to the ground. Soon her body had formed a near perfect arch and the screaming quickly turned to unintelligible swearing. With a hard yank the entangling foliage gave way and slithered off of her.

She was free—even if every part of her body stung or ached. Even if her new, one-armed jacket had been shredded and stained with her blood. Even if her body was still bent in the most impossible way. She was free and it felt wonderful.

For a time.

Her elation fell quickly into dread and then panic as she realized just who had rescued her.

"Put m'down! Let go! Let go!" she cried angrily, punching and kicking her undead savior. The majority of her aimless attacks failed to make any contact, however, one lucky kick did just manage to catch the creature in their already loose jaw. This seemed to be enough for them to release their grip. Lree hit the ground with a thud then scuttled a good distance away from the abomination.

"Don' you ever touch me!" she yelled as she held herself in a vain attempt to stop shivering. "Ever! Never! Ah'll...kill you! Don't think Ah won't!"

The sentinel, with Avery still slumped over their supposed shoulder, didn't respond. They didn't even look at Lree. Instead, they turned around and shuffled back to their original path. She glared at the monster hoping to will them out of existence. As if fueled by that hatred, she picked herself up and followed the creature. Though now at a much greater distance than before.

"So close," she told herself.

Again, this was all a matter of perspective.

The blurry, peculiar object that had been loafing about the horizon gradually came into focus: an enormous archway shaped like an ear that had been chewed on and spat out by some sort of crude, ear-munching monster. The bizarre structure prefaced an even more bizarre bridge of sorts that crept across a wide ravine—but that's not important right now. What is important is that Lree, Avery, and Avery's decomposed chauffeur were now upon the Garden.

Lree had visited the Garden during her many excursions into the shining as the bustling shanty town always offered something new and interesting to see. Featuring a unique mix of smashed debris and colorful foliage, it was full of cobbled together homes, shops, and other edifices one would expect a generic fantasy town to have. It just so happened to look as if a massive botanical garden had been dropped on top of a trailer park from a particularly high altitude.

There was, of course, a more literal reason why the town constantly offered up new and interesting things to see. As if instigated by the plot, the delightful little trash town came under the sudden assault of a devastating tremor. Many of the less-than-prepared structures—the homes, shops, and other types of edifices one would expect a generic fantasy town to have—crumbled instantly while the sturdier buildings toppled comically onto one another until there was next to nothing standing. Curiously, the residents didn't seem to mind much. They barely glanced at one another with a "what're gonna do?" shrug before beginning the laborious task of reassembling their ugly, beautiful town.

Between the destruction and the residents' hilarious catharsis, Lree couldn't help but smile. The only real downside to the recurring restructuring was that it made navigating the town nearly impossible. As the Garden was constantly rebuilding itself there were very few landmarks and maps were enormously useless.

"Hey," she called to the nearest stranger within earshot, "Ah'm lookin' for a florist."

The first person that turned around began to approach her, paused, then scampered away without saying a word. The second person did the same thing, though much quicker. This pattern repeated itself twice more before Lree realized that she had somehow forgotten a very, very important detail.

"Look," she said, turning around to address the eldritch monstrosity and their spoiling cargo, "y'all need ta' hide or something."

Neither Avery's guardian nor Avery replied or, indeed, made any effort to acknowledge that they were listening. Or that they were alive.

"Just...go. Behind that pile of junk over there, okay?" she continued, gesturing the creature to move. "No one's gonna wanna talk to me with y'all freaks hanging over me."

To her mild surprise, the creature complied. They slinked behind a decently sized pile of refuse and placed some flowers onto their head (which promptly died).

Ignoring this, Lree scouted the area for someone who she could catch off guard. There were a couple of potential targets, however, only one of them was wearing a nice pair of shoes.

"Hey!" she called out again. "You, cart guy! With the shoes!"

True to his name, the man was pushing a makeshift cart loaded with parts of his fallen home. He probably had a name but his role in the story isn't significant enough to warrant any creative energy being spent to come up with one. He's just going to get knocked out and robbed of his footwear at the end of this conversation anyway so let's just keep calling him cart guy.

"Me?" he asked, looking first at Lree and then his shoes.

"Yeah, hey, Ah'm lookin' for a florist. Seen one?"

The gentleman sat his cart down to come closer—only to back away again.

"Hoo, ya', but sure ya' be needin' a florist? Yer lookin' rough, sister. There's a bathhouse 'round 'ere somewheres. Or there was."

"What?" Lree asked, more than a bit offended at the suggestion. As she stood there, mouth agape, her eyes involuntarily scanned the area. Despite the fallen buildings, massive refuse piles, and cheerless vagrants that populated the town, the Garden was remarkably clean. Even the soon-to-be-a-victim before her was immaculate—handsome even. Nicely combed hair, clean shaven, and his colorful rags had clearly been pressed.

"Ah'm not from around here," she began.

"Ah' c'n tell," he interrupted.

"But Ah heard," she continued, fighting back the urge to stab the man in the head and walk away with his nice shoes, "about this florist. Maybe you know 'im?"

The well-dressed ragamuffin seemed like he was about to answer her when he stopped to sniff the air. His face caved in upon itself. "You ripe, sister! Hoo!" He waved his hand about to further emphasize his point.

"That's..." not me, it's this gigantic, undead monster lurking in the rubble behind me waiting to carve out my soul as well as yours and everybody else's in town. Lree thought better. "...me. Sorry. Like Ah' said, Ah'm not..."

"...from 'round here, right," he finished, a smile returning to his face. "Ah didn' mean nothin' by it, sister. T'be straight with you, it ain't dat bad. Just, you know, the town has a smell, right? You just don' have it yet. You will, 'doh so is' okay."

Though spoken by the drunken result of a one-night stand twixt a stereotype and a colloquialism, there was some truth in his words. The Garden did have a smell—a pungent potpourri that hung heavy in the air, clinging to everything and everyone like a celebrity-branded perfume. This was, of course, due to the flowers. Those who lived in the Garden harvested flowers, cooked with flowers, and ate flowers. They also wore flowers, bathed with soaps made of flowers, decorated their temporary homes with flowers, and warmed themselves by fires fueled by flowers.

Medicines—as concocted by the florists—were made wholly with flowers. This made the florists quite highly regarded despite being completely ineffective in treating something like anaphylaxis.

As much as she detested the odor, Lree had hoped the belligerent fragrance would mask the skeleton's own offensive aroma quickly. She glanced back to see that the flowers in the debris pile Avery's minion had been hiding behind had all wilted. Still, the aggressively floral scent that blanketed the town was unrelenting. There was a good chance that the creature would be deodorized by the time they left—which was hopefully going to be very soon.

"Now le'see," cart guy continued, "you was lookin' for…"

"A florist."

"Go florists! Goooooooooaaaaaaal!" cheered the wilted refuse pile.

"What was that?"

Lree, shaken, answered somewhat honestly, "Ah have no idea."

"It came from ova' behind dat huge heap o' dead flowers. Sounded like "florists gold" or some'fin."

"Naw, that...was...wind."

The gentleman looked around and then back at Lree. The two stared at each other just long enough to be uncomfortable. Finally, Lree continued with her original question. "Have you seen a florist 'round here?"

"Well, Ah know a bit of floristry!" the man replied, excited.

"Great. Great. But Ah need...Ah'm lookin' for a certain florist. He's uh...he's different.

"Oh, Ah'm different. You should see what Ah..." Cart guy paused and seemed to turn a bit pale. "Wait, y'don' mean *that* florist, do ya'?"

"Ah don't know. Maybe?" She really didn't have time for this. "Who's *that* florist?"

The man with the nice shoes cringed. "The one with, Ah, with the arms?"

Yep. *That* florist.

"Where is he?"

"Ah don' feel right tellin' ya. That thing—that whatever—he's cursed!"

Lree looked around for anyone—anything—else that might be able to help. She saw nothing aside from a literary footnote stating "people in background—description unnecessary."

"Ah need to see him and only him, right? Truth is...Ah'm cursed, too. No matter what Ah do, Ah can't get shake this...smell."

Lree paused, unsure whether or not cart guy was buying any of this. Just in case, she added, "Ah stink, okay. Ah heard that only he can un-stink me. Ah guess."

"You *are* smelly. Like, real smelly. No bath in the world gonna un-stink you, sister, but Ah didn' wanna say as much. Be rude."

"Why?" She thought to herself. "Why am I listening to this? Why am I putting up with this?" She thought about the monster hiding behind her. She thought about Avery slowly dying on the monster's shoulder. She thought about cart guy's shoes and how they really were nice. Too nice for this nameless character, that's for sure.

"Ya' got some pretty small feet," she said.

"Yeah?"

"So, *do* you know where *that* florist is?"

"Oh yeah, yeah. Where was dat scary florist? Ah know, is jus hard to 'memba when you so cold, you know?" he said rather theatrically and staring at Lree's jacket. Of course, by now it was less of a jacket and more a thick halter top accented with trendy tears. And blood but he didn't need to know that.

"Maybe this'll help," she said, handing the "jacket" over without hesitation.

"Ah reckon dat'll do fine like," he replied excitedly. Now sporting an exceedingly feminine top that was fifty years too young for him, he cackled, "Yer in luck! Look dare." He pointed towards a massive hill of beautiful flowers and less beautiful bricks off in the distance. "See dat?

Dat florist's place is prob'ly 'round there. If you don see no one, das where you find him."

"You sure is lucky, yeah," he continued. "Befo' da boom, dar was buildin's all ova da place. You get lost just lookin' dare."

Lree didn't disagree, but she didn't dare say so for fear that it might encourage another conversation with this terrible character. No matter how many times she had visited this particular florist she had never been able to learn her way to his shack. Sometimes she couldn't find him at all. Now, after having just arrived, a direct path had opened up that lead straight to him—like the path that led her to safety out of the valley. This wasn't luck.

Once more, she glanced at the wilted pile behind her. This wasn't luck at all.

"Wells, glad Ah c'd help," said the man, heading back to his cart with a weak wave.

"Right," Lree replied, not really paying attention. She was too preoccupied looking for something on the ground.

"An y'be careful, now, 'kay? Dat guy…he's crARG!" was, thankfully, all cart guy could say before being interrupted by a brick to the back of the head.

Lree strode up to the unfortunate character, half-heartedly looking around for whatever deviant could have thrown the brick. She took her jacket back and liberated the man's shoes from his unusually small feet under the logic that he was no longer using them. Also, since she had lost her own footwear out in the valley, she really needed a new pair. They were a little larger than she had anticipated, but it was too late now and they were mighty nice.

"C'mon, let's go," she called back to the skeletal guardian. "And stay close," she said.

"But not too close," she quickly added.

SEVEN
The Fixer

The novelty of waking up in strange new places had very quickly lost its appeal. Wherever he was this time was somehow even worse than wherever he was last time. It was damp and dark and unpleasant. It was also suffocating and not a little bit alarming. His heart, already working overtime given his woeful physical condition and all that healthy running about earlier, beat harder and harder. To his amazement (and confusion), he wasn't experiencing the early stages of cardiac arrest but rather a feeling that could almost be described as excitement.

Avery groped about the darkness, hoping to find a light switch or maybe a doorknob. His experience groping about dark places, however, seldom led to anything pleasant. At best he might find something sticky. At worst a restraining order.

After an uncomfortable amount of time molesting nothing in particular his curious fingers came upon what felt to him to be a rocky wall. Cautiously, he followed the wall until he came upon a strange blue light. As he grew closer, the light flickered and danced about wildly, soon growing so bright that he had to look away. When he looked back, he found himself in an opulent hallway. At least, it had been opulent. The more he tried to focus on his surroundings the more impossible it became to define them. That thing over there, for example, was probably a chair or a statue or a goat. Or maybe a statue of a goat sitting in a chair. It was definitely red. The entire hall was red. Excessively so—as if it had been painted using a disturbing combination of a large cow and an industrial wood chipper.

Avery turned to leave when he was stopped by a tall, intimidating silhouette. It was as familiar as it was unsettling. The shadowy figure gestured wildly at him, increasing his discomfort significantly. He could feel his body backing up ever so slowly despite the fact that he did not tell it do so.

"You mustn't," he felt someone say. It was a soundless voice, equal parts pleading and menacing. The dark blur seemed to shrink in size yet took up more and more of his field of vision until all he could see was nothing at all. He felt something grab his arm which otherwise would have startled him were it not for the fact that he was plenty startled

already.

"End this," he felt it say. He then screamed as a burning pain shot through his arm. His terrible, high-pitched shrill soon faded, as did every other sound.

Blind and deaf, he felt something push him to the floor. No, not push. Pull. There wasn't an impact, but the floor was very cold and very hard. Slowly, his vision returned—though it was difficult to tell to what extent as everything was masked in a thick haze. He rolled his head over in an attempt to inspect his aching arm but was met with an altogether new face violating all boundaries of personal dominion.

"RAAAAAAARG!" said the face in a manner that was not at all acceptable with most common forms of greetings. Avery's body reacted accordingly, sending him tumbling off the table and onto the floor. Again.

"Not dead."

"Probably is now," followed another voice. Avery knew that voice— that loathsome, acerbic voice that wasn't so much spoken out of a mouth as it was violently ejected out of a murky pit.

The brat—the one with the hair. Of course.

Avery jumped to his feet, an action that proved to be a poor decision based on one's own perspective. He smashed the top of his skull into an absurdly low rafter. This, in turn, caused him to stumble backwards over a chair. The chair knocked over a small table that was holding several misshapen bowls of substances that weren't at all pleasant, as Avery soon discovered.

"Awfully twice of you to redoctrinate my horse, yes?"

"What is your problem?" Lree asked. Embarrassed? Annoyed? Vindicated? Who could tell. "Stop wreckin' his horse!"

Avery felt horrible though not about wrecking the horse. To hell with the horse. No, he was shivering, lightheaded, and his arm was throbbing. His new position—wedged between a fallen table and a wall—did grant him a bit more light, which is how he discovered that his arm was also caked in dried blood and smoking ever so slightly. These revelations went over as well as one might expect them to.

"Varied swell," the unfamiliar voice said, its owner fortuitously hidden in the shadows. "Bacon the tablet with you."

Avery heard none of this and didn't notice Lree helping him up— though we are using a very loose definition of the word help here. Working exclusively with Avery's deadweight, she forced him into the table and then rolled him clumsily on top of it.

"What the hell happened to my arm?!," he asked anyone, still screaming.

"Don' worry about it," Lree said, clearly not worrying about it.

"Don't worry...?! My arm!"

"Yeah, great, your arm and 'e's gonna fix it so shut up."

Before Avery could ask who 'e was, 'e slinked into view. Overcome with panic, confusion, and disgust, Avery could only muster a weak, "Buh?"

No amount of flowery verse could possibly improve the description of the creature that again was hovering disquietingly close to Avery's face. It was, without any exaggeration, the most disgusting thing Avery had seen since his return to the table: a gigantic ball of snot wearing a coat made of week-old road kill. Its head, he guessed, consisted of two large, undulating black orbs that swam about its so-called face like a couple of rotten eggs drunk off of children's cough syrup. There was no nose to speak of, however, it did have a long, arched slit that seemed to form an ever-smiling mouth. Kind of.

This was an abomination created to be an instrument of revenge by some mad scientist. Or worse still, and as Avery correctly suspected, this was the mad scientist himself.

"You colding?" it asked sincerely.

"Wha—yes," Avery responded, rather unsure how one was supposed to respond to a repulsive wad of glop. "Freezing, actually."

"I've some lonely blankets 'round from wares..."

"Did you say blankets?" he asked, surprised and naively hopeful.

"Yeah."

There was a long, blanket-less pause.

"Now," he continued, "let's mistake a look on you." As he said this, one of his eyes wandered off to some unspeakable part of its jellied body. "Oh, there it went. No two worries—little be back in time."

Avery has more than two worries. "Whoa, whoa...in time for what?" he said as his situation was starting to become clearer to him. "I'm okay, okay? Don't worry yourself about me, I'm—" He tried to push himself off the table but his arm crumbled almost instantly. "Damn," he cried, falling back upon the table.

"What a difficultist life you must have been," said the pear-shaped mucus plug.

"What a what? And what's this "must have?" Avery gasped. "Look, I'm..."

"Bessie," interjected Lree. "His name's Bessie." Avery tried to correct her but was stopped by a less than gentle smack to the side of the head.

"That's as a girl's manger, isn't?"

"You have no idea how much it bothers me that I'm starting to understand you."

"Stuff it, Bessie," Lree said. "It's fine. It's a good name."

"Yeah, for a cow," Avery protested, only to be protested himself by another smack to the head.

"Cow, girl, mausoleum, doesn't splatter. I fix them tall."

"Did you say...?"

"I don't know. Moldy when I speak."

"What?"

"Lots your memory, too? You dude knee fixin'."

"It doesn't matter," Lree interjected. "Look, Lupus, just fix 'im, okay?"

Avery snapped. "Why do you keep using that word? I don't need to be fixed! You don't fix people. That's just...not how you say that, alright?"

Wait a second.

"Lupus?" Avery added.

"Yeah," replied the phlegm wad.

"Lupus," Avery said again, this time as straight as he possibly could. "You're name is...Lupus."

"Yeah."

"Name. Your name. Lupus."

"Yeah."

Avery paused for a moment, then asked, "Lupus?"

"Yeah."

"You're called Lupus and you're...a doctor?"

"Beg your garden?" asked Lupus, though it was entirely possible he was responding to some other, unheard voice.

"A doctor. You," Avery scrambled for words, "heal people?"

The sticky creature laughed, sending little ripples throughout its nauseating body.

"No. Justin old forest fixin' those..."

"Please stop saying that."

"Yeah."

"Lupus."

"Yeah."

"Jesus cripes."

"No, still Lupus. Lupus the forest."

"Florist," Lree added, taking her time to pronounce the word.

"Yeah."

Florist, huh. Avery took a good look around the tiny room. Several lamps hung haphazardly from the low, dangerous ceiling, covering the room in a faint and flickering blue light. Bottles, beakers, and burners were strewn about the floor randomly and only a few of those seemed to be there because of his earlier mishap. The patchy walls resembled those of a mid-tier chain restaurant, the kind that guilt-trips you into accepting the paltry Caesar salad featuring exactly three slivers of parmesan with your entree. The key difference was that all of the folksy antiques, disused farming equipment, and stolen road signs had been hung using live grenades.

As Lree was directly behind him he opted not to look at the back of the room. This was almost certainly for the better.

"I don't see any flowers," Avery said aloud, possibly by accident.

Lupus squeezed his one gross eye into a condescending squint. "That's not my probability, mystery."

"Mister."

"Miss?"

"Mister! I'm a guy!"

Bubbles rose up from somewhere in Lupus's body, escaping his mouth as a sigh. "Ain't no markers. Man's just a womb man with a feud unnecessary parts. Don' know why you bother dissevering, honest tea."

"Unnecessary?" Avery argued. He could feel his laughably loose grip on whatever this reality was unravel to the point where he didn't even care that he was mixing up his metaphors.

"Listen tomago on. Let's have a good look—or a look any sway—at the leg."

"Arm," Lree and Avery said, disinterested and panicking. I'll let you figure out who said what and how.

"Arm, leg, cow, mystery...closet really platter?"

As Lupus came closer Avery noticed something about the florist that concerned him. More so than the fact that he was a large ball of jellied cud posing as a doctor.

"Uh, you don't have any arms." Tact was a difficult concept for Avery, especially under pressure. "How are you going to fix—help me without arms?"

"I don't have no harms," he said rather calmly. He then called to Lree. "Help a pile, would you girly?"

This wasn't reassuring at all. Given the choice between having his arm worked on by the blob or the brat, he'd rather gnaw it off himself and be done with it. He was fairly certain he could still enjoy most of his favorite activities with only a single arm. However, before Avery could raise any sort of objection, Lupus added, "Sure, I left them. Hello? Hell no?" He looked around the table, then the room, then at Avery, and then the ceiling—all the while cooing as if he was searching for a lost puppy.

"They're here, Lupus," answered Lree. "Y'know, where they always are?"

Avery managed to prop himself up to look back at Lree and really appreciate both the horror and the ridiculousness of his current predicament. Lree was there, of course, looking annoyed and pointing at something above her. That something was a rack hanging from the ceiling and featuring a meaty arm of what was now a one-armed orangutan.

"What 'bout this one?" she asked, pointing at the hairy appendage. "It's not movin'."

"Tearful reunion! Toss it fear!"

"Okay."

Avery started to point out the flaw in this plan but quickly stopped himself because, despite being more than a little repulsed and absolutely apprehensive, part of him really, really wanted to see how this would play out. Lree hurled the giant arm at Lupus who completely failed to catch it for reasons that probably don't need to be elaborated upon. The appendage bounced off his rubbery chest and fell to the ground.

Yes, that was pretty much how Avery had hoped it would play out.

Lupus dropped to the floor out of Avery's field of view. Peering over the table, he saw the weird blob rolling furiously on and off the arm. This, too, was strangely satisfying until Lupus stood up with the top part of the arm partially submerged in his disgusting body. Contrary to how Lree described it, it was moving.

"What...?" Avery sputtered.

"Tree would be twice but I propose working in to," sighed Lupus. Now that he was able to he began lifting boxes, shifting books, and generally putting his new arm to use searching for another.

The moment lost, Avery collapsed upon the table. Lupus was muttering to himself as he ransacked his ransacked horse—house!—and Lree just looked on. Clearly, she had helped enough.

"Hey," Avery said to her without really thinking, "what's with your ears?"

The question or perhaps its bluntness seemed to shake the young girl. "S-shut up," she stammered. "Ah mean, what's with *your* ears?"

"I saw you runnin' earlier," he continued, completely ignoring her retort, "At least, I think I did. I saw a lot of things earlier and I'm really not sure of any of it...anyway, your hair or whatever you want to call it. Man, your hair is so gross. You have no idea how badly I want to cut it. Like, with a weed whacker."

The only comeback Lree could think of was, "Oh yeah?" which even she realized was pretty weak. Instead, she allowed Avery to ramble on undisturbed.

"And even then you'd need one of those little garden rakes to brush it—y'know, the ones with the three pointy bits?" He emphasized his point by tending to an imaginary garden with the arm that wasn't in excruciating pain.

"Your ears are weird," he continued, putting his invisible tool away, "One of 'em's pointy. What are you, like, some sort of elf?"

Lree didn't know what that was but she was pretty sure it was an insult. "*You're* some sort of shelf!" she snapped, regretting it immediately.

"Whatever, elf. I'm not the one with the jacked up fairy ears."

"Shut up!"

Having already lost interest in the conversation Avery turned his attention back to Lupus. The blubbery florist was still rummaging through his little shack and seemed to have burst into song at some point. The song involved arms. Or maybe it was farms.

A general sense of unease fell upon Avery. As he continued to take in his odd environment he realized he had begun to actually accept a little bit of it. Before he could dwell on this—or at least dwell on it enough to cause any significant concern—Lupus popped back up at the end of the table yelling, "Founder! Founder!" Indeed, he had found something.

"That's a leg," Avery said calmly.

Lupus looked at his new arm carefully. "Got fingers," he said, equally as calm.

"Those are toes."

"Yeah."

Never mind. There would be no acceptance no matter how little. This place was thoroughly abnormal as was its inhabitants. How great would it be to meet someone normal. Really great, that's how great.

"So nice. You'd, too," Lupus said, adjusting his new arm. Leg. Whatever. "Talking, shooting breezes like a cup of old friends. Yeah, friends with crossbows and nothing to lose..."

"We're not friends," Avery and Lree said, nearly perjuring themselves by saying so in a disturbing amount of harmony.

Lupus smiled and released a gross little laugh. "I may be a little blinded and forgetfuled and a little blinded..."

There was an uncomfortably long pause. Avery and Lree looked at each other and then back at Lupus.

"And...?!" Avery encouraged.

"Yeah." Clearly the discussion had ended. Lupus refocused his attention to sifting through and gathering strange liquids, powders, and other curious constituents.

"You said..." Avery fell silent. Engaging the madman, err, blob would only invite anxiety and that was something he already had in abundance. He didn't know how his situation came to be but he lamented it deeply.

The table beneath him shook gently as he shivered and he could feel cold sweat drop down either side of his head. He tried thinking of something—anything—else aside from his throbbing arm, the disgusting marsh monster, and her friend, the other disgusting marsh monster.

"S-so really," he said, his voice cracking slightly, "why're your ears like that?"

"Can't be felt," Lupus replied. "You can't be seething them. Would you like to seize mine tongue?"

"Naw, I'm good. I was talking about her," Avery said, thinking he was gesturing his head towards Lree. As she was now standing beside him he just looked like he was having an episode.

"Ma ears are fine," she said. Her tone was both angry and uncomfortable. It was if she was being asked very intrusive questions by a total moron which is exactly what was happening.

"Yeah, girly. Fine," said Lupus, now busy mixing an ill-scented concoction next to Avery's wounded arm. "Fine and quiet normal."

Avery was incensed. "How would you know normal? You're a weird, no-eared blob with a gorilla arm and a leg from...from...I don't even know what the hell that's from and before you think I actually want to know, I don't. I really, really don't."

"Young mystery," said Lupus with some authority, "normal is what other people have for breakfast."

Avery didn't agree. In fact, he flat out refused to even consider decoding let alone comprehending the florist's ridiculous rebuttal. He knew deep down—though perhaps a little deeper than he would have preferred—that he understood normality. He could not deny, however, that the line that once clearly made the distinction between normal and abnormal had become more than a little blurred as of late.

"Should about dude it." Lupus picked up a small brush with his foot hand, dipped it clumsily in the odorous mixture, and proceeded to baste Avery's arm in the foul-smelling stuff. He then said something akin to "oops." Avery wasn't particularly certain about this procedure and was about to express his concerns through a combination of thrashing and cursing when he realized his aching arm wasn't aching quite so much.

"Shower you feel?" Lupus asked? I guess? There was a new gentleness to his voice that made Avery feel ashamed, even if ever so slightly. He had—well, *maybe* he had misjudged the loathful colloid. Sure, he was repellant—oh, dear lord was he repellent—not to mention aloof and quite possibly senile but isn't that always the way? The revolting, ostracized eccentric is actually just a misunderstood genius?

He really did look gross, though.

"Not bad," Avery said, still in a bit of shock. "It, uh, it doesn't hurt. I don't feel anything!"

"Tearful reunion!" the revolting, ostracized eccentric said, "Cause you're not wanting to felt this." He tugged hard on one of the many lamps that hung from his ceiling, snapping the thin chain that once held it in place. He then shook the lamp, causing it to shine much brighter than it had been.

The sudden departure of gentleness and the near simultaneous arrival of menace concerned Avery. He watched as Lupus tipped the lamp almost completely on its side, sending the twitching husk of what appeared to be an enormous, glowing wasp to splash against the interior of the glass. Fixated on this terrible sight, Avery failed to notice the thick, blue liquid that began to pool at the bottom of the lamp and, very quickly, drip out of it and onto his arm. He did take notice, however, when his arm burst into a raging blue flame.

There was a conversation going on between two parties. One was the blubbery arsonist with the inappropriate arms. His words weren't clear but his manner of speech was. He lathered a strange, sort of false interest all over the beginning of his sentences but by the time he had reached a full stop it was fairly evident that he thought you were an idiot. Then he'd begin again, creating a terrifically awkward tempo similar to a pair of leather boots spinning in a dryer full of live gerbils.

The other voice had to be the girl's. She spoke fast and thick with snide. There really wasn't much else to it other than that Avery found it grating and panic-inducing. He fought hard to eavesdrop, however, passing in and out of consciousness made this a losing battle.

Lupus sighed as he reclined upon himself. "You're friend—she amways scream light?"

What was that? Friend? Or was it bend, send, end, mend, or tend. His mind shut itself down to reboot.

"He's not my friend," Lree was quick to respond.

"Much easier, girly." Lupus arose from himself and oozed over to Avery. "Better to not get tools attached. I plugged the leak but just only. "

Part of the word "attached" dribbled out of Avery's mouth. His mind tentatively loaded into safe mode.

"She salive!" Lupus shouted. "Don't take any comfort."

"Sure, man. No problem," Avery said, his mind clearly still running a diagnostic.

Helping Avery up with his leg, Lupus pointed at the boy's arm. It was no longer bleeding or burning but it was a deep shade of blue—almost an indigo—which naturally caused Avery a decent amount of vexed interest.

"Not sure how to say this," the blob sighed, "It's blue."

"W-what's wrong with it?"

Lupus looked at Lree then looked back at Avery, puzzled. "Not supposed to be blue."

"No, it isn't. But what's..."Avery paused, suddenly remembering who he was talking to. "Is it a problem?"

"Not for me."

"But what about me?!"

"You're going to be die."

"I'm what?! You gotta fix it!" Though he had managed to successfully reboot it was clear that Avery had not thought things through. After all, this was the monster that had just recently set his arm on fire. "You said you could fix it! That's, like, all I heard you say. Both of you weirdoes. Fix, fix, fix!"

"I fixated," Lupus retorted. "You're not leaking all over my horse. You're not hurting many wares, no?"

"I mean, yeah. Or no. But two out of three don't matter when...when the remaining third is still gonna kill me! What am I going to do?"

Lupus thought about this for a moment, then said, a bit unsure, "Die."

It was tempting, at least, at the moment. "What *else* am I going to do?"

"Could..." he paused to think. "Opportunity, I suppose."

For some reason Avery asked the ridiculous and disgusting old snot rocket to explain what he meant. To his credit, he had adequately prepared himself for disappointment.

"Opportunity," Lupus said with an unusual amount of effort. You've got to take opportunity out along the waterfront. Discover just how much he can saver with an assumable mortgage."

Ah, good, disappointment. The one thing he could always depend on. Before Avery could ask what the hell he was talking about Lree interrupted to ask the very same question.

"The heart, girly," he chirped. "The Mistress!"

"Mistress?" Avery seemed to perk up slightly as he repeated the word. Broken visions of his chainmail-clad bikini savior danced around his unabashedly one-track mind. Finally, he thought, things were looking up. Had he noticed Lree wincing at the word "mistress" he might have felt differently.

"That's dumb," Lree said with uncharacteristic clarity. "There's no heart. That's...just a dumb lie."

"'Of course," he a said, continuing the conversation with himself, "Lest gotta truddle the Vineway."

Avery had many questions, such as "What is the Vineway?" and "What exactly does it mean to truddle?", however, his most pressing concern, one of such importance that he felt it absolutely essential to resolve right this very instant, was, "Is she pretty?"

"Pretty something, yeah."

"Great!" he said, clearly ignoring the "something" portion of Lupus's statement. "And she can help me?"

"Spilling tea," he said with great enthusiasm.

"Or just tea," he added with slightly less enthusiasm than before.

"Can you wind a girl's heart? Loves lost, girly. Can you even get in...?"

"Ah can do that," Lree interjected. "Ah can get us in."

"No you can't," Avery argued. Knowing nothing of the place they were supposed to get in to or, for that matter, the world he now inhabited he really had no reason to doubt Lree's claim other than the fact that she was the one who had made it.

"Ah can and Ah will."

"Why?"

Lupus, too, was curious. "Why?" he repeated. "No one really believes in hearts."

"Ah know, but..."

"Who's butt?" asked the one person in the room you'd expect to ask such a question.

"But," she continued, "Ah still...Ah think Ah can get to her. To the Mistress."

There was that word again. Mistress. Forget the chainmail—leather. Definitely leather. And maybe an eye patch! Wait, was she a pirate now?

Avery had just started to organize several choice safe words ("timbers" and "peg leg" topped the list, however, the latter was nixed upon further consideration) when something caught his attention. "Hey," he chimed, "Isn't that my jacket?"

"Donk."

"Did you just say donk?"

"No, I said shut up."

"Where is my jacket, anyway?"

"Crammed up your arse now shut up, I'm thinking."

"It really does look like..."

"If you don't shut your trap you're gonna find yourself in a state of punch...hitting...punchification." Lree punctuated her threat with a nasty sneer and raised fists.

"Oh my god, you sound like the snot ball." Avery laughed. "Punchimawhat? What is that even supposed to mean?"

Lree, unusually accommodating, defined the word punchification through a painfully physical demonstration. She then defined the word again. And again. And again.

"Seriously, what is wrong with you? Why do you always hit?"

Avery asked these questions separately between strikes.

"Because you always say stupid stuff." Well, that and he was fun to hit—like a mashed potato sculpture of someone you really disliked. Best of all, when you punched him, he cried.

Lree's sadistic reasoning wasn't lost on Avery. Unable to counter her attacks—not out of chivalry, of course, but because he simply could not keep up with the girl's absurd speed—Avery yelled, "Why d'ya want to help me, anyway?!"

The pummeling stopped for a moment. After a bit of obvious thought she said, "Ah don't like being in debt is all," and resumed beating the boy.

Lupus, who until now had been enjoying this witless back and forth, took particular interest in Lree's words. "Oh?" he said, "Then why not get startled on my horse?"

"What're you talking about?"

"Don't believe I received compilation for pulling you out of the flower pitcher. Or when tending your words. Or letting your friend mess up my horse..."

Lree recoiled in what might have been guilt. Or perhaps gas. "Idiots," she said quickly. "Ah don't like bein' in debt to idiots. You're no idiot, Lupus."

"Could'a fooled me," Avery said, practically inviting another wave of punches. "And what debt? Does it involve my jacket?"

"Back in the valley. If Ah...you and your bodyguard helped me back there. Maybe saved me. That's all, okay?"

I guess that makes sense, Avery thought. Well, not really but was it worth another argument with the fuzzy spud?

Hang on.

"My what? Oh, crap, you mean...where is it?" He had forgotten all about the monster. That would explain why he hadn't felt any real sense of dread for some time now.

"Ah dunno. Around." Lree sat down then immediately stood back up. She stretched, rolled her head, checked her wrappings, and continued to act busy until Avery finally understood that she was lying and he was now being ignored.

"So you be returbing?" Lupus asked, folding his arms. This action caused one of them, it doesn't really matter which, to fall off.

Lree looked at the ground. "Yeah," she said softly. "But only just once. I mean it."

"Yeah."

"Yeah."

"Tearful reunion," he said with a smile? He then slapped what could have been his belly with his remaining arm and said, "Hedging the Vineway, you're going to need...I've got, uh...I've got...got..."

Lree knew this could take a while. She sat down on something that was either a chair covered in the ugliest carpeting ever created or the stuffed carcass of a rather atrociously furred creature. As she waited for Lupus to assemble his thoughts she stared at the boy fidgeting and drooling on the table next to her. Soon she'd be free. Free of this boy, free from his skeletal guardian, and free from the curse that bound her to the darkness. Everything was going according to plan.

More or less.

"Grim cycle!" the ball of slime suddenly exclaimed. He oozed over to a pile of junk across the room and furiously dug through it with his remaining appendage. "This!" He oozed back over to Lree and presented her with a nasty old hat.

"What is this?"

"A nasty old hat," he replied.

"And this is going to help me?"

"No."

"Then why're you giving this to me?"

"Don't want it."

Lree could feel her attempting to bash its way out of her skull. She knew they had to leave soon otherwise everyone would find themselves punchified.

"We gotta go," she said to Avery.

"So...what's this Mistress like?" he asked. Lree didn't reply so, reluctantly, Avery looked to Lupus for an answer. The florist gave him a big toes up. Then his final limb fell off.

Avery, too, had reached his limit. "You know, I'll just meet you outside, okay?" He slid off the table and, after several failed attempts, found a door that led out into the Garden. Lree followed slowly behind. At the doorway she stopped to look back. Though Lupus seemed to be preoccupied rolling around on the floor again, she said, "I mean it, Lupus. Just once more." She then stepped outside, closing the door behind her.

Lupus stopped rolling for a moment to look at the shut door. "Yeah," he sighed. He then returned to shuffling around the floor.

EIGHT
Comfort within the Chaos

This was a scene Avery had not been prepared for. He seemed to be standing in the most lovingly manicured landfill in existence. Everything seemed to have been buried in millions upon millions of colorful flower petals, resulting in a near-virulent potpourri of aggressively sweet fragrances that wafted upon the breeze in much the same manner as a pyroclastic cloud. It was simultaneously wonderful and awful.

"Where are we?" he finally asked, too stunned to really process any answer he might receive.

"The Garden," Lree said, pushing her way past the boy. "C'mon, let's go."

Before Avery could respond he was startled by the sudden birth of a gruesome funeral arrangement beside him. The creature painfully unfolded itself, dropping trash and flowers everywhere and taking on a frightening yet disturbingly familiar shape.

"Jesus Christmas, don't...don't do that, alright?"

It didn't occur to him that the skeleton had actually responded to Lree's command. It may not have occurred to you either, which makes me regret bringing it up as I've missed a terrific opportunity for some clever foreshadowing. Why don't we just forget I said anything. The skeleton stood up and followed Lree. Period. Don't read too much into it because you're just going to be so hilariously wrong that all of your friends will make fun of you for months. "Hey," they'll say in a mocking tone, "here comes Foreshadow Freddie. What do you think's going to happen next, hmm? What ridiculous evidence can you manufacture that will explain your bizarre conspiracy theory? You're so dumb. You're the dumbest dummy ever. Dummy."

I hate you. I hate you all.

Anyway, another quake shook the Garden hard, razing practically everything and, well, everyone in town. Avery, having become rather used to being thrown to the ground as of late, was able to pick himself back up even as the earth continued to shake. Though his experience with seismology had been limited mainly to Japanese monster movies, he couldn't help but feel that something was different about these quakes. The newly formed fissures, for example, failed to yield any steam or molten rock or mutated lizards. Instead, they brought forth flowers of every kind and color—so many, in fact, that they quickly retook every bare inch of the ground.

Slowly, the townsfolk stood and set to work clearing the flowers, picking up debris, and rebuilding their homes. Curiously, Lupus's shack of horrors was still standing.

"He told me once it's because he uses a special glue," said Lree. "He says 'e "married it himself."

"Yeah, okay, I actually wasn't going to ask," Avery responded, shivering slightly, "because now I know the answer and I didn't want to know the answer. Now I can't not know it."

Lree didn't bother replying as she was too focused on something off in the distance. The quake had been quite helpful in clearing the horizon—another fortuitous and questionable coincidence—allowing her to momentarily overcome one of the many challenges her minute stature often presented her with. There it was—once hidden behind a city made up of shaky buildings and tall, flowering bushes, stood the entrance to the Vineway; the twisted bridge that led to Love's Lost and the Mistress.

Featuring a peculiar series of massive archways, the entrance dwarfed its surroundings. You'd have to be a special kind of idiot to miss it while the town was leveled, which is why Lree carefully led Tweedle Dee and Tweedle Dead over hills of garish detritus, through paths of delightful dross, and across open plains of redolent refuse to ensure they all reached the monumental structure.

Tweedle Dee—Avery—was only barely following Lree's lead as the vast majority of his attention was still keenly focused on the Garden. He wasn't the kind of man to "stop and smell the roses," as it were. The Garden, though, teased his every sense and left him mystified. It was as ugly as it was beautiful. And it was about to get a lot stranger.

"What's that?" Avery inquired, tapping Lree on the shoulder. She didn't appreciate this and responded by slapping his hand away.

"Stop touching me!" she yelled. "And what?"

"That. There," he replied, pointing to that there—an engorged bud of some sort suddenly growing out of a pile of floral debris.

Lree didn't say anything, figuring it would be easier to simply let the moron see it for himself. The bud quickly bloomed into something that resembled a deep, red rose. It was all very lovely, up until the point it unfurled its final set of petals and revealed a rotund and disturbingly naked orange man. Said man, still naked and orange, flopped out of the blossom like a whale being born from a watermelon and hit the ground with a wet thud.

"Uh..."

Lree gave Avery a hard shove. "Don't stare," she said, obviously embarrassed, "Rude."

Avery had many concerns at the moment, however, displaying poor manners wasn't one of them. He watched as a crowd gathered around the recently germinated man. Within moments, he was clothed and going about his business pushing an unclaimed wheelbarrow of junk to and fro.

Predicting the next words out of Avery's fat gob, Lree chimed in, "It's a newborn, stupid. Stop gawking."

"A newborn. Yeah, I don't follow you on that."

"You know, a baby?" Lree replied, making it very clear how little she thought of Avery through her tone.

"That's not a baby."

"Course it is."

"That's a fat guy," Avery said, pointing at the fat guy. "A fat, orange guy that just...popped out of a flower."

"Yeah," Lree sighed. "Like a baby?"

"Baby's don't pop out of flowers! I mean, okay, yeah, if you wanna be crude sure but not literally. And anyway, that's still not a baby! Do you...have you ever seen a baby? A real baby?"

Lree pointed at the newly germinated fellow who, thankfully, didn't seem to realize he was causing such a bizarre debate.

"No. No no, no. That's...that's a man. Right. A grown man. A baby is small, you know. Like a little person."

"Donk! Babies come in all sizes, moron."

"Not that size! Unless you're an elephant. Jesus, could you imagine? That's...hang on. Do you really think babies come from flowers?"

"No," said Lree, as if stating the obvious. "Not just flowers. Sometimes they grow off of vines or fall out of trees."

Avery stared at Lree unsure of whether or not she was joking. "Babies...people...come from people, you know?"

"What?" Lree asked, sounding a little disgusted.

"Moms. You...popped out of...your...mother."

Lree no longer sounded disgusted, she *was* disgusted. "You're sick," she said, absolutely ready to end the conversation. By force, if necessary.

"Don't you have a mother?"

Lree continued walking without saying a word. Her unspoken

response made Avery pause. Since the argument began he had built up a large repository of mean-spirited, plant-central epithets for Lree and had been quite anxious to use them. But her reaction to his question—no, it was the question itself that demolished nearly all of his cruel enthusiasm. He had a mother, of course, and a father, too, though he had never actually met them. Still, he was fairly certain that they were not in any way photosynthetic.

Why now, he wondered. He hadn't thought about his birth parents in a very long time. His closest and, as far as he knew, only relatives were his grandparents who had assumed the dual roles of legal guardians and overbearing employers.

"Aw, man," he said aloud. "They're totally going to dock my pay."

Lree hadn't caught this, however, she did catch Avery stifling an ugly laugh like the creep he was. Whatever. It wouldn't be too long now. They were close to the Vineway and the next step of her master plan was about to begin.

To say the Vineway was massive would have been insulting. It was as wide as many bridges are long and constructed entirely out of, wait for it, vines varying wildly in size. The intimidating structure was draped precariously across a vast chasm, with many portions rising and falling rather sharply.

"What is that?" Avery asked, both genuinely curious and fearful.

Oh great! More idiotic questions! "What do you mean, "What is that?" That's the Vineway, stupid. 'Cross that's Love's Lost."

The that in Lree's last statement either referred to the Vineway itself or the forbidding canyon it more or less extended across. Avery was having none of it.

"I'm not getting on that," he said, assuming both definitions of that were correct.

"We're not going to," Lree said. Before Avery could relax, she quickly added, "Not yet. Just...stay close, alright?"

As they approached the Vineway Avery's curiosity and fear were joined by confusion. The entrance to the great bridge appeared to be gated off by a couple of small guard posts carved into what looked like a lamina. One featured a smartly dressed gentleman who seemed quite content goose-stepping the small area in front of his little building. The other was home to a sad looking man checking papers and shaking his head rather grimly. Those on the receiving end of his disapproval would either argue, cry, or simply turn around and slink away into the flowery chaos that was the Garden. It's worth noting that no one seemed to be actually passing through the gate nor was there a single individual attempting to cross the alleged bridge beyond.

Their path was eventually flanked by a stone wall embedded with, naturally, all types of flowers and what seemed to be cautionary signs of increasing concern. They began straightforward enough with the depiction of an unfortunate stickman falling to his certain doom due to the lack of safety rails along the Vineway. The next sign featured the same stickman, perhaps from an alternate reality where the Vineway had safety rails, and his group of friends in a fit of chaotic revelry, jumping up and down until the bridge breaks, sending them all to their certain doom. This was followed by signs showing the stickman being swept off the Vineway by a strong wind, the stickman being trampled to death for apparently walking too slow, the stickman slipping and breaking his leg for apparently walking too fast, the stickman incurring the wrath of evil spirits for swearing at the Vineway for breaking his leg, the stickman giving a fish to some sort of troll, the stickman lamenting having gotten on the Vineway in the first place instead of staying at home, raising his family, and living a good, ordinary life, and finally a flyswatter that had been partially covered by a skull and crossbones.

"Right," said Lree, taking a particular interest in the final sign. She quickly glanced to her left then her right before darting off towards the former direction.

"Do we need a fish?" Avery asked, still studying the cautionary wall. The absence of a hurtful remark concerned him. He turned to face Lree who was now scrambling over the wall. Avery, too, looked to his left and then his right, though he really wasn't sure what he was looking for. Satisfied that he hadn't seen whatever it was he knew nothing about, he followed Lree, comically scaling the barrier as well as an out-of-shape college sloth with a wounded arm possibly could. The grass on the other side was exceptionally thick and tall, cushioning his fall a bit. It did little to cushion the skeleton's fall, however, as most of the surrounding vegetation had died before it had even touched it.

"Hurry!" Lree whispered loudly. "This way!"

"Which way?" Avery whispered back, rubbing his aching arm and wondering why he was whispering.

"Here! Over here!"

"That's not helping!" he argued in a silent yell.

Avery's nightmare stood up—rather unnaturally, I might add, with bits of the creature bending and folding in directions they ought not to—and ran after Lree's voice. It wouldn't occur to Avery until much later how strange it was to put so much faith into such an affront to nature but for now it seemed like it always had a better idea of where it was going than he did so following it only made sense.

It was a short but nevertheless exhausting jaunt for Avery. They stopped at a clearing that opened up into a chasm without end. At its edge was a big-haired silhouette that could only be Lree brushing or possibly fighting off loose blades of grass. "Why are you guys so slow?" said the obnoxious silhouette.

Yeah, it was definitely Lree.

Avery considered shooting back with a clever, biting remark but A) he couldn't think of one and B) even if he had, he was now really close to the cliff and she was really crazy. Instead, he simply asked, "Where are we going?"

"The Vineway."

"I thought that was the Vineway," he said, pointing his thumb behind him for emphasis.

"That's the skeleton."

"I meant beyond the skeleton. And beyond the wall if you're going to be that much of a smartass."

"Yeah."

"Yeah you're going to be that much of a smartass or yeah that's the Vineway?"

"Yeah."

"Right..." Avery said slowly as he attempted to work out the logistics in real time, "So if we're going to cross the Vineway and the Vineway is back there then...why are we here?"

Lree rolled at least one of her eyes. "Because you can't *just* cross the Vineway. Ah mean, Ah could but you two weirdies? Not like this. But Ah've got some stuff that might work in my secret hideout. It's just down this way."

"You've got a secret hideout?" Avery chortled. "What are you, five?"

"Five what?" she asked, then vanished over the edge of the cliff. Avery dashed over to where she had been and cautiously peered over to see that she was now standing on a less-than-secure ledge several feet down. A gap separated this laughable landing spot with a set of precarious stairs embedded in the wall eventually leading underneath the Vineway.

"I think I'll wait here," Avery announced importantly.

"Fine," Lree said as she began her descent, "Look out for any gorbs or wild voorn and just...try not to die, okay?"

"Ha ha ha," he replied, emphatically pronouncing every ha. He wasn't sure what a voorn or gorb was supposed to be but both sounded too stupid to be threatening.

Avery backed away from the edge and bumped into the skeleton. He apologized for some reason and let the creature pass. Somehow it managed to follow Lree down the daunting path without plummeting to its death. Or undeath. Or whatever.

He was now alone. Alone with the eerie sounds of a crumbling town. And a harsh wind that blew angrily through the interminable chasm. And some jostling foliage that was being jostled by something clearly too large to be cute, cuddly, and have no real interest in eating him.

"Wait up," he said, changing his once staunch "I'll wait here" stance.

Avery carefully dropped to the ledge and swore he felt it crack beneath his feet. He never realized just how big his feet were until he was standing on a ledge he couldn't see hanging over a bottomless canyon. His throat was dry and he began sweating profusely despite the cool gale that rampaged through the chasm. The gap from the hidden ledge to the rocky, pencil-width stairs wasn't great, however, Avery's perception had already been so severely traumatized that a gap only a couple of feet wide now seemed to extend beyond a mile. He closed his eyes, reached out with his foot, and set it gently down on nothing, causing him to first panic then hug the cliff wall. He looked at the staircase again, this time noting that it was actually set lower than the ledge. Avery slid slowly down the wall and, once more, reached for the staircase with his foot. This time he made contact.

Splayed against the canyon wall with no sense of dignity whatsoever Avery carefully considered his next move. Should he put all of his weight onto the foot on the stairwell and carry the rest of his body across the gap or should he do the exact opposite, climb out of the chasm, and find a nice, deep hole to drop in to, assume a fetal position, and cry himself to sleep? Despite his mind winning by nine votes to one for the hole of shame, he pressed forward, crossing over with little difficulty other than the development of a whole new set of anxieties that wouldn't surface themselves until much, much later when it would prove to be a massive inconvenience.

The journey down the steps wasn't nearly as traumatic, even though the staircase turned out to be less of a carefully designed set of stairs and more of a series of unusual rock outcroppings arbitrarily arranged to resemble something that almost look like the remnants of what might have been stairs in a building that had long since toppled over into a canyon. These tragically ill-defined steps eventually led to a large hole in the rocky wall directly beneath the Vineway. Given the option between being overwhelmed with vertigo and falling to his death or scrambling inside a mysterious cave possibly full of beetles, bats, bears, and other baleful beasts beginning with the letter B, he chose the batter. Er, latter.

After a relatively short crawl the small crevice opened into a rather strange fashion boutique lit by the same nightmarish lanterns found back in the blob's shack. That, however, was where the similarities ended. Instead of broken yard equipment and signs featuring adorably racists caricatures peddling harmful products to children, the walls were lined with an impressive variety of luxurious clothing. Massive piles of trousers and dresses seemed to be distributed about the area with deliberate intent while smaller collections of belts, suspenders, and other fashionable accessories randomly accented the floor. Even his skeletal companion had been temporarily repurposed into a frightening coat rack. Every inch of the cave had been covered in something fabulous. It was Lree's private cavern of couture.

"You've got problems," Avery said.

The pile closest to him rustled a bit until Lree popped out of it, rushing to the next mound of clothing as if on a mission. "Not for much longer," she muttered to herself.

"Is this all yours?"

"Sure."

"How did you get all of this?"

Climbing out of the pile with a handful of rather darling blouses, Lree began to survey the room. "Found 'em."

"You found them?" Avery sputtered. "I've found an old shoe before, maybe a coat, but this? It's like you've found a thrift store. You can't just..."

"Can't just what?" It was hard to tell whether or not she was actually participating in the conversation.

"You can't just call something yours because you found it. I mean, not on this scale."

"Well, Ah did."

"I'm pretty sure that's a crime, sprout."

Lree pulled a dress out of one of many carefully arranged piles, simply saying, "Naw."

"It is!"

"It's, ah, Lupus called it something. Appreciation."

Avery sat heavily on a heap of undergarments, realized they were probably used—and not so fresh—and quickly relocated his prominent posterior onto a less personal mound of ill-gotten clothing. "Appropriation," he said. "You know, like theft?"

"Put these on." Lree tossed a small pile of not-quite carefully folded clothing at Avery, including a top made of lightweight chain mail fringed with loud, blue feathers. It was accompanied by another shirt that— sorry, no—it was a dress and Avery was done looking at it.

"This is a dress."

"Stupid," Lree sputtered. "It's called a tunic and it's a fancy one. Probably too fancy for you." As Avery fretted over his new ensemble, Lree prepared herself for hers. She began by removing what was left of her jacket and placing it in a heap of other appreciated outerware.

"I don't know what that is, but this thing goes down to my knees. It's clearly a dress."

"Just put it on."

"Or maybe a woman's night shirt. Looks like I'm going to a slumber party. And hey, what am I supposed to wear underneath?"

"Uh, nothing?" she said as she carefully began to unwrap the remaining rags from her person.

"Uh, I don't think so. I don't appreciate having a winter vortex assault my area when I walk, thank you very much. Seriously, what is wrong with you?"

"Just grab something from that pile," she said, pointing towards the increasingly disturbing mountain of unwashed unmentionables. "Nobody's gonna be checking there anyway."

"They could!" he argued, then questioned what the hell he was arguing about. "Wait, who's going to be checking? And why am I doing this, anyway?"

Lree paused her unwrapping activities as if lost in thought. "You're right, you're gonna need somethin' under that," she said, but not necessarily to Avery.

"Thank you."

"Here, this'll work. Ah've seen some noble folk wearing it." Lree threw a wad of white fabric at Avery who, being Avery, caught it with his face.

"What's this?"

"That's for underneath," she sighed, continuing to remove her rags. "Jus' a little bit longer," she thought to herself.

Avery unrolled the wad to discover it was a pair of white leggings. "I'm not going to wear pantyhoooooo—what are you doing?!" Avery yelled. Slack-jawed, wide-eyed, and holding onto his leggings with a death grip, he didn't know what to make of the sight before him.

"What now?" Lree asked, annoyed and currently quite nude down to her hips.

"Well, that's that," Avery thought, frozen in some sort of curious terror. He was going to jail—there was no way out of it.

"...and while you were rifling through these stolen clothes, can you please tell the court just what Miss Lree was doing?" the prosecuting attorney would ask with a thick Southern accent.

"Nothing. I just pulled the pantyhose down from my face and there she was. Naked."

"Did you say "pantyhose?"

"I did, yes."

"Right. And you said she was naked? Say, "as a jaybird?"

"Well, I...I don't know about that but I saw plenty."

"I'm sure you did. You could have turned around, couldn't you have? "

"Yeah, but, it all happened so fast I..."

"Didn't. You just stood there and gawked at this poor, defenseless creature. Tell me, Mister Hall, why were you even there?"

Avery, intimidated by the accusing eyes of the jury—all PTA mothers from the 1950s—squirmed in his seat. "I was just changing my clothes. She said I had to change my clothes."

"She? Sir, are you trying to tell me that the victim made you look at her? "

"Yes. No! I'm just saying that she told me..."

"And what clothes were you trying on?"

"Pardon?"

"I asked what clothes were you trying on? If you would indulge me."

"There was a, uh, feathery, chain shirt, a dress, and some...pantyhose."

"No further questions, your honor."

Avery looked over to his defense counselor who, instead of

preparing to reestablish the character of his client in a more positive light, was busy killing herself.

"Put your clothes on!" he yelled, spinning around to face a wall of bikini tops.

"What d'ya think Ah'm doin'?" she said. Having now fully emancipated herself from the last bit of cloth covering her absurdly lithe body, Lree walked over to Avery silently and undetected.

"You're still not dressed. Do you need help putting that on?" Her tone, unsurprisingly, was sarcastic.

"I know how to put pantyhose on, okay?" he yelled. Truth be told, he didn't but that was the least of his concerns right now. "Just go! Away! Put something on! Jesus!"

Avery tried to shoo Lree away and, in doing so, unwittingly glanced in her general direction. Through luck and careful editing, he was able to block out anything particularly incriminating from his field of view. He did, however, find himself morbidly enamored by the many, many scars that covered her body. It was as if she had been swimming in a pool filled with sharks and weed whackers and for the briefest of moments he felt the weight of each and every single one of those dreadful cicatrices upon his being.

He hastily turned his head around and pleaded, "Will you put your clothes on? Please?"

"Why're you yelling? Anyways, Ah can't."

Ever since he found himself wandering that grassy field weird things kept happening to him yet his mind had adjusted accordingly. For example, there's the case of the giant skeletal abomination. At one point it both terrified and repulsed him and all he wanted to do was be rid of the cursed thing. Now it was just kind of there, following him like that one friend no one really likes but you invite out anyway because you feel sorry for them. Not that Avery would really know this as he always played the role of that one friend no one really likes but you invite out anyway because you feel sorry for them. At least, in his mind. Avery had no friends.

"Why?" asked Avery, suddenly feeling very depressed.

"You're sitting on Mah dress. Move."

Avery accommodated her request and quickly scuttled behind another pile of intimate apparel as quickly as he could. "I," he started, coughed, and then continued, "I'm going to change now."

"Great."

"So you stay over there, okay? And turn around."

"Why?"

"For the love of...just do it, okay!?"

"You're weird," Lree said, picking up the dress. It was a gaudy, maroon-colored gown speckled with purple, blue, and green gems and featured a neckline that plunged into the most inappropriate areas. Lree managed to control the exposure by wrapping a series of wide, diaphanous belts around her, adequately sealing her shame. Unfortunately there wasn't much she could do about the length of the dress and had to pull it up quite a bit in order to walk without tripping on it and falling on her face. She finished off her violently clashing kit with a couple of mismatched gloves and a veiled hat highlighted by what appeared to be a dead duck garnished by a salad of silk flowers.

"Happy?" she asked.

"You look like somebody's great aunt," Avery said, emerging from behind a pile of clothes wearing his own special outfit. I probably should have put special in quotation marks. "Man, look at this," he sighed, waving his afflicted limb about his side, "it's getting worse. It looks like I used my arm to inseminate a freakin' porta-potty."

"Does it hurt?"

It did hurt. Actually, it had been hurting for a while. Not that Avery would admit this—especially to the human hairball. He was far too macho for that. "Yeah. Lots."

Well, never mind, I guess.

"You'll need a hat, too," she said, seemingly ignoring the previous conversation she had started. "Something big to cover your face."

"What's wrong with my face?"

She had been waiting for this one. The perfect trap had been sprung and now she could pounce on her prey with any number of devastating insults. "It's ugly." No, that was far too straightforward, even if it was true. "Ask a mirror." That one was biting, but would he get it? He was, after all, really dumb. There had to be something she could say that would strike a nerve. Something like...like...

"This one's pretty cool," he said, picking up something that was not even remotely cool. It resembled a cartwheel hat but trimmed with enormous feathers. Though I'm pretty sure it's already been mentioned, it bears repeating that Avery isn't exactly the most fashion conscience young man.

"I-it's ugly," Lree shouted awkwardly.

"Whatever," he sneered, placing the hat upon his head. "You're just jealous 'cause I found it first." Holding his chin thoughtfully, he began to look around the cave. Every couple of seconds he'd pause to make an uncomfortable expression. He cycled through several increasingly disturbing faces before finally looking back at Lree. Lowering his eyelids slightly, he said, "Stylin'."

Utter defeat.

"You never answered my question, spud," he added as he spun his hat around in an attempt to find the perfect angle. There wasn't one. "Why're we dressin' up?"

"You're just now asking that?"

"It's not like I had any other opportunity. The moment I entered your little contraband cave you threw some clothes at me and told me to put them on."

"And you just do everything you're told?"

"No. But..."

"Ah tried to tell why but you got all weird when..."

Avery waved his hands furiously in front of Lree and made several bizarre sounds in an effort to stop her from saying anything else. "Let's not go there," he finally said. "In fact, let's just forget about it. As it is I'm gonna be scarred for life and..." it wasn't until the word "scarred" dribbled out of his mouth that he realized he probably could have omitted that last statement entirely. "Sorry," he said weakly.

Lree either didn't catch what he had said or more likely didn't care. "We're going to Love's Lost, right?"

"I thought we were going to the Vineway."

"The Vineway," Lree said, internally counting to ten, "leads to Love's Lost. We can't enter either looking like you."

"Me?! What's wrong with me?"

"We have to look proper. Important. Noble."

"Not you," she added.

"I don't feel terribly noble," Avery whined as he looked at his absurd costume. "I feel kind of stupid."

"Right, noble." Lree smiled to herself.

Avery fruitlessly fiddled with his ensemble hoping that a tug here or a tuck there might improve his outrageous attire. Maybe if he covered up more? Or stayed in the cave forever?

"Okay," he said, only partially paying attention to his own words, "we're dressed up. Can we go now?"

"Dummy, we've still got to disguise Skelie."

"Whoa, this is fire!" he said, picking up a bright green and blue scarf that most certainly would look better burning in a fire. "Wait, who?"

"Them," Lree replied, pointing to the skeletal coat rack. "Your guardian. "

Avery turned to look at his alleged guardian and shook. "That's not mine, man."

This was not at all what Lree wanted to hear. "What do you mean they're not yours? You're Avery, yeah?"

Avery thought for a moment. He was himself, right? What kind of question was that? What the hell was she talking about? He vocalized this last concern.

"You summoned them."

"No, I didn't," he said, angrily wrapping the scarf around his face like a mask. It still wasn't fire. Like, not even remotely so. It's mere existence was offensive.

"I mean, even if I could do something like that," he continued through the scarf, "why? Why would I summon a monster whose only real purpose is to make me piss myself? And one that smells, too. Like it spent a week in a camel's colon."

"They don't smell."

"Are you kidding me? It smells like..." Avery paused to think of something truly awful. Eventually he followed through with, "like a day-old donkey diaper. It smells. Bad."

"Yeah, but now...?"

He pulled down his tacky scarf mask and inhaled carefully. She was right. His eyes didn't water and his gag reflex seemed to have returned to being an involuntary reaction instead of a alternate form of breathing. "Huh," he said. "That's weird. Good, but weird."

"We're still not naming it," he added quickly.

"But they definitely need a name now. We can't keep calling them...whatever we call them."

"No," Avery contested. "Absolutely no way."

"That's stupid. You're not gonna wear that, are you?"

"Yeah, so?"

"It looks...great. You look great." Lree sighed and made no attempt to hide the fact that she was lying. "Now help me dress Skelie."

"Stop calling them—it—that."

"Why?"

"Look, if you name it you're going to get attached to them. Hey, can I have this bag?" he asked, lifting up a rather large, possibly leather messenger bag from a pile largely consisting of old-time medical bags and crocheted coin purses.

"You don't need it."

"What are you talking about?" he asked, sounding genuinely offended. "Of course I need it."

"For?"

"For putting stuff in it, you know? You should take a bag, too."

"Ah'm not taking a bag and you...Ah don't care. Take it."

"Yay!" If there was a reason why Avery was genuinely happy about this it wasn't readily apparent.

"What?"

"I didn't say anything."

"You said something about not getting attached to them."

"The bag? Too late, it's mine, now. It's cool. Like a...like a paper bag, you know. Look at me, I'm sellin' the Times on the street." Avery proceeded to mime the afore mentioned occupation as well as someone who has never been a paperboy and has no formal training in performance arts could. "Extra, extra!" he yelled cheerily. "Read all about it, hairy little elf girl makes hideous monster her pet!"

Lree knew that the longer this conversation lasted the least likely it would be that both parties would come out alive. "Ah don't wanna make them my pet, I just wanna call them something other than nothing. So it's Skelie."

"Stop it," Avery snapped, accepting fifty cents for his last paper. "I'm telling you, once you name it you'll never be able to get rid of it."

"Name or not, we're still not getting rid of them."

"See? It's already started."

"No, look...if you didn't summon them then they're following us on they're own. They've followed us this far, haven't they? They ain't goin' anywhere...at least, without us."

Avery looked at Lree, then the skeleton, and then back at Lree. So she was right. Again. "Okay," he said, "but we're not calling it Skelie."

Now it was Lree's turn to take offense at having her opinion openly critiqued. "Why? It's perfect! They're a skeleton! Ah mean, mostly."

"It sounds like a character on some kids' science show. Look at it—it's a gross, horrible monster. Everything about it screams death and terror. That's not something you use to teach children how clouds work."

Since she had first met Avery, Lree had great difficulty in understanding anything that came out of his dreadfully obnoxious mouth. At first she had simply figured it was because he was some sort of sorcerer using strange words to deliberately confuse and intimidate her. With the recent revelation that he had not summoned the nameless monster at the center of their current argument she was now beginning to suspect that he really wasn't a sorcerer at all or, indeed, the person he claimed to be.

"Do you have any weapons? Like a sword? Can I have a sword?"

After a notable pause, she said, "So Skelie's good."

"No, it's not. It's cute. They are not cute. How about something like...Trash?" Avery said, now trying on a third, fourth, and fifth pair of boots. Either they were too big, too small, or seemed to be made for a very large duck.

"No."

"Alright," he said, undeterred, "Junk?"

"No."

"Hey, can't I just wear my own shoes? None of these fit."

"No."

"Aw, come on. No one's going to notice—not with this amazing hat, sassy scarf, and fancy new bag!" He patted his fancy new bag for effect. "You're such a good bag, bag."

"Ah said no."

"You're wearing your old shoes."

"Fine, whatever." Lree saw little point in throwing herself into yet another argument with this moron. Besides, he was right. She hadn't changed out of her newly acquired boots and it was very unlikely anyone would notice his strange footwear. From a distance they appeared to be dark sabatons. It was only upon closer inspection that one would discover that they were made of a curious combination of soft, black cloth and thin, stringed laces.

"Oh! What about Offal?" Avery continued, putting his strange shoes back on.

"No."

"Bones? No, that's too obvious. Bones, Bones, Bones. Boner?"

"No."

"Right, definitely no. Did I say Trash yet?"

"Ah don't know," Lree said in such a way that, under different circumstances, could be mistaken as a cry for help. "If you did Ah'd still say no."

"About my weapon..."

"Ah'm not giving you a weapon."

"Why not? Do you have any? You've got that little knife, don'cha?"

"You don't need a knife or a sword or anything like that," she said, astounded by the request. "My dagger is…why would you think you need something like that?"

"I don't know. Self-defense?" He then added, "To look dangerous? Cool?"

"No."

Though he was visibly disappointed, he didn't seem to dwell on it. "I still kind'a like Bones but..." he said, returning to the previous argument. He paused for a moment then blurted out, "What about Jones?"

"Yeah."

"Really? Jones?"

" Jones. Jonesy," she said, not realizing she was saying it aloud. "Ah like that."

It was odd, but Avery couldn't help but feel relieved about naming the creature that haunted him. Relieved and a touch melancholic. "Alright, Jones," he said, facing the newly christened monstrosity, "if you're coming with us, you gotta look at least as fabulous as I do."

It can't be said for certain that Jones actually appreciated their new name as they utterly failed to give a response other than eerie silence and a soulless stare. However, it can be said that by the next chapter they would, indeed, look quite fabulous.

NINE
The Sisterhood

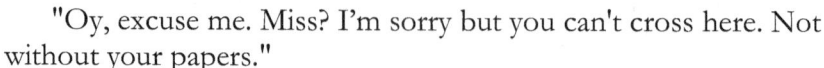

"Oy, excuse me. Miss? I'm sorry but you can't cross here. Not without your papers."

"Are you addressing us?" Lree replied with impressively more disdain than was her norm. "Can you believe the arrogance, sister?"

Silence.

"Sister?" she said to Avery, nodding her head towards the small man in the booth.

Avery's expression shifted from confusion to astonishment to anger in a matter of seconds. "I knew this was a dress!" He hissed at her.

"What did she say?" he asked.

"My good sir," Lree continued in the most posh accent she could muster, "you really must learn to pay more attention to a lady. She asked if you liked her dress."

"I did not!" Avery protested, then doubled over in pain. The latter action was most likely caused by Lree's sharp elbow catching him in the gut.

"I...I'm sorry, mam. It's..." he paused to look at Avery who, even if he wasn't currently folded in half made for a rather homely woman. "Lovely," he said. Slowly. What was the point of all this? His job—as he had been told—was simply to prevent anyone from crossing the Vineway. And since he lacked the wit and physique necessary for effective intimidation he had to rely on a wicked combination of disinterest and bureaucracy to crush dreams.

"See, Bessie? I told you so."

Avery—or Bessie—did not see. He simply said "What?" which resulted in another elbow-based gut shot. Starting to get the hint he adjusted his voice in an attempt to sound less masculine—a task that took considerably less effort than he had wished it did. "Sorry, I mean, I'm Bessie. Thank you."

The gentleman's opinion seemed to change slightly. "That," he said earnestly, "is a very pretty name, if I may say so."

"You may," Lree coughed, nearly breaking character. "Now, if you'll excuse us we're going to be late."

"I'm afraid I can't let you do that. Not without your papers. It's against regulations."

"Regulations?" Lree gasped, sounding out each syllable. "We...are nobility. We do not care about papers or regulations."

"That's as maybe, mam, but you're still gonna to have to show me your papers. No one from the Garden is allowed to cross the Vineway without papers."

"What sort of papers?" Lree asked. She thought, however, "Was this actually worth it?"

"Oh," said the little man in his little booth, astonished, "Phew. I mean, papers. Important papers. Documents. You know?"

She wasn't buying it.

"What are you doing out here, anyway?" he asked, changing the subject with what he felt was grace. "Noble folk don't come 'round here, much." He paused on the word noble long enough to include finger quotes. He did not actually use them, mind you, but he could have and it would have been okay to do so. "They don't come 'round here at all, in fact."

"That," said Lree sternly, "is our business, not yours, mister...?"

" Khauphase."

"Cowface?!" Avery guffawed just before receiving a third and far from final gut shot. For whatever reason—possibly because he's a moron—Avery found the gentleman's name much more interesting than the fact that, like Lree, his speech was completely out of sync with the movements of his lips.

"That's an interesting name," he said, recovering rather quickly from the last attack. "How, uh, how did you come about it?"

"It's me pap's name," said the man, suddenly beaming. "He was a Khauphase, as was his pap and his pap before him. I come from a long line of Khauphases."

"I think I just peed a little," Avery whispered to Lree. She was about to elbow him for a fourth time when she realized he might be telling the truth.

"We—my family—sing a song about it," the man continued unsolicited. "About our name. Want to hear it?"

"Yes, please," Avery said as quickly, straining to hold back a fit of crazed laughter.

"I really don't think we have time for this, dear sister," Lree insisted. To assess her tone, simply imagine her statement presented in dark, dripping word balloon.

"Nonsense!" Bessie yelled, getting all too comfortable into character.

"This strapping young man is about to..." he paused briefly to bite his lip. After a moment he continued. "He's about to serenade us with a beautiful song about his heritage. It would be most...uncouth of us not to listen. Wouldn't you agree?"

"No one's ever wanted to hear it before. Are you sure?"

"No," said Lree.

"Yes," said Avery simultaneously, only much louder. "You'll have to excuse my little, little sister's rudeness. She's feeling a tad testy because, uh, she's ugly."

"Ah'm what?!" a less noble Lree asked with at least one fist raised.

"S'okay," Mister Khauphase consoled Lree. "It's really what's inside that matters, right?"

"Oh, that's even uglier, Mister Cowface," Avery added, glancing at Lree. She was staring at him with a very clear intent to maim and destroy. He coughed and then said, "Anyway, enough of that ragamuffin. Please. I want to hear your song, my good man."

"O-Okay." Khauphase cleared his throat, breathed deeply, and, still within the confines of his little booth, proceeded to assault the strange sisters with an off key and unintentionally ridiculous limerick about his family name.

She wasn't a looker
but still he took her
day after day to the fair

The crowd agreed
she was ugly indeed
and much too much to bear

With a bulging dewlap
that mimicked a tent flap
she was twice the cow as any utter

And this would be fine
were she bovine
instead of my great grandmutter

What little patience Lree had left had been obliterated. Utterly obliterated, one might say well outside of her presence if one had any sense of self-preservation. This was, bar none, one of the worst things she had ever had to endure, including her time in Love's Lost.

That was it. She would knock out the stupid little man, kill Avery, and cross over into Love's Lost dragging his fat corpse behind her. That's just how it was going to have to be.

Lree turned to look at the jerk—the one she had been traveling with, not the singing booth jockey—and reached for her mysteriously placed dagger. The boy was shaking as if he knew what was about to happen.

She then noticed that he was failing to cover a massive grin as if he didn't know what was about to happen and was simply some kind of...

"Idiot," she thought and, just like that, her rage had vanished. It just didn't seem worth it anymore. Nothing did.

"Ah!" Avery exclaimed, wiping small tears from his eyes. "That was lovely. Really lovely."

"What, you think so?" asked the man.

"Yes, absolutely. That was probably the best thing I've heard all day."

The son of Khauphase, blushing just slightly, seemed confused. After a moment, he shook it off and said with a smile, "Oh, go on. It's not that great."

"It is, it is! Thank you for sharing." By this point Lree couldn't tell if Avery was being sincere or not.

"You know," said the little guard in his little guard box, "I've been working here at this post for as long as I can remember and no one has ever asked for my name."

"You have a great name, Mister Cowface."

"Call me Biggphat."

"No, don't..." Avery said out of character.

"Biggphat Khauphase."

Avery doubled over again, stifling a laugh that, were it released, would have easily sent some of the less sturdy buildings in the Garden to the ground.

"Are you alright, Miss Bessie?!" Biggphat asked, rushing to Miss Bessie's side.

"Yes," he replied in a broken and much higher voice. Somehow he managed to get back into his role as a young man impersonating someone's terrible impression of a noblewoman. "Butterflies in my stomach. I'm very excited about visiting that place. Over there."

"Love's Lost?"

Avery shook his head. "Sure."

"Well, look, why don't you just head across the Vineway."

"What?!" Lree screamed. Getting back into character, she asked, "But our papers?"

"Don't worry about it, mam. I know true nobility when I see it." Again, there was a long enough pause on nobility to allow for finger quotes, however, Biggphat Khauphase was clearly above such obnoxious behavior. "Still," he added, "I can't remember when was the last time I came across such nice folk, noble or otherwise."

He watched as the smallest, most confused sister curtsied, lifted her gown, and shuffled away. The middle sister followed suit, though she chose to do a little salute for some reason.

The largest sister, who until now hadn't even been noticed, stood absolutely still. Though her face had been wrapped entirely in a thick, leather-like material, Khauphase could feel her cold gaze upon him. A sudden, biting wind from the chasm tussled the black, blonde, and brown hair that had escaped the confines of what appeared to be a sombrero and caused her jewelry to strike together like miniature wind chimes. She wore something that might have been a coat but it looked more like a number of stained rugs crudely sewn together to create something not quite like a coat. Whatever was hidden within boggled the imagination.

"E-enjoy, mam. And you be careful crossing the Vineway. I'm not even certain it can be crossed."

With a crack and a pop and a jingle and a jangle, she bowed ever so humbly and wobbled awkwardly away towards her sisters.

"Nice folk," Khauphase sighed to himself, settling back into his booth. "Sure hope they don't die a horrible death."

Walking on two broken legs across an ill-kept rope bridge swinging haphazardly over a raging river swarming with hungry piranha would be perilous. Traversing a mile-high chasm while drunk off mouthwash during a windstorm by way of a rotting log would be treacherous. Climbing up, sliding down, and maintaining one's balance on the remnants of Jack's fallen beanstalk in order to cross a bottomless abyss while wearing uncomfortable and constricting clothing was just downright stupid. Yet the one person who you could depend on to bring this sort of obvious danger to everyone's attention was, at the moment, completely oblivious to it.

"That was great," Avery said with a gigantic smile. "I mean really great. I just met a man named Bigfat Cowface and he was happy about it. Like, actually happy. And nice! And then he sang a song and everything just...everything got better."

Lree said nothing. On occasion she'd look back at Avery but no words would come to her. She wasn't quite sure what had just happened but whatever it was didn't make her comfortable. Well, no, that's not right. It did make her comfortable and that's what made her uncomfortable. First Jones and now Avery—it wasn't making any sense. So instead of dwelling on the troubling happenstances she chose to focus exclusively on moving forward—walking, climbing, and sliding. In silence.

"Bigfat Cowface," Avery repeated to himself for probably the hundredth time. "Man, I miss him already. We should've asked him to come along."

That was the most ridiculous thing Lree had heard him say since the last most ridiculous thing he had said which was, of course, the last thing he had said. What really drove her mad, though was that she knew that there was nothing she could do or say to diminish his repulsively chipper mood.

As they reached a particularly high crest in the warped bridge, Avery was given a spectacular first view of their final destination. "I don't see anything," he said. "Where are we going again?"

"There," said Lree, pointing exactly where Avery was looking. "It's right there. How can you miss it?"

"I," he started. Squinting hard, almost painfully so, he asked, "Is it on the hill somewhere?"

Lree thought carefully about how she should answer him: tell him the truth or just treat him like the moron he is. Guess which one she chose.

"Yeah, on the hill," she said as derisively as she possibly could without flat out calling him a moron.

"I still don't see it." There was mild disappointment in his voice which pleased Lree. "Weird," he added and he was right. It was weird. It was remarkably green and formed an almost perfect half circle, like a mountain painted by a three-year-old. And while he still wasn't able to see this Love's Lost place, Avery could make out a number of large flocks of birds that seemed to be swarming the hill.

As he said, weird.

"Is there food there?" he asked.

"There's always food there, though..."

"Great, 'cause I'm starving," Avery said, perking up considerably. "It's like now that I'm not being chased or lit on fire or beaten up I'm suddenly really, really hungry. And thirsty, too. Do they have drinks? Oh, wait. Crap. Do you think it's expensive? You have an in with this place, right? Can you get me a discount?"

Avery's increased curiosity and subsequent enthusiasm only made Lree feel worse. Love's Lost was an apparition, a malcontent ghost that tormented her every moment, waking or otherwise. She wanted to be certain that things would change, that the spirits that haunted her would be excised and her life could truly begin. She wanted to, but something deep down denied her this or any real sense of hope. All she could do, she thought to herself, is push on and see what happens.

"*She wasn't a hooker but some kind of hooker and then something about the fair,*" Avery sang not-at-all quietly to himself.

"That's not how it..." Lree just stopped. The very fact that she knew the correct lyrics made her want to punch something.

"I really feel like I should have a sword."

Not something. Somebody. Avery. She'd punch Avery. Oh, that would be wonderful! Right in the stomach—make him fall to his knees and just wail. She smirked, clenched her first, and was in the middle of spinning herself around to land the satisfying blow when Avery unknowingly interrupted her.

"Hey, I think I see someone," he said.

Ensnared by her own momentum, Lree responded by awkwardly falling to the ground. This, of course, *didn't* escape Avery's notice.

"Why're you such as a spaz?"

Lree didn't say anything—at least, nothing that can be printed here. Still on the ground, she craned her neck in an effort to see just what Avery was talking about. The odd slopes of the Vineway, in addition to its sheer scale, weren't making the task any easier.

Wait, there. Down the path to the left...there was something moving. A lot of somethings.

"Looks like a bunch of joggers," Avery said with just a hint of contempt.

"Bunch of what?" she asked. She was now far more concerned with brushing dirt from her carefully assembled ensemble.

"Joggers. You know, people that run?"

"Run from what?"

"Superior modes of travel? I don't know! Why am I having this conversation with you?"

Meanwhile, as the two bickered, a faint buzzing fell upon the Vineway. It was too faint for Avery to take any real notice but it nagged at Lree. "Shh," she shushed him. "Shut up. Listen."

Avery humored her. For a moment. "Okay?" he said, shrugging his shoulders. "What?"

Lree's eyes, well, at least her one visible eye, widened. Those somethings that were central to their debate were now almost upon them. And they weren't joggers.

The odd little hairball dropped back to the ground quickly.

"Seriously, what is your problem?"

"Get down!" she hissed. "Now!"

Before Avery could ask why he should do such a thing something zipped past his head. A large, buzzing something that instinctively caused him to flail about like he had just been set on fire. Again.

"Stop! What're you doin'?!" Lree yelled. He couldn't be this dumb, could he?

Confident the danger had passed Avery calmly asked, "What the hell was that?!"

He probably could be that dumb.

"Bug!" she yelled. "What color?!"

"What? I don't know. Blue?" As he said this, another creature flew by at an incredible speed. "Red. It was red."

"Get down!" Lree, practically becoming one with the floor of the Vineway, seemed unsettled. "More are commin'! Don't touch them!"

"Why would you think that's something I'd want to do?" asked Avery, the magic of the Khauphase song slipping into the recesses of his mind. Maybe getting down wasn't such a bad idea.

"So," he began, "What would happen if I were to touch one?"

"It'd pop."

"Aaaaand that's bad?"

"You'd pop, too."

"Now when you say pop, what do you..."

Lree lifted her head to ensure Avery could hear every single word in the following rant: "Pop! Means you go from bein' one big fat idiot to lots of little tiny idiots splattered all over the ground, got it?!"

"Right, gotcha'," Avery said, more or less understanding the situation. "But what about them?"

Lree looked back to see Avery pointing at something—someone—behind him. Some tall, confusingly dressed night terror that stood out like the newly cleaned windshield of a car about to drive into a swarm of locusts.

"I mean, they're dead already so are they...?"

"Jonsey!" she yelled as several buzzing cannonballs flew by her, "Get down!"

Jones responded in much the same way they had always responded: by doing nothing. One of the "bugs," as Lree had called them, collided with what was at one point Jones's chest, instantly creating a violent bouquet of smoke, rocks, and flowers. The next couple of strikes and subsequent explosions were large enough to shake the bridge and create an impenetrable, sweet-smelling cloud of dust. It's safe to assume that the remnants of the charging swarm had equally devastating encounters as a decent portion of the Vineway, the portion currently occupied by Avery, Lree, and Jones, was beginning to crumble.

Avery made a decision—probably the biggest decision he had ever made in his entire life and he made it quickly, thoroughly, and without regret. There would be no second guessing and no worries that maybe this wasn't such a good idea. He had come to the conclusion—a conclusion reached without committee—that he was most definitely going to run. Probably in a direction opposite of where the explosions were occurring.

"Run, stupid!" Lree yelled, already a good ways ahead of him.

So he ran. It occurred to him as he stumbled over the splintering ground and barely jumped over ever-widening cracks that he had never been this athletic before. At one point simply thinking about having to walk downstairs to the mailbox used to knock the wind out of him. And now look at him—running around as if his life depended on it. It did, of course, which is why it was at this moment his body chose to protest, putting a complete halt to all movement-related operations (including those involving the bowels, thankfully). The burst of panic-fueled energy had fizzled, leaving behind an inefficient engine of poorly used muscle and aching bones that caused him to lose balance and fall into a large fissure that had fortuitously opened before him. The speed in which the chaos unfolded itself was so immediate that Avery was only able to unleash a small, high-pitched shriek before falling into the dark void below.

TEN
The Boy Who Exists But Only Just

As the shaking and rumbling began to subside so too did the wild panic that had encouraged her to run. Lree had nearly crossed the Vineway in its entirety before realizing that she had done so alone. She had run both far and fast, tearing her carefully chosen dress in the process. Releasing a small, irritated sigh, she came to a stop and proceeded to wait for Avery to catch up with all the patience of a middle school gym teacher.

A disquieting silence fell upon the scene, magnifying her solitude tenfold. "No," she said to herself as she began to retrace her steps. "No no no no no," she repeated, as if doing so would increase the chance that whatever it was she had convinced herself was wrong would turn out to be alright. She was walking faster and faster until she was practically running back towards the origin of the chaos. The air was still heavy with smoke and an unusual potpourri of pyrite and blossoms rained down from wherever the sky was. It wasn't long before she lost her own trail, placing her in an unfamiliar environment with absolutely nothing to orient herself with. That is, until a particularly heavy wind dissipated the enormous billow of smoke that had encompassed a bulk of the bridge.

The Vineway was covered in the strangest arrangement of flowers, some of which appeared to be actively growing. Portions of the gigantic structure had clearly been blown off by the explosions while others were deeply scarred, leaving jagged crevices that led to who knows where.

"Too much," she mouthed, both stunned and a little frightened. The bugs shouldn't have caused all this, she thought to herself. They couldn't have. Just then, something blew past the side of her face and up into the shining sky. It appeared to be a long, flashy something performing a rather erratic dance in the wind. It fluttered about until the updraft had been spent, dropping the object lifelessly to the uneven ground of the Vineway. Lree carefully walked over to its flowery terminus and picked it up.

"Damn it," she muttered, clutching the unfashionably green and blue scarf.

"Damn it," she said a little more clearly, tightening her grip on the increasingly garish scarf.

"Damn it damn it damn it damn it damn it damn it!" she said louder and louder, tossing the insultingly kitschy scarf off the warped bridge and into the abyss. She spun around in a panicked rage looking for something to break or at the very least punch. There was nothing, a fact that only added to her distress.

Overwhelmed by a number of unfamiliar emotions she released a final curse and fell to her knees, creating a small eruption of petals. The plants that surrounded her stirred with unusual life, rubbing up against her legs just enough to be irritating.

"Stupid," she said, grabbing a fistful of the assaulting plants. "You're so stupid." She repeated this several times, pulling up a fresh batch of flowers, weeds, and brush with every insult until she had finally created a sort of moat protecting her from any further verdurous onslaught.

What will you do?

Without the boy she had absolutely nothing to barter with. It's not as if the old bat would give up the heart voluntarily.

As she sat amongst the debris, an angry little castle protected by a tiny fosse of dirt and rock, she pondered that last thought. Something about it felt off.

It—whatever it happened to be—came to her as Avery's offensively tacky scarf returned, rescued once more from the abyss by a fashion conscious updraft. Lree sprang to her feet, catching the awful accessory in midair. Upon landing, she quickly wrapped the scarf around the lower half of her face like a colorblind ninja from a early 90's comic book.

Barter? Ridiculous. She'd force the hag to give her the heart. It was all so simple. Why had she even been worried about this?

Avery's descent had been dallied enough by what felt like an endless series of deliberately sharp tree branches so that his landing almost completely failed to kill him. Not that it was an ideal landfall, of course, but it was soft enough to spare him any serious injury other than a heavily bruised bum. There's a good chance he might have lost consciousness but he couldn't be certain due to reasons that will be revealed in just a moment so relax, already. Caressing his bottom like one would a dying puppy, he surveyed his surroundings—something that was quickly becoming routine to him. Waking up in strange places, that is, not rubbing his butt in such a way that it might be mistaken as being affectionate.

Wherever he was didn't offer much to look at. This was mainly because it was pitch black. Fortunately, all he had to do was waggle his phone a bit to shed some light on his situation. A perfunctory inspection of his person revealed that while he was still wearing his fancy hat and messenger bag, neither offered much of anything to waggle. Certainly not a phone. That device had been tucked away in his jacket which inexplicably went missing around Chapter Five.

Far above him, Avery heard the sounds of crackling and rumbling grow fainter and fainter until finally they faded altogether. He was sitting alone in the darkness with a bruised butt, aching arm, no phone, and absolutely no plan of action.

He could get up...wait, could he get up? Despite the protestations of his posterior, he could and did manage to stand. Now he was standing alone in the darkness with a bruised butt, aching arm, no phone, and absolutely no plan of action. Still, things were starting to look brighter—figuratively and literally, strangely enough. His eyes must have been adjusting to the darkness because he could now make out some details about wherever the hell he was. For starters, he was standing in a large pile of leaves. Soon the walls came into view—walls covered completely in vines, flowers, and other greenery that eventually formed an enormous forest canopy.

Everything went dark the moment he lifted his head in an effort to find where he fell from. When he looked down the light returned. Slowly, very, very slowly, he realized that he was creating the light himself. Or rather, his hat was. An uneasiness came over Avery as he took the gaudy headpiece off to inspect it. It was, indeed, glowing. As his eyes adjusted to the intense light, he found that it wasn't the hat that was emitting the intense light, but the enormous bug that had been caught in it.

As was the case with practically every peculiar situation he found himself in, Avery wasn't prepared for this. He had grown rather fond of the hat and saw a future full of sunny, hatted days. Together they'd do all sorts of fun hat things, such as covering up a particularly bad case of bed head, blocking other people's views in theaters, and concealing the top half of his face dramatically during an intense poker game with a couple of grizzly outlaws in an old Western saloon. But now all of that was spoiled—his hat sullied by a giant roach that could, at any moment, explode.

He sat the hat down as gently as he could and took several large steps back. The bug didn't appear to be conscious, presenting an excellent opportunity for Avery to run away and avoid being blown into bite-sized Avery bits. Even he realized that this was an excellent idea which made it truly puzzling why he chose to ignore it.

Avery got down on his knees and crept up on the glowing insect with the same sort of caution one might approach a toddler holding a test tube full of anthrax. The bug was mostly a golden color flecked with purplish spots, similar to freckles or an early sign of a venereal disease. "Jeez," was all he could say in regards to the creature's size. It was, by insect standards, massive—like some sort of armored chihuahua.

Disturbed but driven by an overpowering intrigue, Avery forgot all about his aches, pains, and sense of self-preservation and slowly—oh so slowly—managed to roll the creature on its side. Was this really a bug? Sure, it had wings—several, in fact—and its legs resembled that of a juiced cricket's, but the more he stared at it the more unbug-like it appeared to be. It had arms, which was kind of weird. And were those hands? Jesus cramps, it had hands, too—complete with tiny fingers!

Most curious was its face—it was unmistakably human. The eyes were a bit large and the mouth was a bit small but all of the essential pieces were there and in the right place. It even had a small, spotty patch of purple run across the bridge of its nose from cheek to cheek making it—her—look rather friendly. Combine this with her frazzled, iridescent hair, her unnaturally long neck, her market-friendly proportions—no, this wasn't a bug. This was a toy—a doll destined to be both treasured and set ablaze by some troubled little girl.

Unable to take his eyes off the perplexing creature—still tangled within a mess of string and feathers—Avery was overcome with a feeling that, up until now, had been reserved exclusively for him: pity. He had just begun to consider helping her when she suddenly opened her curiously large black eyes and revealed a surprise set of preposterously large mandibles.

As hard as it may be to believe, this startled Avery. If he said anything in response it was almost certainly foul. The creature struggled to free herself which only served to entangle her further. Her glowing had become erratic, turning Avery's hat into a fashionable strobe light which, under any other circumstances, he would have thought was pretty much been the greatest thing ever.

This was not any other circumstance, however, and he was becoming increasingly worried that both he and his hat would soon be vaporized by this dangerously volatile roach girl. Swallowing hard, he made the difficult decision to leave the hat behind and tiptoe past the bug before she exploded. He had managed to move several yards beyond the threat when his foot became ensnared in the foliage that infested his surroundings. It was then that he made the mistake of looking back. The bug had managed to flip herself—and the hat—over and was now bouncing around rather comically. Her wings could be heard fluttering turbulently against the floor of wherever this was, followed by struggling, plaintive grunts.

Avery turned to leave—a decent plan thwarted by his trapped foot. For reasons not at all clear to him he turned around to face the creature again. The sight of a dancing, glow-in-the-dark sombrero would have typically brought him nothing but delight because, well, Avery is a rather simple fellow. The way the rim flopped around like a wet newspaper with even the slightest movement would have been more than enough to send him into an uncontrollable giggle fit. Instead, he felt very afraid.

He closed his eyes and shook his head slightly in a weak effort to comprehend whatever it was that was on his mind. It didn't help. All he knew was that he had do something and he had to do whatever that something was right now.

Avery took a deep breath, opened his eyes, and with a sharp tug broke free of the ensnaring vines. Cautiously yet filled with an unexplainable determination, he walked back towards the animated hat. He was going to free the equally terrified and terrifying creature.

As he got closer the hat became less and less exuberant, eventually settling on the ground with only a faint glow. Gently, deliberately, Avery picked the hat up and turned it over. The weird bug had clearly worn herself out. She was breathing heavily and putting very little effort into freeing herself. There's also a very strong possibility she didn't even notice that Avery was there.

He set to his task with unyielding resolve, meticulously untying knots and deconstructing bits of the hat until, one by one, the creature's carapace-covered limbs had been freed. He was about to pick her up when a deep, penetrating chill ran down his spine, paralyzing the rest of his body. "What the hell am I doing?" he thought. This was really more of a feeling than an articulated sentence. At that moment, Avery had actually thought, "nipple flop butterscotch booby sailboat," which does very little to convey the sudden realization that he was about to do something dangerous and stupid. It was at this moment—confused, frozen in fear, and thinking about wind-powered watercraft with breasts—that the bug came to.

Regaining control of most of his faculties, Avery tossed the hat to the ground and awkwardly scrambled several steps backwards. The creature was now airborne and clearly quite agitated. She buzzed around the cavernous nursery like a inebriated bee that had just finished pollinating a powder keg. Each time she struck a wall she'd create a small shower of sparks and each time she created a small shower of sparks Avery would cringe.

"Run!" his mind yelled. "Run as far and as fast as you can! Run now! Go!"

"I can't," said his body. "If I move—like, at all—she'll notice me and come after me! Right now she's fine bouncing off the walls."

His mind gave this argument some serious thought. "But," it finally said to his body, "if she continues to ricochet off the walls eventually she will explode and that will be the end of both you and me. Is that how you really want our story to end? As a sad and aimless tale with no real moral other than "hope begets disappointment?"

"At least it got interesting at the very end," his body tried to argue. "Maybe not. Okay, what if we walk away? Slowly."

"That will not do us much good if she explodes," stated his mind. "We need to put as much distance between the winged hand grenade and us as quickly as possible."

His body knew his mind was right—it always was, the stupid jerk. Still, had his mind even considered just how much abuse his body was being subjected to? No! How about how hungry it was? No! Aching? Of course not. All that selfish bastard cared about was living. He didn't know and didn't care just how painful living was.

"I'm not moving," his body said indignantly. "I'm tired and my arm is hurting again. Figure something out. That's what you're good at, isn't it?"

His mind was taken aback. "I have already figured "something" out. It involves you moving away from the immediate area post haste."

"How long do you s'pose it'll be before that thing...you know...?" asked his body.

Now it was his mind's turn to feel indignant. "Are you threatening me, sir?"

"I wonder," said his body. This was followed by another shower of sparks.

"Can we talk about this later, please?" his mind pleaded. "Surely you must realize that it is essential to our survival—yours and mine—that we leave this place right now."

"Oh, look!" his body cheered as the creature slammed into the wall, "Ah, nope. She didn't blow. Maybe the next one?"

Again, the creature hit a wall and, again, no one exploded.

"Or the next one."

"That is exactly how we are going to die, you know that, right? You are going to become so accustomed to that bizarre bug not exploding that you will forget that it can actually do so and then BOOM! No more you, no more me."

His body was starting to see his mind's point—maybe running away wasn't such a bad idea. Before it could yield itself to the idea of fleeing, however, the flying time bomb made a deliberate change to her trajectory and flew within inches of Avery's face where she stopped. She didn't do anything aside from hover in front of him and make both his mind and his body extremely nervous.

"This is why I told you to run," said his mind smugly. If it had a face it would have been sneering.

"I still can," replied his body.

"Yeah? Try it."

Though Avery was well aware of his body—each beat of his heart hammered his chest with increasing discomfort—he could not actually control it. All he could do was stare into the insect's disproportionate eyes, an act that resulted in less terror than it did empathy. He could feel the creature staring back at him—into him—and he wanted desperately to recoil. Still, he could not move.

"You are so stupid," said his mind arrogantly. "If you had just listened to me we would not be in our current predicament. We would be safe and free from the threat of being blown to pieces. But no. You had to think! As if you are even capable of doing that! You are just a big, dumb body."

Well, that was uncalled for. "Am not!" his body yelled back.

"I'm sorry, I shouldn't have said big. I should have said fat. Fatso."

"Hey now..."

"You look like a pregnant football. And that is why I have just now decided on a new name for you. Do you want to hear it?"

His body did not want to hear it but that wasn't about to stop his mind.

"The Expectant Linebacker," it said.

"Shut up!"

"I suppose that is too athletic for you, isn't it? Very well. How about Chubs Meatface? That has a nice, honest ring to it."

"I said shut up!"

"Muddy Muffintops then. I am particularly proud of that one."

His body didn't respond.

"Biggs Beergut."

"Spare Tire Ted!"

"The Human Colostomy Bag!"

"Enough!" his body screamed, sending a surge of angry energy directly to Avery's motor control. In an instant, he broke free of his crippling fear and empathy, released a soft squeal, and weakly backhanded the creature, burning his hand in the process. Now too busy biting his lip and clutching his hand, he failed to notice the bug buzzing quickly around him. She soon flew off past him, taking all of the light with her. Well, most of the light, anyway. As his eyes adjusted once again to the darkness, he noticed a faint trail of shining golden plants revealing a new corridor.

As the pain receded Avery carefully released his injured hand and noticed that it, too, had a slight golden glow, the epicenter of which featured a tiny flower. It had a comforting warmth to it and actually seemed to soothe his aching arm but it was still growing out of the back of his hand and both Avery's mind and body—agreeing for once—found this to be deeply unsettling. He quickly plucked the flower, almost immediately extinguishing the light and restoring the now-familiar pain in his arm. Looking onward, he noticed that the trail, too, had begun to dim.

There was no time for internal argument, regret, or self-pity—soon he'd be enveloped in darkness with absolutely no chance of escape. He'd follow the trail with the ignorant perception that it would lead to safety or at least somewhere with light.

Besides, there'd be plenty of time for internal argument, regret, and self-pity later.

ELEVEN
Dirty Thoughts

Every step towards Love's Lost reminded Lree of how much she despised it. She could hear the maddening murmur of the privileged carrying on, fancy, expensive glasses clinking together, and the tuneless twangs and bangs of what was supposed to pass as music grow louder and louder. This psychedelic cacophony was enough to drive even the most resilient wedding DJ mad and it was only going to become worse.

As luck would have it—perhaps—her secret exit was still largely intact. And though she passed through it with minimal injury she was almost instantly overpowered and assaulted by the offensive stench of hundreds of sweaty tourists, contradictory entrées, and, least pleasing of all, more flowers.

Aside from being meticulously planted and groomed, the flowers that filled Love's Lost were also significantly larger and far more pungent than any found in the Garden or the valley beyond. For reasons that should come as a surprise to no one except Sally Skims-a-Lot over there, Lree couldn't stand them. The very sight of the bepetaled abominations sent her body into a mild spasm. To be fair, the flowers didn't think too fondly of her, either, which is why she decided to sneak into the otherwise dark complex via a well-lit, heavily guarded, and plant-free path.

Under normal circumstances it would have been easier and smarter to crawl through the field of flowers and slip through the complex unnoticed. However, nothing about Lree's circumstances was normal. Nature had taken a severe disliking to the young girl and went to impressive lengths to make her uncomfortable or, in slightly more extreme cases, end her life in the most gruesome way possible. Even the softest foliage would instantly harden in an attempt to stab, cut, or maim her. Trees would drop their largest, heaviest cones onto her head and, if that failed to do any real damage, they'd try to fall on her head themselves.

For all their beauty, flowers were particularly spiteful. Those with thorns would uproot themselves and launch their barbed stems into her, piercing leather and skin alike, while the more unassuming florae would simply try to smother her with petals—as was the case out in the valley—or by releasing thick clouds of noxious pollen.

Lree paused for a moment to allow her vision to adjust to the limited lighting within the complex. Things could have gone differently, she cursed. Things *should* have gone differently. If that idiot hadn't been wasting so much time lollygagging on the Vineway or singing his stupid songs they'd have made it across together and she wouldn't have to be doing what she was doing now, which was using a tacky scarf to strangle a sentry into unconsciousness. Truth be told, she wasn't exactly opposed to this course of action—it's just that her original plan was so much more straightforward.

After a struggle that went on uncomfortably too long, the guard finally passed out or possibly died. Details. Lree was too busy stalking her next victim to tell the difference. Though the path was lined with lanterns her near insubstantial figure gave her a fiendish advantage even when bathed in the bright blue light, as did the Mistress's commitment to employing the most inappropriate people to fill security positions. Where did she even find these jerks, Lree wondered, felling the next guard who clearly was someone's forgetful grandfather.

Two down, at least four more to go. They didn't seem to be doing much—one was looking for something on the ground while the others seemed to be searching the bushes that lined the path. This would be fun. Easy. Sorry, I meant easy.

And fun.

One, two, three, four—all fell quickly to Avery's tragic fashion sense. Lree crept, dashed, jumped, and rolled her way into the shadow of the large brick wall that surrounded the outer garden. The entrance to the labyrinth was just a few feet away, blocked by a locked gate that she was confident she could climb over.

"You know," said a raspy voice from behind, "I've been trying to think of a way to really insult you."

Lree spun around and was immediately forced up against the gate by a large stone gauntlet. There was no time to react—the impact forced her to drop Avery's scarf which given its equally offensive and deadly nature was probably for the best. She hadn't even realized that she was being held by the neck until her assailant tightened her grip.

"I thought maybe I'd say something like, "subtle as always," or, "how's the boo-boo?," continued the increasingly threatening voice from a conveniently placed shadow. Another hand, one without a stone glove, reached out to brush Lree's hair aside to reveal a series of massive scars covering the right side of her face, narrowly missing her eye. The rather impertinent hand pushed Lree's head to the side and clumsily groped its way to what was left of her ear. There was very little Lree could do aside from struggle, loosening her assailant's grip just enough to gasp for air.

"Look at that. Anyway, I thought, "What if I just ambush her? You know, pin her to the wall and ruin whatever stupid thing she's up to." So here I am!" her attacker said with an awkward cheerfulness.

"What're you doin' here?" Lree coughed.

"I live here," said the apparently less-than-mysterious figure significantly less cheerful than before. She grabbed Lree by the top of her dress and flung her onto the ground into the light of the pathway. "What are *you* doing here, little flower?"

Cobblestone isn't the softest material one could use to create a pathway no matter what type of stone one chooses to cobble. The impact was, without a doubt, painful. Though her body ached, Lree managed to turn herself over to face the most menacing and fearsome coat rack she had ever encountered. Clad in a thick, brown mac and an ill-fitting cloche hat, the creature within managed to hide nearly all of her features. This was absolutely for the better.

Lree wiped a bit of grit and a lot of blood away from her cheek with the back of her hand. "I don't need to tell you anything," she growled. "Now outta my way, sister."

"You're amazing. Truly incredible and so brave," said a sultry-voiced, inappropriately armored battle vixen. "I've never met anyone quite like you."

"Neither have I," Avery sighed, effortlessly pulling a broadsword from the skull of what appeared to be some form of tyrannosaurid.

"I thought you were...I thought you were a nobody," she said, looking away in a futile attempt to hide her flushed cheeks. "But when I fell and you drew your sword against the Lizard King to defend my honor I—"

Avery turned to face his damsel in distress. Shoulders hunched and hands covering her face, she was clearly overwhelmed by his awesome presence. He stood a moment to allow the wind to play with his impressive, barbarian-inspired mane.

"Come on, baby," he finally said, coolly. "Run with me."

"I—"

"Shh," he shushed, moving closer to gift her with a reassuring kiss. "Let's run."

Gently, tenderly, he moved her hands away from her beautiful yet glaringly nondescript face. "Let's run," he said again in a low whisper, closing his eyes as his lips grew nearer. Suddenly overcome with a disturbing sense of reality, he became very concerned that he might actually miss her lips. He opened his eyes slightly to make sure he was still on target and noticed the recipient of his tremendous endowment had vanished. All that was left was a black, empty void. Not entirely empty, actually, as he soon found out when he was ejected from his daydream by a harsh moment of rough intimacy with a wall.

"CRACK!" said either his skull or the wall.

Avery had been following the trail of shining golden flowers far beyond the limit of his patience. They had begun to dim faster than he was able to follow, eventually leaving him in complete darkness. For a while he shut down, dropping to the floor to reconsider his life choices up to this point. "Where did it all go wrong?" he asked himself aloud. He pondered this question for quite some time, counting down each probable mistake until he eventually reached his own birth. Why hadn't he been consulted about that, he thought. No one asked him if he wanted to be brought into existence. What kind of psychotic, selfish bastard would do such a thing?

Before he fell into the self-loathing stupor of an antinatalist and collapse into a ball of tears and sophomoric philosophy, a gust of wind blew against his face. In a flash of uncharacteristic intuitiveness, he decided to follow it.

Any time the wind shifted he'd stop to realign himself so that it was once again flowing directly into him. For a while this seemed like a great plan—until the wind stopped altogether. The corridor had widened quite a bit and the ground had evened out. The entangling vines, inconveniently placed roots, and cruelly positioned shrubs had disappeared, leaving only a carpet of dry leaves and twigs, both of which fell to the mercy of his plenteous weight with a satisfying crunch. With one hand on the wall for guidance and the other in front of him feeling for potential dangers, he was poised to push forward.

And so he did. He pushed forward with the speed, grace, and confidence of an infant attempting to walk unsupported for the first time across a bed of hot coals. It was all very boring, which is why I've decided that the next thing Avery walks into says "KLONG!" and says it in such a deep, hollow voice that it echoes throughout the blackness.

Avery rubbed his forehead and felt around for any signs of lasting damage. It wasn't nearly as sore as he had been expecting which falsely led him to believe he was getting tougher. The truth of the matter is that he was hardly moving when he hit the wall and it was starting to become clear even to him that the wall wasn't a wall at all. He smiled at his little rhyme and proceeded to run his hands along the non-wall before him. He felt stone, plants again—lots of plants, actually—and something that very possibly could have been metal. Focusing on the metallic texture, he groped the object along its perimeter and determined it was some kind of massive door. That is to say, he hoped it was a door. Never mind why would there be a door in a cave. It was a door, Avery had convinced himself, and it would lead him out of the cave. If he could only figure out a way to open it.

There were odd crevices seemingly arranged randomly about the supposed door as well as several insets but nothing felt like a handle or knob. Occasionally he would be able to get a grip on a fairly deep crevice but the door—it was a door, damnit!—wouldn't budge.

Just as he was about to give up, nothing happened. With his back to the wall, he slid down the increasingly unlikely door until he was sitting in a pile of branches and twigs. He slapped some of the nearest sticks away from him, creating a momentary burst of blue light and a small fright. Was he seeing things? What if he really did hurt himself but the damage was all internal?

Avery, quickly approaching a state of hysteria, scrambled to his feet. This sent glowing underbrush everywhere which was both worrying and reassuring. There was just enough light now to reveal that he hadn't been walking on, sitting on, and falling on dried twigs. His reassurance now left him, screaming into the darkest reaches of the cave. A curious sensation of terror and nausea began to sliver up his spine but was quickly squelched with a sudden panic caused by metal clanking and hinges creaking. The door—told you it was a door!—opened slowly, trickling more light into the cave and confirming what Avery had denied himself of deducing: the floor was blanketed in giant, humanoid roach husks. Terror and nausea returned in force as more light revealed that none of the husks had actually been discarded. Each carapace was still full—more of less—of its lifeless host.

He shut his eyes to avoid the sight only to find that the image of the cave floor was much more vivid in his mind. Each mangled body, each twisted expression, each individual scene of horror was neatly placed in a file folder marked "Future Nightmares" and catalogued in the portion of his brain that took a perverse pleasure in remembering terrible things at the most inopportune times, such as asking that really nice girl at the copy center out for coffee or going back for seconds at an all-you-can-eat crab buffet.

One particular image stood out from the distressing slideshow. It was a familiar creature with a head of short, iridescent hair and a freckled face lying atop an offensive pile of bugs far more deceased than she.

A thought occurred to Avery. A horrible, offensive thought borne from his aching arm. It involved the bug. More precisely, it involved the mysterious soothing properties of the bug's glowing blood.

As he picked up the questionably exanimate creature he was overcome with even more troubling thoughts. Thoughts such as "This is really gross," "What the hell am I doing?", and "HAAAARRRRG!", thoughts that should have been at the very top of Avery's list of things to think about when picking up an oversized roach that could explode at any moment, were curiously absent. In their place were more observational and oddly compassionate thoughts ranging from the creature's remarkably light weight to her challenged existence.

The light was still quite dim but did little to deter Avery. It was as if he had become possessed by a life-threatening compulsion to study the volatile creature. It was futile, of course, since his own study of entomology categorized insects as either Should Be Squished or Flee From In Terror. She didn't appear to be breathing or, as stated, alive. The best idea he could come up with was to poke her. There was no noticeable response. If she was alive it was very doubtful she would be for much longer.

Sympathy slowly replaced the panic that had replaced the terror and nausea that had replaced the reassurance that left him in a cave full of terribly, terribly dead insects. This new sensation didn't stick around too long as he realized that he was actually holding one such insect. In his hands. Without a crumpled tissue or shoe.

His immediate reaction was to throw it as far away from his person as possible and he was about to do this when he recalled the words "volatile" and "could explode at any moment." There was also the matter of the creature's —deep breath—blood which, he recalled with no small amount of regret, was the reason he picked her up to begin with.

It was strange, but simply just holding her seemed to ease the pain in his afflicted arm.

Deciding it'd be best (that is, easier) to not think about it right now, Avery began to make his way towards the door and into the light. The sound of approaching footsteps, however, immediately sent him scuttling back into the darkness.

"Shouldn't you be somewhere else?" asked Lree, attempting unsuccessfully to stand, "Threatening people or punchin' things?"

"What do you think I'm doing now?" the coat rack replied. She reached down and grabbed the collar of Lree's dress with her massive, seemingly gauntleted hand, helping her estranged sister up with all the grace and delicacy of a drunken crane operator. As a result, the bulkier, lower portion of Lree's dress tore completely off, revealing much of the damaged figure beneath.

"Those are new," she said, eyeing the many, many scars upon Lree's legs. "You do those yourself?"

"Shut up, Dahlia," Lree snapped back, trying to knock her sister's hand away.

Dahlia pretended to ignore the attack, moving her hand just outside of her sister's reach. "I see your sense of fashion hasn't changed."

"You're one to talk. Look at you," Lree said, taking a slight defensive posture, "You look like an old umbrella."

"Careful, little flower." Dahlia's words weren't meant so much as a caution as they were a thinly veiled threat. She turned her attention to the small regiment of unconscious bodies scattered about the cobblestone pathway. Prefaced by a cross between a chortle and a death rattle, Dahlia said, "Mother won't be happy about this."

"She'll probably thank me. Her guards are stupid."

Dahlia appeared to tilt her head a bit, as if Lree had just spoken to her in algebraic. After a moment, she either chuckled or threw up in her mouth. Though neither would be appreciated at this particular time the former was slightly less disgusting. Lree was incensed.

"This is good! This is so good! Those are...you really think they're her guards?"

Lree had thought that, yes. Now, however, she was beginning to suspect otherwise. As such, she said nothing as embarrassment began to overtake her anger.

"You took out her *gardeners,* you twerp."

"Her what?"

"*Gardeners.* They were *gardening,* not guarding. This is too good! Oh, wait 'til Pentas hears about this!"

Lree's tone swiftly changed to one featuring considerably more panic. "Pentas is here?" she asked quickly. "Right now?"

"Oh yes, she's here, by the way. Or I should say she's back. She spent a while out in the shining looking for you."

"Can you believe it?" Dahlia continued, grabbing Lree by the arms with her massive, stone hands. This was not at all comfortable as one might imagine but Lree was simply too distracted to react. "I heard she even went out past the Garden! Pentas...beyond the Garden. Anyway, she was devastated when you left. I mean, she must have been. I don't think I've ever seen her so..."

"Upset?"

"Angry," she said with what was guaranteed to be a smile.

Lree found this far more distressing than any retribution for assaulting her mother's landscapers. Pentas—the oldest sister—was terrifying enough when she wasn't upset. The thought of her being angry was almost too much. Hastily, Lree changed the subject.

"Why're there so many gardeners out here anyway? What're they doin'?"

"What else would they be doing, runt? Gardening. Some drunken guest has been going through the complex messing up the grounds."

Tightening her grip, she continued, "That's really why I'm out here. I was tracking him when what do I happen to see but my estranged little sister making a complete fool of herself."

Dahlia waited just long enough for Lree to respond then quickly interrupted her with: "Why do you keep trying, anyway? You can't do it. You can't escape your own curse."

"Y-you're hurting me…!"

"Yes, I know. You know what else I know? You're going to die here, little flower."

Lree winced as Dahlia's rocky fingers threatened to bury themselves further into her flesh. "Lemme go! I...I don't wanna hurt you!" She wasn't sure why she said that. As far as threats go this one was empty. It was, in fact, so empty that it was more of a discarded threat wrapper than an actual threat.

Dahlia's laugh echoed the sound of a dog choking on its own snout. "You," she said, catching her breath, "you really are dumb. Hurt me? You barely managed to take out Old Man Willy over there. Come to think of it, wasn't he already dead?"

Releasing her grip, Dahlia dropped her sister back onto the path. It had not become any softer from the last time she had fallen upon it. "You know what?" she scoffed, removing her oversized hat, "Let's see it. Let's see you try to hurt me."

She stared down her little sister in a successful attempt to intimidate her. Dahlia—her face—was dark and earthen, splitting and cracking at even the slightest change in its expression. The top of her cruelly graven head was mostly bare, save for long, sporadically placed strands of singed hair too few in number to discern any actual color. Two dully pointed protrusions sat ill-centered atop of her head.

Not yet satisfied with her effort to intimidate her sister, Dahlia clumsily unbuttoned her enormous coat, dropping it to the ground with a surprisingly loud clomp.

"Come on!" she challenged Lree, striking her own chest several times for effect. She wore nothing but a ragged, uneven pair of pants which might have been titillating were this someone other than Dahlia. Her upper body seemed to be in constant flux, changing shape and shifting from leathery flesh to harsh stone and back again in a matter of seconds. This, along with the chainsaw sculpture she called her head made her very difficult to look at.

She did have some control over her body's disturbing coalescence as Lree very well knew so her boasting wasn't entirely unfounded. Hurting her was almost a complete impossibility. At least, physically.

Lree stood up and retook her offensive stance. Without warning, she struck."Why're you out here?" she asked.

"Are you deaf? I told you, runt. I'm..."

"I know, I know. The guest destroyin' everything. Did you catch him?"

"I'm going to catch him, yeah. Once I'm done with you."

"Unless Pentas already caught him."

"Pentas," Dahlia said with just a hint of disdain, "She could do that."

Lree continued her insidious kata. "No wonder she's mother's favorite. She's so reliable."

"I'm reliable, too!" Dahlia stammered. "I'm just...I've got you to deal with first, you little rat."

"That's a good enough excuse."

"What is?"

"Me. Ah'm your excuse. A've always been your excuse, right? Because you can't..."

"I can! And I will take care of the guest!"

"You mean in there," she said pointing beyond the gate. "Inside?"

Dahlia's fists, previously clenched so tightly they resembled miniature boulders, loosened. It was the opening Lree had been looking for.

"With all the other guests?" she added.

Her strange stone sister didn't say anything. The urge to punch Lree through the gate had vanished. Whatever feeling had been left in that particularly violent void was deeply confusing. Was it jealousy? Embarrassment? Shame? She was flustered and not very good at hiding it. The commixture of odd elements that made up her body began to shift a little faster and with greater irregularity. For Lree, the fight had been going well and now it was time for the final blow.

"Mother give you that coat?"

Dahlia struggled to maintain her dignity, composure, and physical form, ultimately failing to do any of the three terribly well. She picked up her discarded garments, covered herself, slammed open the gate, and stomped past her sister. She trailed steam and melted cobblestone in her wake.

The one thing about being a monster, Lree thought to herself, was that she understood their weaknesses all too well.

Avery watched in horror as an avalanche of meatless invertebrate shells spilled into the tunnel. It wasn't so much the sight that was sickening—though it was incredibly unpleasant—it was the sound. It was like a large cat happily bounding in and out of a huge pile of leaves were you to replace the leaves with giant beetles.

"...does it," said an absurdly gruff voice as the last wave of death settled in the cave. "I'm done with this stinkin' job and this stinkin' place."

"Don't say that," said another, less gruff voice that was at least gruff enough to leave Avery feeling both intimidated and emasculated. "You'll get us into trouble with the ol' lady."

The gruffer voice released a mocking laugh. "Coward. She's just an old woman. I'll tell it to her face! I'll walk right up to 'er and say "This in't what I signed up for. Go find someone else to dump your garbage, sister."

"You'll say that?"

"Yeah."

"Right to her face."

"Y-yeah, sure."

"What about the girls?"

This question was met with silence though it intrigued Avery more than it comfortably should have. Impressively, his mind took the question "What about the girls?"—an ominous inquiry that was quite clearly asked in such a way to insinuate fear and pain and other dreadful things—and repurposed it into something ridiculously hopeful and pleasant. He heard the question repeated in his head. "What about the girls?" his own, internal voice asked, raising its imaginary eyebrow and nodding its imaginary head approvingly. He then proceeded to repeat it several times, eliminating every hint of foreboding nuance until eventually he could answer it with a not-at-all sleazy "Aw yeah."

"What about the girls, Krim?" asked a third voice. This voice— prim, proper, and quite deliberately seductive—piqued Avery's already piqued curiosity well past the realm of reason. Without so much as a thought he stuffed the almost-living bomb he had been holding into his increasingly handy messenger bag and peered around the corner. Squinting until it hurt he barely managed to discern a single, indistinct figure. The much more interesting voice that was neither gruff nor gruffer did not seem to belong to the blurry shape. Fortunately.

Avery's eyes adjusted to the room's luminosity at a pace that was very convenient to the plot. He saw what appeared to be a tall man wearing a horned animal hat, a leather apron, and very little else. Another figure soon came into view—one which the unclothed man creature seemed to be backing away from. This figure—nothing more than a shadow, really—spoke in a sultry, almost comically feminine voice that was more than a little familiar. The more he heard it, in fact, the more it sounded like that of the inappropriately armored battle vixen that he nearly kissed. In his dreams, of course. I mean, come on. It's Avery.

"You have yet to answer my question," she said.

"I-I didn't mean nothin' by it, Cap'n," said the barely clothed beast of a man, inadvertently flashing Avery who didn't realize it was even possible for the human bottom to have a six pack.

"Of course. Still, I am curious as to whom you were referring to—and what you meant by "What about the girls?""

The man's voice was cracking so much he couldn't respond. His friend, the gruffer of the two, interjected from somewhere out of view: "I was just talkin', Cap'n, about the cave. I was saying that maybe...we should find a, uh, a new place to, you know. Dump."

"I see," said the captivating voice, "But that answer does not seem to satisfy either of my questions" Avery still couldn't make out anything more than the owner's shadow, forcing his imagination to create an image for him. She was tall, no...hang on. Not tall. Not short, either. Maybe tall? Tallish? But short, too. Her hair was long, black, and...curly? No curls. Well, some curls. At the end. Full, pouty lips red as blood. Gross—blood? How about an apple? Not one of those green sour apples but a red apple—the kind that don't really taste like apples, more like apple-flavored sponges. God, he hated those apples. Of course, he hated most fruit. Fruit and vegetables. Cripes, now her lips were taking the shape of red peppers. His dream girl was quickly turning into a puppet that teaches grade school children the importance of eating a healthy diet.

"P-please," pleaded the stronger McGruff, rapidly losing whatever composure he had been able to scrabble back together. "It was Dobble who started it. I was tryin' to get 'im to stop."

Avery's eyes wandered as his mind continued to paint pictures of erotic fruit and vegetable trays so he missed the long, exasperated sigh that preceded the troubling series of unintelligible screams. His body reacted accordingly, however, taking complete control and flinging him back into the darkness in an act of desperate self-preservation.

"You can come out now," he thought he heard. "There is no need to hide from me."

The words—her words—came upon a sweet breath that turned just sharp enough to penetrate Avery's heart. He desperately wanted to know who was speaking them but he seemed to be paralyzed from the neck down. His mind, while certainly not an extraordinary one and, on more than one occasion, would deliberately put him into a dangerous situation just so that it could experience a quick hit of adrenaline, was in total disarray. A small portion of it was dedicated to convincing his body to move—though the finesse it had shown earlier was all but gone.

"Move," it said. Over and over again.

What remained of his ability to think focused on creating a solid image of the mysterious speaker or, more accurately, failing to create a solid image of the mysterious speaker. Her body took on what was essentially a humanoid shape though it was shattered and pellucid. Only her head was truly visible and even then it didn't make any sense. If she had hair it consisted entirely of raging flames dyed by the shifting color of her skin. This left only her face as a focal point which, at times, was lovely, intimate, confusing, and eldritch. Eventually it lost all distinction save for a set of large, almond-shaped eyes. They were both beautiful and distressing as they were devoid of any pupils—only green, smoldering sclera.

He felt her warmth first upon him and then around him. Impossibly soft hands gently maneuvered his head so that he had no other choice but to look her deep in her taking, virescent eyes. Strangely, he did not pull away. He could not pull away. Avery felt nothing but pure joy as he stared at the nebulous entity. Pure joy and inner peace. Pure joy, inner peace, and extraordinary self-loathing.

"I'm not hiding," he probably said. He wasn't really paying attention to anything except the mysterious maiden before him. Everything about her radiated sensuality, even if everything was poorly defined. She was real. She *had* to be real. Like...the door.

"Oh?" She placed her hand upon what could have been her bosom, leading Avery's eyes downward. Maybe it was her collarbone. Or somewhere in between.

"I'm just...lost," he said with a noticeable slur.

"And now you are found," she replied without missing a beat. Her voice was much heavier now, almost oppressively so. Avery didn't care—he simply needed to hear her again. These past several seconds without her voice had been devastating. "Tell me, what is it that you wish for? What is it that you desire?"

Avery raised his head—slowly. "I...I want to see you?"

The alluring vision released a charming giggle. "I am right here before you. Can you not see me?"

"Naw, that's not it," he said, no longer sure of who he was addressing. "I can see you or something that may be you. You're kind'a blurry and...not really all there. In one piece."

If she had been taken aback by Avery's words she had concealed such a reaction extremely well. "I assure you that I am of one piece and much, much more than a blur. Please, look harder."

Willingly or unwillingly, Avery complied. He was quite the expert at making the most mundane task look as if it took a monumental amount of effort, however, there was nothing mundane about this. Euphoria and desperation made concentration nearly impossible.

Nearly.

Avery found that if he actually tried he could, briefly, bring small sections of the amorphous figure into focus. These minute moments of clarity—the tip of the nose, for example, or an outline that might have been a cheek—allowed him to create many significant pieces to a truly tantalizing puzzle. Unfortunately, Despite his success the end result was more Cubist than Renaissance. He was no closer to identifying his tormentor and that fact wound itself around his heart, strangling it.

"Well?," said the voice, "Do you see me now? Be honest."

"Yeah," he said, being dishonest. "No," he added, being honest. "I know you're there. I can see a...shape, I guess. And some details around your face but please don't be upset. I'm trying, I'm really, really trying..."

"Shh...It is alright. I am not upset."

"But you're crying."

The mysterious woman, the woman who would one day father all eight of his children, seven of which would be named after a dwarf with a crippling mental disorder while the last one would simply be named Heavy Metal Warrior, pulled away. In an instant, she was gone. Avery's heart, exceptionally tender from the encounter, crumbled into ash and that ash was blown away by a cold, bitter wind. He didn't care where he was, how he got there, or even how he was going to get out. In fact, he didn't care about much of anything. Most of it—life—seemed utterly pointless and extraordinarily painful. Except for those sugary marshmallow chicks that show up in the stores around Easter. Those were good. And fries—like really, really good fries that have just the right amount of salt and crunch. What he would do for some fries right now. Also a comb. What with all of the falling and shrubbery and explosions and punches he wouldn't be surprised if he had any hair left. He checked for good measure. Yes, he had hair and yes, he needed a comb.

An idea struck him. It wasn't a good idea but it was a distracting idea. Avery crawled over towards the light filtering in from the other side of the doorway and sifted through the lifeless pile of carapaces. He managed to find one that appeared to be empty enough and began to examine it closer—but not too closely lest he lose his lunch (had he a lunch to lose, of course). The specimen was intact which worked both for and against him.

He closed his eyes and took a deep, reassuring breath. This wasn't at all awful, he told himself. This wasn't at all awful and disgusting.

SNAP! That's the exact sound it made—a perfect onomatopoeia that one could take real pride in producing were it not associated with breaking a leg off of a not entirely vacant insect carapace. When he opened his eyes he discovered that he was, indeed, the less than proud owner of a giant roach leg.

Coincidentally, he was also the increasingly despondent owner of a giant roach that happened to be missing a leg. Avery tossed the latter aside and rubbed his hand furiously on his pants, completely failing to clean his hand but succeeding marvelously in rearranging the filth on his pants into an enchanting new pattern. Having settled down slightly he looked closer at his latest acquisition. It was, without a doubt, awful and disgusting. But, as he suspected, it was also bristly. Certainly bristly enough to be used as a comb.

Desperate times and all that.

So we're just going to say that yes, Avery used the severed leg to comb his hair and move right the hell along because, Jesus, man. I mean, really?

His hair styled—and now entirely devoid of any color—Avery dropped the "comb" into his bag and returned his attention to the lighted room. Gruff and Gruffer seemed to have left, as did his dream woman. He slipped around the corner of the door and crept into the room with as much stealth as one might expect from a drunken elephant sneaking into a bowl of Rice Krispies. He didn't really think about what had just happened (prior to the sickening salon session, that is) because he didn't remember most of it. All that remained was a vague feeling of longing which, when combined with excessive exhaustion, stupidity, and hormones, was more than enough to push him onward.

He didn't spend long studying the room as it offered very little of interest. It was long, like a hall of sorts, and overflowing with empty barrels. At the end of the hall was an open doorway that appeared to lead to a winding stone staircase. That staircase became his new goal.

Avery was so focused on leaving the room that he walked right on by one of the most fascinating things he would have seen up until this point in the story had he been just a little more observant and a lot less embittered. It was an ash sculpture—beloinclothed, buff, and bipedal. The last descriptor is of particular importance given that the subject was clearly a moose. He was kneeling with his bulky body turned slightly and his beefy arms almost pushing the viewer away. Overall, the piece looked as if it had been taken directly from the cover of an eccentric work of erotic fiction (something like, say, *Elk Lodge Exposé* or *Get Moose & Girl*).

As impressive as it was both in detail and size—even kneeling it was taller than Avery—the bizarre choice of such a fragile medium made it extremely susceptible to collapsing even against the slightest breeze. Avery, not being so slight himself, left a small gale in his wake as he sped along to the exit. The sculpture—this brilliant, absurdist piece of modern art—crumbled instantly into a massive pile of dust.

Not that Avery noticed, of course. Nor did he take any notice of the second pile he encountered just before the staircase. The half dozen or so other piles he encountered on his way up the winding stairwell also went unnoticed.

TWELVE
The Quiet One Who Says Everything

"Look at this," said Kranston, pointing at one of the many damaged hedges that lined the fields outside of the complex. It didn't matter which hedge he was pointing at because no one was paying him any attention. He could have been pointing at a hedge that was on fire or even copulating with another, sexier hedge and the reaction would have been the same.

"Uh huh," said Rans, mindlessly spraying the same healthy rose bush he had sprayed no less than four times already.

Kranston rolled his one eye so fiercely that it slipped into its neighboring socket. He turned around to look at his other apprentice, a young lady named Burnst, hoping for an actual response. Her finger, exploring the depths of her unchartered nasal cavity, was response enough. The old man sighed heavily and wondered how he got stuck with these two imbeciles. Gardening is an important profession. Why, one might say it's absolutely crucial were the one saying such a thing Kranston. Without the gardeners, he believed, Love's Lost would turn into a forest—wild and unruly. He'd seen it happen before, long ago. How long ago he couldn't say. Not because he was forgetful (which he was) or incredibly old (which he also was), but because the passage of time was simply too difficult of a concept to grasp.

For Kranston, time exists in has beens, right nows, and will bes. There are no yesterdays, todays, and tomorrows because there is no such thing as a day. Or a night, for that matter. The word night is a nonsense word that's hardly known outside of Love's Lost. Weeks, months, years—all total gibberish.

That's not to say there are no methods of measuring from then to now and so on. Farmers and cultivators have been known to track small pockets of what we call time using livestock, with each heartbeat counting as an individual unit. Unfortunately this method isn't terribly practical; cows, sheep, and pigs make for awkward wristwatches.

Kranston had, indeed, been tending the grounds of Love's Lost for a long, long time, or several hundred herds in cattle beats. He was among the first recruited from the Garden—handpicked by the Mistress herself! Of course, back then it wasn't called the Garden. It was...something else. Something else entirely. A town, perhaps. Small but lively. There was another town, too, where Love's Lost now stands. He couldn't remember the name of that town, either, but it had the most magnificent temples. And a giant pillar. It was quite impressive, or so he liked to believe. The memory of what it looked like had been lost, long since been replaced with the image of Fortune, the monstrous willow that blankets the complex in constant darkness.

"Look at this," he repeated under his breath. The old man stared at the hedge and the gaping hole in the hedge stared back at the old man. The edges were brown, brittle, and most definitely dead. "Rans," he called. "This. Spray this, please."

Rans, a thin young man with poor posture and an overly apathetic outlook on life, stared through the grousing gardener. "What?" he asked as if responding to a voice inside his head.

"Here. Come here and spray this hole." Realizing his mistake, Kranston quickly added, "Around the hole. The brown bits around the hole in the hedge, please."

His indifferent apprentice shuffled over to hedge and allowed his pump to fall off his back and onto the ground. He then began to prime the device—much to Kranston's dismay. "No, no! Not like that," he interrupted. "You're going to put the needle right through. Here, let me show you. And pay attention this time."

Kranston was a master of his craft but he recognized that the majority of his accomplishments would not have been possible without the bugs that flocked to Love's Lost: the voorn. More specifically, their blood. There were many different varieties with many different uses. His most trusted tool, the ol' pump and spray, was fueled by the green ones. The secret, as Kranston attempted to show his increasingly distracted apprentice, was to pump the device slowly so the needle in the fuel canister would barely puncture the creature. This would almost guarantee enough elixir to revive an entire acre of land.

He pressed the pump slowly. "You'll know when you hit it—you can feel it. The resistance. Then just listen for the chittering. If the bug stops chittering, you've driven the needle in too far and the elixir'll spoil faster."

The older landscaper returned the equipment to his apprentice and watched in dull surprise as the young man completely failed to follow his instructions. At least his aim was on target this time, he thought. Each burst of elixir that fell onto a damaged portion of the hedge repaired it instantly. Within a couple of minutes, the hole was whole.

"That's better," Kranston said using the best smile he could muster. "Now, let's work on the lawn."

It was a simple enough problem to resolve, however, that the problem even existed made Kranston very uncomfortable. He thought he had seen it all—guests had abused the grounds in every fashion from dancing in the flowerbeds to practicing erotic topiary. This was different, though. A path had quite clearly been carved in the lawn—again, not terribly distressing given the surplus of alcoholic beverages available within Love's Lost and the resulting conga lines that can span hundreds of feet in length. This wasn't the result of a runaway conga line. though. The grass wasn't crushed—it was dead.

"Fill in this here, here, and here" he said to Rans, pointing there, there, and there. Kranston turned his attention to his other apprentice who had apparently struck gold during her high-risk nasal expedition and was currently studying her spoils. He then turned his attention back to Rans who had returned to spraying the hedge but this time without his equipment.

The old gardener's thoughts wandered as he began to mend the lawn himself. How many gardeners had he trained? And how many of those gardeners went onto become master gardeners? Had he upset the Mistress? Impossible. The gardens—his gardens—we immaculate. At least, up until now.

He walked further and further into the darkness, griping and mending. It was only when he stopped to prime his equipment that he noticed someone off in the distance. He turned around briefly to verify that his apprentices were where he left them. Though he couldn't quite make out their individual features there was a familiar feeling of stupidity emanating from their direction. "Honored guest," he began, turning back around, "Are you lost? I'm afraid this area's restricted."

No answer.

Kranston drew in closer. This wasn't the first inebriated guest he'd have to escort out of the garden. Still, he couldn't recall ever having to relocate anyone quite so massive.

"Honored guest?" he said again, though this time with a bit more agitation.

Still no answer. The old man cleared his throat and reached out for the imposing figure. As gently as possible, he poked the guest in what he assumed was his or her back; the guest's enormity and strangely ragged clothing made it rather difficult to tell.

"Excuse me," he said, poking a few more times. Each prod from his stubby finger seem to do nothing more than jingle the guest's jewelry. Finally, he reached for their arm or, at least, where he thought their arm should have been. Just as he had made contact he was startled by a loud crinkling noise from behind him.

Hand still in place, Kranston clutched his chest with the other and looked over his shoulder. "What are you two doing?" he hissed at his apprentices as they approached him.

Simultaneously, they replied, "I'm bored," and "Can we go now?" It didn't really matter who said what.

Kranston was seething though he did his best to hide it as not offend the guest. He thought of what happy memories he could to help regain his composure. He thought of the legion of flowers that flourished throughout the complex and he thought of the lovely hedges that formed its natural corridors. He thought of the dancing trees—their brightly colored lights and deafening drums—that never failed to move him. He thought of the way the grass had crinkled when his unworthy apprentices walked up to him. Well, wait. That wasn't quite right. He had just mended that grass. Healthy grass doesn't crinkle, crack, or crunch.

It was, of course, at this moment that the guest chose to respond beyond jingles and jangles. Kranston withdrew his hand as the giant before him slowly turned to face him. The senseless collection of rags, tacky jewelry, and dirty, tumbled hair did absolutely nothing to hide the skeletal horror beneath.

"Honored guest?" the old man asked, his tone changing from mildly annoyed to quietly terrified. Regardless of how the creature replied Kranston was already committed to the idea of running away.

The foppish pile of bone and refuse lurched forward which was all the encouragement the old gardener needed to enact his plan. "Run!" he yelled, turning around to see that Rans and Burnst had already done so and were well on their way to the inner gate. Change of plans. "Wait," he screamed after them, "please, wait!"

While it was impossible to determine his exact age, it's perfectly reasonable to consider Kranston to be doddery. Broken down, withered, and haggard are also acceptable descriptors. And though he was running away as fast as he possibly could, "as fast as he possibly could" didn't amount to a whole lot. Something cold and hard clamped onto his shoulder, forcing him down to his broken down, withered, and haggard knees. He struggled to get back up, due partially to being incredibly old but mostly because the creature's grip was unyielding. When he saw his apprentices throw the gate open (and quickly slam it shut behind them) without so much as looking back his spirit surrendered. He couldn't curse them because he couldn't blame them. No. You know, never mind that. He could blame them and, in doing so, felt just a tiny bit better. Ungrateful, cowardly brats.

Unexpectedly, the monster released their grip, giving Kranston the option of running away (only to get caught again and killed) or turning around (to get killed right away and forgo all of that running around nonsense). Neither were particularly great choices but turning around would at least allow him to die with dignity. If someone was around to watch him die, that is. Like his apprentices. Stupid, spoiled jerks.

So the old man turned around and came face to face with possibly one of the worst things he could recall ever seeing. For a full description, please refer back to the second chapter of this book, around the part where Avery says, "Hello...thing." Nothing's really changed except, of course, for the giant hat, the mass of wigs, and the copious amounts of jewelry that dangled from their neck and shoulder axe, clinking and clanging together like a wrecking ball repeatedly slamming into a pipe organ. Kranston was paralyzed. All he could do was wait for his inevitable but hopefully very quick demise.

The bejeweled guest dropped to what would have to pass as their knees and dug one of their hands deep into the earth. Just as quick, they withdrew their hand and with it a large pile of dirt.

"I'm s-sorry," said the seasoned nurseryman, not really sure if it this was a wise decision. "I'm trying...the grass...the garden. It's...I'm repairing it right now."

Jones—surprise, the monster that's currently sending a cantankerous but otherwise harmless old man into cardiac arrest is, in fact, Jones—brought the pile of dirt to where most of their face used to be. Their hand shook very slightly, allowing the dirt to trickle slowly through their bony fingers.

"MESS. SAGE," seemed to float out of the terror's mouth hole. It was a deep, monotone sound that forced Kranston to cover his ears in pain. Once the final specks of dirt left Jones's hand the terrible noise ended.

Kranston was well aware of what the creature said and were this any other situation, such as someone who was not a gigantic trash monster threatening his life saying the word "message," he would have given an actual reply instead of, "Pardon?" which is exactly what he said.

The monstrosity once again scooped up a fresh pile of dirt and dumped it before their severely fractured skull. As earth fell, Kranston heard the word, "RECLAIMS." None of this made any sense but the old groundskeeper quickly figured that as long as he kept nodding and pretending he knew what the goliath was talking about he could stay alive a little bit longer.

More dirt, more frightful noises. "THIEF," it said, followed by "HEART."

"Yes, yes!" Kranston gasped. The heart—everyone wanted that blasted heart. "It...I don't know where it is. No one knows where it is. Except maybe...maybe the Mistress and look, I don't even think it's real."

As with before, Jones picked up a massive mound of soil and let it fall gently back to the ground. Soon, the first word came. "TELL," it said.

Kranston stared at Jones and waited nervously for the rest of their request. Hours seemed to pass, had the old man any real concept of what an hour was. Let's say pigs. Pigs seemed to pass when finally, as the last bit of dust fell, two more words emerged from the nightmarish construct. They were "ENDS" and "BEGIN" in that curious order.

THIRTEEN
Freedom

It cannot be stressed enough just how out of shape Avery is. It's not that he's genetically prone to obesity or has some sort of physical ailment that prevents him from exercising, it's just that he's extraordinarily shiftless. Let's say his apartment caught on fire, not an altogether impossible happenstance if one takes his appalling negligence into consideration. Given the choice between running down the stairs or using the fire escape to flee from the life-threatening flames, Avery would simply pull his bed covers back over his head and let someone else sort it out.

That's not to insult Avery. Well, maybe it is a little but that's beside the point, which is that it should come as no great surprise that only after climbing a couple flights of stairs we find this well-upholstered college student passed out on a landing.

"How did he even get in here?" asked a guard in a haunting tone somehow lower than bass.

"Honored guest?" asked another guard. Unlike his friend, his voice was more of a contralto being rubbed against pumice. "Honored guest, hello? You shouldn't be here, honored guest."

"He can't hear you, you know."

Of course he knew that. "Of course I know that," he confirmed. "Protocol, Jammess. Pro-toe-call."

Jammess ignored this as he ignored the vast majority of Art's remarks. Security was the lowest ranking and least regarded department in all of Love's Lost, below the garden fauna and even the marketing team. Despite the diverse variety of visitors the complex received—from recognized royalty to infamous crime lords to battle-hardened warriors—there was hardly ever any need for regulatory enforcement. This really had more to do with the Mistress's reputation and those of her daughters than any unspoken concord. The family was feared and respected, though mostly feared, and they ruled dominion over Love's Lost. Admission to the complex was more or less voluntary. Withdrawal was not.

As such, security was simply a fancy title for "too stupid or too dangerous to be anything else" and both Jammess and Art knew this—

the latter simply wouldn't accept it.

"Let's just take him back upstairs and dump him on the lawn, yeah?" Jammess suggested.

"We can't do that!" Art replied in false shock. Although it might have been sincere—it was hard to tell with him.

"Look, he's passed out, yeah? He probably got drunk and, I don't know, thought this was the washroom or somethin'. Let's just..."

"No," said Art. "No. You yourself questioned how he got in here and you're right. We should investigate. He could be a spy!"

Not again. "A spy."

"Yes!"

Jammess looked at Avery and snarled (which was rather amusing for reasons that'll become apparent shortly). "I don't think so. What's he spyin' on, anyway?"

"He's probably looking for the heart!"

"Art, everyone here is looking for the stupid heart."

"Of course! It's the perfect cover. I'm going to interrogate him."

"I hate you so much."

"What?"

"Interrogate him? First of all, you're just a sentry."

"I'm also your senior and I say we interrogate him."

"Don't include me in this. Come on, he's just a drunk that got lost. It happens all the time. Let's just dump him outside and finish our rounds. Please. I'm tired, Artie. I just want to go home."

"Ah ha!" Artie exclaimed, holding open Avery's messenger bag. "He's not after the heart. Look, look at this! He's after the voorn. The fiend! And we caught him in the act, too!" After a few unsuccessful attempts to emancipate the bag—Avery had been laying on the strap—he added, "Don't just stand there, you slug. Help me gather this evidence!"

Jammess wasn't exactly a slug. He was more of a slug-shaped collection of muscles. And though he had enough upper body strength to bench press a bus full of morbidly fat children very few people ever took him seriously. This probably had something to do with the fact that his head was that of a large chipmunk's.

Art wasn't as large as his subordinate and nowhere near as intimidating or adorable. He was, without much exaggeration, similar in shape and size to a twig.

A frail, flimsy twig.

Oh, it would be so easy. A meaty pat on the back would be enough.

Snap. Best of all, it was highly unlikely that anyone would complain—if they noticed at all.

"Are you listening to me, Jammess?" Art asked curtly. Jammess wasn't listening. He was, instead, following his hand as he swung it around loosely in the air. He was also smiling, all of which incensed Art.

"I don't want to have to put you on report, but I will," he threatened. "You know I will. I can do it right here, right now. Do you want that?"

"Please, no," said Jammess, waving his hand even faster. "Any more marks and I'll never be promoted to head of security."

"There is no head of security."

"I know that, you knob. I was being sarcastic. Who do you even give those reports to?"

"No one," replied Art rather matter-of-factly. "I mean, right now. I'll give them to Lady Dahlia eventually or maybe even the Mistress herself and when I do...oh, I wouldn't want to be in your boots."

It's worth noting that Jammess was incapable of wearing boots.

"You'll be up a creek without...a rope. Or a boat. Or something. You'll be in trouble. Big trouble."

"Okay, Artie. Whatever you say."

"Stop calling me that. It's Art. Or sir to you, junior." Honestly, it was a miracle that Art had not been savagely murdered by now.

Jammess looked at Art. Art looked at Jammess. Avery, who had actually woken up quite some time ago, realized it was in his best interest to continue looking at the insides of his eyelids.

Finally, Jammess said, "Art, *sir*, consider you give that report to Lady Dahlia. What do you think she'll say to you?"

Art thought a moment and smiled."Well done," he said.

"No, Art. She's going to ask you why you let this kid in here in the first place."

"But I didn't," Art countered. "We found him here!"

"Under our watch, right? This kid managed to sneak into a restricted area under our watch and steal a bug for some reason." Jammess winced at the word "bug."

"How do you think she'll react to that?" he added.

To be fair, neither he nor Art actually knew how she'd react—other than it would not bode well for either of them.

"We can't just leave him here," Art replied, silently agreeing with Jammess.

"Like I said, let's just set him outside the gate, right? He'll wander into the labyrinth and never be heard from again. No one will ever have to know, right?"

"But," Art asked, setting Avery's bag down, "what if he is a spy?"

"Then we're doing our job," said Jammess with convincing confidence. "I'm sure the Mistress would appreciate us removing such a threat, yeah?"

"I'll grab his legs," said Art, doing exactly what he said he'd do. This was unnecessary since Jammess could have carried the both of them without breaking a sweat but he figured he'd let Art have this one.

"I still wish I could've interrogated him," Art mumbled.

"You can interrogate me when we get back."

"Really?"

"No."

With a soft oof and a bit more effort than she had anticipated, Lree pulled the remainder of tiny frame through one of the least narrow gaps in the outer gate. Strange, though. The bars never used to be much of an obstacle. Just how long had she been gone?

Whatever. She was through the gate and another step closer to freedom. True freedom. Sneaking out to the Garden was liberating, yes, but it was an illusion. She was still surrounded by a murderous environment and in the end she had to return to Love's Lost for sanctuary. Simply leaving the shadowy complex was not enough. She had to find the heart and rid herself of her curse. This also meant she'd have to face her mother—assuming she could find her. None of this was going to be easy and Lree knew she'd have to be careful.

Careful. She tugged on her hair at the thought. She'd been careful up until this point and what had it gotten her? Frustration? Maybe some pain and suffering? Let's see—she had nearly been cut into bold but bloody ribbons by an angry field of weeds, nearly been blown off the Vineway by a bunch of exploding roaches, and nearly been beaten to death by one of her weird sisters. Anything else? Oh yeah, she remembered, she had also lost her bargaining chip and knocked out a bunch of innocent nurserymen, the latter of which didn't actually bother her much.

Being too careful—or careful at all—was what bothered her. A careful Lree would never have journeyed outside the complex and into the Garden. A careful Lree would have given up on finding the heart and lived her life as best she could beneath Fortune's intimidating veil.

The careful Lree had to be left behind. She stood up, clenched her fists, beat her chest hard, and ran deeper into the impossible maze that made up the entire inner garden of Love's Lost.

There are many legends behind the botanic curiosity that is Love's Lost, the most repeated of which involve a heart of some sort. Some say the heart had belonged to a once beautiful maiden—stolen perhaps by an estranged lover. Swallowed whole by the void it left, the maiden became the Nocturne Mistress and created Love's Lost as a reflection of her dark, damaged soul.

But that legend's for sissies. The better and most alluring story claims that the heart of the world itself rests somewhere within the darkness of Love's Lost and that only the Nocturne Mistress knows of its secret location. So powerful is this heart that were you to find it you'd be granted a boon—a blessing that could turn your deepest desires into a reality.

Regardless of which legend you choose to believe in they are all reinforced by the presence of the Mall, the imposing and dangerous hedge maze that surrounds the center of the Love's Lost complex. It's majestic beauty and extraordinary challenge simultaneously welcomes and frightens visitors away. Many first-time guests have never experienced the type of enveloping darkness that Fortune's veil creates. This makes navigating the complicated labyrinth unsettling, terrifying, and often impossible. Maps of the Mall are certainly available, however, they are often exorbitantly expensive and woefully inaccurate. Of course, no one is really aware of this because those who get lost in the maze stay lost. It's said that the guests who have gone missing become part of the maze itself, their spirits set free during the Reconciliation ceremony.

It's worth pointing out that all of the legends discussed here are, to be blunt, grossly inaccurate. Still, legends tend to originate from some sort of truth, right?

Left. Left. Right. Left. Right. Right. Right. Left, again. Right.

Lree stopped for a moment to release a dramatic sigh. This was an enormous pain, she thought. Were it not for her curse, she'd simply climb the nearest hedge and bypass the Mall from above. As if to remind herself that such thoughts were futile, she shoved her hand into the nearest wall. Almost immediately the wall's thorny branches wrapped themselves around the invasive limb and began cutting into her flesh.

Once, she had managed to almost climb to the top of one of the outer walls before being pulled into its leafy interior. The enraged hedge set upon her quickly, winding several thin branches around her throat. That probably would have been the end of her were it not for her eldest sister, Pentas.

Pentas had, or rather has, a way of reading people's thoughts that Lree found unnerving. She always seemed to be there—sitting silently in the back of your mind and just kind of waiting. At the time of the hedge incident she felt Lree's fear and came to her rescue. Or reproach, really. Pentas was none too thrilled about her sister's stunt and her punishment was severe.

Lree jerked her arm free from the hedge. The many, many fresh wounds stung fiercely and bled profusely yet all she did was shake her head. She had to get through the Mall the long way.

While she had memorized the majority of the directions there were times when she ran into unfamiliar territory. In these instances she'd slow her pace to better study her surroundings. A notch in a lamp post, a discolored stone, even the smell in the air provided just enough intimation to get her back on track. On occasion she'd pass by an unfortunate visitor wandering aimlessly through the maze, however, they were usually too drunk or indifferent to notice her.

Eventually she came to what appeared to be a dead end shrouded in almost complete darkness. Far from discouraged, Lree dropped to her knees and began feeling around the edges of the path, careful not to come too close to the walls.

"There," she said with a look on her face that, had you been able to see it, would have said, "I have found this thing that I have been looking for! Huzzah!" This thing happened to be a rock. A large rock, actually, that stood apart from the other rocks—again, had you been able to see it. With a little bit of effort, Lree shoved the rock aside to reveal nothing because, as has been stated, it was too damn dark.

For narrative's sake, let's assume you can actually see what's going on. Lree shoved the unique stone aside to reveal a deceptively large hole in the ground. Taking a deep breath, she crawled into the claustrophobic cavity and proceeded to shimmy her way through the tight tunnel beyond. It wasn't a deep tunnel nor was it very long, however it was extremely tight, more so than she remembered, and it ran directly beneath the murderous hedge wall. That was enough to send Lree into a panic. Her determined composure was quickly overtaken by the thought of being trapped underground by the maze's strangling roots.

With a loud gasp, Lree burst through the end of the tunnel and stumbled into a field on the opposite side of the Mall. She rolled onto her back, outstretched her arms, and stared up at the twinkling lights in the sky. Her heart was beating madly and she had tremendous difficulty controlling her breathing. Gradually she became aware of her surroundings, mostly due to her surroundings poking and lashing her. The grasses in the field were softer than those found elsewhere in the complex and were trimmed exceedingly short, making them more of a nuisance than a threat.

"Aw, dammit," she cursed. This particular activity wasn't uncommon for her.

"Dammit," she cursed again. As previously indicated, this really should not come as any great surprise.

"Of all the..." she said, forgetting to curse.

"Dammit," she said, remembering to curse and ultimately staying in character.

Lree stood up and brushed herself off rather haphazardly as she wrestled with the reality that currently presented itself to her. How did this happen?

Again, she referenced her internal checklist. Item #1: Cross the Vineway. That was more or less a success.

Item #2: Break into Love's Lost without being seen. Well, the breaking in part went fine.

Item #3: Navigate the Mall to get into the Facade. She cracked the stupid maze by memorizing the directions both to and from her secret entrance.

Ah, that was it. That is where things went wrong

Lree looked ahead, despondent. Far across the field was a lone stone outcrop lit by a pale, blue light. The directions she memorized didn't lead to the Facade, they led here. This was her field and that rock was her refuge.

Lree hunched before the mouth of the cave muddled and disappointed. She wasn't quite sure how she got here but she also didn't care. She stepped through the entrance in a trance, running her scarred hand along the cave wall out of sheer habit rather than necessity. It was just as coarse, cold, and damp as she remembered, however, it now also felt cramped and confining. What had she been doing all this time, she wondered. She also wondered, and with considerably more worry, why was she here now.

Slowly, she wandered into the closest cavern, tapping on a nearby lantern until it shone a faint blue light over what could generously be called her bedroom. There was a bed (a rock), a nightstand (a rock on top of another rock), and a large rock that served no purpose (a large rock that served no purpose). For the briefest of moments she felt safe within her private sanctuary—her personal prison. Then the regret, the resentment, and the rage came bubbling back.

What will you do?

A familiar question that, for once, felt appropriate to ask. "Ah don't know," she said, staring at her stony room.

What is it that you wish for?

"Free. Ah wish to be free. Ah will be free," she replied, her confidence returning steadily.

And how will you obtain that freedom?

"Mother," she said. "Ah'll get the heart from mother."

And how will you convince her to do that?

"Bargain. But Ah can't do that now."

What will you do?

"Whatever it takes."

Would you kill her?

"Ah would..." is all Lree could say before a sharp pang in her lower back interrupted her. The pang quickly intensified into a torrent of pain that ran up her spine and clawed its way over the back of her skull. It hammered furiously into her brain and savaged it like a starving beast ripping into its fallen prey. Fire ran through her nervous system and she screamed. She screamed louder and louder as every bone in her body shattered into jagged fragments, puncturing her skin from within.

And then it was over. She found herself on her knees in her bedroom, tears raining from her eyes and spittle dribbling clumsily over her lips. In her hands were clumps of her own hair, evidentially yanked out during the experience. Before she could recover even a little bit of her composure she came to a terrifying realization.

"Pentas!" she gasped, jerking her head around to look over her shoulder.

"Welcome home, little flower," said Pentas softly, striding into the room.

FOURTEEN
Lost in Familiarity

"Hamster," Avery said to himself, scrambling out of the musty corridor and into the brisk night air. "That was definitely a hamster. Hamster head. Super, super cute. Fluffy. Hamster."

It was absolutely abnormal, no question. Still, it wasn't that odd, was it? I mean, compared to the walking garbage monster and hallway of giant wasp carcasses a hamster-headed slug man seemed almost mundane. There was something else, too. Something important he felt he missed. Rereading the first sentence of this chapter, it hit him; it was nighttime.

He couldn't remember just how long it had been since he had seen a star-filled sky. Avery was a city kid and all of the lit office buildings and orange street lamps and blinking traffic lights ensured no one could appreciate the twinkling heavens above. There was so much light pollution that one could comfortably complete a crossword puzzle even in the darkest of alleys. Not that it was recommended to do so nor are such activities endorsed by this book. Please, if you must crossword, crossword responsibly.

Having very little familiarity with night skies that weren't bright and tangerine-colored, Avery found himself temporarily mesmerized by the thousands upon thousands of sparkling stars that flecked the darkness all around him. As enchanting as this was the reality of his current predicament soon overtook his wonderment. He really should keep moving. Before him laid a path lined by dimly lit lanterns and small bushes bursting with a wide variety of flowers. This immediately seemed the best choice given that all other options were either very, very dark or potentially populated by a giant slug with the head of a hamster (no longer appearing as mundane as it had a brief moment ago).

Glancing behind him to make sure he wasn't being pursed, Avery began walking along the lit path. When he heard the sounds of footsteps echo from the corridor he just left he upped his pace to somewhere between a mad dash and a wild panic. Eventually the path came to a massive archway made up entirely of ivy—though in Avery's eyes it was just a big leafy doorway, the kind you'd find on a poor college campus that typically led to a small garden populated by cigarette butts, weeds, and shattered dreams. Feeling that his already limited options were becoming increasingly finite, he charged through the archway and into the Mall.

"What the hell?" he muttered at the sight of the first fork in the path. There were no signs or, indeed, any sort of indication where he should go and why. He shrugged, made a rude noise, and headed down the left path. After several twists and turns, he came to a dead end.

Again, a rude noise.

Aching, hungry, and frustrated, he retraced his steps and found himself back at the entrance. Off in the distance he could see something. Someone. Someones, actually, but only the beefy, hamster-headed someone mattered. Avery dove back through the archway and reached the fork again. "Right," he said. "Left this time."

Unsurprisingly, he found himself stranded at "another" dead end.

This was getting him nowhere. He considered for a moment heading back to the entrance so that he could traverse the maze from the outside. The only problem was he could no longer find the entrance. He must have missed a turn somewhere...or maybe he was taking too many turns. Whatever the case, he was confident that he was completely lost.

In Avery's defense he was hardly the first person to lose his way in the Mall. Though the corridors were mostly lit with lanterns, the flickering lights tended to cast disorienting shadows on the walls and the cruel, almost fractious brick pathways, giving the disturbing impression that the maze was alive. This, of course, was quite deliberate as the Mall had originally served as a means of defense. It was only much later that it became a curious enigma that tempted the rich, powerful, and dimwitted.

Avery was neither rich nor powerful. Dimwitted wasn't exactly a fair description, either, though this was a young man who on more than one occasion had managed to lock himself inside his own bathroom. There was also the time he spent an hour walking up and down the campus parking lot looking for his car, eventually realizing he didn't drive that day and, in fact, didn't actually own a car. And, though it really doesn't need to be said, wet clothes should not be dried in the microwave.

So Avery was a little dimwitted at times and otherwise an ideal candidate for the maze had he entered voluntarily. Under normal circumstances he would have turned around and gone home. Of course, there was no home to go to and turning around—assuming he knew where the entrance was—would lead to certain capture. His only choice then and now was to press on. The problem was: to where?

As he wandered the Mall he'd occasionally hear the sounds of indistinct chatter and tuneless melodies, raising false hopes that he was near an exit. He considered climbing one of the hedge walls, however, opted not to do this based on his severely limited athletic abilities. At one point he had forgotten this very simple fact and reached into the Mall's wall for something to grab hold of. This was a mistake as the leaves were devilishly prickly and coated with something that left a nasty rash upon his arm. The rash itself faded quickly. The burning sensation not quite as quickly.

Onward still. Up until now, Avery had wandered the maze by his lonesome—a fact that was both familiar and analogous to his existence. Every twist and every turn lead to yet another dark, empty corridor and that was perfectly fine by him. He was, in a word, comfortable which is why he suddenly found himself on the ground.

"Sorry, sorry," he hurriedly apologized, turning around to face no one. He had tripped on something other than himself for once—he knew that. He was sure of that. Avery looked behind him, beside him, up, and, finally, down. It was here where he found what or rather who he had tripped over: a rather heavyset old man, though not excessively so on either accounts. Avery kneeled down, apologized again, and then asked, "Are you okay?" more out of morbid curiosity than genuine concern.

There was no response. Upon leaning in closer it was clear that the gentleman had been celebrating or perhaps lamenting something rather heavily and had fallen asleep. In a gigantic hedge maze.

Deciding there was nothing he could or wanted to do, Avery pressed on. He had just turned the corner when he heard the rustling of leaves behind him. He crept back to the corner of the hedge and peered down the corridor. A little blue light appeared from the wall adjacent to the gentleman, followed by a small procession of tiny, tiny ghosts. Each one was no more than a foot high and carried something different. The first one had a lamp and what appeared to be a tripod, the next was clutching onto a medical bag twice their size, and the last dragged an empty sack behind them. The first little ghost set down their tripod and placed the lamp on top of it, giving Avery a slightly better view of the adorable apparitions.

They weren't ghosts—at least, not as far as Avery could tell. Judging from their arms and stubby little legs, they were some kind of fuzzy creature—like a fat ball of Pomeranian wearing spooky sheets made from inexpertly stitched rags. Each featured a pair of eyeholes that had been cut in such a way as to cast a rather serious if not downright dour face that Avery found almost endearing. Indeed, it took considerable effort to stifle an involuntary, "Awwwww."

The adorable troupe waddled over to the unconscious man, signaling to one another using exaggerated gestures. Then they went to work stripping him of all his possessions. His jewelry, his clothes, and even his hairpiece were all carefully appropriated and placed into the sack. Delivered from all of his worldly belongings, the man shivered and looked as if he might wake. One of the fuzzy little ghouls opened up the medical bag, withdrew a nasty looking hypodermic needle filled with a glowing green liquid, and stuck it into the poor gentleman's posterior.

What happened next would go on to haunt Avery at least until the next horrible thing happened. The man's bronzed skin turned leafy green and grass appeared to sprout from every pore on his body. Soon he was covered in vegetation, laying in the middle of the stony path like a flowery lump of pasturage. This wasn't the worst part as Avery soon witnessed. The vegetation continued to grow until it broke apart, the remnants falling to the ground and dissolving into the cracks between the cobblestones. At last, the majority of the disintegrating garden and the man it had claimed were gone, leaving behind nothing more than a few small piles of scattered dirt.

The little ghosts—now far less precious than previously perceived—collected their loot and their tools and marched back to the hedge. The lead ghost tugged on a leaf, opening a teensy hidden door at the bottom of the wall.

"Weird," Avery thought. Aloud.

The three ghosts immediately turned to look at Avery, as did several dozen more emerging from their own doors up and down the corridor. Avery gave a weak wave, turned around, and ran. A small battalion of sour-faced puffballs pursued.

Pentas seemed to glide past Lree, unperturbed by her sister's palpable distress. She took a moment to study the room—cave, really—looking for a place to sit. Given her longer than average legs and extra set of knees this had become a constant challenge with her. With the utmost grace and clearly no regard for urgency, she dusted off the least disagreeable stone outcropping she could find, smoothed out the back of her dress, and rested her alluringly ample posterior upon the blessed rock. This would have almost certainly made all of the other rocks in the room jealous were it not for the fact that they were rocks and therefore not terribly interested in anything other than sitting still for a very long time or occasionally being flung at accused heretics.

"I really do not know how you manage to sleep here," she said, speaking as if in the middle of a conversation. "It is so cold and hard. You know you could always sleep in the Facade with me, right?"

It took a lot to unsettle Lree. Unfortunately, she had faced a lot of such things that could unsettle her quite recently and had just about reached her limit. Having to face Pentas right now was extraordinarily bad.

"Dahlia," Lree gasped, still recovering from Pentas' vision. "She told ya'."

Pentas leaned her back gently against the wall and carefully, almost wontedly folded her arms beneath her pronounced chest, giving her bosom a rather unnecessary lift. For a moment, she simply sat there—jutting and judging. "Oh, little flower," she finally said, "your accent has become so much more abrasive."

She continued: "I am afraid I have not spoken with our dear, strange sister in a great while. Not directly. The moment I became aware of your presence I rushed to the one place I knew you would have to return to. You should have known how worried I would have been—I have been—about you."

"You don't haft'a be," is what Lree would have said were she not paralyzed by her older sister's extraordinary presence.

"You left without telling anyone, as is your way," said Pentas in a tone that made it impossible to tell whether she was genuinely concerned or deeply resentful. A thin stream of dribble fell from the corner of Lree's mouth as she found it increasingly difficult to focus on anything other than her sister's words. "I reached out for you, little flower. Did you know that? I tried to find you out in the shining but you were nowhere. I thought that perhaps you..."

She couldn't take it anymore. Lree cried out in pain as Pentas assaulted her with guilt. Every word dripped with deceitful venom and every statement stung like a rancorous needle. She had to change the subject. Quickly.

"Ah never asked ya'...you didn't...ta' look for me!" she yelled. It wasn't exactly what she had been hoping to say—in fact, it was probably the worst thing she could have possibly said given her situation. However, it was startling enough to break her sister's concentration and relieve the anguish even if only briefly.

"Perhaps not in person," Pentas continued, barely missing a beat as she stood to approach her sister," but your heart cried out for help, little flower. I know you need my help."

"You don't know nothin'," Lree retaliated, her judgment beaten unconscious by her attitude. She glared at her sister who seemed hurt by the statement.

"Hey, uh..." she tried to say but Pentas was already on top of her. She helped Lree to her feet, brushed her off, and tried, in vain, to straighten her aggressively tangled hair.

"Little flower," Pentas said in an exaggerated sigh, "look at you— you are so filthy. I really wish you would take better care of yourself."

"Stop it," Lree tried to say. Instead, she grunted as Pentas picked twigs and leaves from her hair. Her sister then launched into an exhausting rant about personal hygiene that was exceptionally boring but no longer agonizing. At least, not in the same way. Lree also realized that, for the moment, she was alone with her thoughts. This presented an opportunity. She could run, yes, or even fight—either way she'd lose. Any interruption would prompt Pentas to regain her focus and, in that case, both Lree's mind and body would be at the mercy of her sister. If she wanted to escape, she thought, she'd have to make Pentas *want* to let her escape.

This was, of course, stupid. And had Pentas not said the following, it almost certainly would not have worked:

"It would not hurt to bathe once in a while, dear."

Wait, that wasn't it. Hang on, it's coming.

"And your face. You have such a...handsome face. If you part your hair just so you could show it off. After you wash it, naturally."

That's not it either. She really could carry on.

"Will you not tell me how this happened, sister?" she asked, brushing Lree's hair back to reveal her damaged ear and the unusual scars that blanketed a large portion of her face. "Or rather *who* did this? You know that I can find out."

Lree jerked back at the question, drawing yet another pained expression from her sister. Pentas rested her hands firmly on Lree's shoulders and made her mistake. "Is it impossible for you to truly believe that I worry about you?"

Lree's psyche made an almost audible snap.

"Crap," she said.

Pentas released her grip and cocked her head to the side ever so slightly.

"What a loooooooad of crap," Lree continued, singing in a voice not her own.

"Pardon?" Pentas asked.

Lree laughed. It was so obvious now! "All of it," she said. "You, Daliah, mother, the heart, that stupid, fat jerk, whatever happened to him..."

"You are not making any sense, dear," Pentas said, backing up.

Lree's laugh petered into a series of giggles. She was in complete denial and had effectively closed her mind off from any outside influence. And for the second time in recent memory, Pentas felt afraid. She also felt something else she had not expected ever to experience again.

"Why did you come back, Lree?" she asked candidly.

"Ah don't know," her little sister answered, shrugging her shoulders. She pulled out her compact dagger from who knows where and fiddled with the blade. "Nah, Ah do. It's terrible out there. Ah did almost die, you know? A lot. Here...Ah had to."

"Ah can't live this way, Pentas. Hiding in this nasty cave, in the dark. Ah do, and Ah did, but it has to end. Ah need that heart. It's...you can't understand."

For once, Pentas didn't have an immediate response. She watched on as her little sister cut away what was left of her baffling ensemble using her diminutive and mysterious blade. Each scrap that fell revealed another portion of her damaged skin.

Silently, Pentas placed her hands back upon Lree's shoulders. "So many injuries," she said, moving her hands down her sister's arms. "Bruises, scars, scabs, cuts..."

"It's mah life," Lree said, frozen in the middle of an alteration.

Pentas gripped her sister's wrist tightly with one hand and moved the other to cover a peculiar series of wounds hidden on the side of her stomach. Laid out like a ladder, there were eight rungs—scars—in all. "And these?" she asked, running her finger slowly over each scar.

This was more than enough to wake Lree from her trance. She slapped her sister's hand away and immediately wrapped a bit of cloth around her midsection. "Jus' more scars," she said dismissively.

132

Lree continued to shred the remains of her once comically long dress, wrapping the scraps around her arms and legs as tightly as she could. Pentas picked up a particularly long piece of cut cloth and handed it to her little sister. "For your hair," she said softly.

Lree snatched the jagged ribbon from her sister and tied her hair back tightly, creating a tall column with an explosion of hair at the top. "Ah was goin' to pull it back anyway," she said.

Pentas waited patiently for Lree to finish her preparations.

Nearly every part of her body had been covered—even down to her individual fingers. Her hair and a small window across her eyes were all that separated Lree from complete anonymity. Satisfied that she was through, Pentas asked, "Where will you go now?"

Without thinking, Lree blurted out, "Ta' find mother." Realizing what she had said, she turned to Pentas and asked almost accusingly, "Does she know Ah'm here?"

Her sister's tone darkened. "Tell me, what will you do when you find her?"

This was beginning to sound familiar. "Ah'm gonna get her to tell me where the heart is," she said. There didn't seem to be any point in hiding anything anymore. "And Ah know what yer gonna say."

"And that is...?"

"That it's not real. That there's no heart and even if there was it won't...it just..."

Pentas kneeled down to meet her little sister eye to eye. "That is not what I was going to say."

"Where is mother, anyway?" It's not that Lree didn't believe that her sister had something to say, it's simply that she didn't want to hear it.

"You will find her in her study. In the Facade."

Lree tried to put together a cohesive response though all she could muster was a weak, "Ah...okay. Ah gotta get going." She hadn't expected Pentas to actually give her a straight answer. Why would she do that? What was she playing at? Wait, did she ever say whether or not she warned mother? It had to be a trap. Was it a trap?

Will you kill her?

If it comes to that, she thought. If it wasn't real, if the heart didn't exist, what else could she do? She'd have to. Right?

Pentas closed her eyes and smiled. "Do what you need to do, little flower," she said. "And please give her my regards."

FIFTEEN
Crash

No matter how many twists or turns he took the glum-faced ghosts always seemed to be ready for him. He'd be running along a corridor at a quick pace—relatively speaking—and suddenly the walls of the Mall would come alive like a scene out of a Broadway musical. Scores of foliaged doors swung open to the sound of his panic-fueled footsteps and each of these doors unleashed a small legion of dreadfully adorable and adorably dreadful creatures.

What with the poor lighting, uneven paths, and Avery's lack of grace or precision, it was only a matter of time before he made contact with one of the morose monsters. That time was now. He grazed a ghost with his leg, knocking the creature into the hedge wall and then onto the stone floor of the maze. Avery came to a clumsy stop and, as he did, dozens of doors opened all around him, each one featuring a little face fixated on the accident scene. He turned to apologize but couldn't find the words. Before him lay his victim, pantomiming a very dramatic death in the arms of his assumed friend.

"Phillip!" we'll pretend his friend exclaimed. "Phillip, are you okay? Say something. Please, Phillip, say something!"

Phillip—who we will now refer to as Roger because he looked more like a Roger, you know?—raised his hand to reach his friend's presumably tearful cheek. He was shaking violently and it took some time for his hand to reach its mark. When it did, finally, he possibly whispered, "Johnny, 'zat you?"

Johnny smiled what we can only assume was a pitiful smile that said "Yeah, Rog. It's me. It's Johnny. I'm here, man. I'm here." The masks left pretty much everything to the imagination.

"I...I thought my name was Phillip," he might have been heard to reply, almost certainly gazing into his friend's eyes.

"Don't talk. Save your strength, man. Help's on the way," Johnny mimed, looking over his shoulder desperately.

"But you just told me to say something, Johnny," Roger could have chuckled feebly, coughing up something that might as well have been blood.

Johnny pulled Roger closer. "Don't you die on me, man. Don't you do it!" his exaggerated actions suggested. A single tear may have landed upon Roger's forehead.

"It's okay. I'm okay," Roger seemed to say, failing to reassure his childhood friend. "Hey, re...remember that homecoming dance?"

Of course Johnny remembered that homecoming dance. How could he forget? They both had their hearts set on asking Betty Lou to dance but neither had told the other. They ended up getting into a huge fight over who would talk to her first, not realizing that while they were arguing she had died of the plague. Recognizing their foolishness, they laughed and made up over waffles at whatever the equivalent of a Waffle House was in this bizarre world. It was one of many, many fond memories that so perfectly defined their lifelong friendship.

"Not that one," we assume Roger said taciturnly. "The one with the punch bowl."

"No, I don't remember that."

"Johnny?" Roger seemed to have asked, dropping his hand from his friend's face.

"Yeah, Rog?"

"Johnny?"

"I'm here, Rog."

"I can't see you, Johnny. I can't..."

Johnny knew it wouldn't be long now—but he still couldn't bear the thought of having to let go. "Where's that damn medic?!" he silently yelled.

"Promise me something, Johnny. Johnny, you there? Promise me something?" With the last ounce of his strength, Roger barely managed to raise his hand just enough so that Johnny could catch it.

"What is it, man? Anything. Anything for you, man. Anything."

Had Roger been speaking, he would have whispered, "Avenge me." Roger then fell as silent as he had been during this entire performance.

His body fell limp.

He was gone.

Rain poured down out of a watering pail held by a ghost towards the top of the hedge. With his more or less deceased friend in his arms, Johnny lifted his head to face the night sky and noiselessly bellowed, "Noooooooooo!"

As the water pail emptied, Johnny set his friend gently on the ground. He took a stance that clearly stated, "I'll do it. I'll avenge you." And with that, he and every single onlooker glared at Avery who was no longer there. After a while, Roger rose from his puddle and joined in on the collective dismay.

There were a lot of people—well, using the word people might be generous—in fancy suits and elaborate gowns mingling and dancing. Or they could have been fighting—it was difficult to tell from such a distance. Still, it almost certainly looked like a large party. The question of why there was such an enormous celebration in the middle of the maze seemed far less important than whether or not this particular celebration was accompanied by some form of catering. Hot plates, hors d'oeuvres, chocolate fountains, hell, even a tray of vegetables surrounding a heaping bowl of hummus sounded absolutely divine.

Having spent who knows how long getting lost in and being chased through a seemingly never ending labyrinth, Avery spared little thought about slipping into the party uninvited. This party—this massive gala—had the potential of being the least awful thing that had happened to him recently and he was not about to risk missing out on such an opportunity.

The festivities lay just beyond a narrow corridor of weird archways that seemed to contradict the layout of the maze. Had Avery taken the time to inspect the path more diligently or, indeed, at all he might have noticed that the walls had actually been damaged. There's a chance he might also have noticed the dozen or so landscapers working hard to repair said damage. This is why it came as a bit of a surprise when the entryway to the party grounds began to seal itself shut with wiry branches and prickly leaves.

"Not on my watch," Avery would have said if he were at all cool. Instead, he muttered a failed expletive and made a mad dash towards the closing archway. With a mighty and hilarious leap he dove through the narrowing portal, making a spectacularly leafy entrance to the most extravagant party he had never been invited to. Fortunately, no one seemed to notice, which was especially good because Avery would have had nothing to say. His full attention had been thoroughly captured by the sight before him. It wasn't just a party, it was *the* party. As far as he could tell, there had never been and would never be a celebration quite like this one in the entire history of parties.

Not that Avery had any idea of what was being celebrated and if this was normal for the unknown occasion. It's not like he was invited to many parties back home and on more than one occasion even his birthday was celebrated without his presence. Indeed, the largest event he had ever actually attended—that is, crashed—turned out to be a purity ball. Aside from being chased off by a mob of overbearing fathers, it really wasn't all that.

Right now none of that mattered. For all he knew or cared this jocund event could have been the final farewell for a religious cult preparing to part ways with their own earthly existence. There seemed to be an extraordinary mix of people and things posing as people, the latter of which failed to hold Avery's attention. Instead, he was drawn to the sea of blue lanterns floating several feet above the partygoers. As far as he could tell, they weren't being suspended by anything. They just hung there, in the air, attracting small schools of brightly colored fish. They would swim or fly from lantern to lantern, dancing about the light for a few moments before traveling onto the next. It was a strange, confusing scene, but also a jubilant one. Even for Avery, it was a tremendous struggle not to smile.

He followed the lanterns and the fish towards the center of the party, too mesmerized to bother pardoning himself as he slipped between or bumped into the other, permitted guests. At its center—and at the heart of Love's Lost—he discovered what it truly meant to be insignificant. Before him stood what he would later learn was called Fortune, a monumentally imposing willow whose girth rivaled Avery's own apartment complex and whose true height was hidden by the blackened sky. It was a very peculiar looking tree with a massive, gnarled trunk made up of dozens of other massive, gnarled trunks endlessly trying to envelop one another. The entire thing was encircled by dozens of fancy lampposts and a small armada of fancier partygoers, the latter of which seemed to be completely entranced by the sheer majesty of the overgrown plant. It's difficult to say whether or not the lampposts were as enthralled or perhaps more so.

Again, forgoing all conventions of common courtesy, Avery weaved in and out of the masses hoping to catch a glimpse of whatever the next amazing thing possibly could be. A bit beyond the tree stood an impressively large column of thorny vines. Millions and millions of thorny vines. Though not even a quarter of the size of the great willow, it was still absolutely massive. And strangely out of place.

Of course, party decor, flying fish, and absurd displays of topiary are only so interesting regardless of mystique and majesty—in other words, the amazement wore off very quickly. Avery's eyes wandered from the ostentatious centerpieces to the more interesting sights that surrounded them, such as the battalion of buffet tables. Though he was too far away to make out any details his stomach had already decided that whatever these tables offered he absolutely had to bring it into his body.

The buffet would prove a bit of a challenge to get to as Avery found himself pinned between a new wall of portly partygoers and one of the most offensive bands he had ever been forced to listen to which honestly was saying quite a lot given his atrocious taste in music. There were actually quite a few ensembles located around the perimeter, each assaulting diners and dancers alike with a barrage of terrible, tuneless noises. It wasn't until he actively stopped trying to listen that the individual pieces came together to create a medley that evoked emotions he never even knew he had. The once weird and perverse sounds that nearly deafened him now soothed his very being by wrapping themselves around him like an ataraxic blanket made from pure, uncut joy.

The atmosphere was intoxicating. Coincidentally, a portion of the crowd that had ensnared Avery broke off and wandered over to what he assumed was a bar. Guests would stroll up, say something to the octopus behind the counter, and amble away with a glass of something that was almost certainly bad for them. Avery was positively giddy and while once the thought of ordering a drink from an octopus would have seemed crazy or at the very least stupid, at this very moment it didn't bother him. This was now his party and he would enjoy himself, anxiety and common sense be damned.

"Hey there," he said, strolling up to the bar and trying his hardest to act casual. "I'm, uh...what? Hey, there. Hi."

The octopus—or what Avery had once perceived to be an octopus, turned around and said with what we can only assume was a smile, "Good evening, sir. How may I serve you this all night?"

So octopus might be a little misleading. It was more of a floating ball of tentacles with a creepy eye stalk at its top. Again, though, no big deal—except the way he pronounced evening and night gave Avery a slight pause. Evening was stretched into four syllables and night sounded like he added an N to the word height. It was odd, but Avery was now far too focused on getting smashed to give much thought to anything else.

"What, uh, what do you recommend?"

"Perhaps something to drink, sir?"

He wasn't entirely sure if he was supposed to smile at the joke or frown at the jape, resulting in an expression typically reserved for difficult bowel movements. As Avery thought up a clever comeback—or tried to think of one, really—the horrible little ball of bartender excused himself momentarily and hovered over to serve another customer. He pulled out a corpulent glass that could have easily doubled as a fishbowl and filled it with blue, liquid flames. The guest, a squat, well-dressed creature wearing an all-too familiar cloth over his or her head, thanked the bartender and walked away.

"My apologies, sir," said the bartender from some secret orifice." Have you decided then?"

Play it cool, Avery. You've got this. "Yeah. I'll have what that guy had."

"A lantern, sir?"

"Is that a drink?"

"No, sir. It's a lantern."

He wasn't about to give up. "Kidding. Haa! What's the strongest drink you've got?"

The tentacled bartender...the bartentacle...the octotender? Bartopus? Let's go with bartentacle. The bartentacle thought briefly and then suggested, "Well, there's the Hollow Man, sir, though it isn't particularly popular."

"Is it any good?"

"That depends on your individual appreciation, sir. It does have a significant chance of liquefying your insides which you may or may not find agreeable."

"Pass," Avery replied quickly.

"There's also the Magmatic Discharge, but that one..."

"Pass."

"A Diarrhetic Donkey, sir?"

"Jiminy Christ."

"Pardon?"

"Pass."

"Yes, sir. How about an Amber and Gravel mix?"

"Which consists of...?"

"Amber and gravel, sir," the bartentacle replied straight-faced. If it had a face. "Mixed."

"Yeah, I knew that was coming. Can I just see a menu?"

The floating barkeep uncurled one of his tentacles to reach within itself and retrieve a rather fancy piece of parchment. "Yes, sir," he said, placing the paper in front of Avery. "While it doesn't quite contain everything we offer, you will find some of our most requested drinks on this menu, sir."

Avery unfurled the parchment and mulled it over. Actually, he pretended to mull it over because he had no idea how to read it. It looked as if someone had tried to write a message for help from the tip of their bloodied finger while being struck repeatedly with a battle axe. Before he had the chance to lose all hope entirely, he pushed the menu back towards the bartender and pointed at a random ink blot.

"I'd like this. This will do."

"Why, thank you, sir."

Silence.

"Well?" prodded Avery.

"Sir?"

"My drink?"

"Yes, have you chosen one yet?"

"I just did," said Avery, pointing once again to the blot. "Right?"

"That's my slogan, sir."

"I know that. I like it."

"That really is very nice of you to say. I always thought "Share a Glass with Death" was catchy."

"No. I take it back. That's...that's a really awful slogan and I don't like it. Anyway, I...this one. I want this one." Avery pointed at another ink blot.

The bartentacle's single eye widened, then settled back down. "Ah, I see. I didn't realize you were one of *those*."

"One of who?" Avery asked, not really wanting an answer. "Look, never mind, how about you just mix me up something from those bottles over there. And don't...don't say anything. No comments, no judging, no...just nothing. Otherwise I'm gonna be here all night. Sober."

Avery looked at the mass of horrors before him. Deeply. "I can't be sober right now," he sighed.

"One moment, sir." The strange barkeep went into immediate action, pouring a variety of mysterious liquids into a mixer with some of his tentacles while preparing a glass with others.

"Thank you," Avery sighed, exhausted.

"This should do you well, sir." The mass of fright sat a jaunty little glass in front of Avery. It was filled almost to the very top with a shining, greenish yellow liquid trapped in a perpetual whirlpool.

"Six-hundred and eighty petals, if you would," he added.

"Petals."

"Petals," the bartender confirmed, holding out a tentacle and bobbing it slightly.

"Right, petals." Avery correctly surmised that these petals must have been a form of currency. A currency which he was not in possession of.

"Petals," he said again, clearly stalling so that his brain could come up with some way out of this that didn't involve returning the drink or getting arrested.

Oh! Oh! That'll work!

Playing it cool, Avery reached for a wallet he didn't have in a pocket he didn't have while nonchalantly scanning the vicinity for a wealthy-looking scapegoat—preferably one that didn't feature steak knives for teeth or claws that could tear through metal (or fleshy twenty-somethings).

There! Attached arms, a single, normal-sized human head, nice tie, probably had only two legs, table made it difficult to tell—yeah, that's the guy.

"Him," he said, pointing towards a regal, sepia-skinned gentleman eating alone at a table cut off from the rest of the celebration. "He told me to order any drink I'd like and just put it on his tab."

"You're with him?!" the bartentacle gasped, which was kind of gross, really. "Are...are you joking, sir?"

Let it be known that had Avery chosen to say anything other than, "Does it look like I'm joking?" he would have saved himself a tremendous amount of stress and torment in a future not that far from now. Avery, a savant at making spectacularly poor decisions, did indeed choose to say, "Does it look like I'm joking?" He even raised an eyebrow for effect.

"N-no, sir," the tentaball replied. Tentaball—that's a keeper. I am sorry, sir, had I realized...well, please give my regards to the Lord Larse."

Avery, who was already walking away with his ill-gotten drink, waved a hand and yelled back, "Sure thing!"

Once again, Lree entered the diabolical hedge maze, though this time across the stone path and through the thin trestle that had been constructed specifically for her. This was the safest and most direct route to the center of the complex. Beyond that, she'd have no problem reaching her mother. Well, almost no problem. The Mistress's study, where she spent the vast majority of her time plotting, scheming, and lording, was located on the top floor of the great Facade that overlooked the central pavilion. Its gaudy interior was well lit and teeming with guests. The actual study itself was almost certainly being watched by her least doltish guards.

She'd worry about that later. Her priority was getting through the Mall, a task she found to be disturbingly simple. It wasn't disturbing because the task was simple—it was disturbing because of *why* the task was simple.

Pentas.

She felt her sister's presence in the back of her mind; suggesting, guiding, warning, and advising. And while it bothered her immensely— she had not asked for help nor did she appreciate being manipulated— she knew just how much more difficult the trek would have been without her sister's interference. Unsurprisingly, that bothered her even more.

Lree's animosity and anger drove her forward faster and faster until she soon found herself at the entrance to the center pavilion. The festival was in full swing, which was a rather silly statement given that the festival was always in full swing. An endless rotation of guests trickling slowly in through the maze and staff brought in from the Garden meant the party never ceased. Its existence had become accepted as a natural occurrence— sempiternal and ever present.

It was smelly, sticky, sweaty, and utterly intemperate. Oh, to be rid of this place. Lree nearly delighted in the thought. To bathe in the sunlight, to run unfettered through open fields, to listen and hear nothing but the wind—thoughts like these bolstered her resolve and punched her doubt in the gut, kicked it down the stairs, and then laughed at it as it laid there twitching on the landing.

"I'm not done yet," said her doubt, rising unsteadily to its knees. It took a shaky step up the stairs. Then it took a second step. And a third. A fifth. And an eighth. "You really think you can do this? You? Alone? Please, you already had to get help from Pentas just to get here!"

"Shut up!" Lree yelled as her doubt climbed higher and higher. "She didn't help me. Ah used her."

Her doubt laughed hard, fierce, and familiar. "Keep telling yourself that, little flower. She's using you and you know it. Look where she led you."

"Ah'm where Ah want to be, " Lree said.

"Liar! You've been set up. Look! Over there, beyond the Truth."

Lree was looking. Intently. There, past the dining tables and buffets, past the bands and the dancers, and past Fortune and the thorny tower, Truth, just before the entrance that led to the Facade. There it stood, tall, solid, and draped in an ugly brown coat that left everything to the imagination.

"Dahlia," Lree said, teeth clenched.

"Told you so," gloated her doubt.

Lree knew that she got lucky—very lucky—during their last run in. Attacking Dahlia's fragile self-esteem would not work a second time (at least, so soon). Worse still, for all her faults, Dahlia was an extraordinary tracker. Just because Lree hadn't been seen—presumably—didn't mean she had the advantage. Dahlia's position was no coincidence, either. The Facade lay beyond the marketplace and the entrance that led to both was being watched carefully by a vaguely woman-shaped lump of rock with a terrible attitude.

On impulse, Lree readied her dainty dagger and prepared to charge. Just before she could launch herself, her sister seemed to turn to face her. Lree leapt into the nearest crowd, rattling them only slightly, then underneath a dressed table, rattling it a bit more than slightly. She hated to admit it but a frontal assault was an astonishingly bad idea. Her only option—and she absolutely detested the thought—was to come up with yet another plan. Whether or not her mind would settle long enough to devise a course of action that required at least a hint of forethought was certainly questionable.

Avery faced a most difficult conundrum. He was, to put it lightly, famished and there in front of him was the largest display of food he had ever seen. There were at least five rows of tables partially encircling the party grounds with each individual table overflowing with items that he desperately hoped were both delicious and edible, though not necessarily in that order. From afar, he spotted a table that exclusively offered baked goods—breads, rolls, muffins, pastries, that sort of thing. Another table featured a menagerie of mysterious meats from creatures he was comfortable with not recognizing. Then there was the dessert table, clearly one of the most popular tables judging from the crowd gathered around it. The only reason he even knew it had desserts was because of the gigantic cake at the center of the table that towered over the hungry patrons. This exquisitely decorated cake—with piping as large as a person and simply too many tiers to count—was large enough for a squirrel to live in, raise a moderately sized family, and retire to, provided they don't die from diabetes before that.

The conundrum—which I apologize for getting a little sidetracked there—was that only one of his hands was free. The other, the one attached to his blue, aching arm, was holding the spoils won from the battle with the bartender. A solution came to him much faster than he expected and he finished off the drink then and there. It had a texture like poorly mixed cement and an alcohol content a touch less lethal than an industrial-strength cleaner but its flavor was magical. It was sweet—but not overly so—and very, very insidious. The second sip tasted better than the first and the third was better than the second. This pace continued until the glass was empty and Avery's inhibitions had been liquefied. If he cared very little about his current situation before it's safe to say he cared even less now.

He set the now empty and partially melted glass down on the ground by releasing his grip and letting it fall from where he stood. Evidently accustomed to this sort of behavior, a tiny, masked waiter managed to make an impressive diving catch, preventing the glass from shattering on the brickwork and ending the inning, leaving a man in scoring position. Avery staggered out of the batter's box and swayed over to the buffet table with the smallest crowd. There were stacks of plates and bowls at the head of the table, accompanied by all manner of silverware. He snatched a plate and a handful of random utensils. If he ended up with a salad fork instead of a place spoon he'd make it work somehow. His priority was to fill his plate up with as much food as possible and then spend the next week or so eating the aforementioned food.

Even in his less than sober state, he quickly began to realize why this table was receiving far less patronage than the others. The spread on buffet was laid out like an extraterrestrial autopsy. If there was anything edible hidden within the offensive display he certainly couldn't tell.

"Really?" he said to himself rather loudly and, as he did, the table shook ever so slightly. This, in turn, caused the, uh, food, I guess, to jiggle and wobble in a deeply disturbing and mildly erotic manner. He was just about to turn away when an enormous and obviously quite entitled claw passed by him and reached deep within the trough of terror.

"Excuse me," said a raspy voice as it yanked out a mess of bright, green hair that appeared to be in a bit of distress.

"Oh, pardon," said another, high-pitched voice. This time it was accompanied by some sort of purplish tendril that wrapped itself around a pile of orbs that Avery wished dearly weren't actually eyeballs.

As more strange voices excused the actions of their stranger extremities, Avery took the hint, grabbed a few handfuls of whatever seemed least likely to spring back to life and attack him or his bowels, and scuttled away from the buffet disappointed. There he stood, alone with a large plate full of mysteries in his hands and a faint sense of reality threatening to sober his spirit. Tables were plenty, however, so were the alarming number of bizarre beings already occupying them. Just before his worry and excessive anxiousness made a sad return, he remembered something—someone, really.

Past the general assembly of dining tables and off by himself in the dark was a lone gentleman tending quietly to his meal. He had just brought an exceptionally rare piece of what we'll assume was steak to his mouth when he was very suddenly interrupted.

"Oh man, you've no idea how happy I am to see you," said a voice, followed by the sound of a plate crashing down upon the table. "I'm Avery. Can I sit here? Thanks!"

SIXTEEN
Darkness Personified

He was a gaunt, slender man of indeterminable age with warm, brown skin and black, silken hair that ran down the entirety of his back. He wore an expensive-looking azure suit fringed and frilled to the point of being excessive even for a Victorian vampire. Indeed, looking closely one couldn't help but notice that his ears came to a bit of an unusual point and his angular goatee defied the laws of physics. He appeared human enough, though, like someone you'd find cynically flicking through LPs at an independent record store. Were you to make eye contact there's a chance you'd be taken back by his solid black eyes and aggressive assertion that music is dead.

He raised his hand in either an awkward attempt to wave or to stop some invisible force behind him, then asked, "Avery, is it?"

"Can I sit here?" Avery asked, sitting down.

"You seem to have already done so."

"Cool," Avery said rather absently. He was far too preoccupied with how the eclectic collection of weird entrees and appetizers on his plate seemed to have become intimate with one another to provide his forced host with a proper reply.

"I take it there is something you want of me," the gentleman continued, picking up a glass of water, sniffing it, and then promptly returning it to the table.

"Yeah," Avery said again, unable to take his eyes off the torrid scene taking place upon his plate. "Should I eat this? I don't think I should eat this. It looks...bad. Not week-old pizza under my pillow bad, but, like, I'm gonna throw up my large intestine if I swallow any of this. That bad. I'm so hungry, though..."

If the man's expression was anything to go by, he did not have an opinion on the matter.

"I'm Avery," said Avery.

"So you've said," said the man.

"I guess I did. This place is crazy. Who are you?" It's important to note that Avery's tolerance to alcohol tops out at cough syrup.

Again, the man picked up the glass of water but this time he stared at it—into it, actually—and appeared lost in thought. "Who are you?" he repeated solemnly. "Every time I look in the mirror..."

"Uh-huh."

"Every time I look in the mirror, I see a face altogether unfamiliar to me. "I am Larse," that strange reflection always says to me. I believe him, but deep down I suspect that this Larse person is nothing more than a mere name." He sat the glass down and looked away from the table at some unknown distant object, disappointed. "Yes, only in name."

Avery, biting his bottom lip, stared at Larse hoping he'd explain whatever the hell he was talking about. After a terribly awkward period of silence, it was clear that this was not going to happen.

"Cool," he said, followed by an even longer period of terribly awkward silence. Small talk had never been his forte and he pleaded with his brain to come up something, anything, to break the silence.

"So, come here often, Larse?" Damn you, brain.

"Hmm?"

"I'm not trying to pick you up or anything," Avery said quickly, stumbling over his words. "Not that I wouldn't want to if I was attracted to you. I'm not, but if I was I would. I mean, I don't know you very well but you look fine, I guess. You've got that whole super skinny, moody, broody thing going for you. Like, you should be in a band with a bunch of other skinny guys and...take pictures of tombstones and railroad tracks and..."

Larse looked on in silence.

"Memorials. Like, the ones with angels or those fat, baby angels. I really hope there aren't any fat baby angels in heaven, you know? Jesus Crispy, that would be horrifying."

Larse continued to look on in silence. This time, Avery took notice. "I'm not judging you or anything. And especially not on just your looks! I mean, it's what's inside, right? I don't judge."

Oh god, it was his second grade Valentine's Day party all over again. Unlike the other kids who brought in cute, harmless cards with ponies or turtles or super heroes spouting such pun-filled lines as "You're a Knock Out!" or "You've Captured My Heart!," Avery had brought in a bunch of overstock cards from his grandparents' shop. They were absolutely lovely cards, far fancier than even the ones that came with lollipops, and everyone was sure to be impressed.

The issue was one of demographics. On that cold, February day, Diesel, a child destined to be a bully thanks to his parents' inability to come up with a name that didn't punch you in the face, became "The

Most Special Wife in the World" and Avery's teacher, Ms. Aberdeen, was subject to a number of very long and costly inquiries upon the noted revelation that "Only She Touched Him in That Very Special Way."

"I'm just making chitchat," Avery stammered, suppressing one of his more haunting childhood traumas. "Small talk. I'm not hitting on you."

"Is that supposed to be a threat?" said Larse in an unexpectedly sinister tone.

"What?!" Avery exclaimed. "No, no! Look, I just," he slowed down, trying his hardest to reword his original statement. "Want," he continued.

"To know."

"If, uh..."

"You come here."

"Often."

Damn it.

"No," said Larse. "Yes."

Avery blinked. "So...yes?"

"No."

"Okay," Avery said blankly. "Nice night."

"Hmm," hmmed Larse. "Oh, yes. The night, as I'm told it's called. It's very dark."

"Yeah it is. Dark," Avery was beginning to think that maybe he should have chosen a table with a monster after all.

"I relish the dark," Larse added, somehow managing to sound both giddy and depressed. "Darkness is one of the few things I can take joy in. It is both a tragic lover and a bitter enemy. I welcome it and it turns on me, blinds me, hiding that which I do not want to see."

"Sometimes," Larse droned on, "I wish that I might actually be blind. Though I can't help but wonder that were I blind, would I find the world any less ugly?"

Without thinking, Avery advised, "You could just close your eyes for a while and try it."

Larse smiled. I think. It was really, really hard to tell. His face was so haggard and his skin was stretched so tight he had a sort of permanent grin. "Even if I close my eyes, my mind replaces my sight with its own imagery. Sometimes it's obvious that it's based on my own perception of how awful I assume the world is and when I open my eyes I see a world that's dramatically worse."

Avery stared at Larse. Larse stared at Avery. It's not clear if either of them blinked.

Half an ill calf earlier beneath an empty dining table Lree was silently demanding that her sister move out of her way. Her words, however, may not have lined up exactly with that objective and could have easily been misconstrued as petty insults which is why we're not going to repeat them here. Not that it matters, really, because she never actually said anything. She dared not even mouth the words for fear of attracting Dahlia's attention.

True to her statuesque physique, Lree's sister stood her ground and continued to survey her surroundings. Maybe there was another way in, thought Lree, but from her current position it was impossible to tell. Satisfied that her sister wasn't looking directly at her, the lissome little miss dashed from beneath one table to the next, often using the crowd of pickled partygoers to hide her presence in between. Though not every table was vacant she managed to never cause anything more than a minor disturbance. She was so quick that by the time any of the startled guests bothered to look beneath the table she had already left it.

Eventually Lree found herself under one of the many buffet tables near the great tree—but not too near as the closer tables were set upon the lawn. One such table had been dedicated to desserts and would have served as a much nicer hiding place than her current location. Despite standing on less-vindictive brickwork, it was immensely uncomfortable. Whatever loathsome slop that was being passed off as an entree above was, to put it mildly, pungent. To put it less mildly, it was as if the odor had taken the form of a giant, infected foot that was attempting to squash Lree. And as if the smell wasn't punishing enough the heat and humidity from the hot plates above left the young girl feeling beaten and drained.

Just as she started to leap out from the nicely set torture table she was blocked by a guest's sabatonned feet. She had moved to the other side of the buffet to ready her escape when she heard someone cry out "Really?"

It was so loud, so obnoxious, and so familiar it startled Lree, causing her to bump her head on the underside of the table. She held her skull tight and stifled any sort of curse that was sure to follow. Through teary eyes, she stared at those shuffling sabatons that continued to block her escape. Those soft, black sabatons with thin, stringed laces.

Avery looked solemnly at his plate, as yet untouched. "Up until a little while ago I was starving. I would have eaten anything," he said to either himself or his morose host. "I'm beginning to doubt my conviction."

"Look at this," he said, stabbing a blue slab of gelatinous meat with his fork and lifting it into the air. "What is this? What do you see here?"

"I see pain and suffering," said Larse. "As it has always been."

"Exactly!" Avery exclaimed, though he wasn't sure if Larse had actually been referring to the mystery entree or the world in general. "I see this and think, "Avery, this is going to kill you. Don't eat it.""

"But you will."

"I will," Avery agreed. "And you know why?"

Larse seemed to consider the question rather intently. "Because," he finally said, "your body is a selfish beast. Insatiable, demanding, cruel, uncaring..."

"No, that's crazy. It's really because today...today is the first day of my new life. Did you know that?"

Before Larse had a chance to say that no, he did not know that, Avery stood up from the table and thrust the fork full of intrigue before him. "I'm going to experience new things," he said with rehearsed conviction. "Leave my bubble! Patronize local restaurants! Patronize local restaurants! Eat unfamiliar food—like this thing!" And with that, he took a larger than life bite out of the questionable comestible. It was everything he hoped it wasn't.

"And?" Larse inquired.

"New things!" Avery choked, fighting back tears. "This is awful. It's like the afterbirth of a canned ham. This has got to be the worst thing I've ever tasted."

"You've got to try this," he added. And yes, he was serious.

Larse, fortunately, had lost interest and was mumbling the word darkness quietly to himself over and over again. Fearing the repercussions of swallowing the vile entree, Avery quickly ducked below the table and clawed the offending meal out of his mouth.

Lree's first reaction was to grab the owner of those soft sabatons by the ankles and drag them beneath the table. Actually, that was her second reaction. Her first reaction was to stab the owner of those soft sabatons in the soft sabatons many, many times and she came very close to doing so were it not for the arrival of more feet. Now any sort of violent action would likely cause a scene which would alert Dahlia and end both her personal mission and her life, the latter of which she was resigned to continue at least until she was able to see the former through.

She waited patiently—as patiently as Lree could wait, of course—as those stupid sabatons shuffled from right to left and then wandered off. Lree got as flat on the ground as she could to confirm that it was, indeed, Avery—the fat, talentless, useless pig with the funny accent and funnier hair that was now white for some reason. Feelings of anger and frustration clashed with those of relief and expiation—she was thrilled and deeply furious to see that he was alive. Then came a devious smile. Her plan—her original, better plan—could still work.

Another brief round of musical tables brought her a touch closer to her ire and salvation. As always, he looked utterly baffled and lost. Had he not been so far away she could have nabbed him easily. Maybe it would cause less of a ruckus if she waited until he sat down somewhere. Yeah, then she could sneak under his table, grab him, and do...something. Her biggest problem—that being her sister—hadn't resolved itself and, in fact, became much more difficult now that Avery had to be added to the equation but whatever! All that mattered right now, right at this very moment, was that the person calling himself Avery Hall was alive, here, and so very close to capture.

After what seemed like an eternity of indecision, Avery finally moved towards a table. He half walked, half stumbled through a large crowd towards the edge of the pavilion. A couple more dashes from table to table allowed her to see his destination.

"You what?" she said to herself. Again, this is what she meant to say but it may have sounded a lot like a deluge of ugly insults. Past the many tables filled with painstakingly arranged fruits, vegetables, breads, and meats, beyond the throngs of guests chatting and dancing and romancing, and outside of the gala itself was a single table tucked away in a pocket of darkness. At that table sat a man—a most dangerous man—protected by an etherial sentinel that was both an impenetrable shield and an indiscriminate killer. And Avery—the slobby, weighty, aimless fool—wobbled right on through the deadly blockade, dropped his plate on the table, and took a seat?

All Lree could do, aside from gape at the situation before her, was wait. Again.

On a good day, Lree's patience could be best described as lacking or even absent. At the moment, her already limited supply of patience had run out. It took a considerable amount of effort to stop herself from flipping the table over, especially as more and more guests took their seats. At first it was a single diner eating by herself. Not quite the lonesome loser Lree assumed her to be, the guest was eventually joined by another and then another and then two more losers. Now the entire table was full of losers and Lree spent less time watching Avery babble on and flail about as if he had been set on fire and more time dodging clumsy feet, dropped silverware, and wagging tails. Her presence went entirely unnoticed thanks to the wicked combination of inebriation and ineptitude that was quite common with guests in Love's Lost. Such a combination presented Lree with a unique opportunity.

Despite the cramped space and poor lighting, Lree quickly and expertly liberated the guests of their clothing from the waist down. It required a startling amount of skill, not to mention liberal use of her mysterious dagger, to collect enough articles necessary to create a decent disguise. The one with the tail—he was wearing some type of skirt—was the easiest target. The others wore either long dresses or tight pants, all of which had to be cut just right and then carefully peeled away as their respective owners shifted their respective weight around.

The party was now pantsless, save for the quiet woman at the head of the table. There was something off about her—something intimidating and repulsive. Having come to the conclusion that it would take her far too long to suss her out, Lree turned around and began work on her new disguise. In a surprisingly short amount of time, she assembled an outfit that would typically be considered conspicuous were it not being worn inside of Love's Lost. As this was the case, she now perfectly resembled any number of the fashionless guests that plagued the party.

"Have I told you about my sadness, Avery?" Larse asked with an uncomfortable sincerity.

Larse had not told Avery about his sadness, however, Avery was hesitant to tell him so. As exciting as it was to be having a conversation—a real conversation featuring genuine, back and forth dialogue—the actual act of conversing had become exhausting. Larse's sullen tone wasn't making things any easier. Avery ransacked his brain for anything that might steer the conversation towards something that wasn't suicidal.

"I'm a hairstylist."

Well, less suicidal.

"I'm afraid I don't follow you," said Larse. "You're a...stylist?"

"Hairstylist, yeah."

"And that is...?"

"Uh, a stylist? Someone who cuts hair?" Avery responded. Somehow he managed to stifle the "duh" that he desperately wanted to add to the end of his reply.

"And what do you do with this hair?"

"Excuse me?"

"The hair that you cut," Larse reiterated, "What do you do with it? Do you weave it? Make clothes out of it? Use it to create effigies of ex-lovers so that you may remember their scent as you weep softly into them?"

"No. I sweep it up and throw it away."

Larse leaned back in his chair and gazed upwards at nothing in particular. "That's life, isn't it?" he said with a heavy sigh. Avery didn't respond. At least, not verbally. Internally, he was fighting a desperate battle to save what little sanity he had left—and he was losing.

"Is that all you do? Cut hair?" Larse added.

"Well, yeah. I mean, no, I do other things, too, but I've gotta pay the bills, right?"

"I don't know," said Larse, looking accusingly over his shoulder. "I've never heard of the Bills, though I'm curious why you feel compelled to pay them. Are you being extorted?"

Initially Avery figured they'd both talk about their jobs, complain about their low wages and overbearing bosses, and celebrate the weekend with another round of whatever the hell that magical drink was. It was clear that Larse and, let's be fair, Avery's poor interpersonal skills weren't going to allow that to happen. And just as soon as the excitement of meeting someone new had arrived—someone who was actually willing to speak with him and not ask if he wanted to super size his order—the stress and pressure and effort required to nurture and maintain this new relationship obliterated that excitement and his mind wandered. There were the usual stops—regret, depression, loathing— but the previous conversation struck a particular nerve that left him with a rather extraordinary thought: he didn't *have* to be a hairstylist. Not anymore.

"I don't know how I feel about that," he said aloud. Realizing this, he continued: "I hate it. I've always hated it. You have no idea the kind of crap I used to get at school."

Larse listened in silence. It wouldn't be incorrect to refer to it as satisfied silence.

"I never could ask anyone to the prom or homecoming or whatever 'cuz I was always the one doing their hair. It was awkward, you know?"

"And what's worse? I'm real good at it," he said, pointing at his own hair for justification. "My grandma taught me. Forced me, really. She had me practice day after day on the shag carpeting in their den. Have you ever trimmed a den's worth of shag carpeting? With styling shears? I felt like my arm was gonna fall off."

"Ah," said Larse, "I see now. I had thought that perhaps it had simply turned blue as a reflection of your soul. It must hurt."

Of course it hurt but after his hairstyling rant he wasn't about to admit it. "Like crazy," he admitted. Before he could regret it he slammed his hands down on the table and jumped up from his seat. "Crap! I still need to find the Mistress! "

Larse gave Avery a look riddled with doubt and despair. "You," he said in his menacing voice, "know Mistress All?"

Calming down—slightly—Avery retook his seat and stammered, "Kind of. I know of her. Lupus—he's this, well, thing. Anyway, Lupus sort of said if I could win her heart she'd fix me. My arm. So I figured I just gotta put the ol' Hall moves on her, you know?" Avery illustrated this by firing off a pair of finger pistols.

"No, I don't," Larse replied quickly. Clearly, Avery was firing blanks.

Larse leaned back in his chair, leaned forward, then back again. "Do you like games, Avery—I'm sorry, Mister Hall?" he asked, slowly entangling his fingers to bring his hands to a close.

"Yes," said Avery, extending the word "Yes" nine seconds more than it needed.

"Of course. You have to. We all have to. Life is an endless game filled with winning and losing—mostly losing."

"I like games," he continued. "It's one of my few pleasures in this tormented world. And your proposal sounds like a wonderfully interesting game."

"My what now?"

"Unsurprisingly," said Larse, "I am also seeking the heart."

Avery, picking the least disgusting things off of his plate, snorted slightly and said, "Actually, that is surprising. I didn't think she'd be your type."

"And what type would that be?"

"No type, no type," Avery blurted. "You just...I thought...you're so skinny and well dressed and broody. You're hair's immaculate."

"As is yours. The white is deceptively innocent."

"Yeah, it's pretty amazing what you can do with hair gel and a quarter of an insect."

Larse didn't respond. At least, not immediately. He allowed the silence to go on long enough to be uncomfortable and just when Avery had worked up the nerve to ask, "Did you say white?," the skinny, broody, and well-dressed man with immaculate hair spoke up. "Mister Hall," he said, "let's make a wager. If you capture the heart first, I..." Larse leaned back in his chair and almost immediately leaned forward. "I'll treat you to a meal."

Avery flicked one of the larger and more disgusting blobs from his plate and onto the ground where it promptly scuttled away. "Go on," he said.

"An actual meal. Not this endless trough of lies and disappointment. This meal would be catered specifically to your personal desires."

"Deal."

"Perhaps," said Larse, taken aback, "you should hear the rest of the wager?"

Avery shrugged his shoulders. Larse continued: "Now if I take the heart before you, you'll return with me to Yaatana."

Avery shrugged his shoulders again. "My home," Larse added.

"So either way I'm probably going to get fed, right?"

Larse stroked the top of his goatee. "I suppose that's true," he said.

"Then yeah, like I said: deal." A thought occurred to Avery. "Hang on, wait. Um, just so we're clear—what would I...? Why do you want me to come with you?"

"You are very interesting, Avery Hall. In truth, I had given up on ever finding anything—anyone—truly interesting in this world."

Avery tried to respond but was too awestruck at being called interesting. In his short, bitter life he had been called many things, none of them interesting. Most of them were the exact opposite.

Larse sighed heavily. His brief bout with enthusiasm came to a tragic end, like a middle-aged mother, having searched the better half of her life for her long-lost child, finally spotting a familiar face in a crowd. Just before she can call to them, she awakens to the realization that she never actually had any children and is, in fact, dying of an inoperable brain tumor. "This resentful world," he said, "that threatens to drown you in the murmurs of the meek and for what? Hope? Hope is an illusion for ill-fated idiots."

Avery stared at Larse with eyes as wide and as bloodshot as the vile plate before him. A voice inside his head screamed, "Run away!", "This guy's crazy!", and "Please don't eat any more of that disgusting food! I seriously think we're about to die!"

"Hey, I'm going to go see if I can find something to eat that's actually meant to be eaten," Avery said. Weakly. "Want anything?"

"I want the world to embrace despair like a lamentable liaison, enveloping it in a warm but uncomfortable blanket woven from threads of self-satisfaction and loathing."

"Right. They've got a dessert bar, you know. I saw a big ol' cake on the way over here."

"A slice of cake would be an acceptable substitute. Perhaps one without icing. I refuse to accept that anything sweet can truly exist in this world."

"I," Avery said slowly, waiting for his brain to filter the dismay out of Larse's request. Slowly, nervously, he rose from his chair. "I, uh, I'll see what I can do. Save my seat, okay?"

"Is anything truly worth saving?"

As Avery was well on his way back towards the legion of buffet tables he missed what Larse said next.

He said: "Follow him."

There, that should be far enough. Avery looked over his shoulder and breathed a sigh of relief. The dark pocket of depression at the edge of the pavilion was well out sight and he was, once again, surrounded by strange, beautiful, and horrible creatures. He—Larse—was a nice enough guy. A bit intense and kind of a downer. Also kind of psychotic. But he had managed to have some semblance of a conversation with him that didn't result in someone getting punched, burned, or knocked out and that, for Avery, left an extraordinary impression.

Punched, burned, and knocked out. Lree. Funny. In a way, he almost missed the little germ. It's not that he enjoyed the abuse, but he began realize that in between the punching, burning, and knocking out they, too, had shared quite a few normal discussions—relatively speaking. Whether or not one would consider a conversation about naming an undead horror while arguing what stolen garments are the most fashionable normal varies from person to person.

But that's the thing—that was the difference between Larse and Lree. His conversations with King Brood were civilized, absolutely, but they were also tiring. Talking to the seedling was almost effortless and felt conventional.

Now it could very well have been the drink from earlier, but a smile managed to creep across Avery's face as he thought of Lree. Sure, she was a dirty little tumbleweed with an appallingly bad attitude, but she was also kind of sweet. In her own way. Almost like a kid sister that also happened to be a rabid Pomeranian. Or just a Pomeranian. He could almost hear her now, yelping or threatening him or just generally being unpleasant. "Hey, stupid!" she'd say, utterly disgusted. And then she'd punch him. She'd punch him hard, real hard, in a low-lying, ill-conceived area of the male body that's particularly sensitive to blunt force trauma. "Donk!"

Avery dropped immediately to the ground, making a face to complement the action that took place at the end of the previous paragraph. "I refuse to accept," he said, a pitch or two higher than usual, "that anything sweet...can truly exist in this world."

SEVENTEEN
Mistakes Might Have Been Made

It began with a grinding, deafening drumbeat. The cacophonic music that had once been loud and lively came to a slow silence. Dancers stopped dancing, diners stopped stuffing their faces and other parts of their bodies featuring eating orifices, and guests who were simply mingling and engaging in small talk stopped being boring old farts, if just for a few moments.

The drumbeat then grew faster as all eyes turned to Fortune, its gigantic roots unfurling to the rhythmic pounding. Cracking and popping, the loosened tendrils wrapped themselves around the smaller, adjacent column—the Truth. They then lifted the Truth into the air, revealing that it's true size had been hidden far beneath the ground. Each root would raise the thorny column as far as it could reach before passing it off to another. The Truth itself never titled or turned—it simply went up and up and up and the guests were absolutely enraptured by the whole ordeal, laughing and applauding as the dangerous tower reached its apex hundreds of feet in the air. Even Avery, doubled over and cupping his damaged manhood, found himself completely enthralled by the event.

Fortune left the Truth suspended in the air and the crowd came to a hush as they stared, dumbfounded—and rightfully so—at the unnerving sight looming above them. What was going to happen next? Was the show over? Would Fortune return the Truth to the ground and, if so, would it do so gently or just drop the thing, killing everyone and ruining what was otherwise a very nice party?

The drums stopped and it was during this moment of tense silence that Lree made a mistake. This mistake would serve as the catalyst for a series of events that would ultimately result in the destruction of Love's Lost.

"Let's go," she said in a harsh whisper, tugging on Avery's tacky tunic.

Far across the pavilion, in front of the entrance to the marketplace, Dahlia tilted her head slightly. "Oh, little flower," she thought, grinning, "You never learn."

The crowds were still thick and there were many, many tables in the way, but now Dahlia knew for certain that her sister was here and where she could be found. As she took her first steps towards an act of vengeance she had been so looking forward to, Fortune released its captured column.

Frightened and fascinated, Avery could not tear his eyes away from the sight of the falling pillar. Somewhere, off in the distance, a handful of guests began screaming but the rest of the partygoers seemed almost elated. Somehow the Truth managed to fall back into the hole it was lifted from, creating a massive quake that threw nearly everyone to the ground. The terrifying boom that preceded the quake left him unable to hear anything but a high-pitched ringing that was losing its appeal rather quickly. Still, he could see that the guests were as happy as ever—happier, even. They were insanely jubilant, clapping and laughing and cheering as if they had just watched the ball drop from One Times Square on New Year's Eve, except instead of a wire orb of extra large Christmas lights it was One Times Square itself.

It soon became evident even to Avery why everyone seemed so excited. Tiny explosions of light began to erupt from the visible base of the Truth, each a different color and each resulting in a unique flower. These explosions rapidly grew in number, carpeting the column with a myriad of brilliant hues. Upon reaching the very top, the glowing flowers faded away and, within a breath, the Truth ignited in a dazzling display of reds, yellows, blues, violets, and many other colors Avery wasn't familiar with. Then the sky itself erupted in a burst of fiery flora. Glowing petals gently fell from above like radioactive snow and soon the entire complex looked as if a rainbow had just thrown up on it.

The Reconciliation ceremony was, without a doubt, the most beautiful thing Avery had ever witnessed. It also left him with a powerful sadness unlike anything he had ever experienced.

The ringing had been replaced by the sounds of a party at its peak some time ago, however, Avery hadn't noticed. He was staring hard at the base of the Truth, slack-jawed and breathless.

"Are you really crying again?" Lree asked, ready to mock him mercilessly.

"No," Avery said, coming to his knees. He then realized that he had, indeed, been crying. A lot. And he still was. He turned his head to face Lree. She was wearing what appeared to be a large pair of trousers over her head. Eyeholes had been cut out of each cheek and her hair sprung from the crotch like a giant palm tree. It was, all in all, a gloriously stupid sight and he had to tell her. He said: "Why won't it stop? It needs to...it hurts..."

At first, Lree said nothing. Avery's tone was altogether different—almost as if someone else was talking through him. "What've you been drinkin'?" she asked and accused him.

"I haven't. It was just one drink but...I don't want to be here anymore."

Lree, reluctantly, sniffed the air around Avery. "What is that? Glass cleaner?"

"Ass cleaner?!"

"Guh-lass," she said, looking over her shoulder. To her surprise—and relief—the entrance to the marketplace was clear. "Glass cleaner."

"Oh, right," he said, now feeling a bit more like himself. "Wait, no. That's not...it wasn't glass cleaner!"

"C'mon," she said, kneeling down beside Avery to help him to his feet. "You wanna get out of here, right?"

The Truth was about to drop and the once noisy guests were now so quiet that you could hear a mouse squeak from all the way across the pavilion. In this case, said mouse had squeaked, "Let's go."

She had to act quickly. Her anger and frustration fueled her transformation and, as a result, made her transformation much more difficult to control. After only a few steps, her feet had almost completely turned from flesh to stone and she was beginning to crack the brickwork beneath her extraordinary weight. The rest of her body, shrouded almost entirely in either a large poncho or small tent, had begun to swell with a superheated cocktail of resentment, fury, and ecstasy.

Dahlia quickened her pace, moving from an impolite hurry in a shopping mall to an entitled runner on a narrow country road. If a guest was in her way she would stop and politely excuse herself before proceeding onward. At least, that's what she thought she was doing. In reality, if a guest was in her way she'd simply plow through them.

Too late. The Truth fell—as did the majority of the partygoers. Dahlia, feet planted firmly within the brick patio, didn't so much as shift. Then the lights went up and there, off in the distance, stood—

stood!—her little sister. Wearing what appeared to be pants on her head.

She would still be standing, Dahlia grumbled to herself. It would have been impossible for something already so close to the ground to topple over.

And even though she already knew Lree was here, actually seeing her—especially wearing such a stupid getup—left her incensed. Well, more so than she already was. A surge of heat erupted somewhere deep within her core and she charged her sister. Had anyone been watching, it would have looked like a curtained emergency shower station pouncing upon its prey. As it turns out, nobody was watching.

Almost nobody.

Dahlia came onto her sister like an avalanche of earth and rage. Though she was still many paces away she leapt at Lree. On her descent, her poncho billowed from below like a parachute, revealing her molten body. She twisted herself in an altogether uncomfortable and unnatural way, as if redistributing all of her muscles into her right arm. She was either about to pitch a mean fastball to close out the inning or punch her sister into the patio. Given that her flaming fist had grown at least three times its normal size and that she was midair, thus instituting a balk, it's safe to assume that her goal was the latter.

Lree, clearly unaware of her sister's enthusiastic greeting, took to her knee. Dahlia screamed as she brought her fist down upon the top of her sister's brushy head. Or at least, she would have had she not been punched into the patio first.

"...and then I said, "You taste awfully rich..."—pause for effect—"...for someone so poor!"

And the party erupted in laughter so practiced it was difficult to tell if anyone had actually listened to the story at all.

"So droll, yes yes. So droll," said an older, wider gentleman in between an odd mixture of choking sounds and drink names.

Across the table a noble couple seemed to agree. First with the old man, then with each other. "Oh yes, quite amusing," one said.

"Very witty," said the other. He then turned to the woman at the head of the table and asked, "Very true, too, I believe, yes?".

The woman sat quietly at the head of the table, her black, blonde, and brown hair bouncing playfully in the evening breeze. Though her face was covered by an absolutely enormous hat, she more than likely agreed with the nobleman. Or at least, that's what he assumed because, really, who would disagree with him?

"Say," said the noblewoman to the weird dragon man, "do you think we'll see her?"

The dragon man, attempting to remove a piece of what we'll assume is not a person from between his horrible, pointed teeth using only his horrible, serrated tongue, simply said, "Hrrm." Upon freeing the vestige of his meal from his fangs, he added—with a belch, mind you—"You're referring to the Nocturne Mistress, I take it?"

"Yes, yes!" she replied, nearly showing an actual emotion.

"I don't believe so," he said coolly. "I very much doubt she exists. She and her silly heart."

"Here here, yes yes," said the old man next to him. He then took several drinks, some of which were actually his.

"Oh, she exists for sure," countered the noblewoman. "My great cousin's second aunt's cupbearer swears he once caught a glimpse of her. I do hope we see her. We've travelled all this way, haven't we dear?"

"Yes, quite a long way, yes," dear replied.

The noblewoman leaned inward, acting as a source of gravity for the more vocal guests at the table. "You know what I've heard?" she whispered. "I've heard the heart, too, exists, and she stole it..."

Dramatic pause.

"...from a voorn queen."

Somehow, the scaly man with the giant, fanged lizard face managed to look disgusted. "Vulgar!" he hissed, throwing himself backwards.

"Disgraceful!" shouted the old man.

"Dear! Really now," gasped the nobleman.

All eyes turned towards the woman at the end of the table. It was silently agreed upon that she, too, found the comment distasteful.

"Hrrmph," grunted the dragon, "if that's so then it can stay lost." His eyes shifted slightly and he lowered his voice. "Speaking of all things repellant, did you happen to notice who's sitting at the table just across the way? In the shadows?"

The old man hadn't but didn't wish to be left out of this riveting conversation. "Quite right, quite right."

"What? Who is it? Who is it?" the noblewoman asked impatiently. This was all very, very exciting. For her.

"Don't look! Don't make eye contact," the dragon man snapped. "I suppose they'll let just any riffraff in."

"I-I-I don't understand," said the nobleman, stumbling over his words. "Who is that man?"

"It isn't. No, it is!" his wife replied, gently touching her bottom lip with two fingertips. "I never would have expected...I've heard he's quite handsome. Oh, let's go see!"

"I say, has it gotten colder in here?" interrupted the old man. No one seemed to be listening. "Quite, quite cold," he grumbled to himself.

The dragon man lifted himself out of his seat just enough so that he could send his clawed hand to the opposite side of the table, stopping the noblewoman before she could get up. "Don't be foolish!" he yelled as quietly as he could. "That creature—attractive or otherwise—is Jharana Larse. There's no mistake. Simply looking at him..."

There was an audible gulp from the couple across the table. The old man was busy trying to restart his heart.

"...means your doom," the dragon man growled. He then sat back in his chair—a chair that seemed much colder than before—and laughed. Slowly, the noblewoman and her husband also laughed.

"You really had us going there, chap," chortled the nobleman. "Hook, line, and, uh, sinker as they say."

"Filthy Yaatanan scum." It seemed as if the dragon was preparing for a long, ignorant rant on the people of Yaatana when suddenly—thankfully—the pavilion was blasted by the sound of a banging drum. A low hush fell over the party as the guests continued their banal conversations in a most extraordinarily genteel fashion.

"Oh, look! It's starting!" the noblewoman whispered. A general feeling of excitement fluttered about the table, however, there was one guest whose excitement had reached a level bordering on madness.

"Wake up, old girl," said the nobleman. "You don't want to miss this." The rhythmic drumbeat was soon accompanied by the creaks and pops of Fortune's roots. One particularly loud pop caught the nobleman by surprise, sending him into a comical spasm. One of his flabby arms flew wildly into the air while the other flew wildly into his silent neighbor, knocking her forward into a plateful of ugly pastries.

"Oh dear, oh, I am so sorry," said the nobleman. There was no reply. A thought crossed his mind but he dismissed it. It came back quickly—too quickly to be dismissed this time. He turned his head to match the woman's previous line of sight and squinted. It was rather dark now but he was almost certain that she had been facing the shadowy pocket of the party hiding that Yaatanan gentleman.

"Dooooooooom," he heard the dragon say in his thoughts.

At that moment, the woman lifted her head from the plate and fell awkwardly back into her chair.

"Hogwash!" he muttered, reaching for the hat she had left behind. Try as he might, he could not fully ignore the chill that persisted in rattling his thin spine.

The Truth fell and soon the sky was filled with bright, colorful lights.

"Marvelous!" cheered the nobleman, attempting to return his neighbor's extravagant hat. "Simply oh...oh dear..."

"What is the matter?" asked the noblewoman with a total lack of concern in her voice. She then noticed what was, indeed, the matter. "Oh my..."

All eyes turned to the pastry-faced woman at the head of the table.

"She is quite the tasty dish, isn't she?" said the dragon man, quite pleased with what he considered to be his wit.

Not to be outdone, the noblewoman added, "You are just so sweet, my dear."

Everyone giggled and chuckled and chortled—it was all terribly amusing. At least, up until moment when the large sticky bun that had been obscuring her face fell onto the table with a satisfying splat.

Without any prior rehearsal, the nobleman, noblewoman, old drunk, and half-dragon performed the following actions in complete synchronicity:

- They screamed.
- They stood up.
- They realized they were naked from the waist down.
- They sat back down, embarrassed.
- They glared at the mangled skull that belonged once to their charming dinner companion.
- They screamed again.
- They stood back up.
- They each ran their separate ways. Pantsless.

No longer obligated to entertain their guests, Jones politely stood up and returned their chair beneath the table. The Truth had managed to knock the majority of the partygoers off their feet, giving the bejeweled nightmare a clear path to the great willow.

Jones's sluggish shamble turned into an athletic sprint, their shallow steps into airborne bounds. They were moving so fast and so fiercely that it would have been impossible to stop. Even if you were to, say, throw a girl-shaped boulder of flaming magma at them, they would simply knock it down and proceed onward unflinchingly.

The girl-shaped boulder of flaming magma flattened the palms of her hands against the ground and pushed herself upwards, wrenching her head out of the brickwork. She shook it a few times to not only orientate herself but dislodge the earth and stone stuck to what we'll generously call her face. Other than being a bit dazed, she seemed to be uninjured. Physically, that is.

"Lree!" she said to herself, panicking. The party was back in full swing, everyone had returned to their feet, and Lree was gone. What had happened, she wondered. She was right on top of her! Her fist—which was no longer made of molten rock and had returned to its normal size—was so close to her sister's skull that the enormous bushel of hair atop her ugly little head should have caught fire. It was as if she hit something. Or rather, something hit her.

Dahlia stood up and readjusted her cloak. No one seemed to have noticed her or the large hole she had inadvertently created in the patio (which she filled in discreetly with debris using the side of her foot). Assuming Lree would be headed to see mother, the walking coat rack started back towards the entrance to the marketplace. She had made it just past the great willow when she heard a most awful sound—a low, monotone moan that pounded her temple. This, in turn, was followed by a series of ear-piercing screams that treated her temple with even greater disdain. The guests were running towards her—past her, really—and away from Fortune. At its base stood a massive figure with an equally impressive cloak. She couldn't tell what they were doing, but Fortune seemed to actually be recoiling from them. This in itself was alarming, but Dahlia's attention was drawn to the area of decay that surrounded the cloaked assailant.

This had to be the intruder she was told about. The little flower would have to wait.

"Hey, jerk, back off the tree," she called out to the figure. You can guess she wasn't into the whole "honored guest" thing. To enhance her threatening presence, she cracked her stony knuckles several times. To the average person, the sound would have been intimidating, maddening, and painful.

The cloaked figure turned out to be anything but the average person as they didn't react to her presence at all. There is no possible way they didn't hear her which meant they were ignoring her. While this did bother her to an extent it also delighted her. She would make her presence known.

Dahlia grabbed the figure by what was probably their shoulder and pulled them away. Or tried to. The intruder wouldn't budge.

Her skin began to harden. "I said back off," she seethed, pulling once again but with considerably more force. This time, the figure went flying backwards, landing on the dessert table and scattering the finest sweets in Love's Lost all over Love's Lost's largest patrons. This of course meant that dessert would not be served during the festival which was a great tragedy. This would, however, prove to be the least disappointing of the many tragedies that would befall Love's Lost during its final night.

Slowly, awkwardly, the figure raised itself from the broken buffet, leaving their cloak stuck to a tray of preposterously large lemon-ish tarts. The partygoers who were brave or simply dumb enough to stay behind to watch the ordeal now fled as Jones reached full height. Covered in tarts, cakes, toffees, taffies, puddings, and pies, they were a most delicious looking terror from hell, but still a terror from hell nonetheless. In a flash, they rushed Dahlia who stopped them hard by reaching through their bejeweled chest to grab their spine.

For a moment it seemed as if neither party could move. Just as she had flung the giant garbage creature into the unsuspecting table of sweets, she swung them around hard and threw them back at Fortune, an act Fortune did not appreciate. Dahlia leapt upon the intruder in a bewildering fit of rage and joy, pummeling Jones with a rapid succession of powerful punches. Like a piston engine of pain, Dahlia slammed her fists into the creature so quickly and fiercely that the attack created sparks and molten spray, lighting the surroundings on fire. This was another act Fortune did not appreciate.

Dahlia hadn't noticed the damage she was causing but even if she had it wouldn't have concerned her. Truth be told, she wasn't even really concerned about the strange invader. They had simply given her all the excuse she needed to go wild and vent her numerable frustrations—though it was difficult to tell which was fueling the other. Her attack had devolved into a sort of blind rage and she was hitting Jones less and less. Each stray hit created a cloud of dirt and debris that eventually blanketed the two in a dusty haze. Dahlia threw her right arm up and behind her, preparing a final blow. Down came her fist, gorged on malcontent and absolutely inundated with resentment. Though she could not fully see her target she was confident she hit them—but the impact was far less devastating than she had anticipated. She tried withdrawing her fist only to discover it was stuck. Pulling with all her might, she was able to budge it just enough to see that it was being held tight by a grotesque, skeletal hand.

The last thing she heard before being sent to the edge of the courtyard—leaving a fiery path of destroyed tables, chairs, and guests in her wake—was a strange and haunting voice say, "FINE."

EIGHTEEN
Smattering

Dodging and weaving her way past awestruck tourists, Lree quickly led Avery out of the pavilion and into the dome's infamous marketplace. Before them lay a near endless street absolutely packed with people and, this bears repeating, things that looked almost like people. On either side of the street—and sometimes down the middle—were vendors hocking, bartering, cheating, and generally doing the sort of thing vendors do in thronged bazaars like this.

Lree took a quick glance over her shoulder to see that a crowd consisting of tourists, shoppers, and fleeing guests had effectively clogged the entrance. It wasn't entirely clear to her how they managed to escape the pavilion but the fact of the matter is that they had and the burgeoning bottleneck would make it difficult for her sister to follow them.

Without so much as a word she grabbed Avery by his azure arm and pulled him deep into the sea of hot, sweaty commerce. This would have otherwise excited Avery as very few members of the opposite sex had ever voluntarily reached out to touch him and of those who did the majority consisted of aged phlebotomists.

"What're you doing?" Avery asked in a pained whisper. He tried taking his arm back but found this action both uncomfortable and impossible. The arm had begun to ache again and Lree's grip was unusually tight, the latter of which turned out to be a bit of a blessing as he was quickly being consumed in large bellies, rank armpits, and overpowering body odor. Just before he was completely lost to the monster that is poor hygiene Lree yanked his arm hard enough to pull him into a small pocket of personal space. Avery gasped, horrified to be sharing said personal space with the sprout but was relieved to be out of the crowd, at least for the time being.

"Follow my lead, alright?" she said. "Even if she comes in here she'll never find us. Just keep bein' your stupid self and blend in."

Avery had several questions he would have appreciated answers to, such as:

• Who was "she?"

- Why would "she" want to find us?
- What would "she" do if she actually found us?
- What do you mean "stupid self?"
- Why are you wearing pants on your head?

It was obvious even for Avery that his questions would not be answered and in the unlikely event that they were such knowledge would confuse him more. Lree, noticing his befuddled expression, lifted a portion of her ass mask and said, "Right, good, just like that." She then pulled Avery down a narrow opening of less-than-savory vendors.

Temporarily free from the crowd and ignorant of the danger they were in, Avery took a brief moment to acclimate himself to the marketplace. It was very much like an outdoor flea market except the air didn't taste of boiled peanuts and knockoff designer fragrances. There were stalls filled with beautiful decor, elegant clothing, a bizarre smattering of jewelry, and a few other things that were neither beautiful nor elegant but definitely very bizarre. And they were all probably smattering, too.

Avery, being Avery, stopped at one such stall that lay oddly empty save for a table featuring a potted, nondescript flower and a yellow silly straw. He looked around, behind, and beneath the table but could find no one.

"Hey, buddy," said the flower in a low, raspy voice. "I'll give you six petals for the kid."

Avery turned to Lree and whispered, "Is that a lot?"

"No," said Lree, suddenly remembering what an enormous pain it was to travel with this idiot.

"Nah," said Avery to the potted flower. The fact that he was bartering with a flower didn't seem to faze him. Perhaps it was still the drink from earlier.

"Nine petals."

"How about nine?" Avery asked Lree.

"How about Ah punch you in the stomach and stab you in the face?"

"Sorry," Avery said, moving away from the shifty flower, "Maybe next time."

Being knocked to the ground—twice, no less—should have made Dahlia very, very angry. She was excessively prideful of her strength, a trait that even her mother recognized as her best. Truth be told, she *was* angry. Very, very angry. But she was also elated which was causing chaos within her body. Pockets of magma began to move rapidly from one extremity to another, eventually setting fire to her precious and hated cloak. She didn't even bother to take it off, choosing to simply let it burn away as she walked back towards Fortune.

Guests were still screaming, fires were still raging, and the creature was still attacking the gargantuan tree—unaware that Dahlia had returned. All of their clothing had been burned away by her previous assault, revealing the intruder for what they really were: an enormous, skeletal junk heap festooned with flashy jewelry. This revelation would make no difference to Dahlia as she wouldn't hesitate to and actually did attack the uninvited guest from behind.

Amazingly, Jones dodged the assault and retaliated by flinging the back of their boney fist directly into Dahlia's face. She, too, dodged the attack and retaliated the retaliation. This back and forth exchange of near hits and artful dodges went on and on until one or the other was dodging a retaliation of a retaliation of a retaliation of a retaliation of a retaliation of a retaliation of a retaliation of a retaliation of a retaliation of a retaliation of a retaliation of the initial attack. Out of sheer frustration, Dahlia finally decided not to dodge. She took a fistful of metal and bone square in the cheek, resulting in a frightening crunch but not much else. Before Jones could recover its arm, Dahlia struck them in the center of what was probably their sternum, resulting in a equally disturbing crack but no damage to speak of. This set off an exchange of blows so intense that it could have easily been mistaken for machine gun fire had anyone in the area known what a machine gun was. The sight was as awesome as it was comical—like a couple of brick walls in a slap fight.

Each strike came harder, faster, and hotter, like the tagline to next summer's action-packed, blockbuster sequel. The heat was so intense that the majority of Jones's jewelry liquefied, ultimately fusing to their already weird skeletal frame. Strangely enough, their metal plaque was largely unaffected. Not that Dahlia noticed. The warm-up had been exhilarating and she was finally ready to get serious.

A blinding beam of light shot out of a large fissure that split her left shoulder. She laughed. She laughed louder and louder and louder—as did each of the dozens of slits that now riddled her body. Both the sound and the scene were maddening. And then things got real ugly.

One by one, the boisterous crevices were silenced by violent gagging. A tendril of searing rock shot out of each slit, waving about wildly and ultimately doing a fantastic job of bringing down a once rather jovial celebration.

Though the battle only occupied a very small portion of the pavilion, Jones and Dahlia had managed to damage or outright destroy most of it. Fortune, agitated by Jones's presence, was whipping its roots about with a wanton fury. This helped to spread the flames caused by Dahlia's unrelenting attacks and grotesque molten appendages.

It might have been proper to label the situation as "out of control" well before Dahlia had been thrown across the courtyard. Calling it such now would seem sarcastic. It was bedlam, which is why neither party noticed the volley of faintly glowing arrows that were headed their way.

The arrows, each carrying a small, green vial, whizzed by Dahlia and landed at the intruder's feet. Most of the vials broke upon impact, instantly entangling Jones's legs in thick, wooden vines. These, of course, began to rot away rather quickly, which is why they were assaulted with a second volley, and then a third, a fourth, a fifth, and so on. Eventually Jones was cocooned in what appeared to be a miniature version of Fortune.

Dahlia had backed off after the first volley and a deep, dark sense of foreboding replaced the ecstasy that had half allowed her to continue fighting.

Calm yourself. Remember yourself. Regain yourself.

The words had a cleansing effect, like an enema for her conscience. When she felt the touch of something warm and gentle upon her arm—her arm that was still a volatile mixture of solid and boiling stone—she turned to see her sister, Pentas, at the edge of the pavilion with a small battalion of archers and guardsmen.

"Enough!" Pentas told her troops. "The creature is subdued. Sual, take your squad and see to the injured. Everyone else, extinguish the fires with due haste."

"Captain, what of the creature?" asked a guard with a funny helmet. She was probably a lieutenant or something. Dahlia never saw much point in memorizing the security and defense hierarchy since she outranked them all. She did take particular interest in the officer's face, however. Even from this distance she could tell it was flushed and it had nothing to do with the heat from the fires.

"The safety of our honored guests must come first, commander. Now hurry." And with that the blushing woman with the funny helmet joined her squad to assist with damage control. Pentas glided effortlessly across the chaos to join her sister as if she had choreographed her route ahead of time. The broken brickwork, broken tables, and broken guests that littered the pavilion could not break her elegant stride. She held in her arms a folded cloak.

"I had it handled," said Dahlia, panting breaths of hot ash. Her body had begun to lose its heat and was returning to normal. Well, normal by Dahlia's standards. "You didn't need to call in your disciples."

"I know, dear sister," she replied, making it obvious that she had chosen to ignore the latter comment. "I have no doubt that you would have subdued the creature on your own. Eventually. However..." Pentas finished her thought by simply looking around the war-torn pavilion.

Dahlia took the hint. "I need to talk to mother," she said, snatching the cloak from Pentas and quickly hiding herself within it.

Are you sure about that?

"Pentas," she said, aghast at the question. "You saw what happened, right? That thing did something to the tree. That's not...that hasn't happened before. She needs to know about this I mean, what if it really damaged..?"

"Yes, I understand," her sister replied softly. She then added, "But would it not be best to wait before discussing this matter with mother?"

Dahlia wasn't sure what her older sister was playing at. She was always scheming something, of course, but this was unusual even for her. "We have to tell her. We...this was an attack!"

"That has yet to be determined. I simply do not think it is wise to go to mother with assumptions. And disappointments." As Pentas spoke, she seemed to be commanding her battalion without so much as a word. In short order, the injured received the treatment they needed and the destruction was being undone in one way or another.

"Would you really want mother to know that you let an intruder onto the premises?"

"I didn't let anyone in!" Dahlia tried to argue.

Pentas continued undeterred. "Would you really want mother to know that the intruder then went on to assault Fortune and that you

172

destroyed the pavilion in a futile effort to stop it?"

Dahlia backed down. Unfortunately, Pentas hadn't finished.

"And what of Lree? Are you going to tell her that you found our estranged sister and then let her go?"

This struck a nerve. "That's not what happened at all! That thing came out of nowhere..."

"That thing being the intruder you were supposed to have taken care of, correct? Dahlia, think. You cannot approach mother like this. You will be punished again. Severely. We both know this."

"But we can't just let this go!" Dahlia replied, shirking at the thought of further punishment.

"We can," said Pentas, carefully straightening her sister's posture and adjusting her long coat, "and we will. For now. Look, Fortune will be fine, the tables can be fixed, and the guests can be replaced. There is something else, something of far greater importance than a single disappointing party at the center of this confusion. I believe it is in our best interest to learn all we can about it."

Dahlia had lost track of the conversation, becoming flustered and more than a little embarrassed. "Well...what about Lree?" she asked, almost unconsciously.

"Patience, sister," Pentas said with a sweet smile. "The two of you will meet again. Soon, I suspect."

"Commander!" she called out suddenly. Within moments, the same commander with the same funny helmet came running up from behind and gave her a brief but formal greeting. "When you and your squad are finished here I want you to secure the creature in one of the stronger cells down in the voorn lab."

"Aye, mam, " she said. "Is that all, Captain?"

"U-use a briar cell. Those roots aren't gonna last forever and that thing could easily punch its way out of an old cell," Dahlia chimed in, suddenly feeling important again.

"Mam?" asked the commander, looking at Pentas. Dahlia returned to feeling less important.

"If you would, Commander," Pentas ordered and off she went.

Dahlia peered out from beneath her high-collared cloak, clearly frustrated but unsure of what to do about it.

Patience, sister.

NINETEEN
Glass Wishes

The marketplace was home to merchants from whereabouts uncared about hawking curiosities to less-than-discriminate tourists with a great sense of wonder and not much else. Avery was one such tourist, making the challenge of blending in with the other guests remarkably easy. He was such a spectacular example of a—as the merchants liked to call them—sucker that his naively enthusiastic curiosity had managed to ensnare Lree. She would grouse and insult him when he dragged her into yet another tent, however, she wasn't exactly in a hurry to move on. She even made a few purchases of her own, though they may not have been purchases in the traditional sense. Her acquisitions—a lovely silver bracelet, a black, leather belt clearly made for a person several times her girth, and, best of all, a pair of goggles with absurdly large, yellow lenses—were received through involuntary donations instead of some form of agreed upon trade.

Of course, Lree never lost sight of her goal nor did she ever forget about the rock-like individual who threatened to stop her from achieving said goal. Though they spent quite a while browsing and occasionally pilfering they were still moving forward—and that meant they were getting closer to the Facade. What's more, there hadn't been a single indication that they were being pursued—which was odd but, Lree thought, not odd enough to really dwell on.

And so they ventured deeper and deeper into the marketplace, each passing vendor offering stranger and stranger goods. By this point, Avery had learned to stop touching things if he didn't know what he was touching, which was practically everything. Still, anything remotely shiny or bouncy or noisy would instantly grab his attention, like a two-year-old in a steelworks, which is how he found himself standing in front of a table full of small glass orbs, each one containing a tiny, crimson flame in the shape of a heart.

"Whoa," he said.

"Hello, friend," croaked a rather low, froggy voice. "You look like the kind of suc—man who knows what he wants, am I right?"

"I don't know, mysterious voice," he responded absently, still entranced by the lovely flames, "I think so."

"So wha'dya say, friend?" continued the voice. Just beyond the orbs, sitting behind the table, was a small, frog-like creature smoking a long, thin pipe.

"Whoa," said Avery again. He turned his attention back to the orbs. "What are these?"

"What, these?" asked the frog, pointing to the orbs with his pipe.

"No, these," Avery replied, pointing at the orbs he happened to be looking at. It should be noted that all of the orbs on the table were identical.

"These are anything you want them to be."

"Oh. Okay," Avery replied, disappointed and already turning his attention to whatever Lree was looking at. Some kind of crossbow encrusted with poorly cut gems. It was shaped like a rather uncomfortable-looking bra.

"No no, wait," said the vendor picking up a nearby orb. "This is the heart of Love's Lost."

Lree, who had until now been largely ignoring Avery and his frivolous interactions, crept closer to listen to the strange vendor.

"Right," said Avery, "Does it do anything?"

"Does it do anything? Does it do anything! My good sir, each of these hearts has the power to make any wish come true! Just like the real thing!"

Avery was, surprisingly, unconvinced. "Uh-huh."

"It's the truth! Make a wish, give it a good whack, and..."

"And...?"

"And you get your wish. Just one, mind you. It's only good once."

"So why don't you?" Avery asked, picking up one of orbs.

"Sir?"

"Why don't you make a wish?"

"I did!"

"Yeah? And it came true?"

"Of course. That's why I'm here."

"You wished to be a frog selling flaming glass balls to total strangers at a flea market?"

The little amphibian released an exasperated sigh. "No. I...I wished the same wish everyone wishes for. I wished for more wishes. Now I can't get rid of the damn things even if I wished it which I can't because I already made a wish.

"Everywhere I go," he continued louder and with increased bitterness, "wishes. My house is overflowing with wishes. I sleep on

175

wishes. I bathe in wishes. I wipe my ass with wishes..."

Avery sat the orb down and rubbed his hand on his shirt. "So I guess it really is true what they say."

"And what do they say, sir?"

"You know. Be careful what you wish for?"

"Who says that?"

"I don't know. Everyone."

"Why would they say that?"

"Because you...I mean, you got your wish."

"Yes."

"And it was bad?"

"Oh no no no. It worked spectacularly well, as you can see, sir."

Avery looked around at nothing in particular and simply said to himself, "I wish I'd stop having conversations like these."

"With one of these you're sure to get your wish!"

"You just..."

The frog looked at him curiously.

"Look, I don't have any money or petals or whatever fruity thing you people use for currency around here so it's not like I could afford one of your cool little balls anyway." Avery paused for a moment as a rare, devious idea popped into his head. "Unless," he began, "unless you let me wish for one."

"I don't understand, sir."

Neither did Avery, really, but he tried to work it out as he spoke to the frog. "Like this, right? I'll wish for...I mean, I'll make a wish to purchase a heart from you."

The vendor thought for a moment and then smiled."Okay, " he said, "you've got yourself a deal."

"Really?"

"I am a man of my word."

"Ribbit," Avery thought. He then said, "Alright, how much for one?"

"For you, sir, just fifty petals."

"Forty-five," said Avery.

"Why are you bartering?!" the man said, nearly dropping his pipe.

"Hang on, how much are these again?"

"Fifty-five petals, sir." The vendor's tone suddenly became a tad less enthusiastic and much less friendly.

"I thought you said they were fifty."

"Why did you ask how much they were, then?"

"I dunno. Felt right. Anyway, you're supposed to go down, not up."

"I'm sorry, I forgot to mention the five petal surcharge for wasting my time."

"Fine," Avery sighed, picking up another orb. "I wish to purchase a heart for fifty-five petals. Or whatever." And with that, he smacked the glass ball. He smacked it again. And again. He finally threw the ball at the ground and something happened. The pretty little flame trapped within the orb vanished in a sad puff of smoke, leaving behind one hell of a shooter.

"Very good, sir," said the frog man. "I hope you enjoy your wish. Good night!"

Avery stared at the vendor. "So, can I just take any of these?"

"No sir. Well, not without paying for one."

"But I just did," Avery argued.

"That was for the wish you just used."

"That's not what I meant and you know it. Anyway, it's broken now. There's no light comin' out of it. You owe me a new one."

"Sir, you bought a heart already..."

"And it's broken," Avery insisted, picking up a lit wish. "Not to mention it didn't even work. I wanted a cool flaming orb, not a glass cantaloupe. What the heck am I supposed to do with that?"

"I don't know, sir," said the frog, lying. At present, he could think of at least a dozen things Avery could do with the orb, most of which involved sticking them up rather specific places on his person.

Avery dropped the new orb into his satchel and pushed onward. "You knowingly sold me a defective product and you won't even make an exchange? What kind of business are you running here?" He turned his head and spoke loudly to no one in particular, "Hey, this guy's selling busted goods! Busted goods here! And he's being kind of a jerk!"

There was no way to win in an argument with an idiot. The vendor slumped back in his chair and gave out a little croak, defeated. "Just take it and get out of here, kid!" he said, drawing in a rather large breath from his pipe. His intent had been to blow a puff of smoke into Avery's face, however, the boy was well on his way back into the throng of simple-minded shoppers.

Lree, who had witnessed the majority of the weird exchange, caught up to Avery and said, without a hint of irony, "You're cheap. Really, really cheap."

Sure, Avery thought. He was cheap. He was also a cheap guy with a sweet, flaming orb.

Two by two and then one by one, the shops and booths and kiosks grew further apart until finally there were no more. The marketplace came to an end at a brightly lit fork in the road. To the left lay the Facade; to the right, guest lodgings, servants' quarters, garrisons, and a few other buildings not worth mentioning, especially since none of them will be left standing by the end of this book. Lree led Avery to the left.

The great Facade was, in a word, shabby. In a few more words, it was small, decrepit, and potentially very, very hazardous. Prefaced by a tinier, less attended version of the terrible hedge maze, it didn't exactly fill one with confidence. Abandoned fire training towers were more inviting and hospitable.

The two guards that flanked the entryway did nothing to soften the building's image. They were nearly identical and wore very little aside from a pair of menacing scowls that suggested neither guard was into tickling puppies, getting caught in rainstorms, or happiness in general. They were most definitely into bodybuilding, however, and seemed to be able to will muscle mass into existence.

Lree passed by the towering guards undisturbed. She paused upon reaching the entrance, wondering why mother had placed the guards there to begin with. Seeing as how she was able to walk right by them wearing scraps of other people's clothing and giant, yellow goggles presumably meant they were expecting her or failing rather spectacularly at their job. If the latter, they were now more than making up for it with Avery. The dope found himself blocked almost immediately by a wall of chiseled pectorals.

"I'm sorry, sir," said one of the guards—it really didn't matter which. "No unauthorized entry."

Before Avery had the opportunity to say something that would have inevitably gotten himself pounded into portly pudding, Lree chimed in with, "He's mine. Let 'im through."

"I am *not* yours, you little creep!" Avery protested. Despite this, the guards silently (and perhaps a tad belligerently) moved aside. "How about, "He's with me" or "He's a friend?" he continued. "Not "He's mine." Like, what is that about? You're so weird."

"You're definitely not my friend," Lree reminded him. Avery said nothing, choosing to follow the little dirtball into the condemned building without an argument. The party still weighed heavily on his mind, specifically the overwhelming feeling of despair that nearly knocked him out. It wasn't that he was unfamiliar with despair—it could be said that he was a bit of an expert on it. It was that the despair he felt wasn't...didn't seem to be his own.

The sound of a jingling bell brought him to attention. It was a small bell set just above the doorframe, the kind used in trendy salons to alert staff of the arrival of their three o'clock. In this case, said staff consisted solely of an elderly woman. That's all—somebody's grandmother sitting behind a heavy wooden desk. You can picture just about any little old lady and it would be an accurate description of the Facade's concierge. Also, now all you can think about is little old ladies. There they are, inside your mind. All day, all night. Especially all night. As you drift off to sleep, exhausted after a long day of telling your friends that they really should buy several copies of *Ever Day* for themselves and every member of their family, you can't help but wonder about these words. Why did you read them? They had nothing to do with the story and you could have easily moved on to the next paragraph but no! Your dreams now belong to her. You're next to her at the grocery store and she tells you that you shouldn't buy the package of sharp cheddar you just placed in your basket because it was made in China. Now she's in front of you in a no-passing zone going 35 miles per hour when the speed limit is 55— and her left turn signal is permanently stuck in the on position. Will she ever turn? And when?! Oh no, look out! She's walking up to your door with a Bible in one hand and a purse full of fuzzy licorice in the other!

Much like the staff, the interior was small, stuffy, dusty, and plain. It might have had a carpet but if we are to assume that's a euphemism knowing this little fact certainly won't help you sleep any better tonight now, will it?

Aside from a couch that seemed to sit rather high off the floor, there really was nothing interesting enough to take note of. In fact, the only thing truly interesting was that everything was so blasted uninteresting. Avery found himself disillusioned.

"What is this?" he whispered to Lree. "Are we in the right place?"

"I told you," she replied, annoyed, "this is the Facade."

"Yeah, I get that but does it ever stop being a facade? And who's that?" Avery asked, pointing rudely at the elderly woman behind the service counter. And in your dreams.

"That's Ethel."

"Ethel?"

Lree never quite understood why Avery insisted on repeating the answers he received back to her as a question. Maybe he was hard of hearing. Or just stupid. "Yes," she said, "Ethel."

Avery scratched his head. "I don't know why, but all of this is...disappointing. There was this thing at the bar that looked like this giant...mass...of purple spaghetti, right? That was pretty wild. And then there's the talking flower, frog, and dog back there..."

"That was a dog."

"I know. A talking dog."

Lree sighed. "It wasn't a talking dog. It was a dog you just started talking to. People were staring."

"He was nice," Avery said, ignoring Lree completely. "Even shook my hand. No one ever shakes my hand. Not even car dealers. You know, one time I actually went to a dealership just to see if..."

"Stay here," she said, cutting him off and shaving several hundred words off of this chapter. "I've got to talk to Ethel."

"Where else would I go?" called Avery as she walked to the service counter. He might have heard her reply with a "donk" or perhaps something much ruder.

The kindly old woman bowed her head slightly and smiled as Lree approached. Lree did the same, save for smiling.

"Can I help you?" asked Ethel.

"Miss Ethel, it's me," Lree said, raising her goggles.

"Oh my!" gasped Ethel, springing to life as best she could (by which I mean lifting her head and widening her eyes). "I haven't seen you around here since...well, look at you. You've grown so much, dear."

"Ya' think so?" Lree asked feeling slightly embarrassed.

"Not really."

Avery snorted.

"Is mother in, Miss Ethel?"

"Your mother," said Miss Ethel, regaining her composure if you looked hard enough, "is always in, dear. You'll find her in her study. Shall I tell her to expect you?"

So...she wasn't expected? "Please don't," Lree said curtly."Ah want to surprise her."

"Oh, I see. Well, best of luck with that, dear. Here you go."

Without any fanfare whatsoever, the tiny room began to fold in on

180

itself. Almost as if by instinct, Avery threw himself under the couch and watched the once cramped, old-fashioned lobby unfold into a vast, elegant receiving hall. The double doors that made up the rundown entrance vanished, tables, chairs, lamps, and chandeliers materialized out of nothing and all of the existing furniture was reborn, including Avery's hiding couch. Beyond the front desk—which it, too, had been transformed into something far lovelier—now stood a spacious hallway flanked by a number of important looking rooms and a pair of shining staircases. These coalesced into a single, spiraling stairway that ascended steeply into the upper levels of the Facade. The many, many upper levels.

Avery crawled out from beneath a newer, fancier couch, brushed himself off, and nonchalantly walked over to Lree.

"So where is the study?" Avery asked, expecting the worst possible answer.

"On the top floor," Lree said without even looking at him.

Of course. "That's a lot of stairs," he said flatly.

"Ah guess."

"Can't we just take the elevator?" To his dismay he could not find anything that even remotely looked like an elevator.

"The what?"

"Elevator. Goes up and down? No walking required? Or can't we magic our way up?"

"Donk" was the only answer Lree was willing to provide and it didn't leave Avery with much hope at all. Slowly, silently, and bitterly, the two began to climb the stairs. Separately.

TWENTY
Wings of Hope & Sorrow

The climb up to the Mistress's study was a long one, as well as fairly uneventful aside for some childish name-calling and copious amounts of whining. Indeed, the only difference between this arduous, upwards journey and a brutally dull family road trip was that dad wasn't there to threaten to turn this car around right now so shut the hell up! I swear to god, I mean it this time!

So let us break from all of this laborious, stair-climbing drudgery to explore elements of our story we may have overlooked, such as the importance of Avery's bag. From the moment he discovered it back in Lree's four-finger discount clothing cave Avery had not once removed the accessory from his person. Yet in all that time he had only placed three items within it, one of which is rather significant. His most recent acquisition was a glass heart—a curiously crimson flame imprisoned within a large marble. If you don't remember anything about the heart that's on you. It's not like it was briefly mentioned back in one of the more boring chapters at the very beginning of the book. It was described, in detail, only a few pages ago. I mean, clearly you have nothing better to do so what's the point in skimming?

One of the other items Avery acquired—an item that has a thirty-three percent chance of being the most important thing in the bag—is something Avery himself doesn't fully understand why he did so: a dead bug. Well, unconscious, really, and that was only until Avery dropped a glass orb onto her.

The creature awoke dazed, fatigued, and aching terribly. The warm red light emanating from the strange globe revealed that she was in a large sack of some sort—and that she had been captured.

Quickly—and quietly—she scrambled her way to the top of the bag. A heavy flap kept her sealed inside, however, she was able to sneak a peek beyond her leathery prison thanks to a convenient fold. The sudden burst of brightness took her by surprise. Indeed, she was briefly fooled into thinking she was outside once more. As her eyes adjusted to the light she received another shock—one that sent her tumbling back into the bowels of the bag. It was a frog. A giant frog that looked either hungry or angry or perhaps both. Escape would have to wait.

She sat down next to the glowing orb, frightened but not necessarily for herself. She, like the rest of her kind, had been lured by a melody—a pitiful song that didn't just drift on the wind, it became the wind. It invoked a sense of despair and called—begged—for help. And if help could not be given, then perhaps mercy.

They had traveled a great distance, over both sea and land, to an enormous tree—certainly the largest one she had ever seen. It's branches were so thick and so heavy that it formed a beautiful, impenetrable dome. Nigh impenetrable.

As she flew about the tree, dumbfounded by its majesty, she failed to notice that the rest of her kind had penetrated the leafy barrier and were now worming their way through layer after layer of tremendous foliage. When she grew bored of the tree's enormity she returned to find that all of her friends were gone save for one.

He was younger, perhaps weaker, but his wings—trimmed like a snowflake and glittering from all vantage points—were beyond elegant. They were also beyond practical, which is how he found himself ensnared in a series of unfortunately placed twigs.

She approached him coyly at first, smiling a slight gap-toothed smile. He didn't seem to take notice so she fluttered around him once or twice or three times. Maybe four or six. Eight. After the tenth flutter she lost count. He wasn't responding and that was just uncalled for. Taking exception to this rude behavior, she circled him angrily and buzzed away.

Still, he did seem to need help—rude as he may be. With what appeared to be a little sigh she turned and flew back to the discourteous cutie with the gorgeous wings.

There he was, still dangling in the branches helplessly like some sort of adorable puppy that had found itself stuck in a tree due to a mishap with a World War I-era artillery cannon. Carefully—and with more than a little bit of embarrassment—she went about liberating him. A gentle pull on his wings here, a snap of a twig there—finally, he was free.

He didn't thank her. He didn't even turn to look at her. He simply dove as hard and as fast as he possibly could into the dense layer of branches below. Soon, he was gone.

And she waited.

She waited some more.

She clenched her tiny hand into a fist and declared to take action.

She waited again just in case.

She sighed and then took action.

The tree top had been far more dense than she had expected. After no small amount of effort she broke through what she assumed was the bottom of the tree's woody crown—it was so dark she didn't know for sure. The pretty boy with the prettier wings was nowhere to be seen but that could be said of pretty much anything at the moment. A few pinpoints of light had managed to pierce the tree's heavy plumage but their irregular blinking made it impossible to orientate herself.

To make matters worse, she could still hear that dreadful song as well as the buzzing of wings from all directions. On occasion she'd feel something brush against her but she was always too startled to try to catch it.

So she hovered there, deep within the abyss, until her wings, which had been fluttering nonstop for who knows how long, had reached their limit. Despite giving her best to control her descent she fell at an uncomfortably rapid pace. This otherwise would have ended her story were it not for the fact that she landed almost immediately onto what she presumed to be a soft, leafy branch. Maybe not leafy. Grassy. It really didn't matter. What mattered was that she now had a chance to rest and that was good enough. Oh yeah, and it saved her life. That was alright, too.

She rolled over onto her back, bending her wings in a rather awkward manner. This didn't bother her as much as the darkness. Half of the time she couldn't tell if her eyes were opened or closed, even when she saw a faint glitter directly above her.

Invigorated by an unhealthy combination of hope and desperation, she jumped to her feat and chased that glitter. It didn't take long to reach as she had greatly misjudged the distance. She stopped just short of colliding with it—him! It was him! And, like before, he utterly failed to react.

She didn't care. Well, she did and when it was appropriate she'd punch him hard in the arm but right now she was just happy to not be alone.

Lit by his shiny and increasingly meretricious wings, his face was devoid of any emotion. His eyes were vacant and his expression was lifeless. It was as if he was stuck in a trance which, of course, he was.

Far off in the distance (or perhaps nearby—her depth perception had been all but obliterated by the darkness) there was a colorful light, flickering gently but never dying. The longer she stared at it the bigger and brighter it became. It was clear that the boy was being drawn towards this light—and not just him. All of her friends. They were all there and not a single one seemed to notice her.

This was getting ridiculous. Unable to think of a better idea and fed up with being ignored, she decided to simply follow the boy as he descended slowly towards the lights to see what all the fuss was about.

Fuss, of course, was the wrong word to use as it implies taking action and even having a sense of urgency. Had there been an actual fuss amongst the others things might have turned out quite differently.

"There, those two!" someone yelled as a net swooped by her left side, snatching up one of her friends.

"Yeah, yeah," another replied as another net just barely missed her from the right.

It was a trap and a terrible one at that. Though she was able to easily outmaneuver her would-be captors—giants wielding large nets and other ensnaring tools—the others were not so fortunate. Showing no sign of awareness and clearly not interested in any form of self-preservation they were plucked from the air with ease.

Some of the giants—those without nets—were busy segregating her friends by color. Those with hints of red were placed in steel cages. They seemed to be the luckiest of the bunch. The blues had their wings torn off and were stuffed into tiny glass boxes. Many of the greens had their juices drained on the spot, their lifeless husks thrown into dirty barrels.

She hovered far above the horrible scene, safe from capture but not from trauma. She wanted it to stop—actually, she wanted to stop *it*—but her wings were pulling her back away from the nightmare. They might have actually succeeded in doing so had she not spotted a familiar set of wings below.

In a flash she returned to the carnage, weaving around nets, ropes, and even giant, clawed hands until she reached him. She pleaded, she pulled, she pushed, she tackled—all in vain. Soon a net was upon him and he was pulled to the ground.

It should be noted that he was green.

She wanted to look away but couldn't which is why she failed to notice a particularly large group of entranced victims falling from above.

They came upon her suddenly like a rogue tidal wave, knocking her hard towards the awaiting giants.

They were quick to surround her but not quick enough to run away. She snapped the pole of the first net that came down with a magnificent flying uppercut. The following six or so nets were dispatched in similar fashion. The giants were stunned.

After splintering the last of them, she returned gracefully to the ground and chittered. This seemed to be enough to jolt at least one of the gigantic creatures out of his paralysis. He lunged at her with his gauntleted fist but his sheer size made him clumsy. Also, stupid and ugly. She shot straight up into the night sky like a bottle rocket launched from the mouth of a profoundly irresponsible teenager, performed a sharp, steep arc, and came down on the giant's funny helmet with remarkable force, driving the beast into the ground by a good three feet.

Most of the disgusting brutes wisely scattered, however, a couple of them decided they were tired of life and confronted her. The first was dealt with before she could even finish posturing, lain flat by an armor-shattering blow to the sternum. Her comrade—thinking she had not seen him approach—lunged at her with a hammer designed specifically for causing serious harm to one's body and not for hanging awkward family portraits above the mantel (unless, of course, you hate your family) (or mantle). Without turning around, she lifted her left forearm just above her head, completely negating the weapon's force and momentum. The giant struggled, pushing as hard as he could and losing traction as he did so. He then lifted the hammer away and swung at her again, this time from the side. And again, she stopped it—catching its riveted face with her mandibles.

She looked at him and smiled. He was in shock—so much so that he wouldn't let go of the handle. "Impossible," he was probably thinking to himself. "Nothing this small or this adorable can be so strong!"

Just to prove him wrong—well, maybe not "just" as scaring the piss out of him shared the same priority—she crushed the hammer's head with her powerful, bisected jaw—face, bell, claw, and all. The front of the massive creature nearly scrambled over its own back in an effort to run away as fast as possible, leaving nothing behind but splintered steel and a foul-smelling puddle.

She tilted her head slightly and spit out a piece of the hammer in a way that said, "You're not even worth my time, scum." With the last of the giants taken care of she could now begin freeing her friends. They had been cheering for her and celebrated her good looks and many victories. "No, no, please. I just did the right thing," she would have said could she have spoken.

The cages were smashed and the barrels were broken. Every trap—every prison—had been dismantled save for one. It was a glass box that shone a bright, green light.

"And why am I looking at this disgusting thing again?" she heard from behind the glass.

"Its color, Mistress!" said a deeper, more excited voice. "Look, look!"

The light grew dimmer as a figure began to take shape from within the glass. She pressed her face up to the translucent wall to get a better view and was sent hurtling back into an adjacent wall when the strange figure did the same.

"Gold! Gold and violet! Isn't it marvelous?"

The following silence made it clear that the Mistress did not think this was marvelous.

"A-and," the deeper voice stammered, "look! Look at its eyes. They're not like the others at all. Have you ever seen anything so...so...marvelous?"

"Karn..."

"Kran. I mean, Kranston, mam, and just..."

"So you remember the last time you approached me with something marvelous? I do, sadly. I was presented with two blades of grass, one of which you claimed was greener than the other."

"And was it not marvelous, mam?"

"Before that," she continued, ignoring his comment completely, "it was a new species of mushroom..."

"I'd never seen the likes of it. It was so big why you could wear it like a hat!"

"That's because it was a hat, you old goat."

The Mistress plucked the glass box from Kranston's hands and studied it. "Hm. I'd say it's more yellow than gold. Not that it matters—this is just a voorn, Korn."

"Kranston, mam."

She sighed heavily. "You've tended my gardens for a long time, haven't you?"

"Why, sometimes it feels like that's all I've ever done."

"Yes, and I value your work. I really do."

"Thank you, mam, that's the..."

"But that doesn't mean I value or even welcome your input on the goings on of my resort."

"Of course not, mam. That's not what I..."

"Or that I'm interested in anything you have to say."

"Or," she continued, dropping the box, "that I want any sort of interaction with you outside of me telling you to keep my gardens neat and tidy."

Kranston, who had spent far too much energy in a mad scramble to catch the glass box, gasped, "Of course, mam."

The rejected old man took a few steps backwards before fully turning around to leave. As he entered the hallway he slowly closed the door behind him. "Until next time, mam," he said cheerfully. The Mistress didn't say anything, however, there was a loud thunk at the door followed by a crash. That sort of thing seemed to happen every time he visited her.

As he made the long hike down to the lobby he wondered why she didn't welcome his discoveries anymore. He had found so many interesting things—rare things—for her collection. Okay, so maybe they weren't all quite as marvelous as he had thought but this one, this voorn—it was special. He was convinced of that.

He had been sorting through a pile of bugs that had fallen rather hard to the ground—all greens, thankfully. Had they been reds...best not to think about it. At the very bottom was a voorn with the most unique combination of colors he had ever seen. This alone was fascinating—at least for a boring old groundskeeper and amateur entomologist—but when it picked itself up he knew he was onto to something truly, well, marvelous. He grabbed the nearest container he could get a hold of and scooped the creature into it. By now its eyes were wide open and it was displaying what could easily be assumed to be agitation.

This voorn was resisting—as if it was aware of its surroundings and, more amazingly, its own existence. Oh, he just had to show someone!

Thinking back on it, this had been a bad idea. No one else was around except for a handful of sentries and his apprentices. Neither party had any real interest in or respect for the resort's fauna or flora. Still, maybe this would spark some inspiration in the young folk.

"Here, look at this," he had said, then cringed slightly at the memory. He handed the box over to Rans, the least moronic of his two apprentices. Rans, of course, promptly dropped it. The box hit the ground hard, as did the contents within. Thankfully, the voorn was alive but now it was acting in much the same manner as its kin. That is to say, it wasn't reacting to anything.

Even stunned, he had thought, this creature was still interesting. Certainly the Mistress would want to know about this.

And the rest you're familiar with. If not, reread this chapter from the part where the Mistress says, "And why am I looking at this disgusting thing again?" If you're still lost, follow these instructions again. Don't do this too many times, though, as you may find yourself caught in a dangerous time loop from which there is no escape.

"And why am I looking at this disgusting thing again?" she heard from behind the glass.

"Its color, Mistress!" said a deeper, more excited voice. "Look, look!"

The light grew dimmer as a figure began to take shape from within the glass. She pressed her face up to the translucent wall to see that it was too late! You'll never escape this chapter! Never!

Her dusty prison had long been placed high on a shelf in a dingy room full of terrible things. There were many other glass boxes like hers, as well as a plethora of sharp, pointy tools, strange plants, and strange, giant creatures.

"Burnst!" barked a particularly strange, giant creature, the ancient one called Kranston. Also Senile Old Fart. "Bring me a green, no. Two greens, please. And a blue. There's a blue on the shelf somewhere."

After a moment one of the other giants lumbered over to her shelf.

It stood before it as one might a urinal in a nightclub. "Senile old fart," she mumbled, then called back, "How do I know which one's blue?"

The beast did not receive a reply or if she did she was unable to hear it. Whichever the case, she began to open and examine each prison individually starting from the bottom.

Her prison—the glass cage—wasn't especially well made. The latch could be lifted simply enough with the tip of a wing. Of course, the majority of her friends that had been locked away in such cages had no wings and even if they did they had no will to escape.

She had a will to escape. At least, initially. She had made it as far as the outer wall when she witnessed another group of her friends fall victim to the giants. The scene was every bit as horrific as her first encounter with the monstrous creatures and she realized she couldn't leave—not without her friends.

She returned to her cage just as easily as she had left it. Evidently, her rarity had already been forgotten which, were it not for the fact that she had been imprisoned by a group of cruel giants hell-bent on torturing and murdering her friends, would have annoyed her. Slightly. However, her ephemeral popularity had given her a considerable advantage. Her prison would become her base of operations. A safe haven inside the enemy stronghold! She could observe the giants and their twisted work unnoticed. She could even leave her cage for a while to explore or perform reconnaissance missions.

And so she did. She reconnoitered and observed. On occasion, she even performed a bit of sabotage. Sometimes it was even deliberate.

Now, all of her hard work—everything she had learned, everything she had planned—was in jeopardy. The creature known as Burnst was exceptionally inept. If she reached her cage and got her meaty hands around her...

That wasn't going to happen. When she got to her, she thought, she'd tear off the creature's arm with her mighty mandibles and use it to beat down anyone standing in her way of freedom. Not only was she cute, she was fierce!

Sadly, the giant never got to her box. Somewhere along the way she had decided that opening then closing each prison one at a time was simply too tedious.

"What are you...?!" was all she heard before she was sent flying backwards. The shelf came down with a terrific crash, sending shards of glass, chunks of wood, and scraps of metal every which way. Dozens of prisons were shattered and their prisoners freed. Technically. None of them seemed particularly keen on leaving.

"Found one," said the giant, picking up a wingless voorn. He was blue, though it wasn't clear whether this was his natural color or because he was dead.

An argument amongst the enormous creatures ensued but she didn't pay much attention to it as she was far more concerned with the condition of her cage. The glass walls, naturally, survived the fall but the latch—the latch that had once been so easy to lift—had been dented and was now stuck. Before submitting completely to panic, she noticed that the roof (the lid to the box, really) had been loosened. With a little effort she could shift it just enough to escape—only to be caught immediately if she did, of course. She was on the top of the pile in the middle of the room, after all. She'd have to wait until the creatures left. Assuming they didn't try to clean up the mess first.

Those familiar with Burnst and her counterpart Rans know that there was no chance of this happening. "Just...I...look," Senile Old Fart stammered, "I'm going out for a while—never you mind where. I want you to have this place cleaned by the time I get back, right?" And with that he left, slamming a large wooden door behind him.

A moment later, the door swung open. "Never mind. You two are coming with me," said the old one. "If I leave you in my shop alone I won't have a shop to come back to."

The two slothful beasts shuffled past the older one who closed the door behind them. Satisfied they weren't coming back, she went to work pushing the roof aside. Soon she was free of her cell and on her way to a decently large crack running along the ceiling.

They were all dead—dead or dying—and there was nothing she could do to change that. She knew this. She knew she had to escape because maybe...maybe she could find help beyond the tree. Tell others what she had learned. Tell them that she had to leave everyone behind.

The golden voorn with the violet freckles had managed to squeeze her entire upper half through the crack in the ceiling when she suddenly pushed herself back into the shop of horrors. She returned to the pile of prisons, searching frantically but finding little else than shattered glass and broken bodies.

She then moved on to the old one's desk. It was as ever filled with frightening objects; sharp metal blades of increasing length, a grooved wooden block obviously used for crushing, a long, stained cylinder with handles at each side, and jars. There were dozens of jars, each filled with a colorful extract ground from her friends. Beside the desk rested a number of large gardening tools and stacks of cages, the occupants of which had long expired.

If she could just find someone. Just one. That would be enough, right?

Her search continued—from corner to corner and top to bottom. Her friends were everywhere yet she was utterly alone. She fluttered down to a barrel painted with red crosses and collapsed. Escape—were it even possible—had lost its appeal. Her drive, her battle, and her story was over. And she began to cry softly. Then not quite so softly. Streams of tears ran down her cheeks and she bellowed as a giant wasp would, which is to say awkwardly and uncomfortably.

This horrible sound stirred something from within the barrel, to the point where it began to shake. She wiped the tears from her giant eyes and flew about the barrel, looking for an opening of any sort. There, through a large crack, she saw them—dozens of them! Red, winged, and, most importantly, alive.

Now, to open it. The lid had been sealed tight but that didn't really matter because it was too heavy to lift on her own anyway. If she could tip it over somehow then maybe it would pop off, but if she couldn't even lift the lid then lifting the barrel was definitely not happening.

Then she remembered the tools over by the desk—in particular, the long one with the three metal prongs. With a considerable amount of effort she dragged the garden rake over to the barrel. Made of a combination of wood and dirt, the floor was naturally uneven. This provided plenty of room for her to wedge the metal end of the rake beneath a portion of the wooden prison, creating a crude but hopefully effective lever.

Pushing on the end yielded very little success, so she zipped across the room and raced back as fast as she could, putting her full force into the effort. The rake, the voorn, and the barrel went tumbling to the floor. The lid popped off as planned and out shot a single red voorn. It collided with the adjacent wall and exploded, shaking the room and inadvertently providing a superior solution for escaping by removing a quarter of the stone shop from the equation.

The others trickled out of the barrel at a much less destructive pace. There were nearly thirty of them in all. They never said much and, truth be told, they may not have even been aware of what was going on, but they did follow her out of the small building. She kept them low and outside of their brethren's light, choosing a path that led to the side of the dome instead of its labyrinth-like top. As she had discovered some time ago, the branches that formed the walls around the base of the bizarre dome were much thinner and easier to navigate—even if they featured a much greater number of flowers and leaves. Within moments they were free.

It felt good. The sun felt good. It was warm and bright and comforting. She didn't want these feelings to end. The others didn't seem to share the same fuzzy experience. It was searing and blinding and maddening. The hysteria grew quickly, escalating into a swarm of screaming panic. Without warning, they took off, still flying low to the ground but at an ever increasing speed. By the time she caught up to them she had become a part of the deranged swarm.

Onward they went, scorching the grasses and flowers beneath them as they raced towards an enormous chasm. A fierce wind shifted the swarm's direction, slowing them down only slightly. During this brief reprieve, she caught a glimpse of something peculiar just beyond the great ravine: a series of massive stone archways.

Another harsh current and another course correction. It was clear that the swarm had become a plaything to the wind. A few voorn had separated from the main swarm and formed a small clique that inadvertently directed the others. Tethered to the ground, the rebellious offshoot led everyone towards a series of warped roots that bridged the chasm.

They didn't see the giants walking along the roots. She probably wouldn't have noticed them either had it not been for the voorn ahead of her that ran into a rather large, bejeweled giant and promptly exploded. The shockwave scattered the voorn in all directions, triggering even more explosions.

In the chaos she had become tangled in one of the giant's hats. Her energy spent from keeping up with the swarm, she collapsed—as did a sizeable chunk of the bridge.

She climbed back up to the top of her awkward cell and peered out from the flap. The frog was gone, but she—her cell—was moving. Carefully, very, very carefully, she poked her head out from beneath the flap to gain a better view of her surroundings.

The voorn scrambled back into the bag. She had, indeed, been captured again. As she devised a dozen new escape plans her gaze wandered towards and became enraptured by the glowing orb. Flaming orb. It was a flaming orb. And it was really, really cool—whatever that meant.

Well, anyway, back to planning her escape. The best she could come up with was waiting until they had traveled outside of the crowd and then make her dramatic and daring exit. And it would be dramatic, what with her arm hurting so much.

Her arm wasn't hurting. Not even in the slightest. And yet she found herself rubbing it to soothe that nonexistent pain. Also, she felt inferior to everyone and had an inexplicable urge to brush her hair. She then passed out which was absolutely for the best given that there was only a single styling tool available and it had been made from one of her friend's legs.

The voorn go by many names, most of which are unflattering if not altogether wrong. The most common term is bug which, while technically true, is really pejorative. They may display attributes similar to other insects, however, as demonstrated, they also possesses a very real sense of self-awareness and sapience. Indeed, it would be much more accurate to refer to them as fairies, brownies, or sprites. Fairies, brownies, or sprites with hard exoskeletons and bone-crunching mandibles, of course, which is why no one refers to them as fairies, brownies, or sprites.

Through some unfortunate incidents and many cruel experiments the voorn have proven themselves to be far more than miniature monstrosities. They actually offer a multitude of uses based on their color, such as providing light, controlling the weak minded, encouraging rapid plant growth, turning flesh to stone, and even creating massively powerful explosions. As such, they have become somewhat of a valuable commodity within certain empires.

Careful harvesting is required for maximum yield (and less unfortunate incidents) and only the purest voorn extracts fetch the highest prices. It is for this reason—though far be it from the only reason—that the term bug has been so widely spread and accepted. Capturing thousands upon thousands of gentle, peace-loving faeries, crushing them into a sticky paste, twisting and squeezing the juices out of there broken bodies, and keeping them in a state of perpetual torment sounds like, on the outside, the epitome of bad behavior. Bugs, though. Bugs are pests and can be caught and exterminated with gusto. No one bats an eye at a swatted fly—at least, no one worth talking to. Hippy.

Many empires have been built around the practice of pest control, but none so powerful as Love's Lost. For at its heart is a woman of such genius, such drive, and such confidence that she will do whatever it takes to achieve her goals. Morality, honor, loyalty—these are all silly words that needlessly bind the shortsighted. She is known as Miss All, the Mistress of Love's Lost, and Lree and Avery are currently standing outside her private study completely unaware of how much danger they are actually in.

TWENTY ONE
The Girl Who Listens to Rain Inside Her Head

It had taken Avery quite some time to recover from the grueling climb to the giant doors that presumably led to the Mistress's study. At first he had kept count of the number of stairs but lost track around one hundred and fifty when he blacked out. How he made it to the top floor was a mystery but not necessarily one worth investigating as even the thought of all that climbing exhausted him. All that really mattered was that he had made it. Now all he had to do was stroll into the Mistress's office or whatever, woo her with his suave, sexual advances, and have her treat his arm.

And then what? What was he supposed to do after that. It's not like he had anywhere to go—he still didn't even know where he was! The only thing that he was certain of was that he couldn't go back.

Right?

I mean, even if he could would he want to?

Avery released a sort of frustrated growl and began hitting himself in the head. Clearly, he thought without the slightest hint of irony, he was still drunk.

Typically Lree would have taken a great amount of satisfaction in watching Avery abuse himself however she, too, had lost herself in thought. How would mother react to her return? Would her original plan work? Why was she starting to enjoy this?

Lree looked over at Avery who was losing a fight with himself. He stopped when he noticed her staring at him. "What?" he said, annoyed.

"Don't do anythin' stupid," she sighed, repositioning her goggles onto her forehead. "Let me do the talking."

"So what are those for?" he asked, pointing at her stolen spectacles. Lree replied with a disgusted "Donk!" and that was the end of that conversation. Whatever. At this point it really wasn't worth exploring. He simply wanted to get on with it so he could stop worrying about dropping dead and start worrying about getting the hell out of this place. Still, he had to admit that this place—this world—was pretty amazing. Then again, so was a chocolate-dipped waffle cone stacked with two scoops of salted caramel ice-cream and that never tried to kill him. At least, overtly. This amazing place could lick him.

"Leave the bag here," Lree ordered Avery nonchalantly.

"W-why? What's wrong with it?" he retorted, gripping the bag's strap.

"Mother...the Mistress doesn't trust anyone with bags or sacks or purses or stuff like that. She'll think you're gonna steal something." It's important to note that Lree's tone was less explanatory than it was accusatory.

Avery gestured at his colorful ensemble. "*I'm* gonna steal something?" he scoffed.

"And it's just rude. So leave it here," she said with a straight face. Avery was incredulous.

"You know what's rude, Miss Manners? How about punching someone in the nuts, huh? That's the sort of thing most normal people would consider rude."

"How was Ah s'posed to know you had nuts?!" Again, she said this with a straight face. "Why're you so weird?"

With his jaw thoroughly dropped and eyes bulging well beyond acceptable safety limits, Avery stood there in front of the giant set of doors unsure of what he was supposed to do. Arguing with Lree seemed to be the best idea but where would he start? "Oh yeah?" or "Well, where do you keep *your* nuts?!" were combative dead ends and that was all he had. He could...

"Wait," he stopped himself. "Are we talking about the same thing?"

"Ah'm not talking about anything."

"No, you were. We were. About...you know? I don't think I want to have this conversation anymore."

"Fine. Drop the bag."

"No."

"Drop. It."

Avery relented. "No one's gonna take it, will they?" he said, placing his precious purse upon the offensively ornate marble floor.

Lree didn't respond because she no longer cared. She walked up to the pair of doors that lead to her mother's sanctuary and gave them a disapproving stare. Each door was only half as wide as most doors but three times as tall. They always made her feel insignificant, which is exactly what they were meant to do.

This is stupid.

Really, really stupid.

She took a deep breath in secret, placed both hands upon one of the doors, and pushed . With no small amount of effort, she managed to open the door just enough so that she and Avery could squeeze into the Mistress's study.

Study might have been a bit of a misnomer given the room's massive size. It was designed like a great gallery, its walls overflowing with strange artifacts, extravagant banners, and paintings clearly produced by artists with deep-seated issues. The room was large and somewhat cylindrical, dimly lit by halos floating just below the ceiling. Looking a bit closer, Avery realized that they weren't just glowing halos but illuminated fans. Fans! Given his arduous battle with the infinite staircase, the fans—working in harmony to create a soothing and satisfying current—were, by far, the most impressive and appreciated feature in the study.

"Were you raised in a barn?" snapped a voice, crackly—yet incisive—and absolutely dripping with sarcasm. "Close the door, little flower. You're letting the stench in."

Lree, shutting the door behind her (and almost catching Avery's cursed arm in the process), responded immediately with, "It's not a barn. It's a hole in a rock."

"Disagreeable as ever, I see," said the voice which Avery correctly assumed belonged to the Mistress. "If you've come back looking for a fight I'm afraid you've wasted your time as well as mine. Particularly mine. I'm really not in the mood, little flower. Now, if you've come back to apologize I might be persuaded to listen."

Slowly, Lree began to walk down the thin red and gold carpet that lined the floor. Avery followed suit, now taken by how soft the carpet was—it was like walking on a bed made of hundreds of live lamb. Between the cool breeze from the fans and extraordinarily soft and not-at-all PETA-approved carpet it was difficult not to lay down and take a short nap. Not that a nap would be possible what with all the yelling.

"Apologize?!" Lree screeched, giving Avery a bit of a start. "Ah've nothin' to apologize for!"

Lree came to a stop a few feet before a short landing, atop of which sat a wooden desk, plain in such a way that it actually clashed with the rest of the room. There wasn't even much on it; a book, something that looked like a pen, a cigar box of some sort, and a baseball, terribly beat up and obviously very, very old. The fans and the carpet were great—no argument there. The artwork was weird and fancy, sure. But the desk? It was normal which, in this place, wasn't.

"You're either lying or simply ignorant of your own actions," said the Mistress, her back still turned away from her daughter. She sat in a massive, leather-like chair that faced the ludicrously lofty windows at the end of the room. They provided a fantastic view of the pavilion below as well as of Fortune's unique majesty.

"Knowing you," the Mistress continued, "it's probably a little of both. For starters, you damaged the bridge leading to the Garden. You then assaulted some of my most dedicated gardeners who were doing nothing more than repairing the grounds. Oh yes, that leads me to the next item: your pet. You seem to have lost control of it. Do you have any idea how much it's going to cost to repair the Mall? Let alone the Vineway?"

Lree looked at Avery accusingly. "It wasn't me!" he said.

"I've also been told that you were seen conspiring with Jharana. Now that can't be coincidence, can it? Jharana Larse? One of the Chain's most colorful magnates?

Again, Lree looked at Avery accusingly. "That...might have been me," he said. "Though I wouldn't really call him colorful."

"And finally you cause a scene during a Reconciliation. We've only now gotten the largest fires under control."

"None of that is my..." Lree began, attempting to defend herself.

The Mistress's chair turned just enough to reveal a distinctly feminine face. "Oh it is. And I'd say you have quite a lot to apologize for, little flower."

Lree said nothing as she saw no point in arguing with her mother. Better to get right to the point before she loses control of the conversation.

"I see your time spent out in the Shining was pointless," her mother continued as Lree lost control of the conversation. "I would have hoped at the very least that you'd have gained a sense of self-worth out there. Or maybe a sense of fashion. What are you wearing, daughter of mine? You look like, well, you but worse."

Avery had never seen Lree look so flustered and, ever the tool, took some joy in the Mistress's incessant needling. That is, until she turned her attention to him.

"And what is that fat little thing that's following you? Is it even alive?"

"Hey, now!" Avery interjected. The Mistress didn't seem to care for his input as she ignored him and continued laying into Lree.

"I swear, little flower," she said, "the only thing you excel at is disappointment. This is why your sisters..."

Truth be told, Lree wasn't flustered by her mother's endless barrage of insults, revilements, and disgraces. She wasn't even flustered—she was anxious. Though the fans—powered by leashed voorn mindlessly flying in circles—kept her mother's study cool and comfortable, Lree was sweating through her raggedy disguise. Her arms felt numb and her legs were shaking so hard she was having difficulty standing.

The Mistress was oblivious to her daughter's distress, carrying on about how ungrateful she is or how she should learn to behave like Pentas or how she had her head chef thrown into the labyrinth because her soup was cold and she didn't even like soup. Lree had actually stopped listening to her some time ago, though this was more out of distraction than in any interest to preserve her own sanity.

"Give up," said her doubt, returning with a vengeance. "You know you can't do this."

You can do this.

"You're so dumb," her doubt insisted. "Do you really think you can get away with this?"

You can do this.

"You're going to be stuck here forever."

You're going to be stuck here forever.

"PHWARG!" Lree blurted out, snapping Avery out of his funk. He had still been reeling from the "fat little thing" comment a few moments earlier. He wasn't fat—or little. Filled out, maybe. Even pudgy in certain places. But fat? No. Average. Average was fine, wasn't it?

"Temper, temper, little flower," the Mistress said, annoyed. "Was that even necessary? Just what are you...?"

"This's Avery!" Lree shouted, pointing wildly at her bargaining tool.

"Really! I've had just about..." her mother stopped. "Avery?" she inquired, her tone changing dramatically.

"Yeah?" said Avery.

The Mistress spun her chair around to face her guests. "Yeesh!" Avery said, recoiling with a complete lack of subtlety. She—Lree's mother, the Mistress of Love's Lost, the Nocturne Mistress, she who must be wooed—was a thin, ancient woman inappropriately clad in a glittery flapper dress accented by far too many strings that hung from the neckline. Her skin sagged and was slightly green, a color that when used to describe skin typically indicates serious signs of infection and requires that certain portions of the body need to be removed immediately. Her hair was a dirty gray that had been immaculately bobbed to the point of looking like a helmet and did a poor job of covering up her three sets of extra eyes.

200

"Well, that changes things, doesn't it? Avery Hall, I presume?" she said, getting up from her chair. Lree tensed up and took a few steps back. As for Avery, hearing his full name somehow managed to shock him more than the fact that the one who said it was a dolled up, green-skinned, spider-faced old bearcat.

"I guess?" he squeaked. As much as he wanted to, he couldn't take his eyes off of her and the longer he spent looking at her the closer he came to screaming. Her face was worn yet cunning, sad yet menacing. At its center was something that approximated a nose, discolored, flattened, and cut with deep indentations that reached beyond the corners of her mouth. It looked more like an electrical socket that had been responsible for a house fire than an olfactory organ.

"How do you know my name?" he said weakly.

"Oh, I know everything about you, Mister Avery Hall. Do you mind if I just call you Avery?" the abnormal old woman asked as she slinked around to the front of her normal old desk. "I actually know more about you than you do. At least, more about your predicament. I should say that you are quite fortunate as to..."

"Stop!" Lree yelled, pulling a darling little knife from who knows where . "One more step and Ah'll gut him!"

Avery was confused, perhaps justly so this time. Had she been talking about him? As if to answer that question, Lree darted behind Avery and swung her leg around to hit him directly behind the knees. Her sudden and violent actions forced him to change his earlier assessment of the carpet. It wasn't at all soft and did little to cushion the back of his skull as he hit the floor. Before he could even so much as swear Lree was on top of him with the knife—now starting to lose its adorable aesthetic—held far too tightly against his face.

"Get offa' me, you weed!" he grunted carefully as not to cut himself grimacing. She wouldn't budge. The lissome little creature suddenly seemed to weigh hundreds of pounds, successfully immobilizing him. The best he could manage was to glare at her but she wouldn't even look at him. Her eyes were frighteningly determined and focused on who he could only assume was the old lady thing.

The old lady thing in question laughed. "You are just full of surprises, aren't you? Gut him? *Gut him?* I'd say you've been hanging around Dahlia too much. Tell me, little flower, why would you do such a thing? Why would you want to, as you say, "gut him?"

"Stop calling me that!" Lree yelled, nearly crying.

"Oh, how awful of me. You're embarrassed. Well, what should I call you, then, little flower? I certainly don't wish to risk offending your delicate selfhood."

"It's Lree."

"That is a boy's name, my dear."

"Ha!" Avery shouted, feeling simultaneously triumphant and terrified.

"Shut it!" she cursed. "And you! Ah'll kill him! Ah will!"

"Yes, I recall you saying something like that, though to be honest your crude accent does make it difficult to discern your message sometimes, little—sorry, Lree. You realize I only started calling you that as a joke, right? I suppose it's appropriate since you're acting so foolishly. Tell me, what would killing the boy accomplish?"

"Yeah!" Avery agreed.

Finally, Lree thought to herself. Finally something was going according to plan. She knew—well, hoped, really—that her mother would ask such a question as she had prepared the perfect reply.

"Satisfaction," she said coldly. And rehearsed. "He dies, he's outta' mah life. You've no idea the sort of crap Ah've put up with hauling this idiot here. And you—you'll know you'll never have another chance like this. You'll die filled with nothing but regret."

Avery felt drained, stupid, and most of all scared. This went well beyond giant skeletons made of garbage, creepy blob monsters setting fire to people, and adorable ghosts performing amateurish theatrical productions. Now would have been the ideal time to pass out, however, his mind was far too invested in the unexpected drama unfolding within the extravagant study to allow his body to do so.

"If and when I choose to die I guarantee you that I will do so filled with regret regardless of whether that boy lives or not, dear," said the Mistress, rubbing her forehead in a combination of frustration and annoyance. Frannoyance. "My life is full of regret. At the moment, I regret not locking those doors."

"I suppose," she continued, "there's a point your little performance? Are you waiting for me to say, "Is there anything I can do to persuade you to stop acting so foolishly?"

"Yeah," Lree replied curtly. "Answers."

"I don't recall raising you to be this vague."

"Ah don't recall you raisin' me at all!" Lree snapped back, her doubt now almost completely overshadowed by her confidence.

"Do not test me, young lady. I believe I have humored you and your meatball hostage long enough. Now tell me: what questions do you expect me to answer?"

"Tell me," Lree paused to look down at Avery. She saw fear in his eyes as well as something she'd later look back on with a tiny bit of repentance. Right now, sitting on his chest and holding a knife to his throat, she didn't care. "Tell me everything you know about the heart. Where it is. How to use it."

The Mistress released a heavy sigh. "And here I thought that you were actually being serious. The heart is a legend, dear. A fairytale. You of all people should know..."

"Don't give me that!" Lree yelled back, the desperation in her voice taking command of the room. "Don't you dare! You know what Ah live with. You know mah life. You tell me what Ah need to know to change it. You tell me about the heart."

"My poor girl," said the Mistress in such a way as if to solicit a reaction from Lree. An involuntary twitch of the eye would suffice.

Lree complied.

"Very well," she continued. "I'll tell you all I know about "the heart." But don't you dare blame me if it's not what you want to hear. Now, release the boy."

"No way."

"I have to verify him." The Mistress moved within a few steps of the hostage situation before being stopped.

"Ah said no way! Take another step and..." To complete her sentence, Lree shoved the side of the blade underneath Avery's right cheek bone. This was met with some disagreement from Avery in the form of high-pitched screaming.

"Please, little...Lree, you're giving me a headache," the Mistress said, closing her many eyes. "And your fat friend isn't helping." One by one her eyes opened and with refreshed intensity. "Anyway," she said rather loudly in an attempt to squelch Avery's screams, "I'm not impressed with your little tantrum. I will verify your claim and then decide whether or not we have a deal. Is that understood?"

Lree didn't move. She didn't say anything. She did, however, glance at her hostage. "Fine," she sighed, turning her attention back to the Mistress, "but you give me your word that you'll answer...you'll tell me about the heart. Ah want to hear you say it."

"Does my word really matter to you?"

"No, but it does to you," Lree responded sharply. And she was right.

"Clever," her mother sighed. "For you." She waited for another reaction and got nothing. "Very well, I give you my word. Now, if I may inspect the merchandise?"

Merchandise? What is she talking about, Avery thought. Did she want that cool glass ball he haggled off the frog? Or the...oh, ick. He still had the bug, didn't he? Why would she be interested in that? Or no, wait. Wait, wait, wait. He had left his bag outside and he didn't recall ever mentioning it or its contents. She meant him. *He* was the merchandise.

Oh. Oh my.

Avery's mind worked hard to invent logic that would justify that statement. He was in a large, elegant hotel surrounded by perversely provocative art. The Mistress—I mean, it's so obvious now, right? She was called the Mistress. She might as well have been called the Madam. She was old, had authority, a bunch of weird spider eyes—at least two of those met the general Madam stereotype. This was quite the career change, he thought, but was he ready? Could he really keep things professional? What would he do when his clients inevitably fell in love with him?

"I think of you every night and day," she'd say in a vague, Middle-Eastern accent. She, in this case, being a thirty-something executive with short, black hair, thin-rimmed glasses, and a penchant for mini-skirts and tight blouses. Surrounded by corporate yes-men with 401ks and self-confident jerks with unnaturally white teeth, she was looking for something different. Something exciting. She thought she had finally found it and for a time she had—but it was all just a sad illusion. "You. You took my heart. Then you took my pride away."

Avery knew it would be difficult. Being this awesome was as much of a curse as it was a boon.

"Seasons must change, love," he'd say, cool, confident, and collected. There's a good chance he wasn't even looking at her. "Separate paths, separate ways and all that."

"No!" she'd scream, beating his back with her fragile fists. "No, no, no! I can't break free from the things that you do!"

He still wouldn't look at her. What had caught his gaze, I wonder. A sailing ship? A freight train? Maybe even a rocket ship? Well, it didn't matter. There really was nothing left to do.

"Come on, girl, "he'd say, denigrating her feelings. "There's no need to go away mad. Just..." he'd paused to sigh. "Just go away."

"Here it go," he added. "Dreamin' 'bout the lovin' you do."

"Don't want you mad," he also said, and quietly, creepily, giggled to himself. Lree lept off of him in a hurry.

"Er, what's wrong with him?" her mother asked.

"That's your problem now."

"Please, Mister Hall," said the Mistress in a friendlier yet aggressively more uncomfortable tone, "if you would stand up. I assure you, you will not be harmed."

Half lost in his bizarre fantasy, Avery hadn't heard anything the Mistress had said. He did, however, notice that Lree no longer had him fastened to the floor. He jumped to his feet, became very dizzy, and fell onto his backside. This did little to deter him as he stood back up almost instantly, striking a pose that he thought reflected everything that made his fantasy self so incredible: it was the thoughtful gaze.

Several moments passed. No one moved and no one said anything.

"I am sorry for the way my daughter treated you," said the Mistress, taking charge again. "As I am sure you are no doubt aware she is rather boorish and can be quite difficult to deal with. She can't help it, though. It's just in her nature. You understand, don't you, Mister Hall?

Mister Hall, whose posture was still demonstrating a presumably intense level of philosophical pondering, understood only one thing: he had been gazing thoughtfully for far too long and now had no way of breaking the pose without looking or sounding awkward.

"Has something caught your eye? You seem a bit distracted." Miss All asked.

"These pictures," Avery said, looking and sounding awkward.

"Paintings."

"Okay. They're very..."

"Yes...?"

"Art," he said weakly.

"Idiot," Lree muttered. Avery shot her a dirty look that went entirely unnoticed. He hadn't realized that she was facing the opposite direction.

"That's quite enough," said her mother tersely. "I believe it's time you left, my daughter."

Lree spun back around to face the Mistress. "That's not what Ah agreed to...!" she sputtered.

"I said that I would tell you about the heart after I...speak...with Mister Hall for a short while. That was implied, wasn't it? You don't expect me give in to your adorable demands without verifying him first."

The Mistress stared down at her daughter who was practically seething with frustration. Best to calm her down a bit to avoid another scene. "Breathe, little flower—Lree, excuse me. I will tell all about your heart. Soon. For now, wait for me in the dining hall. The large one. I will be along shortly—I don't expect this to take very long." She gave Avery a cutting glance that made him jump slightly.

As reasonable as she believed her request to be it was clearly not what Lree wanted to hear. "Ah don't think so!" her daughter replied with a snarl. "You're going to tell me right here, right now!"

This was clearly not what her mother wanted to hear, either. "Up until now," she said in a low, guttural voice, "I have allowed you to perform your ridiculous minstrel show." The room seemed to darken as did the Mistress herself. Her gravy-colored eyes took on a luminescent quality, casting uncomfortable shadows across her face. "But it is over. The performers are to leave the stage immediately and await payment. If you cannot carry out this task, I will be forced to terminate your contract. And by contract I mean you. You and your fat little friend."

Lree looked over at Avery who was seemingly oblivious to the danger he was in. "He's not my friend," she snorted as she sheathed her blade. Somewhere. She had pushed her luck far enough and gotten what she wanted. She could wait. "Ah'll go—but you'd better..."

"I wouldn't, if I were you," the Mistress interrupted, raising a single finger. "I will speak with you soon. In the meantime, Mister Hall and I have much to discuss. Now leave us. And close the door on your way out. Without slamming it."

Lree stormed out of the room, making sure to slam the door behind her.

The Mistress looked agitated but unsurprised. "That girl," she sighed. "I'm starting to think she'll never grow out of this phase."

"Kids, right?" is what Avery thought about saying but wasn't confident that he could pull it off convincingly. Plus he kind of hated that girl right now. Well, more so than he had before. What the hell was all that about, he asked himself. No answer came—just the same question again and again, increasing in vitriol each time.

"Now then," she said suddenly, clapping her hands and giving Avery another start. In the blink of eight eyes, she was violating the boundaries of Avery's personal space. "Let's take a good look at you," she said with a smile that otherwise would have had him calling out for an adult.

TWENTY TWO
An Idiot Unbound

It took some doing but Lree managed to shut the ostentatiously oblong door with a satisfying BAM! She had gotten exactly what she'd wanted under the best possible circumstances but was plagued by an unexplainable sense of disappointment. It was the sort of disappointment a child experiences having kicked and screamed for a box of cereal—a cereal they don't even like—that advertises a really neat toy. Mom or dad finally relent, placing the carton of sugar-crusted wood chips into the shopping cart to placate the child while secretly rethinking their puritanical stance on contraceptives. Come the morn the child wakes up extra early unable to hold back their excitement. Oh my god, a new toy! A new toy! You don't understand! It's new! And it's a toy! Open the box! Open it right now!

Of course, this is when reality up and smacks them in the face. There is no toy, only the severed finger of poor Mister Stevens who but a few weeks earlier had gotten his hand jammed in the NP-506b Cardboard CrimpMaster while trying to retrieve his glass eye which, coincidentally, had been discovered in another box of cereal by a slightly less disappointed child.

A terrible pressure had been swelling deep within Lree's chest before she had even stepped into her mother's study. It had now reached bursting point and she had to bite her bottom lip to stop herself from screaming. She stood by the doors for a moment, shaking and fuming. Her plan—the original plan—had gone smoothly and that was the real problem. There was no finality, just frustration. Lree took that frustration out on the object nearest to her: Avery's stupid satchel.

The first kick sent the bag sailing through the air until it was abruptly interrupted midflight by a wall. The second and third kicks scuffed it and partially drove it into the molding. The fourth and final kick sent it sailing back across the room and into the double doors. The latch that held the flap closed came undone, releasing some of the bag's contents onto the floor.

Lree watched with mild interest as a glass ball with a suspended red flame rolled slowly towards her. Before it could come to a stop, she walked over to pick it up. It was that idiot's wish.

"Stupid," she said, staring at the flickering heart within the orb. It was awfully tempting to toss it down the stairs—there were a lot of stairs, after all—but watching the tiny flame dance around calmed her. It was ridiculous, of course, though it might be good for a laugh.

Holding the orb out before her she said, very softly, "Ah wish it all would disappear."

Nothing happened. Maybe it wasn't good for a laugh after all. Lree dropped the globe and let it roll back towards the door. She would be the one to make her wish come true, not some frog's balls.

Lree readjusted her goggles, turned around, and began down the stairs. She might as well go along with her mother's plan and learn everything she could about the heart. And what if it all amounted to nothing? What then? Well, she'd worry about "what then" when and if then actually happens.

Avery was standing in the center of the Mistress's study—a sort of shrine to opulence filled with extravagant sculptures, paintings, and otherworldly oddities—naked down to his boots. Mind you, he wasn't aware that he was mostly nude as he found himself completely distracted by the Mistress's uncomfortable actions.

After Lree had left the Mistress quickly walked back to her desk. She fiddled with something in the box next to the baseball and came back wearing a strange, glass cylinder beneath her nose. It used a pair of small, curved tubes to hook into her nostrils, feeding her a supply of brightly colored powder with every snort.

She then began circling him. Slowly. Occasionally, she'd rub the back of one of her spindly fingers across his face, lightly pinch his arms, or blow his hair aside with her ancient, dusty breath. Avery wanted to say something—specifically, "You're making me intensely uncomfortable"—but the Mistress had been carrying on a constant conversation with herself from the start, making it impossible to politely interject.

"Remarkable," was one of the many things he had heard her say. Other things include: "This isn't...oh! But it is!", "Look at this. It's a shame, really," "This can't be your natural hair color," and, "Well there you have it."

She carried on for some time—circling, critiquing, prodding. Avery had begun to tune it all out. This wasn't what he had expected when he agreed to come here. Not that he knew what to expect, really, but he was definitely sure that whatever it was, this wasn't it. The appeal of being forced into a world of high-class prostitution had lost whatever sliver of luster he naively believed it had. All he wanted to do now was leave. It didn't matter where. Home was fine. Yeah, that's it. Let's go.

To his surprise, he couldn't. He couldn't move or even speak. What the hell had she done?

"I am sorry, Mister Hall—Avery. May I call you Avery?" the Mistress cooed, somehow sensing Avery's distress through his motionlessness. "Wonderful. You can call me Miss All, by the way. So, Avery, I had to bind you otherwise I wouldn't have been able to do this." And with that, she pinched his right buttock. Hard. It was most unwelcomed.

Something didn't feel right, aside from a spidery grandmother fondling his rear end. It wasn't the pinch itself, either, which was more of a "there's some good meat on this one" pinch than a "I'm making a rather inappropriate pass at you" pinch (and Avery was quite thankful for this). No, it was that the pinch—regardless of motive—was startlingly tactual.

"Or this," she said, slapping the same cheek. He definitely felt that one as she had struck skin. The Mistress released a cackle that would have otherwise shaken him could he move. "You've got nothing to worry about, Avery, because you've got nothing I want."

"Even if you did," she said, coming around to face him, "you couldn't handle it."

Avery's eyelid twitched, surprising him. The terminally erstwhile fondler didn't seem to notice as she had already begun circling him again. Circling and taunting like a vulture days before being placed on a list of registered sex offenders.

"That's not to say you're useless to me. No, no—not at all. My little flower really did bring me something special, didn't she? I suppose I'll have to be more truthful with her when we speak. I owe her that much."

He could now move his eyes, however, he did his best to conceal his newfound ability. When she had made yet another lap around to his backside he took the opportunity to investigate the local area. There didn't seem to be anything that he could use to protect himself. He did discover that he was almost entirely bereft of clothing.

"WHAT THE HELL?!" he yelled. Apparently, he could now yell, too.

"And more surprises!" she said with glee. "To think you could free yourself that quickly. Or at all!"

"Why am I naked?! Where are my clothes?" Everything else would certainly have to wait.

Miss All laughed a laugh that would make children cry. "So prudish! I wonder..."

Avery could now move his arms and hands, allowing him to rather awkwardly conceal his most inappropriate bits. He wasn't particularly ashamed of his naked physique—indeed, his self-image was extraordinarily high, if not delusional. Avery had always pictured himself as having a bold, noble, fantasy-type body, but in reality he was less a Boromir and more of a Bombur. Regardless, he was comfortable with himself. He was not comfortable putting himself on display for an increasingly creepy spinster. "Give me back my clothes," he said, nearly crying.

"I never took them," she replied, still cackling to herself. Cripes, she was unsettling. "If it will make you more comfortable I—"

"Yes!"

"Please, don't interrupt," she interrupted. She then drew in a large breath through her nose, released a weak cough, and continued. "As I was saying, if it will make you more comfortable I will restore your clothing."

Avery now had complete control of his body, however, he was hesitant to move. At least until he was dressed again. The Mistress began waving her hands before her as if she was conducting a symphony of blind musicians. Piece by piece, Avery's mismatched clothing reappeared on his person as if they had never left. Many things went through Avery's mind as he slowly became presentable again, however, the most pressing thought that had escaped his lips was: "Can you teach me how to do that?"

"And have you undress me? I really don't think so," she said, regaining her composure.

"I wouldn't use it on you," Avery said. Convincingly.

"That was meant as a joke, Avery. I..."

"I so wouldn't use it on you," Avery said. Again, convincingly.

"Yes, I see..."

"Good god, no."

"Enough. I believe you. Anyway, it doesn't work quite like how you imagine it does."

"You made my clothes disappear," he argued, ensuring that all of his clothes were back in their proper places. "I get it. I mean, what's not to get?"

"Strings, Avery."

"Okay."

"Not just strings, either. Ropes, chains, leashes, irons. Can't you see them?"

Avery wasn't exactly disappointed in not being able to find any of the items the Mistress mentioned, specifically the ropes, chains, leashes, and irons. Especially the ropes, chains, leashes, and irons.

"I thought as much," she said with a condescending smile. "To be fair, not many people can. But they are everywhere—all different lengths, all different sizes, all different strengths—binding everyone and everything together."

"Oh god," Avery thought he thought to himself. Instead, it seemed to claw its way out from the back of his throat and dribble out of his mouth. Setting aside all of the abuse and running and starvation and betrayal there was the small fact that he was dying and now...now it turns out that he placed all of his hopes in some cracked up cult leader spouting a silly new age philosophy about invisible soul strings or something equally as stupid. If she handed him a pamphlet, he thought, he was gone.

Miss All took notice of Avery's doubts as they were written rather plainly across his disappointed face. She inhaled deeply from her vial and clapped several times. "Move," she said.

Avery could not. He couldn't even speak.

"This," she said, pulling the strange device out from under her nose, "is filled with a substance...a mixture of substances you won't find anywhere else. It is my creation and I assure you I came about it with a great amount of difficulty."

"Even the slightest miscalculation in the measurements," she continued, "can result and has resulted in removing the subject's skin instead of their clothing. As you may be aware, skin plays a rather important role in keeping most of us alive."

Miss All replaced the device, inhaled, and clapped once more, releasing Avery. She explained: "Unfortunately, I cannot make things disappear. Well, I suppose I can but not so much in a literal sense."

Avery didn't reply. He was too confused and too uncomfortable to really concentrate. His entire body ached from the Mistress's multiple enchantments—most likely the ones that held him in place and not the one that stripped him of whatever dignity he might have had. All he could really do was let his tormentor continue to torment.

"I pulled on those strings attached to your curious clothing and bound them to something else. The floor, actually. Look."

Avery obeyed. He looked down and watched as his tights turned to a kind of liquid dust. The unearthly substance seemed to pass right through his legs then his boots, finally staining the carpet beneath with a pattern that resembled a crumbled pair of tights.

"And now," Miss All said, waving her hands again. As predicted, the stain coalesced beneath Avery and began to rise up. The ethereal sludge then slowly reverted back into the boy's silly tights. "Well?"

"So you put my shoes on the wrong feet?"

"What were you watching? I didn't touch your shoes. I shifted your tights to the floor."

"Oh," he said, disappointed. He then became very alarmed and asked, "Couldn't you have just taken off my shoes instead!?"

Miss All laughed again which was clearly not Avery's intent. "No, and that in itself is just part of the mystery. Did those funny shoes come with you?"

"What do you mean?"

"I mean, are they...yours?"

"I didn't steal 'em!" Avery said defensively. "Yeah, they're mine, okay? I bought them. What does that...?"

"Yes, I thought as much," the Mistress interjected. "They are completely unbound. As are you. It's as if neither your shoes or you, yourself, exist. You're just a waste of space."

That last bit was unnecessary, Avery thought, and definitely the last straw—whatever that meant. Was it really a big deal to take the last straw? Let's say you're at the minute market squeezing a syrupy frozen beverage out of a loud, clunky metal box and there's a guy next to you—a big guy with arms as large as truck trailers and a face that says yeah, I've killed people, wanna make something of it?!—getting a cupful of Boppin' Berry Blast. You pick up a straw out of the little steel cubby and discover that, shockingly, it's the last one. To make matters worse, the guy—the same guy who road in on a horse made of fire and hatred—saw you take it. In that scenario, the last straw certainly insinuates impending finality.

But how does all that apply to this situation, Avery wondered. He was upset at being called a waste of space—an insult not entirely new to him—by this elderly arachnid but wasn't sure where or how the guy with weaponized arms and flaming horses came into the picture or what the hell straws had to do with any of it.

Miss All stood by watching over Avery as he frittered to and fro. While she wasn't certain he was who Lree claimed him to be, he was quite a rare specimen and worth further study.

"Avery," she said rather curtly, bringing him to instant attention. "Why have you come here? Why did you seek me out?"

"What?"

"Why did you seek me out?" she repeated. "I know you came here on your own accord. I doubt very seriously that my daughter was able to take you prisoner and force you all the way up here to my private study."

To be perfectly clear, the Mistress was not insinuating that Avery was too powerful or too clever to be taken prisoner by her demonic daughter. As proof, she added: "My little flower lacks the patience and subtlety for such things. She would have slit your throat and left you to rot in the sun long before you even reached the complex."

Avery wasn't so sure—though he couldn't really disagree with her, either. Especially after being suddenly taken hostage by the little dirtball.

"Careful, Mister Hall. As uncouth as she may be at times, that little dirtball still happens to be my daughter."

Crap. He was thinking out loud again. "This," he said quickly, pointing at his blue arm.

"Yes, I had been wondering about that. I assume you weren't born that way."

"No. How would that even be possible? Look, apparently I fell on a rock and cut myself and I guess it got infected. I was told by a ball of snot that the infection would spread until I die and that if I could win..."

Avery stopped to clear his throat.

"I was told," he continued, "that only you could help me."

"You say you fell?"

"Apparently, yeah."

"Apparently?"

"Well, I wasn't awake when it happened. I passed out, I guess."

"You guess."

"I guess."

Miss All stared at Avery. It was an incredulous stare that made Avery feel just a bit foolish. "Out of curiosity," she said, "how do you know you fell on a rock?"

"The sprout—your daughter told me. She said I passed out and...fell..."

"My little flower told you," she said with a smile, "and you believed her?"

"Apparently," Avery admitted, now feeling far more than just a bit foolish.

The Mistress circled Avery again and stopped at his arm. "May I?" she asked, already lifting his sleeve. Avery gave a weak nod anyway. He wasn't keen on having her weird, spider-eyed face so close to him again but he was even less keen on dying a slow, excruciating death which is what he assumed would happen if he didn't get his arm taken care of immediately.

"Infected, hm?" she said, poking the area around the initial wound. This hurt a great deal. The Mistress lifted his arm and dropped it a couple of times, rotated it both left and right, and bent it upwards and downwards. This, too, hurt a great deal. More so, really. "Infected," she said again.

"Can you fix it?" he asked, wincing. "I mean, can you make it normal again?"

The Mistress released Avery's arm and walked back in front of him. She rolled her hand into a fist and set it atop her bottom lip to draw out Avery's anticipation. Finally, and with a great deal of theatrics, she said, "Of course I can restore your arm. I am the Mistress of Love's Lost, after all. I can do anything!"

Avery was awestruck by the old woman's confidence. There was no doubt in his warped little mind that she could, indeed, do anything. "Okay," he said, "Great! Let's go, let's do this!"

"Not here and not now," the Mistress said tersely, deflating a portion of Avery's enthusiasm. "Don't look like that. I have some matters I must attend to first."

"...but my arm..." Avery tried to argue.

"Is blue, yes, but otherwise of little immediate threat. Still, it certainly shouldn't be put off." The Mistress's statement was punctuated with the creaking of the large doors at the front of the study. "Ah, perfect," she said. "Pentas?"

Avery cocked his head to the side to see who the Mistress was talking to. He then returned it to its previous position, allowing both his mind and his body time to grasp the questionable image his eyes had given them.

"Mother, I thought you should know..." said the subject of the questionable image in a tone that was alarming and alluring. Also, familiar. The cave! The voice from the cave!

"It will have to wait, Pentas," the Mistress interrupted. "As you can plainly see, I have a guest."

Perfect, agreed his mind and body. The Mistress had just provided them—sorry, him—with the perfect opportunity to turn around and introduce himself without coming across as a creep. In his excitement, Avery spun around so fast that he made himself dizzy, sending him spiraling to the floor.

Pentas kneeled down beside Avery and offered her hand. "Are you alright, sir?" she asked in a voice that was almost offensively sincere.

"It's nothing," said Avery, holding his head in his hand. "Happens all the time." For all of his many faults, Avery was, at the very least, honest. Of course, one could make the argument that this, too, was a fault.

"Please," Pentas insisted, offering her assistance once again.

Avery gave a half-hearted "Yeah, thanks" and grabbed her hand as calmly as one would a railing while falling down an icy staircase. It was soft and warm, smooth and delicate, and it belonged to a woman whose appearance could only be described as mythical. Rushing streams of turbulent black hair fell from the top of her head, accenting a pale, illustrated face immune to critique. Her figure would make an hourglass blush and was very difficult to ignore. Not that Avery bothered to try. Once his eyes fell upon her chest he could not and would not remove them—as if he was engrossed in a deeply provocative documentary on the Civil War that happened to be playing in her cleavage.

Gently and with practiced control, Pentas guided Avery to his feet and again asked if he was well. He shook his head both yes and no, not really knowing how to respond. She was perfect in every way.

This indecisive seizure momentarily released Avery from the spell the mysterious woman's breasts had clearly cast upon him, enabling him to continue his objectifying gaze. She was, as already noted, perfect in every way. Well, actually...

The words "most ways" stumbled out of his gaping maw. He hadn't noticed before because of her dress. It was long with lovely little accents and mirroring slits that didn't seem to end. This was in part due to her large, weirdo legs that first bent one way—the normal way—and then the other. Her gigantic cloven feet certainly didn't win her any points, either.

Just be to perfectly clear, Avery's a bit of a pig. You got that, right?

"Pardon?"

"Did you say that or did I say that?" Avery asked.

"And what was that?"

"I don't remember. Hi, I'm Avery."

"It is a pleasure to meet you, Mister Avery. I am Pentas." Pentas released Avery's hand—much to his disappointment—and turned to face the Mistress. "Do you need something of me, mother?"

"I do," said Miss All returning to her chair at the head of the study. "This poor boy is afflicted with quite a nasty infection. I am going to remove it. Be a dear and please prepare the necessary arrangements."

"Arrangements?" Avery said nervously. "This isn't going to be like a surgical procedure or anything, is it?"

"Please, Mister Avery, there is nothing to worry about," soothed Pentas. Despite Avery complying almost instantly to her suggestion, she continued: "These things are often very complicated. We will make every precaution to ensure your safety. Am I wrong, mother?"

"Hm? Yes, of course. Your safety is paramount, Mister Hall. You have nothing to fear. Now please, if you will? As I said, I must attend to a few pressing matters but will be along shortly."

"Oh, and Pentas? Mind your manners, hm?"

"Of course, mother." Pentas turned back around and headed towards the enormous double doors. "This way please, Mister Avery," she said.

"Just Avery's fine," he said. For a moment he felt that maybe, just maybe, something was not quite right. The exchange between mother and daughter sounded warm but felt very, very cold. It was altogether different than the heated exchange between the Mistress and Lree. And why was the Mistress being so accommodating all of the sudden? Surely that was suspect.

But that moment of clarity was lost as soon as she had said his name. "Avery, of course. That is quite nice. Well, this way please, Avery."

Was it a demand? A request? Oh yeah, it was definitely a request. Cool. Gotta act cool. And smooth.

Avery said, "Uh-huh," took two steps towards Pentas, tripped over his wrong-footed boots, and fell flat on his face.

TWENTY THREE
Three of a Kind

This may come as a bit of a shock to you, dear reader, but Dahlia, Lree's hot-tempered, mean-spirited, and violently aggressive older sister and part-time fireball, is not a very patient young woman. Indeed, insisting that she sit quietly and wait would be like telling a half-starving hyena not to leap jaws first into the bloated belly of a day-old mule deer carcass just yet. Legs splayed and back hunched, she sat in her chair like a dying barbarian king. On the floor in an ugly pile lay the massive trench coat given to her by Pentas.

Pentas. Like Lree, she both respected and feared her older sister—but mostly feared. Though she had never seen her really angry, Dahlia had witnessed her sister take down large and powerful guests—drunken warriors, rival crime bosses, and even an ill-tempered demigod—without so much as lifting a finger. She could effectively will anyone into submission.

Which is how Dahlia found herself sitting alone in one of the Facade's larger dining halls. She wasn't sure what her sister was up to—Pentas was impossible to read and unnecessarily cryptic—but felt it wise to go along with whatever her plan happened to be. After all, she was the oldest and was always looking out for her best interest.

Wait in the dining hall. Hide the wine.

Dahlia rarely came to the Facade and when she did it was even more unlikely that you'd find her anywhere near a public dining hall. Like most of the rooms in her mother's sanctuary it was absolutely enormous and littered with treasures. A single table ran the entire length of the room, ending at an imposing hearth flanked by two massive stone columns. There were dozens of available chairs meant for dignitaries and other seemingly important guests. The empty seats unsettled Dahlia as she much preferred to eat in her room deep below the complex, alone. And right now that sounded like a great idea.

She had just crouched down to pick up her coat when she heard footsteps coming down the stairs. It was a familiar, clomping sound—one made by callused feet wrapped in cloth scraps.

"Oh, little flower," Dahlia said, adding a sinister grin just in case anyone was watching. She had just about decided how best to ambush her younger sister—either leap on her from the doorway or rush her as she came down the stairs—when she realized she had missed something.

"Hide the wine?" she asked aloud. There was a trolley of sorts across the room almost bursting with bottles but what of it? Lree didn't drink so what did it matter? Maybe Pentas meant it as a metaphor? Why was she so obtuse? She just come out and say what she meant!

Dahlia cursed a highly inappropriate curse, ultimately deciding to ignore the potentially figurative advice and hide instead. Given her unique stature, her choices were limited. She could duck beneath the table—though with no table cloth to conceal her she'd be spotted fairly quickly—or behind one of the gigantic columns near the fireplace. The decision making process took far longer than it probably should have given that the majority of her thoughts were still focused on assaulting Lree in various terrible ways. Eventually, she settled on the columns and barely managed to dash behind one before her little sister entered the room.

Lree, too, was not a regular patron of her mother's dining facilities. Despite this one in particular being free of plant life she never cared for the company. She quickly found a chair—the only chair not neatly tucked beneath the table—and sat herself down. Her heart was racing— she was close now. Closer than she had ever been before to being truly free and all it cost was one really annoying guy. Any feelings of regret about luring Avery to Love's Lost and leaving him to the mercy of her mother were almost immediately overtaken by feelings of hope—real hope! Her new life was about to begin.

She placed one foot on the edge of the table and pushed herself back in her chair. "Wonder what mother'll do to him," she caught herself thinking as she rocked back and forth. Not that it mattered, of course. What her mother would do to him, not the rocking back and forth bit.

"Probably put him in a cage or something," she continued to think. It really wasn't her problem anymore.

"Drain his juices like a bug. Stuff him and put him on display." What. Ever.

"Idiot."

"Are you sure you are alright, Avery?" Pentas asked, shutting the giant door behind her.

Avery wasn't alright. How long had it been, he wondered, recounting the numerous incidents, humiliations, and near-death experiences he had fallen victim to since waking up in that grassy field. He no longer felt like he was in complete control of his own actions. His reality had slipped into a sort of lucid dream that he was incapable of waking up from.

"Mister Avery?" she asked politely and possibly sincerely.

"My bag," Avery responded. "Where's my—oh, here it is." Indeed, there it was, crumpled by the entrance to the study with its contents spilled upon the floor. He knelt down to pick up both the bag and the orb, noticing that one of the two items was no longer as cool as it once was.

"Aw, man. It's broken," he lamented. And he was sincere. Despite no longer containing a tiny, dancing flame and thus being nowhere near as impressive as it used to be, he had gone to an awful lot of trouble to acquire the orb. And, you know, the sheer size of it made it just interesting enough to be worth hanging on to.

It occurred to Avery that since the orb had fallen out of the bag then he should probably check to see if the bug was still there. The bag, however, was in a terrible state of disarray when he found it. If the bug was still there then it, too, would be in a terrible state of disarray and that was a sight he didn't feel his psyche was ready for at the moment.

He turned to Pentas who had been waiting patiently at the top of the stairs. A smile crossed his face then a frown for the thought of having to once again tackle that chapter-long staircase filled him with dread. It was a very wide, winding stairwell flanked by rather plain white walls. Every few dozen steps there was a small landing featuring a painting or sculpture or something clearly designed to stop you and be appreciated. As neither a lover of the arts or physical fitness, Avery found little to appreciate.

"Have I done something to upset you, Mister Avery?" Pentas asked, urging him towards the stairs.

"I don't think so," Avery said plainly. "It's just I'm not looking forward to the trip back down."

"Is my company that poor?"

"What? No!" he exclaimed. He had been so caught up in his own personal loathing and pity that he had completely forgotten just how attractive his guide was.

"It's," he began slowly, scrambling for an explanation that was at least somewhat plausible. Other than, "I'm lazy and totally out of shape," of course. "It's a long way down. It's boring, you know?"

"Super boring," he added unhelpfully.

Pentas seemed to consider his words. Finally she smiled, clapped her hands, and said, "Shall we make a game of it then?"

Oh no. She wanted to race down to the lobby, didn't she? Yeah, that sounded great. He might as well just throw himself down the stairs since his heart would have exploded by the first landing anyway. At least then he might stand a small chance of winning.

"I don't..." he tried to say.

"I will ask you a question and you will answer it. Then by the next landing you will ask me a question and I will answer it. How does that sound?"

"Why do you get to go first?" Avery asked.

"You may go first if you wish."

"I don't care," he said.

Pentas took the lead and Avery followed a step or two behind. Already he felt the sickening sensation of vertigo wrap itself around his head—squeezing it, suffocating it.

"Where have you come from?" Pentas asked. Like before, her voice snapped him out of his stupor. Temporarily.

Avery thought for a moment then said, "Not here."

"You will have to try harder than that, Avery," Pentas cooed. Avery felt himself being cooed and blushed slightly as a result.

"Really. I don't know where I am or how I got here, but I'm starting to feel like wherever this is it's definitely not where I'm from. Like, not even close. So me telling you, "Oh yeah, I live outside of East Orange but I'm actually from a little town in the dead center of Nowhere Ohio called Pataskala," wouldn't mean much, would it?"

"It means much more than you may realize," she replied politely. "Though I admit I am not yet familiar with such places. Are they beyond the Chain?"

Avery stepped onto the first landing and said "I don't know what that is," followed by, "Is it my turn now?"

"You have the advantage." The way she said this made Avery blush harder.

"Alright, um, what's this chain about?"

Pentas, already descending the next flight of stairs, said, "I feel that you may be toying with me, Avery." He wasn't, of course, and nearly gave himself whiplash shaking his head so hard. This odd spasm of denial seemed to have convinced Pentas.

"Very well," she continued. "The Chain, or the Great Chain depending on who you are speaking with, is a series of more than a dozen shards making up the lower portion of Raltor Tark. Some of the more noteworthy shards include Finfal, Yaatana, and La'lapu La'fala. We are on Mora, the anchor."

Avery responded wordlessly with a series of blinks. He wasn't expecting much of an answer let alone one so well rehearsed. After a while, he finally admitted, "I don't think I understood anything you just said."

"Just as well," Pentas said with a smile, "because it appears to be my turn again. Tell me, why did you bring my sister back?"

"Your what?" Avery asked, figuring out the answer to his own question internally by the time he reached the last syllable. If Pentas was the Mistress's daughter and Lree was also the Mistress's daughter, that would make Pentas and Lree...

"Sisters?!" he shouted. It was difficult to tell whether he was shocked or simply disappointed. "I guess that makes sense," he muttered. "Technically. You're talking about the sprout, right? Miss Stabs-You-In-the-Back? The human hairball? You're not much alike, you two. Not at all."

Avery stole a glance of his guide's stunning profile. "Oh man, not at all."

Pentas displayed remarkable patience. "I suppose we are not. However, she is still my sister."

"I guess. Anyway, I didn't know I was bringing her back. Wait, I didn't even bring anywhere. She brought me! 'Cause of my arm." In an effort to convey his distress he gave his afflicted appendage a nice, hard slap. The resulting stream of loud, angry, and completely unintelligible noises indicated that such an effort had been successful.

Pentas clearly had more questions but Avery, quite worked up, was quick to throw out his own as they reached the next landing. Rubbing his arm like a creep, he squeaked, "Are you seeing anyone?" After a less than pleasant throat clearing, he repeated his question in a slightly less comical tone. He was still rubbing his arm like a creep, however.

"I see you," was her response. It wasn't quite what he had been hoping for but it also wasn't the worst answer which would have been, "yes." Well, that's not true, really. The absolute worst answer would have been, "Yes, yes, dear god yes so don't even think about asking me out you overstuffed Boston cream doughnut. And stop rubbing your arm like a creep!" That would have been pretty devastating. And delicious! He was so, so hungry.

"I mean, do you have a...boyfriend?" he asked more clearly. Pentas's expression changed from believably pleasant to being as pleasant as she had to be in order to up-sell a deluxe icemaker on a new refrigerator so that she could meet quota. The dreadful silence that followed Avery's question lasted for, by his own account, a hundred million years. The Permian age gave way to the Triassic and the Triassic gave way to Pentas's response. "No," is all she said.

Avery, ever the master of subtlety, shook his fist by his side and shouted "Nice!" through clenched teeth.

A seemingly genuine smile returned to Pentas's face. "You are an odd one, Mister Avery."

"I'm an odd one?" Avery said, raising his voice back into a squeak. Pentas was very obviously taken aback. "Pfft. Listen, sister, I've seen some truly weird stuff since I woke up here. Walking skeletons, anthropomorphic bugs that explode on contact, a squirrel-headed snake man with a chest as big as two of me, and a dude named Cowface."

The pair had reached the next landing, however, Avery was too busy ranting to notice. "I stole a glass of Windex from a floating ball of worms and guess what. It turned out to be the best damn drink I've ever had in my entire miserable life. I then had a dinner-less dinner with the secret lovechild of Edward Scissorhands and Morrissey. I was felt up by a woman old enough to be my grandmother's grandmother and who also happened to have like eight freakin' eyes."

"And the absolute weirdest thing—the one thing that I can't stop thinking about—is the baseball."

Pentas, who had been polite enough to allow Avery to finish his whiny, rambling, and bewildering outburst, suddenly took a very keen interest in what he had to say. She stopped on a step just below him and, less than gently, grabbed him by the blue arm. "Did you say the baseball?" she demanded.

"Y-yeah?" he grimaced. He honestly wasn't sure whether to be intimidated or turned on. "The baseball on whatsherface's desk."

Unconsciously tightening her grip and drawing in closer, Pentas said, "You know what the baseball is?"

The pain was beginning to reach unbearable levels, triggering his mind to release a soothing, distracting, and embarrassing ramble. "Kind of. I mean, duh, yeah, but I'm not very into sports. My grandma forced me to play tee ball when I was like six or something. I only got up to bat once and I...struck out."

Pentas released Avery's arm and repeated, "You know what the baseball is?"

He began to rub his arm again though this time it seemed significantly less creepy—even if he was panting slightly. "But that's not weird, right?" he said, painting slightly. "It's not weird and that's what makes it weird! Everything here is weird. Your mother's weird, your sister's weird, you're weird..."

"In a good a way," he stuttered.

"But the baseball isn't weird because it's just a dirty ol' baseball."

Something was very different about this boy. It was little wonder why mother, too, had taken an interest in him.

It was in the refuse tunnel. She had tried reaching out to him but his presence vanished. It was as if he ceased to exist up until their reunion in mother's study. Even then she could only see him. Her mind would not accept that he was actually there in the room and that disturbed her.

And frightened her.

And angered her.

Indeed, something was very different about this boy and she would find out what that something was before mother could.

"Mother is what you might call a collector. The baseball must be one of her most prized possessions. No one is quite certain what it does or why she values it so, but it is absolutely off limits. No one is allowed to touch it. Not that anyone would even dare touch her other treasures, of course, but the penalty for defiling the baseball is," Pentas took an inappropriately long pause here. "...severe."

"Uh-huh," Avery said, chewing on one of his longer fingernails. "You know what else I just thought is weird?"

Pentas's head had begun to throb and her polite demeanor was showing signs of significant fracturing. She would not lose to a mere boy even if he was more of a mere boy and a half. "Please, do tell," she said in a manner that would seem threatening to anyone paying attention. Unsurprisingly, Avery was not anyone.

"What? Oh, the flowers."

"I am afraid I do not follow you."

"Flowers," Avery urged. "This place—outside—everything is covered in flowers. I've never seen so many flowers anywhere, it's crazy! I just think it's just weird that with all those flowers there's no sign of 'em in here. I mean, look at all that crap in the study—there weren't even have any pictures of flowers."

"They are not pictures," Pentas corrected Avery, "they are paintings. And you are very observant."

"I *am* observant."

"Yes, I believe I just said that." Pentas sighed. This was getting her nowhere. "To tell you the truth, mother does not like flowers. You could even say that she outright despises them."

"Garish, pungent, hateful things," said Pentas. Her tone had dropped a few notches and she appeared to be speaking through Avery instead of to him. "That is what she once confided in me. So much effort for so little return."

"And they die far too quickly," she added.

"Then why this place? Why all the flowers?"

"Mother is not so arrogant to allow her personal grievances to get in the way of smart business decisions. The enormous variety and large volume of the offensive flora that spawn from the voorn have become very popular attractions. Most guests visit specifically to tour the gardens. She would never dream of denying them their simple pleasures—especially if they are willing to pay."

They had reached another landing, one highlighted by a bright red painting set inside a small recess within the wall. "Is it my turn? I've got a question," Avery said, raising his hand with some enthusiasm.

"I feel as though we might have skipped a turn or two."

"What's a voorn?"

Pentas gave Avery a look that effectively repeated his question though in a much more condescending way. Had she been over thinking this boy's potential? Had her calculative and delusory lifestyle made her immune to the obvious? She was confident that Avery was unique, however, unique didn't necessarily equate to important. There's a very real possibility that they were not locked in a battle of wits and, had Pentas been privy to practically any of the previous Avery-focused chapters she would have realized that this was the case.

Regardless, he still had value—but what of it? Pentas pondered on her predicament while watching Avery touch one of her mother's paintings with his pudgy, greasy fingers. He drew in closer to study the piece and at one point she was sure she saw him stick his tongue on it. This was confirmed when he said, "Yeah, that's paint."

"What did you expect?"

"Looked like a strawberry. I thought these were magic pictures, like how this place is magic and all, and you could lick the pictures. You can't. I mean, you can but it won't taste like anything in the picture. Unless it's a picture of paint. Then I guess it works out."

Pentas, dubious and fearful, frustrated and bewildered, did something she found quite unexpected: she laughed. The outburst of merriment caught her so off guard that she was utterly incapable of stifling it. It was a genuine laugh that brought her to mild tears. It would also magnify her doubts and fears and frustration and confusion tenfold but right now she felt a strange relief.

Avery thought about laughing along with her but he didn't know why she was laughing which would mean he'd have to fake it and he was terrible at doing that. "Ha ha haa!" he'd bellow, just like that, just as it was written in a comic book. Then he'd be asked to leave the funeral.

Laughing was out of the question so he settled on responding with an awkward smile. It seemed to work.

"Forgive me," said Pentas upon drawing in a deep breath. "I am used to entertaining guests, not having guests entertain me. They try, of course. But..."

"Forgive me," she repeated. "You wanted to know what a voorn was. You are serious, yes?"

"A what?" Avery responded. "Oh, oh, right. Yeah. You were talking about flowers and said blah blah voorn blah blah blah. I was listening. What is it, like, plant food or something?"

Pentas had regained much of her composure and felt a bit more generous with her answers. She still wasn't completely sure he wasn't toying with her but if he was she decided it would be wiser to allow him to lead the conversation for now. She was, as has been noted, patient. She'd simply wait for the opportunity to take it back—no use expending any energy doing so at the moment.

"In a way, yes," she said. "The green ones are often used for growing, feeding, and repairing the flora throughout the complex. Others have different uses, all based largely on carapace colors."

"Carapace?"

"Yes," Pentas continued, "the shell."

A startling image flashed through Avery's mind. It was an image of a glowing lantern stuffed with the rotting remains of something quite horrible. "So," he hesitated, "the voorn are like an animal? Like a crab or clam or...?"

"An insect. Nasty little creatures, too. Some have pincers that can cut through solid stone. That is one of the reasons why they are so difficult to harvest."

There was also the cave, its floor carpeted with creatures either dead or dying. That's where he got to see one up close.

"At least, difficult for everyone else. Mother has created a system that not only attracts the voorn but pacifies them, allowing us to harvest and process them at a speed no one else can match."

Her face had been human. Mostly human. Humanoid. She had a little nose, cheeks dotted with freckles, and large black eyes filled with actual emotion. Fright, mainly, but also something else.

"It may not look like it, but Love's Lost is as much a processing and production facility as it is a resort for the wealthy and powerful. We tend to downplay the former, however, as it can put off our guests."

Avery slowly opened the bag hanging next to him and peered inside, afraid of what he may find. A thin shaft of light shone into the bag and from deep within he saw that freckled something else staring back at him with unnaturally large, black eyes.

"Despair," he muttered.

"Disgust, actually," Pentas replied, unaware of Avery's obvious befuddlement. She seemed to be enjoying herself—so much so that she had just only now realized they were off the stairwell and on their way to the lobby.

"What is especially amusing is that the facility is intimately entwined with the resort and yet the guests can't see it."

Avery closed the satchel and his eyes as a dreadful, uncomfortable feeling consumed him. It was malicious and resentful, desperate and miserable, sad and lonely. Worst of all, he didn't know whose feelings these were.

"That's not right," he murmured. His words didn't register with Pentas but his judgmental tone had more than a passing familiarity about it.

"Pardon?"

"I don't know why I said that," Avery admitted. He then immediately contradicted himself by saying, "Wait a sec, yes I do. That's messed up. They're living things, aren't they?"

"The guests?"

"The bugs! The voorn or whatever."

Was that it, Pentas wondered. Was he after the voorn? If so, he was much more of a threat than she had previously suspected and she needed to do something about it. Now.

Pentas lead Avery towards the middle of a great hall not far from the main entrance. He had been ranting almost uncontrollably about the voorn the entire time and was just about to explain why it was okay to squash a roach but not a little person when he was mercifully silenced by the sweetest, softest, and only pair of lips ever to touch his own.

TWENTY FOUR
Success & Failure

Lree sat neatly in her chair, kicking her feet while humming an entirely improvised tune. She smiled a pleasant smile. Her mother would be along shortly with the heart and together they'd discuss the nature of and resolution for her terrible affliction. Her smile, now well beyond pleasant, took up at least a quarter of her face.

Hands resting softly in her lap, she swayed gently from side to side to the melody of her newly invented song. Occasionally she'd sing a lyric or two, most of which involved sunshine and words that almost rhymed with sunshine if you were phonetically challenged, such as saccharine and praline. This was going to be wonderful, she thought. Once all was said and done she'd hug her mother and her mother would hug her.

"Won't you join me for tea?" her mother would ask. Lree knew what this really meant, however.

"You're just looking for an excuse to open that special tin of cookies you've been saving."

"Guilty!" she'd sing. Then they'd both laugh and hug again.

"I love you, Lree," her mother would say.

Lree screamed, jerking her head free from a puddle of drool. It was an absolutely breathtaking body of dribble, complete with a complicated system of working inlets created by the numerous gashes that may or may not have been a result of her picking at the table with her ever curious dagger. One can't say for certain as the alleged knife was now nowhere to be found.

The room was cold. Freezing, really, thanks in part to soaking her head and ample hair in her own saliva. It was odd—though she didn't think about it until much later. Between the everlasting dark and her cavernous prison she had gotten quite used to the cold. But for whatever reason the cold she was experiencing at this moment was unbearable.

Lree rubbed her arms and looked at the hearth at the end of the room. Inside was a large charred log and a pile of tiny embers beneath incapable of melting a miniature butter sculpture. She didn't see any fresh wood to speak of though her view was limited due to the two massive columns that flanked the fireplace.

The columns. Right. The wood, the bellows, the shovel, the tongs—they'd probably be hidden behind the columns as not to sully the appearance of the dining hall. Appearances meant everything to mother and her obsession with order bordered on mental illness. Everything had a place and a purpose. Everything and everyone.

Of course there was a fire-starter behind the column. A tall, bulky, trench-coated fire-starter of foul temperament overly eager for Lree to get closer.

"I love you," Lree recalled and, consequently, shivered. Let's...let's just stoke the fire and get warm for now. Put everything else far, far out of your mind.

She leapt out of her chair and bounded towards the dying hearth. Her hand had just reached around the column when she withdrew it suddenly. There was a commotion out in the hall (this wasn't exactly true, however, since the hall had been dead silent up until this point so that even a flatulent field mouse would be enough to cause a commotion), presenting her with an opportunity to alleviate at least a portion of the tedium she had been forced to endure.

Lree felt the same way. Stealthily but quickly she tiptoed around the perimeter of the room until she came to the entrance. The far door was still open so she slid to the very edge of its closed twin to get a good listen. And maybe a peek if warranted.

Don't judge. It's something to do, alright?

Proving in part that this book has at least some semblance of taste the commotion had not been caused by a colicky critter. It was just Pentas carrying on and on as was her wont. Or so it seemed. Something was off—either her tone or volume or...something. Lree cupped her crippled ear in an effort to hear exactly what she was saying and, more importantly, to whom.

"Despair."

Wait, was that him? Her part-time punching bag, hostage, and aggravator? The idiot? Huh, guess mother decided not to kill him. Whether she was relieved or disappointed by this is better left a mystery. And speaking of mysteries, why was he with Pentas? And why were they talking about bugs?

Lree's mind whirred as each question she thought up was answered by yet more questions. For example, "What was Pentas even doing here?" was followed by, "Why didn't I hear here coming down the stairs?" which was followed by, "How long has she been here?" Her train of thought not only returned to the station but to the factory in which it had been manufactured.

Lree and Dahlia peered carefully around their respective corners in search of answers that weren't just other questions. What they found left them more perplexed than ever. Also, angry and a little embarrassed.

He kissed her. The idiot was kissing their sister! He's not dying! Why isn't he dying?! Why isn't he dead?!

Lree and Dahlia, mouths agape and shaking slightly, were so astounded by the bizarre scene that neither had noticed that they were both now standing out in the open. Pentas noticed, however. With her face still pressed intimately against Avery's, she glared at her sisters. Then she smiled.

It wasn't a pleasant smile.

Later—much, much later—the Mistress made her way down to the dining room. Though her head was held in a way to obscure her expression the way she carried herself made it quite clear that she wasn't in the best of moods. Not that Lree particularly cared. It's not like her own mood was any better. Setting aside her absurdly long wait there was the incident between the idiot and her sister that was equal parts disgusting and unsettling. So much so, in fact, that she had all but forgotten about the room's inhospitably low temperature.

"It's freezing in here," the Mistress said in an accusing tone. "Would it have really been that difficult to start a fire? Honestly, you've been down here long enough. Have some consideration."

Lree stared at her mother. It was really the only appropriate response she could give other than throwing the tableware at her. The Mistress had picked up on this but wasn't looking for an argument. Not right now. Instead, she fitted her strange, glass device into her nostrils and inhaled deeply. She then waved her hand in the air, ending with just two of her fingers pointing straight up in a rather suggestive fashion. In a flash, a raging fire burst into existence within the hearth and almost instantly began to heat the room.

"Honestly," she said again, taking a heavy seat at the head of the table. She removed her breathing apparatus and rubbed her temple furiously. "Dear," she said a bit unsteadily, "Let's have our little chat another time. I just had the most unpleasant conversation with that kook of a groundskeeper and I'm...I'm exhausted. I think it may be time to have him purged. Shame, though. He is a fantastic groundskeeper. Raving mad, for certain. Skeletons? Wind chimes? I need a drink."

As if filled with renewed purpose, the Mistress stood up and strode over to a silvery cart resting against the wall in the middle of the room. Bottles full of colorful and presumably volatile liquids occupied the top shelf while carefully stacked towers of thin glasses created a crystalline cityscape below. She spent a few moments deciding on which drink would adequately satisfy her, finally settling on mixing several of the bottles together into a glass and finishing off the questionable concoction in a single impressive gulp.

Perhaps out of shock or even sympathy Lree didn't say anything. At least, at first. When her mother started in on her second glass, Lree spoke up. "You promised," she said coolly.

After another gulp and a sigh her mother, wearily, agreed. "So I did, little flower," she said. "Very well, ask away. But please, don't...let's keep things nice and quiet. For mother's sake."

Lree began to say something about being called "little flower" then stopped. She had been anticipating this moment—this confrontation—for so long that she wasn't about to get sidetracked by mere quibbling.

"Is it real?"

The Mistress brought her glass to her lips, taking a slower, more appreciative sip this time. "It being...?"

"The heart. Is it real?"

Another sip. "Yes, I suppose it is."

Struggling to contain her excitement, Lree burst out with, "Where is it? Tell me where is it!"

"Why is it so important to you?" her mother responded. "What do you plan to do with it once it's found?"

"Ah'll destroy this place!" It was an honest answer, if not all that subtle.

The Mistress failed to hold back a chuckle. "And that's supposed to encourage me to tell you where it is? I'm going to need another drink." She then followed through on her declaration.

"Ah mean it!" Lree added. "Ah want to...Ah need to be rid of this place."

Returning to her seat, the Mistress took a quick sip of her latest drink and asked, "And why is that?"

"It's," Lree paused long enough for her mother to take several more sips. "Ah mean, it's the only way to fix me."

The Mistress was expectedly confused. "Fix you, dear? Fix what, exactly? Your hair? Your manners? Your attitude? Your posture?" The Mistress looked at Lree, most of her eyes slightly glazed over. "Your hair?" she repeated. "Believe me, little flower, I have tried "fixing" you. We all have. You just can't..."

"*Your* curse!"

"*My* curse?" her mother replied, taking a bit more amusement out of the accusation than Lree was comfortable with. "How am *I* cursed? Outside of having an impatient and impertinent daughter. Daughters. At least two of you."

Lree slammed one of her tiny fists on the table, rattling dozens of empty plates and glasses. "You know that's not what Ah meant!" she yelled. "The curse you put on me to keep me here! Ah know it was you!"

"What *are* you talking about?" the Mistress asked, setting her glass down. "How am I keeping you here? More importantly, *why* would I want to do such a thing? It's not as if you actually contribute to the business. The most I've ever seen you do is clean some glasswork. At least your sisters have the decency to show some gratitude."

"Ah can't go nowhere without being attacked. Everything is after me. The trees, the flowers, the grass—everything!" Lree's words were weighted heavily with equal parts anger and frustration—so much so that the Mistress relented. Slightly.

"Ah. You're referring to your curious affliction, yes? I'm sorry to disappoint you, little flower, but the origin of your curse, as you so quaintly call it, has little to do with me or Love's Lost."

"Ah don't believe you."

"I wouldn't expect you to," the Mistress countered quickly. "However, it is the truth."

"Oh, you had potential," she continued. "So much potential. I thought for sure that you would be the one. I still do, really, but...how to explain this to someone like you..."

Lree had no idea what her mother was babbling on about but she was fairly certain that it wasn't what she wanted to hear. If she wanted any answers—any real answers—she'd have to keep her mother on track.

"Start from the beginning," she said with uncharacteristic patience.

"Did you know," said her mother, "that you are my eldest daughter?"

Lree did not know this, as indicated by her reply of, "Huh?"

The Mistress stared into her empty glass longingly. "More, please," she said simply.

"O-okay."

Lree got up from seat to take her mother's glass over to the cart and froze. What was she doing? Why was she doing whatever it was that she didn't know she was doing? She looked back at her mother, desperate.

"Anything will do," her mother said. "Mix some together if you have to."

Lree complied, sloppily pouring a glass full of whatever bottle happened to be within her reach. She returned the glass to its owner where its contents met their immediate demise.

"What d'ya mean eldest?" Lree asked.

"Hmm? Did I say that? I suppose I did. You are the eldest, though I couldn't tell you in years because you don't even know what those are."

Wonderful. She was drunk. Still, this might provide an opportunity to receive some honesty from her mother if she was careful.

"But Dahlia and Pentas..."

"Are...bigger, yes. Older," her mother interrupted, "But you are the eldest. You've been my daughter longer than those two. It's really not that complicated."

"It was somewhere. That's not important. I just happened across you. Saved you, actually."

"You saved me?" Lree asked with a significant amount of incredulousness. By now she had taken a seat a bit closer to her mother.

"Your curse, if you want to call it that. You were being strangled. Of course, I didn't realize what was happening at first but no one else was helping so I..." her mother's voice trailed into an embarrassing silence. "It was only later that I realized your gift."

"Mah what?!" Lree screamed. Of all things to call that which had only sought to destroy her from her earliest memories, gift was the very opposite.

"Oh dear, I'm beginning to think letting you visit the Shining so much wasn't such a great idea. Your accent is atrocious. My. Say it with me: my. Mmm. Eye. My."

Lree ignored the critique and pressed further. "Why...why'd you call it that?"

It took the Mistress a bit to realize what her daughter was referring to. "Oh," she said. Eventually. "Your gift? It is, little flower. How can you not see that?"

"'Maybe cuz Ah'm too busy makin' sure mah gift doesn't kill me?'"

"And that's the reason why you're such a disappointment. Well, one reason, I suppose. You have to look beyond that, dear. Look at the bigger picture. You make the world react to you. The world reacts to you. It should be the other way around but it's not with you. Don't you see?"

"No," is all Lree could think of to say. So she did.

"You matter," her mother said. "No one else in this damned world matters. I could, right now, sink that detestable ghetto across the chasm into the sparkling depths and the world wouldn't even blink. I could also do nothing and still the world would not notice. But the world notices you and that, little flower, is real power!"

Lree wasn't convinced nor was she impressed or flattered or in any way emotionally impacted the way her mother thought she should be. "This is stupid," she said more exhausted than angry. "Ah came here for answers. If all you're gonna do is lie to me—and don't tell me you're not—then Ah'm takin' back the idiot and leaving."

Her mother sat back in her chair to take the full brunt of Lree's threat and yet her expression never changed. While she was obviously in the same room as her daughter, her thoughts were somewhere else entirely.

"I studied you carefully. Very carefully. And I started to think that maybe I could improve you."

"You tried to remove mah curse?" Lree asked hopefully.

"Heavens no," the Mistress laughed. "Pay attention. You weren't providing results so I sought to create something that could. In retrospect, I went about this rather haphazardly, I'm afraid. Dahlia was a miserable failure."

"She was little more than a blank slate when she was brought to me so I was convinced the...I was convinced it would work. Can you guess what happens when you combine a child devoid of emotions with the world's ire?"

Lree, leaning forward so that her shoulders were slumped, stared down at her lap with widened eyes. She felt she should say something, however, she didn't know what that something should be. Was this how it was supposed to go? How were these answers supposed to set her free?

"Dahlia happens. Still, it wasn't a total loss. After a while it was clear they possessed some unique gifts, as I'm sure you're well aware. But they're useless to me."

"Why're you tellin' me all this?" Lree asked, secretly hoping her mother would stop.

The Mistress rose from her chair, snatched her glass from the table, and haphazardly walked back over to the silver drink cart. She cleared her throat and, in a particularly convincing impersonation, said, "Tell me everythin'. That's what you said." She poured herself yet another drink and slowly made her way back to her seat. "So I'm telling you everything. If you can't handle it I'll be more than happy to end this arduous conversation now and never return to it. This isn't easy for me, either. I don't like dwelling on the mistakes I've made."

Lree's chest was pounding hard and she became visibly shaken. Mother was right, though. She had demanded to know everything and she'd be damned if she'd let a few disquieting feelings stop her from achieving that goal.

"Ah can handle it," she said.

"I know you can," her mother agreed and Lree almost believed it. "You're willful and stubborn. Much like me in that regard."

Now she was shaken *and* nauseated, with the former cruelly antagonizing the latter. Unlike before she now had plenty to say on the matter, however, the fear of spilling most of said matter all over the table prevented her from doing so. Instead, she let her mother continue her rambling narrative of regret.

"I can't help but pity her. Your sister. I suppose that's one reason why I've kept her on."

Lree, too, pitied Dahlia—at least, she did now and that was troubling. Hatred, jealously, bitterness, fear, longing—her relationship with her sister had always been overwhelmingly selfish and that was fine. That was comfortable. But to feel sympathetic towards her— towards the cruel monster that had helped make her life miserable—felt wrong. So Lree did exactly what Lree does when she became uncomfortable. She lashed out.

"That's all you got?" she sputtered. "You pity her? After turnin' her into a freak and...and you pity her?!"

Without so much as raising her voice, her mother replied, "I did no such thing. You did."

"What?!" Lree snapped. "Ah'm..."

"If it weren't for you," she interrupted, still irritatingly stoic, "Dahlia would never have had to go through those...changes. If it weren't for you, she'd never have had to experience the pain and suffering wrought by your gift."

"You wanted the truth, did you not? Can you now see why she resents you? Why *I* resent you?"

"You call your gift a curse," she said, pressing on so quickly that Lree had no time to respond. "It's not. Don't you see? You're a curse. Your *existence* is a curse."

There was a slight pause—slight enough for Lree to retaliate. "So why d'ya keep me here?" she screamed. "If Ah'm so terrible why haven't you thrown me out, huh? Why haven't you had me killed? Or am Ah just another failure you feel sorry for. Like Pentas and Dahlia."

"Careful, little flower," the Mistress cautioned with an inflection dripping with disgust. "Pentas was not a failure. Pentas was a mistake."

For whatever reason her mother's cryptic comment seemed to calm the tension in the room. Lree sat back down and asked in a barely polite voice, "So why d'ya keep me?"

The Mistress leaned back in her chair as if seriously considering the question. "I suppose," she began, "I suppose it's because you remind me of myself."

"What?"

"You remind me of myself," she repeated. "Not completely. Heavens no—that's almost obscene. But compared to the other two—to everyone—you have, uh, you have moxie."

Lree gave her mother a look that perfectly conveyed the message: "What the hell are you talking about?" Only quite a bit ruder.

"Pentas and Dahlia are...they're tools. That's all they aspire to be. Tools to run my business, to make my life slightly less agonizing. You, on the other hand, you clearly have aspirations. Flawed aspirations for sure…"

Taking a moment to finish off her drink, her mother continued: "But you're reckless and undisciplined. Like I was. I'm trying to protect you—can't you see? When I feel you're ready I'll let you loose and you'll be able to seek out those flawed aspirations."

"Is that all?" Lree asked.

"Hmm? Oh, sure."

Lree stared at her mother unconvinced. The Mistress, for her part, stared at her empty glass. The fire from the hearth blazed on, crackling and popping in that pleasing why fires do when roasting marshmallows, cylindrical meat products, or accused witches. Indeed, it appeared to be burning with excessive vigor in a vain effort to compensate for the lack of pleasantry in the atmosphere. This may or may not have had something to do with Dahlia's proximity to the hearth or the fury she was struggling to contain within her.

"Tell me about the heart now."

"Fetch me another drink, little flower," her mother said, rubbing all of her eyes in succession. "And...and I'll consider it."

"How did I get here?", "What have I done to deserve this?", and even, "When I get out of here I'm gonna kill that no-good lawyer of mine!" are all perfectly acceptable things to consider upon being recently incarcerated. Prison cells are, after all, restrictive by nature and often provide those within time to reflect, worry, and plot.

Avery was doing none of these things. Instead, he sat motionless on the damp dirt floor at the back of his wooden cell with three fingers resting upon his bottom lip.

"She kissed me," he either thought or thought he said. He thought it again to determine whether or not he had said it. Hearing nothing, he said it aloud. Now he was certain he had said it. He wasn't certain that it had actually happened, however. It, of course, referring to his original statement: "She kissed me."

He always suspected that he was a powerful force. It was simply unavoidable, wasn't it? With no other course, she'd almost be obliged to conform.

Or wait. Was he getting his ego confused with a Robert Palmer song again? It didn't matter. "She kissed me," he thought. Now was the time to live it up live it up and head for the Nineties with Ronnie's new gun.

That...that wasn't right either. Though if you squint hard enough the lead singer from The Escape Club does kind of look like Robert Palmer.

Damn his grandparents and their obnoxiously catchy oldies! They reigned dominion over the music that played both in the house and the shop. If the artist wasn't in a neon pink headband or faded flannel shirt they weren't worth listening to. That was the rule. Horrifically, he had grown so accustomed to the synth pop, rock ballads, and overemotional grunge and, like grandma and pops, would grow to find modern music repellent.

"Why am I in a cage?" Avery asked himself. Temporarily shaken free from his self-induced trance by his self-induced trauma, he took the opportunity to scan his surroundings. He was in a cell of sorts made from impenetrable walls of thorny latticework. There wasn't much else in his personal prison aside from a mysterious bucket that he absolutely refused to investigate further and a twisted log that ran from the front of the wooden cage right up to the very back. He had a sinking feeling that it was meant to be his bed.

Lit by the same ghastly lanterns that littered the complex, the room outside of his cell offered very little in the realm of peace of mind. Dangerously large cracks splintered the walls, the floor, and the ceiling. From these cracks sprang the same diverse variety of flowers found throughout the rest of the complex. As for the room's purpose, Avery assumed—correctly for once—that it was meant to be a laboratory. There were beakers and burners and cages and enough sharp objects to convince him that he had to leave right away.

"There's no door," he said aloud, clearly unconcerned with the alarming frequency in which he had been talking to himself. "Why isn't there a door?"

To answer this question, Avery would have to remember how exactly he came to his latest sorry state. He sat down on the least uncomfortable section of the gnarled log that took up the majority of his cell and struck a pose that suggested either deep thought or concerning constipation. He had been talking with, uh, shoot. What was her name? Cripes, she was gorgeous. Pentips? Or was it Pengo? He loved Pengo! What a great game—the way your little red bird thing would trip upon completing a stage. Classic. Yeah, it had to be Pengo.

Pengo was talking but he hadn't really been listening to her. Avery remembered that quite well which was actually kind of strange for him. Typically his brain tunes out lengthy conversations for fear that the deluge of inanities might push out some of his more important memories, such as the embarrassing changing room incident or the combination for his seventh grade gym locker. He hadn't been ignoring her, per se, but his attention was certainly elsewhere.

"My bag!" he yelled. Again, to no one as it was just him, a bucket, and a log alone in a wooden cell in the corner of a dimly lit laboratory. "Where's my bag?"

Avery frantically searched his entire being and as much of his surroundings as he could for his lost bag, all the while trying to process exactly what he had last seen within it. The bug was there—or voorn as Pengo had called it—but every time he tried to picture the creatures face he was overcome with horrific scenes of torment and despair and utter hopelessness.

Avery shook his head just enough to feel unbalanced. As he regained his composure he happened to spy a familiar messenger back hanging on a rack far across the room. He wasn't completely sure it was his but the thought that it might be managed to fill him with just enough relief to calm his nerves for a moment.

Alright, moment's over. He still hadn't figured out how he ended up in this angrily latticed cage. Setting his hazy memory aside, the lack of a door rendered his situation impossible and that wasn't sitting well with him. Avery hopped back onto his wooden cellmate and attempted to make himself comfortable. He failed though this was no fault of his own.

"Ah!" he shouted, sitting up suddenly. There was an old lady. The old lady...the plain one in the lobby. Pengo had spoken with her and the room reconstructed itself again. The next part was especially difficult to recall as all the twisting and turning and imploding and exploding produced a series of favorable gusts that flirted with the lower portion of Pengo's dress.

"Nice," Avery whispered to himself in a not-at-all creepy way.

"Weird legs, though," he added because he's a terrible person.

The images began to fade and he brought his fingers back to his lips. It was odd. Great, definitely, but odd. His lips tingled as if the kiss never stopped. I hope she comes back, he thought. Don't I?

A sudden, violent tremor prevented Avery from answering that question and from falling into a deep well of self-loathing. He instinctively flung his body upon the gigantic log and clung to it like a basiphobic koala. The shaking grew worse and he felt the log rise and bend beneath him, loosening his grip and sending him tumbling to the floor. What followed was a chorus of cracks, pops, and high-pitched hisses that threatened to forcibly evict his remaining sanity from his person.

Now folded into an almost perfect L, the log—most of it, anyway—began to disintegrate. Large chunks of wood fell to the floor and turned almost immediately to ash. The half of the log that had set itself upright fell back to the floor, kicking up the ash to create a dense, black cloud that encompassed the area in and around the cell.

Avery coughed. A lot. This continued rather unpleasantly until the cloud fell to about knee level. Of course, Jones chose this moment to quickly rise from the ashen fog.

"Jesus, Jones!" Avery screamed. He then began coughing again.

Jones—naked but looking quite glamarous thanks to the mosaic of metals melted to their frame—stomped over to what was probably the front of the cell and placed their decrepit hand upon the thorny wall. In an instant it withered and crumbled into dust, creating the door Avery had been seeking.

"Wait!" Avery yelled as Jones began to step out of the cage. Curiously, the macabre monstrosity postponed their escape. They didn't turn, they didn't acknowledge Avery—they just stopped moving.

"I," Avery began, "I kissed a girl. I mean, s-she kissed me. We kissed. With lips. On the lips."

It really was the only thing he could think of.

To his surprise, Jones turned their head to just barely look back at Avery. Slowly and followed by more painful snaps and pops, they lifted their hand to their side and formed a fist. From that fist rose a bony thumb.

TWENTY FIVE
Love's Lost

It was as it always had been: bright and hot. Even the shade cast by the great willow did little to lessen the discomfort. Indeed, it only seemed to enhance the melancholy of an everlasting summer's afternoon.

"She's late," All thought. In fairness this had more to do with her anxiety and impatience than any agreed upon future convergence given that time was, at best, an abstract concept. Maybe there was an accident. Maybe she just got tied up in the square. Maybe she just didn't want to come.

"Hello!" called a sweet voice, pulling All back from her personal precipice of pity. There she was coming up the hill, smiling, waving, and still yelling, "Hello!" Clearly she had been hurrying though she appeared hampered by her clichéd girlishness. Her elbows were locked hard against her waist and she seemed to be clutching something closely to her bosom as she trotted awkwardly along the path. Her steps were fast but deliberately diminutive as to keep her skirt from flowing too wildly.

"Sorry," she said upon reaching the willow, breathless. She called herself Fortune—Fortune Lree—and spoke in a soft, inviting manner highlighted by a comforting accent.

The young woman drew in a deep breath, immediately coughed it out, and drew in another. "Late. Worried?"

All looked up at her friend. She wasn't particularly tall but stood more than a few inches above herself and her shape was, to be perfectly blunt, impossible. And contrast to her own ordinary persuasion, every curve, every muscle, and every dimple of Fortune's rich umber skin seemed to be deliberately designed to reflect the ever present sunlight in the most brilliant ways. Even her hair—long, dark, and absurdly smooth—defied logic, rippling in the gentle breeze as if it rested on a carefully choreographed pond.

"Not particularly," she lied.

"Oh?" she said, still attempting to catch her runaway breath. "I suppose I shouldn't have bothered picking these for you." Fortune unlocked her arms and presented All with a hastily assembled bouquet of violet, white, and yellow flowers.

All eyed the oddly colored floral arrangement as if she had just been presented with a week-old rat king but graciously accepted the gift. "Lovely," she said in reference to the sentiment rather than the gift itself.

"I knew you'd like them. I have something else, too," she added, rummaging around a petite satchel she wore over her shoulder. "At least, I thought I had something else..."

"The flowers are more than enough. You didn't have to bring me anything else."

"That's good because it looks like I didn't. I'm..." Her voice was drowned out by an increasingly loud buzzing. Two large, faerie-like creatures, one red and the other a pale violet, flew up from behind her carrying what appeared to be an identical satchel.

"Ah," she said, comparing the two bags. "I ought to label these."

She loved that about her. She was perfectly imperfect. "Hello, Dahlia. Hello, Pentas," said All with a smile.

The creatures dropped the bag at Fortune's feet—spilling its contents—and flew over to All beneath the willow.

"Don't spoil them," she said, picking up the strange fruit that had escaped the satchel. "Those two have been nothing but trouble lately."

"Oh? Is Her Majesty having difficulty keeping her subjects in order?" All extended her hand to allow the slightly violet creature to land upon it. "It must be tough caring for such an ungrateful queen."

"Don't call me that. I'm no more their queen than they are my...things. Subjects. Here," she said, handing her friend the larger of the two pieces of fruit. We're going to call them apples despite actually being pink, potato-shaped gourds covered in dark red cysts. They are, quite clearly, not apples or even apple like. Calling them apples simply conveys the message that they are being treated like a tasty fruit snack instead of a fistful of rotting tumors torn from the braincase of a recently deceased elephant which is exactly what they look like.

She sat down next to All and angrily took a large, crude bite out of the juicy tumor. Apple! The juicy apple!

"Oh my goodness, Fortune, stop!" All cried. "Look at you—your dress! It's everywhere!" She quickly came to her knees in order to lift her long blouse. A belt loaded with tiny purses, pouches, and knickknacks secretly hung from her waist. She retrieved a minute knife with a not-quite-so-minute blade and gestured for the odd fruit. "Please, allow me," she said, adding "m'lady" with a wry smile.

Fortune returned the smile with one of her own. It was a smile so wide and so genuine that All couldn't help but feel guilty for teasing her. She watched as All carefully sliced the apple with her silvery knife and gleefully accepted the perfectly prepared fruit when she was done. "Why're you wearing that?" she asked, nibbling on the "apple."

That in question was a silken veil that partially covered All's face. Turning away, she simply said, "Let's not do this, please."

Fortune failed to oblige. "It's ugly. You don't need it," she said, reaching over to remove the veil and ultimately revealing All's extensive collection of eyes. "I suppose you might. But not around me."

All scrambled to replace the veil. "You always know just what to say, don't you?"

"I'm serious. You know it doesn't bother me," said her friend in earnest. All did not reply. After a respectful moment, Fortune said, "Oh, I bet you're wondering why I called you out here."

In truth All hadn't wondered. She leapt at any opportunity to see Fortune regardless of the reason.

"It's not just for the flowers and fruit?"

"No. Dahlia!" she called. The little sprite responded, flying from All's shoulder to her friend's hand. "Show us what you've got."

The crimson faerie launched herself into the air with a fury. When she achieved a satisfactory apex—just short of touching the bottom branches of the willow—she began to spark. Soon she was raining a shower of harmless red and yellow bolts upon the two. All was enraptured.

"You taught her to do that?"

"Of course not," she responded. "She did it on her own."

"Beautiful."

"Isn't it?"

All tried to stifle a smile but utterly failed. "You know..." she said quietly, pulling down her veil as far as she could to hide her embarrassment. Unfortunately, all it seemed to do was call attention to it.

"Avery? What is it?"

"I love you," she whispered.

"Hmm?" said Fortune. "Oh, thank you."

And so they sat beneath the willow eating appalling fruit, playing with faeries, and talking about nothing in particular. They were happy. Avery was happy. The happiest perhaps she had ever been.

It was as it always had been: uncomfortable. Avery sat beneath the ailing willow idly fingering the pages of a well worn book and failing to ignore the heat of the endless day.

"She's late," she thought. Fortune was always late—as if she just assumed Avery would always be there for her. She would, of course, despite being stood up on a number of occasions. There was always an excuse and seldom an apology. At least, a sincere apology.

Still, Avery wasn't about to risk missing out on the opportunity to meet up with her friend. Even a brief "how do you do?" would keep her going for a great while. Did that make her tragic or just pathetic she wondered.

"Hello!" called a sweet voice. There she was. Finally. Fortune was in a typical hurry, running awkwardly up the hill as if burdened by glass slippers. She was accompanied by her two favorite faerie tagalongs, Dahlia and Pentas. No doubt they had something to do with her tardiness. The faeries demanded her attention and she was obliged to give them it.

"Sorry," she said upon reaching the willow. She drew in a deep breath, immediately coughed it out, and drew in another. "Late. Worried?"

Avery looked at her friend and felt simultaneously frustrated and relieved. "Not particularly," she said.

"Are you sure? You seem...I don't know..."

Why would she know? "I'm fine, really. Now you said you had something to give me?" Arg! Why did she say that? Why not, "Nice weather," or "Is that a new dress?" or practically anything else to draw out the conversation. Getting right to the point was the very last thing she wanted.

Fortune appeared lost in thought for a moment. "The poor tree," she sighed, staring up at the wilting branches of the willow. "Oh, sorry, I do."

"Did," she added, rummaging through her bag. "Somewhere."

Avery sighed quietly to herself. Even if she did find it, she thought, it would still end up disappointing. It's not as if she knew her—the real her.

"I'm sorry. I think I put it in the wrong bag."

"That one?" asked Avery, pointing at an identical bag floating behind her friend. It was being carried with some difficulty by more faeries, none of whom she recognized or really cared to recognize.

"Oh, thank you!" Fortune exclaimed. "Thank you, thank you, Here." She gingerly took the bag from her faerie friends and retrieved a large book from deep within it. Avery did her best to conceal her total lack of enthusiasm.

"I was hoping that you'd take a look at this and tell me what you think."

Was that it? "I'd love to," Avery replied, smiling. "What is it?"

"That's the thing, we don't know."

"We?" Avery thought.

Fortune opened the book and thoughtlessly flipped through the pages. "We think it may be related to the pillar but the words...the manuscript doesn't...well, no one's been able to make any sense of it. You, though. You have a gift for this sort of thing..."

Avery closed the book she had been reading and sat it down beside her. "Let me see," she said, unsure of whether to be annoyed or flattered. Fortune handed her the obviously ancient tome and Avery opened it immediately with an obvious bitterness. Was this all she was good for? She looked up at Fortune—this dark, lovely woman superior to herself in almost every conceivable way—and smiled.

"So...you think you can...?"

She looked back at the book, though this time she actually gave it more than a passing glance. The pages were filled with compact passages of fine calligraphy and meticulously drawn sketches. She could read it, she thought. It was as plain as English. It *was* English!

"I can," Avery began, her bitterness giving way to excitement. "I can read this! Where did you find this?"

"La'lapu La'fala!" Fortune replied, herself quite excited now. "It was during our last expedition. We were doing some digging around the pits and..."

Avery's excitement began to fall back into a sickening mix of bitterness, anger, and worry. She went all the way to La'lapu La'fala alone?

"...wouldn't let us take it all. Some ridiculous local law or something. Do you know what they do with the artifacts they find? If it can't be weaponized it gets destroyed. Destroyed! It's so...barbaric!"

No, not alone. She didn't go alone and, even worse, she went without her. That would explain why she hadn't seen her in however long. She could have at least told her she was leaving. With someone else.

"Anyway, we managed to smuggle a few things out. That book, obviously, some small bits of jewelry, and," she said, extending the word "and" into obnoxious territory, "a little something for you."

It was going to be a rock, wasn't it? Not a geode or a gold nugget or even a fossil but a rock. A plain, boring, stupid old rock that "reminded me of you" or some such rubbish.

"Catch!"

Instinctively, Avery dropped the book onto her lap and held out her hands to catch what was almost certain to be a heaping helping of disappointment. As the gift landed in her cupped palms she fell victim to a whirlwind of conflicting emotions. Her face became a cascade of mucus and tears, the latter enhanced significantly by her many extra sets of tear ducts.

"W-where did...?" was all she could manage to blubber. She had pulled the gift close to her chest, her fingers eagerly fondling each of the one-hundred and eight stitches that covered its surface in a familiar figure eight pattern.

"Same place," Fortune laughed. "Is it alright? I mean, is it a baste ball?"

Avery nodded furiously before sputtering a weak yes. She then continued sobbing.

Giving her a moment, Fortune asked, "Are you okay?"

"So happy," Avery mouthed silently. "I'm sorry, I'm..." Why had she doubted her? Why did she think she didn't care? Her guilt had become overwhelming, causing her to whimper, "I'm sorry. I'm so, so sorry."

"You're so funny. Sometimes I think the only way I can get a smile out of you is to get you to talk about your Yancheese."

"Yankees," Avery corrected her between sobs. "I can't believe you found this. A baseball. A real baseball." She held the dirty, brown orb up first to show her friend then the faeries. "Look at that. See the tobacco stain?" She turned the ball slightly, adding, "And look—it's even been spiked!"

Her friend smiled that same warm, comforting smile. "I'm just happy you like it. I wasn't completely sure it was the same thing. I mean, the color's not quite right but that stitching's so unique it had to..."

"It's perfect, thank you. Thank you thank you thank..." And with that, Avery lurched forward into an uncontrollable crying fit. Dahlia and

Pentas gently buzzed about her, confused and curious. Fortune placed her hand upon Avery's head and ran her fingers through her hair. It felt wonderful.

Fear? Doubt? Jealousy? Bitterness? Anger? She had been a terrible friend. She had been a terrible person.

"I love you," she sputtered.

Fortune continued to rub her head. "Thank you," she said. Probably while smiling.

It was as it always had been: frustrating and humiliating. She was late. If she was lucky she'd get an apology or maybe an excuse but then it would be dropped—never to be brought up again. At least, of course, until the next time she was late.

She gripped the baseball tightly, occasionally rotating it in her hand as if selecting a pitch. How long had she been doing this, waiting for Fortune under this dying tree? Certainly years—the cavernous crow's feet and tear troughs were evidence of that—but how many years exactly? And for what? A moment of happiness? What was a moment anyway in a world without time?

"Hello!" called a sickeningly sweet voice. There she was, Little Miss Sunshine, coming up the hill. Thoughtless and oblivious.

"Sorry," she said upon reaching the willow. Avery stared at her. Fortune was as young and as beautiful as she ever was. Avery, meanwhile...

Fortune stared back with a curious expression. "What is it?" she asked.

Avery took a deep breath. "I wanted to show..."

"Have you seen the girls?" Fortune interjected. "I've...neither Dahlia nor Pentas have been around lately and I've looked everywhere."

"Right," Avery said without empathy. "Everywhere. I can see that. Anyway, I wanted to show you something important."

Avery lifted the bottom of her blouse just enough to reveal a small pouch that had been tied to her belt. Still gripping the baseball, she managed to slide two of her fingers into the top of the tiny bag. With a gentle nudge the drawstring loosened, allowing her to retrieve a pinch of dust from within. "Watch," she said, bringing the dust to her nose.

"What is that?" her friend asked.

"Just watch." Avery closed her eyes and inhaled deeply, drawing in every bit of the mysterious substance in one long breath. Slowly she uncurled her arms beside her and waved her free hand about as if she had been conducting an orchestra for the blind.

Fortune continued to look on perplexed and now more than a tad concerned. When Avery opened her eyes again they shone a deep red and were devoid of pupils.

"Are you okay? Your eyes—what have you done?"

"Did you even notice? I'm not wearing a veil. I'm done with that."

"Good," Fortune said. She might have been genuine. "I've always hated that silly thing. You look so much better without..."

"Don't you dare," Avery snapped back. "Don't you even or so help me. Look at you. You're the same exact person I met however long ago. Me? This leathery hide, these spindly arms, these sagging breasts—this god damned nightmarish face. I'm a monster with or without a veil so don't you even..."

"So you've matured a little," Fortune interrupted with a fair amount of adversity. "Most people do. What matters is..."

Avery burst into an uncomfortable laughter. "A little? Is that pity or sarcasm?"

"No, I mean it. I really do. Look, I didn't come here to argue with you again. I'm not even sure why we're arguing."

This seemed to agitate Avery even more. "No, you wouldn't. You're so damn thick, you know that?"

"Are you going to tell me why you called me out here or are you just going to continue insulting me?"

"I'm sorry, I didn't realize I needed a reason to see you."

"That's not what I—"

In a flash, Avery placed her right hand before her friend's face, silencing her. She then held the baseball up to her lips and christened it with a silent whistle. Almost immediately the murky orb became enveloped in a fiery yellow aura. When it looked as if it were about to burst into flames Avery tossed it into the air. Like a tiny meteor, a trail of fire followed the ball both on its way up and on its way back down. It landed back in Avery's hand with a loud pop and a burst of crimson and gold sparks. Fortune, understandably startled, fell backwards onto her timelessly pert posterior. "What? That's...how?!" she stammered.

As the final sparks faded away so, too, did the frightening color that enveloped Avery's eyes. "Well?" she said, pupils restored, "What do you think?"

"Where's Dahlia?" Fortune asked calmly yet still sitting uncomfortably upon the ground.

"I can't tell you how long it took me to perfect that. This. The first time I tried it I nearly set fire to the room. The ceiling is still covered in soot and..."

"Where is Dahlia?" she asked, this time with a heavier, wavering breath.

Avery didn't reply. At least, not verbally. She just looked at her friend without expression, as if she were watching a fifth grade production of *Judith*.

"Where..." Fortune began again.

"Do you know what entomology is?" she asked, dropping the ball behind her. "It's the study of insects. One of the books you had me look at—one of the many, many books you had me look at—was on entomology."

"You never said anything about that."

"No. At the time I was just looking for a way to save our...save your precious tree. It was supposed to be a surprise."

"Oh."

"It has worms, you know. If you look hard enough you can see them—thousands of them. Only I discovered that their not really worms so there wasn't much I could do about them."

"How sad."

"I suppose, but it wasn't a waste. I did discover something else interesting while pouring over that raggedy old book. Do you know what it was?"

Fortune indicated that she did not know. This really didn't matter because even if she did know Avery was going to tell her anyway. It was clear she had been preparing for this moment for quite some time and it would be rude to stop her now.

"Your faeries—they're actually bugs, "Fortune." Ordinary bugs called voorn. Not faeries."

"I don't understand what you're trying to tell me. To me they—my friends—they're faeries. They always have been and they always will be."

"And that's why your own research hasn't led you anywhere. My god, how long have you been studying that damn pillar? I'm honestly not sure if you're naive or simply dumb."

"That's not fair," Fortune argued, tears pooling in the bottom of her eyelids. "We have learned things—many things. But every...with every discovery there are more questions. You can't tell me that you've never wondered about it? About our research?"

Avery smiled, pleased that her prey had walked right into her trap as planned. "Actually I had wondered which is why I've been doing some research of my own."

"On the faeries."

"Not just the voorn. And not the tree, either. On the pillar and the town. Oh, and on you."

Though Fortune had returned to her feet she was finding it quite difficult to remain upright. Her legs had gone weak and she felt as if her knees were ready to buckle with the next light breeze. This wasn't like her friend at all. Had she done something to set her off? Had she not done something? How did things come to this?

"M-me?"

"Especially you," she said bitterly, adding, "Avery."

Fortune's eyes widened as her mind was suddenly and violently emancipated from thought. "What?"

"But like you said," Avery continued, "every discovery leads to more questions. Why you hid your identity from me, for example. Or why you pretended you couldn't read. I've thought and thought about it and the only conclusion I can come up with is that you simply don't want to share your gifts."

"No—I wasn't trying to hide anything from you. Avery was my name, yes, you're right. Once. But that was a lifetime ago. I...I let go of that name long before I met you."

"I'm sorry," she added. "I didn't think it mattered."

"Didn't matter?!" Avery's thoughts became turbulent as she imagined her friend looking down on her all this time. Humoring her. Patronizing her. Pitying her. Mocking her. Her body wanted desperately to react—to slap something, punch something, shove something. Closing her eyes—all of her eyes—she managed to focus her rage into her hands which quickly took to clenching the sides of her blouse. When she opened her eyes again she saw a woman before her. No longer a friend or a lover but an object of ire and scorn, of bitter memories and betrayal.

Avery smiled. "I suppose you're right. It didn't matter. None of it matters."

Fortune took a step closer, reaching out to embrace her friend only to recoil out of a something that could almost be described as fear.

"Please, I don't understand any of this. I don't know what I...it...you. You're an entirely different person."

"This is me. The real me. This is who I am. Who I've always been. If you would just open your god damn eyes..." Avery found herself powerless to stop the torrent of resentment escaping her lips. Powerless yet relieved.

"That's not true at all. You're still...when I met you, you were different, yes, but look how far you've come. You've grown. You've changed in so many ways."

"I have changed. Before I met you I was confident. Self-assured. Independent. I made things happen. When we met I—that person you met—was a shell. Broken and twisted and hideous and lost."

"For a while," she continued, "I thought you were my salvation. Embarrassing now to admit it but, as you pointed out, I was different back then. Impressionable. That's the word. I was so impressionable. I became what I thought you wanted me to become and I waited here for you. You knew I would be waiting, didn't you?" Avery drew in a deep breath and tilted her head skyward, avoiding Fortune's bewildered gaze. After exhaling, she continued, "You could always come back from your escapades knowing that I'd be right here where you left me. In my willow cage."

"Stupid, really," she whispered.

Fortune had reached her limit. Her head was swimming and she was quickly losing faith in being able to resolve whatever arguments her friend had been throwing at her. "I should go," she said quietly. "I don't know what brought this on so suddenly or why you're being so, well, like this, but maybe after we've had some time apart to think about it..."

This did not please Avery. "Do I have to spell it out for you? Oh, that's right, you're supposed to be illiterate. Should I paint a picture instead? Would that be easier?"

"Maybe? I don't know. I just need to be by myself for a while." Fortune turned to walk away, only to turn back around to say the one thing she absolutely should not have said.

"Just...just know that I forgive you."

Avery's face seemed to collapse upon itself and turn a dark shade of red. In a flash, she grabbed Fortune by the top of her blouse and flung her friend around, smashing the back of her head hard against the trunk of the willow. "You," she hissed, "forgive me?!"

The decaying willow was not only hard but unusually knotty, making it one of the least ideal surfaces to be violently thrown into, second only to an irritable metallic shark. The base of Fortune's skull took the brunt of the force though her neck, shoulders, and back absorbed their fair share. Fortune, gasping, cradled her head in an effort to ease the pain. It was because of this awkward position that she completely failed to notice that Avery had replaced her baseball with her silver knife. It's unclear whether Avery was aware of this herself.

"You selfish, arrogant, tactless..." she said, stopping to rub her temple with her knifeless hand. "You forgive me? All I've done...everything I've done for you. Everything! You used me—took advantage of my weaknesses, trapped me in this nightmarish cage, and used me and you have the...the...audacity to blame me for it?! I was a fool not to see it earlier. This is who you are, Avery. Maybe this is who you've always been."

Fortune was silent.

"Say something!" Avery screamed. "Say something. Go on, take the higher ground. Show me the error of my ways like you always do! Show me what a better person you are!"

Fortune's silence continued. If Avery hadn't already been pushed over the edge she was certainly over said edge now and well on her way to a dark pit of which there would be no return. She stormed up to the woman she once thought of as a dear friend—a friend she could not bear to live without—and punched her in the side of the head. When she received no response, she hit her again. And again. And again.

Fortune slumped to her knees and rested awkwardly, painfully against the willow. Avery lorded above her. She felt nothing—not the pain in her arthritic knuckles nor her blistering grip on the knife handle she held.

A buzzing sound. They were coming—as expected—and would be here soon. It was almost over.

Avery knelt before her friend and placed the blade of her knife near Fortune's left breast. After a deep breath she threw the entirety of her weight against the silver handle.

"The worst part...do you want to know the absolute worst part?" she said softly as she fell deeper into Fortune's bloodied chest. "I still love you."

Fortune lifted her arms and placed them around her friend. With what little life she had remaining in her she squeezed Avery tightly, driving the knife in even further.

"Thank you," she said.

"So?"

The Mistress blinked. There was a full glass of something resting in front of her on the table and, beyond that, her daughter giving her an intense stare. "So what?" she asked innocently.

"So where is it?"

Picking up her drink—and then promptly setting it back down—All said, "You'll find the heart in the pavilion...though I dare say it is impossible for you to reach."

Lree jumped out of her seat and nearly threw her entire body onto the table. She wouldn't lie about this, would she? What would be the point in that?

"And does it do what they say?" she asked.

"And what do they say, little flower?"

"That it makes wishes come true!"

The Mistress smiled. "I suppose it does," she said. She picked up her drink again but this time finished it off. Very quickly.

TWENTY SIX
Demolition

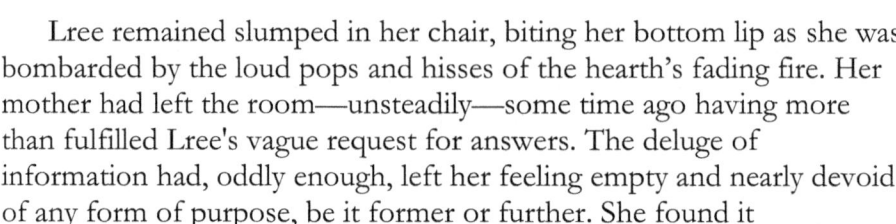

Lree remained slumped in her chair, biting her bottom lip as she was bombarded by the loud pops and hisses of the hearth's fading fire. Her mother had left the room—unsteadily—some time ago having more than fulfilled Lree's vague request for answers. The deluge of information had, oddly enough, left her feeling empty and nearly devoid of any form of purpose, be it former or further. She found it outstandingly difficult to put her newfound knowledge to use, let alone make sense of it all.

"At the base of the tree—the true base—you'll find it," she had said. When asked what she meant by that her mother rambled on about how much more clever she was than everyone else and the topic was never broached again.

A lone bead of sweat slipped from beneath the band of her goggles. The rags she wore as clothes now clung to her, chafing her skin at even the slightest movement. She felt flushed but only because the room was so hot. Almost unbearably so.

In an astounding display of inertness, Lree barely managed to cut her eyes towards the silent hearth. Mother's spell had succeeded in reigniting the cinder of the previous fire into a fierce blaze but those remnants were now gone. There was nothing left to burn.

At the risk of killing any sense of suspense, Lree wasn't at all curious as to why the room was growing hotter. She simply didn't want to accept it. If there was ever a more inappropriate time for what was about to happen it would be now.

"What d'ya want, Dahlia?" she asked, her eyes still fixated on the empty hearth.

Dahlia, who was standing behind her sister, steaming, said, "I want to hurt you." There was no inflection in her voice which made Lree very uncomfortable. And just a little bit excited.

Lree turned her head slightly so that she could sort of look her sister in the eyes. She seemed angry. Angrier, perhaps, than Lree had ever seen her. Her coat was gone and she was exposed, a bright yellow fire burning between the cracks in her jagged skin.

There were a number of things Lree could have said in response to

"I want to hurt you" that may not have provoked her sister into pursuing the action her statement implied, saving the main floor of the Facade from fiery destruction. As this was, indeed, what she had wanted Lree chose to ignore such options and said, "Lookin' at your face is painful enough," instead.

Dahlia brought her engorged fist down fast, reducing Lree's chair—but not, unfortunately, Lree—to cinders. Obnoxious and persistent as ever, the little flower leapt out of the way without so much as a singed hair on her stupid, ugly head.

Quickly, Lree bounded backwards into the general vicinity of the empty hearth. As she had hoped there were all manner of tools hidden behind the column, as well as the ashes of what was once a rather nice black and brown coat.

"How long were you spyin' on me, huh?" Lree asked, now waving an iron poker about menacingly.

Dahlia didn't respond. More precisely, she didn't respond using words in an effort to establish a civil discourse. Instead, she punched a large chunk of stone out of the column that Lree had been using as a partial shield.

"What's your problem?!" Lree yelled, rolling to the adjacent column.

"Shut up!" is all Dahlia bothered to say as she was far too busy trying to do serious harm to her little sister. She hit the new column harder than the last, nearly shattering it. Under cover of dust, Lree scrambled behind Dahlia and struck her as hard as she could with the poker. The iron tool ricocheted off of her sister and was vibrating so fiercely Lree was forced to drop it. The attack didn't seem to faze Dahlia in the slightest, however, it did leave a sizeable crack across her lower back that seeped magma. Satisfied she had caused at least some damage, Lree turned and bolted towards the exit at the opposite side of the room. She wouldn't be able to talk her way out of this fight nor was this a fight she had any chance of winning. Escape was the only option.

Her sister agreed completely. Before Lree could reach the entrance she fell to the floor screaming. A searing pain gripped her ankle and bound her in agony. She rolled onto her back and saw that her left leg had been ensnared by a molten tendril. The strange appendage seemed to have been birthed from Lree's attack and it wasn't alone. Unfortunately she hadn't noticed this as she was desperately—and fruitlessly—trying to untangle the fiery lasso without causing even more damage.

Dahlia turned to approach Lree and, in doing so, severed the tendril at its source. Very quickly it solidified into rock, cementing itself to the floor. She took an exceptionally long time to reach Lree for reasons that should by now be pretty obvious even to our less-than-attentive readers (you know who you are). Her sister was writhing about the floor, gripping her leg in a vain effort to stop the pain from spreading and it was delightful. She even said as much.

"Delightful," she said, as I said she would. Dahlia reached down and grabbed the rocky mass that pinned Lree to the floor. With a disturbing lack of effort or, indeed, care, she wrenched her sister upwards by the leg, shattering the tendril, bits of the floor, and probably bits of her sister. Dahlia was a great deal taller than her little sister and her weird, shape-shifting arms could grow and stretch almost at will. Both of these facts made it possible for her to lift Lree high enough so that she could look her sister in the eye. Upside down.

"Mother's right. You do have a gift. You can take a whole lot of abuse, can't you?"

Lree, who had been falling in and out of consciousness as her sister haphazardly dangled her by her wounded leg, was obviously having trouble coming up with a response. She had to be careful about her words. Saying the wrong thing would deplete what little remaining consciousness she had left real fast. However, if she could say the right thing she might be able to wriggle herself free and make towards the exit. But what was the right thing? What do you say to a homicidal brick oven hell bent on calling your existence into question in the slowest, most painful way possible?

During a brief moment of awareness, Lree came to the conclusion that she was over thinking things. Instead of deliberating what was right or wrong she spat in her sister's face. And even though it evaporated into a tiny puff of steam almost instantly it was enough to encourage Dahlia to release her captive via tossing her over the dining table and across the room. Plates, glasses, and utensils of all manner followed Lree to the floor, crashing with a most terrible sound. A number of linens—doilies, napkins, hot pads, that sort of thing—were also pulled into the chaos, however, they didn't sound nearly as impressive when they hit the ground so it's hardly worth mentioning.

"Get up, runt!" Dahlia commanded. "I know that didn't hurt now get up!"

Dahlia's impression of her sister was flattering but not altogether correct. It did hurt. Being thrown across a lavishly set dining room table, falling victim to a shower of breaking glass and ceramics, and having a leg caught in a lasso made of lava—not a single one of those instances failed to produce an uncomfortable sensation.

Despite her tenuous condition Lree soon popped up from behind the table armed with what would have otherwise been a stunning dinette set were it not being hurled at and consequentially shattered against a molten monster. She began with the dessert plates.

"Why're you comin' after me for?" she asked as she pitched a fast ball of flatware at her sister's face.

Dahlia showed no interest in dodging. "Shut up," she said. Clearly she showed no interest in having a heart-to-heart chat with her sister, either.

"You were listening, weren't'cha?" Lree yelled, moving onto the relish dishes. "It's all her fault! She made you like this!"

"I said," Dahlia began, lifting both her flaming hands into the air and balling them into boulders. This wasn't going to be good. "Shut up!" she cried, bringing her stone fists down onto the table. It had been a sturdy piece of furniture crafted from a wood that sounded like a zesty exotic seasoning, like padauk or muninga. No doubt, countless conversations such as "Please pass the muninga," "Surely you mean padauk," "Ah ha! I do! I am such a middle class simpleton!" were volleyed over the top of this lovely centerpiece that had just been splintered in two like a thin piece of balsa which I'm pretty sure is also a wood and not something you'd sprinkle over your chicken nuggets for a fabulously feisty flavor that's sure to surprise your family tonight!

Lree was rapidly running out of bowls and plates and was down to the silverware. Not that it mattered much. Dahlia managed to deflect every single soup ladle, pastry server, and dessert spoon thrown at her. Once the napkin rings were launched her ammunition had been spent. Dahlia pressed slowly forward, forcing her sister to back up against a familiar cart. She reached behind her back, fumbling around for something she suspected would prove to be a much better distraction than a tossed gravy boat.

"I never liked you," Dahlia seethed. "Not even a little."

"Don'cha think Ah know that?" Lree replied, trying to stall her sister. "Ah kind of figured it out after you tore my ear off."

Dahlia stepped forward and onto the remnants of the fallen table. "I'm going to tear off much more than a pointed ear when I get a hold of you."

"I hate you," she continued. "You...repulse me."

"Ha!" Lree said, though only because she thought she had found what she had been searching for. Had she been paying more attention to her sister her reply still would have been "Ha!" but with significantly more derision.

"Now I see," Dahlia said, stopping to rant dramatically. "I know why I can't stand you. Can't stand the sight of you. It's all your fault."

"Were you even listenin'?!" Lree asked, her hand firmly gripped a bottle behind her. Just a little bit longer. "Mother did this to you! Not me! Mother! She said so her-..."

"Your fault!" Dahlia screamed. At the height of her retort several more cracks appeared on her body. "If it weren't for you, you rat, I'd be...I'd be able to do things, you know? I could walk around without wearin' a damn tent! I could be more to mother than just an enforcer."

"But you!" she rambled on. The cracks had become so numerous that her skin began to take on a striking mosaic quality. "You bewitched her with that freakish curse of yours."

Dahlia took another step though before her foot even reached the ground she found herself under attack from a flying wine bottle. She blocked it with ease, shattering the bottle with her forearm and, coincidentally, loosing the highly flammable liquid that it once contained over everything. Particularly herself. A bright white flame engulfed her and sent her stumbling.

"You little brat!" she yelled, stopping just short of rubbing her eyes. Given the state of her weird body this would have been devastating—like rubbing one's eyes with coral after having been dunked in a vat of lemon juice.

Now was the time to act. Lree ran towards her sister, scooping up napkins and hot pads in both hands along the way. As if she had predicted her sister's plan, Dahlia, still blinded, swiped her arm through the air. And as if Lree had predicted that Dahlia would predict her plan, she leapt upon the attacking arm, using the hot pads and other linens to protect her palms as she unfolded herself into a perfect handstand. She quickly pushed herself off, vaulting over her sister and landing catlike behind her. Her leg was throbbing but she was simply too caught up in the moment to care. Now facing the door, Lree mule kicked her sister in the back, adding a monotone "Donk!" because she knew it would annoy her.

Neither of these actions were well thought out. For starters, Lree had no way of knowing whether her sister's back was solid enough to kick or if she'd lose her one good leg as her foot passed through her molten target. Not to mention that annoying Dahlia, no matter how gratifying it may be in the moment, almost always resulted in painful and disfiguring retribution.

While the fruition of the latter consequence remains to be seen, the former turned out to be lucky indeed. Lree managed to hit a portion of her sister's back that had briefly turned solid. Blinded and unbalanced, Dahlia stumbled into the wreckage of the table and onto the floor.

It took a great amount of effort not to stay and gloat. Lree had already come up with four putdowns perfect for the situation and had narrowed the choices down to two when she saw her sister prop herself up on her knee. The insults would have to wait. She had to get out of here right now. And that's precisely what she did.

Lree bolted out of the flaming battlefield that had once been a dining room and into the opulent lounge that made up the ground floor of the Facade. It was mostly empty save for the old woman knitting quietly behind the counter at the center of the massive lobby.

"Miss Ethel!" Lree called, "Miss Ethel! Exit, please!"

"Yes, dear," said Miss Ethel in the most grandmotherly voice possible. The room folded and unfolded itself around and upon Lree until once again it resembled the cramped, dirty foyer of a no-tell motel. Even as the final vestiges of the former lobby were being replaced, she threw the newly formed front doors open without hesitation.

"Thank you, Miss Ethel!" she yelled from outside, running past the guards and into the courtyard. She then ran back to the entranceway and poked her head inside. "You can turn it back now," she said.

"Yes, dear," Miss Ethel replied and immediately set to restoring the Facade's opulence. Through all the shifting and falling and stacking Lree saw a furious ball of burning rock and charred flesh burst through the dining room entryway, destroying the doors, the frame, and a good portion of the surrounding lobby in the process. Dahlia, suddenly realizing what her sister had done, glared at Lree. Very quickly all signs of the rundown front entrance—including Lree—erased themselves and she was trapped within the burning lobby.

"Miss Ethel, no!" Dahlia cried. "Turn it back! Turn it back right now!"

Miss Ethel—being Miss Ethel—obliged Dahlia. "Yes, dear," she said as if the vengeful lava monster had asked for a warm glass of milk and a gentle kiss on the forehead before bedtime. Again, the fancy and fiery lobby began to shift back into a decrepit little foyer.

"No!" Lree yelled back as the entrance returned. "You gotta turn it back! Mother said so!"

"Yes, dear," Miss Ethel replied, as if Lree had just asked her if she could lick the cake batter off the beaters.

Lree turned to face the guards. "Great job, guys," she said. "Keep it up. Doin' great." They didn't respond but even if they had she wouldn't have heard them as she was already in the street and well on her way to the marketplace.

The room outside of the lab looked very much the same as the lab itself: damaged but festively so. There were flowers of every kind sprouting from the countless cracks and crevices that made the room less of a fixer-upper and more of a burn-it-to-the-ground-and-start-over type of project. Clearly, the Mistress had not concerned herself with the resale value of this place.

But what was this place, Avery wondered. There were dozens of barrels stacked high to the ceiling as well as a number of large, bronzed boilers bubbling and belching steam quite loudly. A brewery? That wouldn't be too weird, would it? Love's Lost was a resort, after all. And despite the dilapidated look of the room the equipment within was clean and seemed to be in working order. It wasn't weird at all.

Well, maybe a little weird. I mean, he had just escaped from a wooden jail cell in the room next door. Though he had never actually been to one, Avery was almost certain that most breweries did not feature their own prisons. Evil-looking laboratories, possibly, but no prisons.

Avery came to the conclusion that the longer he hung around trying to make sense of the room the more disturbed he'd become. "Let's keep moving," his mind said reassuringly, "and forget we ever saw this." It was, perhaps, one of the wisest thoughts he had since even before he woke in that grassy field however many days ago.

There were two possible exits, not including the door that led to the prison from which he came, of course. Don't be stupid. The most obvious escape route involved a set of double doors at the end of the room that appeared to have been forced open against their design. That was probably Jones's doing though Avery couldn't say for certain. He had left the lab some time after the walking refuse pile, having taken his time retrieving his bag and poking around the various workstations. Seeing as how the only other exit—a large, red door tucked into the shadows adjacent to the boilers—was still sealed with a complicated system of locks, it was a safe bet Jones hadn't left through there.

"Red door, then," he said to himself. He had considered and, indeed, accepted that the terrifyingly macabre construct knew where it was going which was all the reason he needed not to follow them. Besides, nothing ever good seemed to happen whenever he walked through a set of double doors.

Supported by ignorant confidence, Avery strode across the room and over to the locked door. It was garishly decorated in strange knobs, chains, latches, and other mechanisms designed to both keep intruders at bay and test the intelligence of chimpanzees. Avery, well established as having the coordination of a large pile of wet noodles, spent an absurd amount of time fiddling with the afore mentioned knobs, chains, and latches. Satisfied that he couldn't possibly unlock the door further, he grabbed hold of the largest handle and gave it a tug.

The door didn't budge. Somewhere, a chimpanzee was smirking.

"Come on," he moaned, tugging again without any success. He inspected the door carefully, noticing one or two or ten knobs that hadn't quite been turned all the way and even more latches that been left latched. Correcting most of these oversights he tugged on the door again.

The door still refused to budge. And now he heard something not entirely unlike footsteps echoing in the distance.

"Come on, come on," he pleaded, pulling harder and harder. Once again, he reviewed his work on the door. A twist here, a turn there, and lift. He was sure that this time it would open. For whatever reason— perhaps the door was jammed, he missed a lock, or even that the author took a perverse pleasure in watching Avery panic—it did not.

"...like...better to...right?" said a voice so low that it shook the room slightly.

"No way," Avery whispered, halting his fruitless unlocking exercise to focus on the voice coming from outside the double doors.

"Better? Jammess, you wouldn't know better from something that's...not as good."

The unnecessarily thick hair on the back of Avery's neck stood up. Reacting with unusual perception and speed, he ran across the room to close the laboratory door and then found a nice, dark crevice behind a boiler to hide behind.

Why was he hiding? He had done nothing wrong, at least that he knew of. When the guards come in—because of course they're going to come in—he'd stroll cautiously into the light and explain the circumstances that led him to this strange predicament. That sounded reasonable and, really, it was quite reasonable. Then again, at least one of the guards had the head of a gerbil and a body sculpted out of industrial piping so forget all of that, we'll just cower behind this boiler, thank you very much.

"Didn't I tell you to close the doors last time?"

If Jammess responded, Avery didn't hear him. The cacophony of whirring and hissing that had escaped the boilers dominated the room. Still, he watched as quietly as one could while fighting a panic attack as two strange yet familiar men walked through the double doors. Art, the smaller, thinner, more obnoxious one made an immediate line towards the red door while Jammess, his offensively cute and bafflingly constructed subordinate, stood in the doorway. Avery squished himself further behind the boiler.

"Strange," said Art, "Someone's already...no, that's not right. Who did this?"

"What?" Jammess asked, unable to hear above the noise of the room as well as being entirely uninterested. He considered bringing up the fact that the entrance had been damaged somehow but knew it would only excite Art and they'd spend the rest of their shift filling out tedious paperwork.

"What are you staring at?" he called back as he gave the monstrously secure door a heavy push, opening it inward. Avery glared at the door, embarrassed and disgusted.

Art, the gentleman who didn't have a hamster head, stomped over to the one who did and began discussing something that may or may not have been important. Avery, meanwhile, channeled all of his personal problems and misgivings onto the door.

That door. That stupid door. It wasn't the first time he had been humiliated by an inanimate object nor would it be the last but he couldn't let this one go. His ill-placed ire paid off, however, as it allowed him to witness a strange sight he otherwise would have been completely oblivious to. A large chunk of the complicated system of shadows that cut across the doorway dislodged itself and floated curiously to the top of the door. It quickly blended back in with the surrounding darkness, leaving Avery to believe that it was probably just a trick of the light. When it moved again, however, it did so with a gentle sound that caused

Avery no small amount of distress. It was the sound of fluttering wings.

TWENTY SEVEN
Hooks

Avery wasn't exactly sure what he had expected behind the needlessly complicated door but this—whatever this was—wasn't anywhere close to being within the realm of possibilities he hadn't thought up. He had watched the strange sentries walk through the doorway and almost immediately walk back out with armfuls of tiny steel cages. Well, one of the sentries had armfuls of tiny steel cages. The other one, the smaller, more obnoxious one, seemed burdened only by his massive ego. They left the boiler room together but Avery wasn't convinced that they wouldn't be back.

It took some doing, but his mind was able to trick him into believing that okay, they will be back and if he was still there they would undoubtedly discover his rather obvious hiding place. Best to hide somewhere else, somewhere new. Behind that weird door, for example.

Unfortunately that which made the door so weird wasn't limited to its endless series of locks, switches, and cranks. A few steps beyond the door stood another door at the end of a narrow, poorly lit hallway. This door was much simpler than the previous, however, it didn't seem to want to open. After a great deal of trial and error Avery discovered that this door would only open if the other door had been closed. Having discovered this trick he continued proudly through the newly opened doorway.

Several more steps down another narrow, poorly lit hallway led Avery to yet another sealed door. After significantly less but still enough trial and error to be embarrassing he came to realize that, like the previous door, this one would only open when its predecessor was shut. This scenario repeated itself a number of times. So many times, in fact, that he had begun to wonder if he had at some point died and been sent to purgatory. He didn't remember dying and he couldn't think of why he would have been sent to purgatory other than for all those movies he pirated as a kid. And as a teen. And as an adult.

Another hallway and another shut door. It wasn't just movies, either. Television shows, music, games, comic books—all downloaded illicitly and without a second thought given towards any potential consequences. Had the various publishing houses only mentioned spending an eternity in purgatory instead of boring him with the same indecipherable block of legalese things might not have turned out this way.

Another hallway and another shut door. This was starting to become a tad worrisome.

Another hallway. Another shut door. And another. And another. This was no longer worrisome, it was terrifying. Breathing heavily, he turned himself around and began the long journey back to the boiler room which he reached immediately.

Avery didn't have long to reflect on his rushed passage through space and time as he came face to pectorals with the slug-gerbil-man known as Jammess. This sent Avery into an amusing panic back into the endless corridor. He slammed the door behind him and threw his ample bulk upon it hoping that it would be enough to prevent the emasculating sentry from opening it.

Jammess did not try to open the door. Art, unsure of whether or not he had locked the door, had sent Jammess back to check for him.

"Sorry, Artie," he scoffed in a tone that would have otherwise been ugly but hey! Hamster head. He then flipped a few switches, turned a couple of cranks, and finally pulled a tiny lever on the door.

"This one's all on you," he added, snickering.

"What," he gasped, looking to his left.

"The," he gasped, looking to his right.

"Hell?!" he gasped, looking at the enormous, dome-shaped cavern before him. Avery then slipped down the door, landing gracelessly upon his backside.

It was an abattoir of sorts. A cold, mechanical slaughterhouse lit almost entirely by an obscene orange light radiating from a giant, circular pit at its center. Hundreds of pipes of all different sizes rose from the sides of the pit, snaking their way rather wantonly along the ground and up into the earthen ceiling. It was, in fact, the ceiling that left Avery quivering on the slick, dirt-covered floor.

There were hooks and chains and hooks and gears and hooks and roots and, surprise, hooks. There were an awful lot of hooks. Some of these hooks hung by their lonesome, simply looking sharp, pointy, and terribly menacing. Others held cages, jars, crates, and other containers that may or may not have been filled with something utterly horrific. Avery was siding very heavily with "something utterly horrific" given that the rest of the hooks were being used to decorate the butchery with insects in various states of decay. Worse still, everything was moving. The hooks, for example, were being carried along an absurdly complex system of chains and pulleys all throughout the factory of horrors. The cargo—the crates, cages, and corpses—all seemed to bounce merrily along as they were ushered to who knows where.

Avery slowly came to his feet, worried less about the terrible scene before him and more about the scene's limited impact. Already his mind had shifted from "I desperately need to change my underpants and get the hell out of here!" to "I desperately need another one of those amazing drinks and hey! What's that sparkling thing over there?!" and he found that very troubling. He was, he feared, getting used to this madness.

In a surprising moment of forethought Avery locked the door behind him. At least, he thought he locked the door behind him. He definitely locked something behind him. In Avery's defense, the problem wasn't simply because he lacked any form of what could possibly be mistaken as basic intelligence but that the door he had come through—the door with all of the locks and knobs and what-have-yous—had shut and was now lost in a wall of locks and knobs and what-have-yous. He pulled and pushed on various areas of the wall but there was no sign of the exit. He began locking all of the locks on the wall that he could find—just to be safe. The small amount of peace of mind this action yielded, however, was rescinded when the last lock triggered a loud siren and a flashing red light. Almost all of the macabre activity in the room came to a grinding halt.

Avery, feeling unusually aware, suspected that whatever he had done probably wasn't supposed to have been done. The violent tremor that shook the entire room seemed to confirm this. The hooks high above clanked and clattered as they hit one another, resulting in an unfortunate rainstorm of dusty insect bits. This alone would have been plenty distressing, however, matters were about to become much worse. The massive and at one point innocuous roots that had once clung tightly to the ceiling unfurled themselves, snapping many of the chains that made up the complex conveyor system overhead. As the chains fell so too did their cargo.

It was in the middle of this lengthy, chaotic scene that a question popped into Avery's head. It was a basic question but nonetheless important. As he thought about how to answer it the space around him seemed to slow. The dangling chains and hooks clanked a bit less and the falling cages and flaky remains hung in the air like dust in a beam of sunlight.

"I," he began to say, interrupted by a powerful tremor that sent him stumbling back into the wall. He then tried to say, "What," however, this, too, was interrupted by the sudden collapse of the ceiling. His answer would have to wait.

The question, by the way, was something along the lines of: *"What will you do?"*

"Tell me," the Mistress began, wrapping her arm around Pentas's, "what do you think of our guest?"

Pentas tried to break free of her mother's grip, though subtly as not to draw attention to her actions. She failed on both accounts. "And which guest would you be referring to, mother?" she asked.

"Avery, of course. The young man you escorted down to the lab. What do you think of him?"

"He is very...interesting. I believe that he will..."

"Interesting," her mother repeated, mimicking Penta's tone. Her grip tightened ever so slightly. "Let's be frank, dear daughter: he's a bum. He's dull and homely. He's utterly ordinary in every conceivable way. How could anyone—you, of all people—possibly find such a witless lunk interesting?"

Regaining some of her composure—though none of her freedom—Pentas replied with confidence. "It is quite a journey from your study to the laboratory, even for someone in such excellent health as yourself. But Mister Avery—well, you are aware of his physical challenges."

"We took many breaks and discussed many things," she continued. "He is outwardly simple and, as you mentioned, plain but I found that plainness unusual and intriguing."

The Mistress led Pentas to a large set of familiar red doors. They were open which wasn't particularly odd, however, they were opened outward instead of inward which was particularly odd. "Insightful as always," she said, releasing Pentas to inspect the doorway.

Pentas smiled. "You have taught me brilliantly."

"You know, daughter of mine," said mother, ignoring the doors and returning to the conversation, "there are three types of people I hate."

She turned to face her daughter and raised a finger before her face. "Flatterers," she said.

She raised a second finger. "Liars."

She raised a third finger. "And Red Sox fans."

"So," she said, balling her fingers into a fist, "tell me again: how could you possibly find such a person interesting?"

"I looked into him," Pentas said rather defiantly. She then took in a slow, deep breath. "I had traveled down into one of the outer refuse tunnels believing I would find our little flower."

"And did you?"

She thought for a moment then shook her head. "Her presence was there," she said, "though she was not. That's when I found the boy— Avery, as we now know him. I reached out to him, albeit instinctively."

"What did you see?" the Mistress asked.

Pentas didn't answer. At least, not right away. A mysterious fear had momentarily taken control of her mind and the only form of communication she could commit to was a blank stare.

"Pentas!" her mother snapped. "What did you see?"

"Nothing," said Pentas, coming very quickly to her senses. "Nothing at all. He saw *me*."

Lree was, to put it lightly, in a jam. She had rather easily made her way through the marketplace and back to the pavilion—back to the inane chatter and noxious odors she never wanted to return to. It was this brief moment of embittered reflection that placed her in the afore mentioned jam.

"Get off! Let me go!" she cried in between spitting out mouthfuls of dirt and grass.

"I don't think that's going to happen," Dahlia replied. She was straddling her sister in such a way that made any and all escape attempts futile and embarrassing. She pinned Lree's head down with her engorged right hand, releasing just enough pressure at times so she could scream. Other times—more often than not, really—she'd apply an excessive amount of force to drive her sister's face further into the ground.

It was, as one might imagine, uncomfortable.

"Ah'm," she began.

Push. Release. Spit.

"Gonna kill you!" she finished.

"I don't think that's going to happen, either," Dahlia chuckled in that same dreadful way that nearly mimicked a duck gagging on a sponge. She then pushed her sister's face back into the pavilion's lawn with a loud crunch which either originated from her goggles or her nose. Lree might have been heard to say something a bit rude towards her sister regarding this action or she might have simply been informing her that she had a "monstrous itch."

"Listen carefully," Dahlia said rather calmly for someone drilling their little sister's head deep into the earth. "First I'm going to burn every last bit of unmarred skin from your body. Know what I'll do next, little flower?"

"Kill!" Lree managed to scream before being forced back into the pavilion lawn.

"Not yet. I'll then cripple both your legs so you'll never be able to run away again. Mother will appreciate that."

If Lree said something it was either incomprehensible or unpublishable.

"I'll probably break your arms, next. I can't think of a reason why, honestly, other than because I really hate you." The disgusting chortle that followed made it clear that Dahlia believed she was being rather witty.

There aren't many things a person thinks of when being buried face first by a giant, chortling molten rock other than, "Ouch," and, of course, "I would like this giant, chortling molten rock to stop burying me into the ground face first." And while both of these thoughts had been bouncing around Lree's head for some time now they were greatly overshadowed by those of regret and anger, though not necessarily in that order. If only she had been more careful. If only she hadn't been in such a hurry. If only her sister hadn't been sitting on top of her.

Dahlia, rather uncharacteristically, presented her sister with the opportunity to explore a number of previously unobtainable options by suddenly standing up. Lree, fully capable of running away but unwilling to do so, waited. She waited and listened.

"What's going on?" she heard Dahlia ask herself.

Lree's curiosity was piqued further yet still she did not budge. She laid flat on the grass silent and motionless. Gone were the not-so-subtle vibrations born from the many feet of the many, many guests. So too had the obnoxious chattering born from those same guests vanished. A few whispers here and murmurs there, sure, but otherwise the pavilion was silent. And, of course, the pavilion was never silent unless...

Perhaps forgetting her predicament, Lree lifted her head out of the dirt and scouted the area around her. Everyone was staring up at Fortune. No, not at Fortune. At what Fortune was holding: the Truth.

"Something's not right," Dahlia said quietly.

"It's just the Reconciliation," Lree said in a tone that made it clear she had indeed forgotten her predicament. Dahlia curtly reminded her.

"Quiet, you," she said, pushing her club-like foot down on the middle of Lree's back. The name-calling and obscenities that followed were drowned out by the deafening boom of the Truth as it slammed into the pavilion. The blast sent the sisters—as well as a number of guests—flying across the venue. The dust hadn't even settled before the Truth was again airborne with rubble and many of the afore mentioned guests—at least, parts of them—trailing from the bottom of the thorny pillar.

Dahlia, already on her feet, watched in awe as the Truth slammed back into the pavilion again and again. Each time it left a sizeable crater and what can only be described as a horror pancake within. This was far beyond something not being right. Something—this thing, in particular—was very, very wrong. As if to confirm this, the Truth came crashing down a few yards in front of her. Though her unusual physique allowed her to stand her ground she was unable to dodge the ensuing wave of party and pavilion shrapnel. Dozens of tiny and not-so-tiny stones tore straight through her strange flesh while some of the larger debris found themselves trapped within her grotesque body.

Unsurprisingly, this caused a lot of pain but Dahlia tolerated it as best she could, which is to say she violently emancipated the imprisoned chunks of rock and earth while bellowing incomprehensible insults and threats. "I'm going to kill her," she thought to herself—though perhaps not in so many words—while removing the last of the larger pieces of debris from her leg. "Her," as should come as no great surprise, was in reference to Lree who was no longer beneath Dahlia's massive foot. The billowing dust clouds and panicking guests pretty much guaranteed that finding her tiny sister at this exact moment would be nearly impossible. Fortune seemed to have stopped its terrible assault, however, the threat of being crushed by a twenty-story column of thorns remained as it held the Truth high in the air.

Every passing moment that didn't involve punching a hole through her sister frustrated Dahlia more and more. There was, of course, the very real possibility that Lree had been crushed by the Truth but this didn't stop Dahlia from scouring every inch of the pavilion multiple times. Her long, vengeful pursuit came to a sudden end when a thought not of her own entered her head.

Please make your way to the Nest. Quickly.

The Nest, yes. That would explain why Fortune had gone berserk. At least, partially. Dahlia spit, unintentionally setting an unfortunate guest ablaze with her fiery projectile. She didn't even bother to pretend not to notice, choosing instead to roll her eyes and stare off into the opposite direction. The little flower was still out there. She had to have survived and probably fled into the Mall during the chaos. She'd catch, torment, and kill her sister soon enough. She just had to be patient.

As the trail of flaming guests she left in her wake could attest to, what little patience she did have had almost certainly run out.

TWENTY EIGHT
A Matter of Forced Perspective

"I have managed to calm most of them," Pentas said with a soft grunt as she locked a large lever into place. "I will not know the extent of the damage until I can study the system in greater detail. Whoever did this..."

"Whoever?" The Mistress had a unique way of making anything she said sound both sincere and dubitable. "Whoever. Could it possibly be the young man you escorted down here, Pentas? The young man you were meant to lock up in the room next door?"

"He is," Pentas replied, unmoved. "I did exactly what you insinuated."

"No," the Mistress replied sharply. "Not exactly. If you had "exactlied" we wouldn't be here now, would we?"

Pentas said nothing knowing that it would be fruitless to argue with her mother. That and this is what she more or less actually wanted to happen.

"This place is a mess," her mother continued. "Look around. Find him. I'll tend to Fortune."

"You believe he is still here then? Mister Avery?"

"I do. The maintenance entrance has been destroyed and..." the Mistress paused to walk over to the glowing pit. Cautiously, she craned her head over the rim and looked up and down the shaft. "You saw him, didn't you? That boy couldn't climb out of his own pants let alone the Nest. He's here."

Pentas knew this, of course, but given the level of destruction around her it was doubtful he was still alive. She couldn't help but consider this whole exercise futile and filthy. Only a fraction of the systems were running and only a fraction of that fraction of the systems were running almost correctly. Chains had been snapped, countless cages were toppled, and large piles of earth lay strewn about the Nest in varying degrees of inconsideration. Dozens of mindless voorn hovered about the room running into walls, machinery, and each other. Digging through refuse for the boy's remains was far, far beneath her. Which is why she called upon her sister.

Please make your way to the Nest. Quickly.

"Are you going to look for him or not?" the Mistress asked.

Any grievances or frustrations Pentas might have felt were perfectly masked behind a practiced expression denoting collectiveness and authority. "Of course, mother," she said. "I was attempting to reach out to him."

The Mistress had already turned around and was fiddling with some buttons and valves along the wall. "I doubt that you'll have very much luck with that. Not with him. You're better off putting those hooves to good use and start digging."

"Yes, mother," Pentas replied, smothering a sigh with a heavy feather pillow. She tiptoed over to a particularly large pile of refuse—a feet unto itself since she didn't actually have any toes to tip upon—and stared at the chore before her. How did things turn out this way? She had been so careful planting the seeds of chaos throughout Love's Lost and expected that at least one such seed would grow to bear fruit. Or control, in this case.

Of course, that's the thing about chaos. By its very nature it can't be controlled. Nor can it be planned or predicted. It was troubling enough that virtually all of the seeds she had planted were sprouting simultaneously, but now there was this boy—this Avery—clearly set on harvesting the finest of the crop for himself.

She scoured the pile of rubble for a stone or brick to remove. It had to be large enough to make a difference but light enough to not require any significant effort. There, towards the top, was the perfect candidate.

"Hey, let me get that for you."

"Thank you," she said, withdrawing her hand. Where did he come from? What was his end game? Just who or what was Avery? This awkward, barrel-shaped boy crouching down in front of her. Struggling to lift a chunk of brick from the very top of a large pile of rubble. Pushing aside smaller, lighter debris from around said brick chunk in an effort to make it look like he had every intention of lifting the chunk. Now blocking the chunk with his extra girth in an effort to hide the fact the he couldn't move it and, in fact, was already bored with the idea.

"Avery!" Pentas screamed with an audible gasp.

"What? I'm not...nothing! No brick!" he said as he spun around to face Lree's menacingly attractive sister. Naturally, his lack of coordination sent him onto his bottom.

Though it defied her build somewhat, Pentas effortlessly swept Avery up by his shoulders, bringing him almost instantly to his feet. "Why...how are you here?" she asked, dusting him off. "What happened?"

Avery looked to his left, his right, and then his left again before finally releasing a weak, "I didn't do it. It was...like this? Already?"

"It does not matter. You—"

"Oh," said the Mistress slinking into view from the shadowy far side of the room, "but it does matter. Greatly."

"She did it!" Avery blurted out, pointing furiously at Pentas. "Shame!"

Pentas reacted accordingly. "What?!" she said, her face taking on a robust shade of violet.

"Sorry, I don't know," Avery whispered. "I panicked."

"Are you alright," the Mistress asked.

"I am fine, mother."

"I wasn't asking you."

Silence.

"Avery?"

Avery stood to attention. "Yeah?"

"Are you alright?"

"Me?"

"Who else would I be talking to?"

"Her?" he said, pointing at an unusually flustered Pentas. She was grateful that neither of her sisters were witness to her unprecedented distress.

The Mistress sighed. "I already said that I wasn't...you know what? Never mind."

"Never mind what?"

She—the Mistress—needed another drink. Desperately. Still, she kept an extraordinarily calm demeanor. "Just tell me...tell me how did you manage this? What did you do?"

"I didn't—"

"Did you mean to block the pacifying agent?"

Avery looked at the Mistress with the same look a puppy gives its owner after it piddles on Great Great Grandmother Victoria's antique Kashmir rug. He was preparing for a swat on the nose with a rolled up edition of the Polk County Post when the room suddenly lit up in a bright, yellow light.

"Ah, that's something, I suppose," said the Mistress.

Something, thought Avery, was right. It certainly was something. Something along the ceiling that was horrific and terrifying and truly, truly awful. Something like an infinite mass of wooden anaconda violently slithering over one another. Occasionally, a portion of the frenzied nightmare would eject itself and slam against the wall, floor, or ceiling before being sucked right back in, like a yeti sucking on a swim noodle.

Avery considered saying something akin to, "Look out!" or perhaps even "Quick, over here!" but the Mistress had made it perfectly clear that she was neither ignorant nor afraid of the worming roots.

"They're not roots, if that's what you're thinking," said the Mistress. She then added, "They're not snakes either. Or worms."

Roots, snakes, and worms were actually only three of Avery's guesses. He had a shopping list full of increasingly awful possibilities but every time he attempted to voice one the Mistress would immediately reject it. Eventually he realized that if he just stopped trying to guess then she would reveal the true answer—but did he really want to know?

"S'krolaliatharium tomethius," she said proudly. "Or simply skro'tom, if you're so inclined."

The look of shock and terror that had become Avery's default expression as of late cracked ever so slightly as he held in a volatile round of childish giggling. Pentas glanced over at the shaking boy, confused and concerned, the latter for her own sake.

"Skro'tom," the Mistress said. Avery had crossed his arms and pulled in his lips. "Skro'tom," she began again, slowly, "aren't a living thing. Not really—not the way you understand. They're a bit like an element, though I wouldn't call them natural. Especially these. Skro'tom aren't usually this large." She looked up at the writhing mass, casually shooing off an ousted root as one would a gnat.

"I see," Avery gasped. He took a few deep breaths and regained something that could almost be mistaken for his composure. Sensing that he was still in a great deal of trouble he felt that stalling was currently his best course of action. "So why are these giant skro...sk...why are they here? I mean, what do they do?" He then pulled his lips back in.

The Mistress stared at Avery. Avery, lipless, stared back. "Are you sure you're alright?" she asked. Avery nodded furiously which seemed enough to satisfy her. "Skro'tom penetrate," is all she could say before Avery burst into hysterical laughter. After a few moments and quite a few "woos" and "oh mans" he came to a startling realization.

"Why is no one else laughing?" he asked aloud.

Pentas, visibly and uncharacteristically agitated, said nothing. The Mistress, completely within character to be agitated, scolded Avery.

"Skro'tom are a plague. Kingdoms have fallen due to unchecked skro'tom. They can't be stopped."

"Have you tried cold showers? Maybe a jigsaw puzzle of a kitten or something?"

"What?"

"Aw, c'mon! You're totally setting this up for me, right? I mean, c'mon," he said, almost pleading. "Eh?"

"There is nothing funny about skro'tom," said Pentas in absolute seriousness. "Mother is correct. They are an uncontrollable and invincible menace."

While Avery missed most of what Pentas had said due to another mirthful outburst, he did catch onto one word. "Uncontrollable," he said. "Then how..."

"I can control skro..." the Mistress began to say. Noticing that Avery was struggling to hold back another round of boisterous merrymaking she corrected herself before continuing. "Them," she said. "I can control them. I'm the only one who can, in fact."

"Gross."

"Excuse me?"

"I said," Avery began to say. "I, um, how? Because you're, like, a witch or something?"

"To the ignorant and superstitious I suppose I am. But I'm a scientist, Mister Hall. You do know what a scientist is, yes?"

"Well, yeah," said Avery, a bit taken aback by the sinister tone in the Mistress's voice. "But you can't just be a scientist. Like, who puts that on their resume? Occupation: Science. Work History: Science. Graduated with Honors from Science University. Majored in Science. I mean, what are you a scientist of?"

"I am..."

"Oh! Is it scrotums? Please say it's scrotums."

"No."

"What then? Magic?" Avery interrupted. "If it's magic then you're a witch, not a scientist. Also, that's dumb."

"I am," the Mistress began again, secretly imagining herself sitting at a table with a large glass of wine before her, "an entomologist."

Avery's blank stare encouraged her to explain herself further. "Insects, Mister Hall. I study insects."

"This goes way beyond bugs," he replied. "Look at this place. The cages, the machines, the rectum over there..."

"Skro'tom," the Mistress corrected.

"Whatever," he said with a snicker. "This isn't...what kind of, uh, research do you do? Really."

"You're oddly astute, you know that?"

"Thank you."

"That wasn't meant as a compliment."

"Uh-huh."

"Quite the opposite, actually." She waited patiently for a response but Avery gave her nothing beyond digging in his ear with his pinky finger. "Everything you see here," she started after a sigh, "is a result of my research."

The Mistress strode over towards the giant pit in the center of the room, peering over the edge. "Very good. Not that it would matter, I suppose." She then straightened herself up and vaguely pointed at the remaining cages above her. "Voorn are vile little creatures. Disgusting and very, very dangerous—the latter being the reason for my research. No one else was brave or clever enough to even consider the possibility that they might be exploited. It was my genius that created this place. Everything you see up there—that was because of me."

It should be noted that by now Avery had managed to unwittingly erect an invisible barrier that completely enveloped him, like an igloo of ignorance that effectively censored him from the Mistress's masturbatory lecture. His jaw went slack and his eyes glazed over as the Mistress of Love's Lost droned on about her utter brilliance and unrivaled intelligence. Just as his eyelids had achieved half-mast he was struck with a thought—a vision, really. It was dark and muddied and mute but one thing was absolutely clear: it was a voorn, anguished and screaming.

Avery shook his head gently, an action Pentas picked up on. The Mistress had not been so observant. Feeling a great sense of personal satisfaction in explaining her brilliance and having enough alcohol in her to make her highly combustible, she rambled on without giving Avery as much as a glance. Avery, for his part, was actively trying to ignore her. His barrier had been shattered by the strange vision and now all he could do was distract himself, lest he succumb to Miss All's endless monologue and his brain makes a desperate and potentially deadly escape through the back of his skull.

"...properties," she had been saying. "11As, the most common, produce a chemical that enhances plant growth dramatically."

A thick needle, thicker than a needle had any right being, punctured the creature's carapace in much the same way a railroad spike would a pink, Mylar balloon exclaiming "Mis Quince!" in an aggressively cursive font. The ear-piercing squeal that followed, however, came about as a result of the assault and not from Camila discovering a brand-new Honda Civic from Mimi in her parent's driveway.

"...red coloration, specifically 17f through 19f..."

The same needle, or at least a needle sharing the same, nightmarish size as the one in his previous vision, was being filled with a sludgy, orange substance. It wasn't clear where the substance was coming from though Avery was afraid he knew where it was meant to be going.

"...Fortune calls. They come here in droves—pacified and completely harmless. No hunting, no danger—simply catch..."

A different scene but familiar. The dome-shaped cavern, the walls lined with strange machinery, the giant, central pit—it was the same room he might have accidentally destroyed. The only real difference, if you insist on nitpicking, is that instead of being littered with fallen rock and debris it was blanketed by beakers and burners and all sorts of glass tubes. This, combined with the absence of the hooks, chains, and cages that typically ornamented the ceiling, made the room appear much less like a poorly regulated slaughterhouse and more of a state-funded research lab that would not be passing this year's inspection.

As much fun as it was to play spot-the-differences, Avery's attention was inexplicably drawn to a scene unfolding near the center of the room. There were a number of...people? It was difficult to tell. He thought they might be people as they were perfectly people-shaped, however, they lacked any sort of detail or definition. Anyway, the things that may or may not have been actually people were pouring barrel after barrel of trash into the pit.

Now even Avery had a feeling it wasn't just orange peels and empty potato chip bags being thrown away, however, he had absolutely no desire to verify his suspicions. This was, of course, when he was pushed close enough to the pit to see that it was, indeed, being filled with those disturbing, anthropomorphic bugs. Hundreds and hundreds of them; alive but only by default.

He was now close enough to reach into the pit which he almost did if he wasn't stopped by the enormous, thorn-covered pillar that came crashing down into it. Avery gasped and his body trembled as if awakening from a frightful dream. Feelings of relief and disappointment overtook him upon realizing that he was back in the destroyed-version of the pit room still being assaulted by the Mistress's extraordinary ego. He bit his lip, shook his head, and even clawed at his wounded arm—try as he might, he could not wake up from this dream.

Avery was unable to contain his distress and Pentas was quick to slip into what passed as his thoughts. Given her past experience, she was taken by surprise at how simple it was to penetrate his consciousness. She was taken further by surprise when his consciousness seized her own, trapping her within his mind.

"...brilliant containment methods, if I do say so myself," the Mistress droned on. What was she talking about, Avery wondered, albeit briefly. Surprisingly, the drunken ravings of a spider-faced madwoman who may or may not have been trying to kill him rated fairly low on Avery's personal concern scale. His spontaneous and increasingly uncomfortable visions were much more alarming. If they were only a little less spontaneous then maybe he could get back to worrying about more important issues, like asking Pentas out on a date. He looked over at her and smiled a ridiculous smile that screamed, "I'm terrible with people!" Pentas didn't respond. She didn't move in any way. She simply stood there, frozen, staring wide-eyed at Avery with a disgusted expression that pummeled his ego.

Dejected, he lowered his head and came eye to eye with a giant bug. It was the same giant bug he had pilfered from the cave of horrors. The same giant bug that had led him into this terrible room. And while he had many questions regarding her presence here, her current proximity to himself demanded that he swat the nasty creature away. Avery had just lifted his arm high enough to achieve maximum swatting momentum when he made an observation he wished he hadn't. The volatile little insect was clutching onto his right leg as if seeking protection. It—she—was afraid but clearly not of Avery. Her fear had been caused by something else. Someone else.

He looked at his hands. They were small and lithe, like that of a child's. They were reaching for something or pushing something away— it wasn't very clear. A blurry figure suddenly approached him and his view faded into blackness.

He was now looking down at an operating table of sorts—heavy emphasis on "of sorts." There were bright, silver instruments strewn about and what appeared to be a patient in the midst of a seizure. Unable to look elsewhere, he focused on the patient—a young boy with dark, nearly black hair wrapped almost entirely in a long, dirty dressing gown with many, many thick leather straps holding him down. It soon became clear that he had not, in fact, fallen victim to an epileptic episode but had been struggling to free himself. At one point he managed to loosen the restraints around his leg enough to kick a number of utensils off the table with his hoofed foot.

The violent crash of clattering metal jolted Avery back into reality, or at least, what he had begrudgingly accepted as reality.

"And what are you?" the Mistress asked.

"Uh," said Avery, unsure whether or not she was addressing him. She wasn't. "Curiosities and rarities with secrets so easy to unlock a child could do so. Not a child. Me. To me, it's as simple as child's play. To me..."

Avery's brain, muddled by a relentless barrage of strange visions and stranger emotions, disabled all auditory sensation in a valiant attempt to mute the Mistress's narcissistic diatribe. This brought little comfort, however, as it only changed his predicament. He was still cornered in the crumbling ruins of a horrific factory by a beautiful, ostrich-legged statue, a soggy, blithering fossil, and an uncomfortably large wasp that he would have long ago smashed with a book were it not for its terrific potential to explode.

It was at that thought—of his surprisingly volatile yet ultimately disappointing demise—that Avery found himself treated to another vision. And another. Simultaneously.

He was screaming—he could feel that. The strain on his jaw, the scratch in his throat, the dampness on either side of his head from the flow of tears. It was a fearful, sorrowful scream that had been rendered mute by a chorus of screams.

He was being torn apart. His wings, legs, arms—one by one they were ripped from his being and drained or mashed or stitched or simply thrown away into the pit and yet he felt none of it. Instead, he felt a deep, penetrating shame.

For once, Avery's selectively conscience state of mind provided him with a distinct advantage. He realized that he hadn't been strapped to a table and that he wasn't in any immediate danger of having his nonexistent wings forcefully removed from his person. These realizations gifted him with a limited sense of awareness outside of his subconscious.

More or less used to this kind of thing, Avery's mind forced his fractured perceptions to coalesce onto the sight of the old woman ranting and raving before him. Everything—the world around him and those from within—went black as his mind attempted to reboot itself. As it did, Avery heard a voice thrice over.

"You disappoint me," said the Mistress of Love's Lost.

TWENTY NINE
Fortune Favors

The violence ended almost as soon as it had begun, leaving behind a gentle but no less disconcerting rumble. Fortune and the Truth were dormant once more, though the latter had only done so after a final catastrophic blow to the pavilion. The enormous, thorny pillar was currently resting at a rather precarious angle that leaned towards its master.

Lree stood up from behind a smashed dining table formerly full of presumably delicious pastries, brushing a mix of splinters and powdered sugar off herself while looking around for her sister. Dahlia could not be found anywhere and, for a moment, the thought that she might have been crushed by the Truth during the chaos filled Lree with something akin to hope. A trail of scorched earth and guests that lead out of the pavilion, however, quickly dashed that feeling.

It didn't matter—she had bigger things to worry about. Quite literally. The fantastical tree never seemed more massive or more intimidating than it did right now. The huge roots kept climbing up and up into the sky, converging on a single point before blossoming into an umbrella of branches so thick and so numerous that it blocked out the sun almost entirely.

That was it. The point. That was the real base that mother had talked about. She had to climb it, she thought. No, she would climb it. Probably.

The twisted collection of creeping roots that formed Fortune's titanic trunk knocked Lree's enthusiastic determination out cold and dumped it into a bottomless well. Each root was as large as a full-grown tree. Larger, even. Certainly large enough to smash embittered little girls averse to nature into horrific blobs of resentful jelly.

Of course she could just be over thinking things. What was there to be afraid of? The great tree had never attacked her before, right? Right. Then again, it had never lost control and destroyed the entire pavilion, either, so...

Lree slammed her fist against the toppled table, an act that hurt considerably more than she would ever admit to. "Stupid," she thought. Her salvation was right there, right in front of her. She wasn't going to allow fear and hesitation to stop her from reaching it no matter how justified such feelings might have been.

She took a step forward off the brickwork and onto the grass, waiting for a reaction. The lawn was agitated instantly, lashing at her wounded ankle as violently as a carefully manicured lawn could. Lree barely winced. Her focus was on the wooden behemoth before her. Its roots remained remarkably still. They were so still, in fact, that one might even mistake Fortune for a proper tree.

It's important to note that Fortune was anything but a proper tree. This will become evident soon enough.

Lree took another step. It was a slow, difficult step hampered by the increasing hopelessness of her situation. At this distance she noticed things about Fortune that she had never noticed before, such as how its bark clearly wasn't designed to protect the great tree. It was knobby and spiky, providing very little opportunity to grab a hold of without seriously harming oneself. This bark—this tree—was poised to attack.

Another step and still no reaction. Maybe it wasn't after her, she thought. To Fortune she was no larger than a crumb that had fallen off another crumb. Even if it could sense her presence, why would it care?

Another step. And another. And another. Her confidence was growing so fast that she didn't even notice that her feet were bleeding profusely. Another step. The tree didn't seem to take any notice of the tiny, dark-skinned girl at all.

It was on the eighth step that the question "Why would it care?" suddenly became rather relevant.

"Pentas," said the Mistress with heavy inference, "If you would...?"

Avery assumed correctly that it was he who was being inferred towards and that the rest of her request wasn't "...bake this nice young man some of your famous blueberry muffins." Miss All's cold, exasperated tone was enough to convince him that he should leave right away.

Despite having a substantial amount of experience being caught in awkward situations he wasn't terribly skilled at getting out of them. Eyes still on the Mistress, Avery took a small step back, startling the bug that had been cowering behind his leg. The voorn fluttered a bit along the ground but ultimately returned to her original position when Avery stopped. He quickly realized that even if the volatile bug hadn't prevented his escape, the giant, glowing pit behind him would have.

"Of course, mother," he heard Pentas say with a slight stutter. He was too embarrassed—and too ashamed—to look at her, let alone talk to her. Suffice it to say, he would not be running towards her to escape. Avery took the only remaining option and bolted to his right, the voorn following closely behind. Their progress was cut dramatically short by the sound of crumbling rock and crackling fire.

"Impeccable timing, Dahlia," said the Mistress, clearly more disappointed than impressed.

Avery watched in terrified silence as an enormous, vaguely human-shaped meteor trundled out of the shadows and into the open room. It—she—seemed to be an overinflated toddler that had been set on fire, only somehow worse. As he stared at this new, smoldering threat he couldn't help but consider the sudden benefits of jumping into the giant, glowing pit.

"E-excuse me," he said, slinking by Dahlia. Dahlia looked at her mother who simply shook her head slowly.

"I don't think so, boy." Dahlia quickly grabbed Avery by the shoulder. Being in the presence of the Mistress, she had cooled her hand significantly and used only a moderate amount of pressure. Avery screamed.

"Dahlia," her mother called.

"I barely touched him!" she retorted, noticeably rattled.

"I wasn't accusing you, dear. Please, bring him here."

Embarrassed but mostly enraged, Dahlia complied, shoving Avery back before her mother and sister.

"Thank you, that'll be all."

"But..."

"That will be all, Dahlia. I need to speak with Mister Hall calmly, you understand. Your presence doesn't exactly inspire an atmosphere of serenity, does it? Now please, give us some space." The Mistress waved her hand weakly, gesturing towards the far side of the pit. "Start cleaning up this mess," she said. "Oh, and cover up, will you dear?"

Dahlia looked over at Pentas, expecting at the very least a wily smile. Pentas wasn't smiling. Her bottom lip was curled beneath her top teeth and her eyes—her pupils, inordinately small, were shaking wildly. What had happened here, she wondered. Was it the boy? How did he do so much damage to the room? And what did he do to his sister? She then glared at Avery who, upon receiving the glare, flinched hard enough to pull what passed as a muscle in his neck.

"You," she said, slapping Avery on the back of the head, "Don't even think about escaping."

"That was unnecessary, wasn't it?" her mother said rather coolly.

Dahlia lowered her head slightly and turned away. "Sorry, mother," she said, glancing at the Mistress then quickly looking back at the ground. "I didn't mean to...not really."

"I wasn't talking to you," she snapped back. Their conversation was now over.

Avery, who had been too preoccupied with cradling his head and sobbing, hadn't witnessed this exchange. He was only reminded of his situation when he saw Pentas's hoofed feet come into view.

"Avery," she said, striking a pose before him that may or may not have been deliberately provocative. He dared not look her in the eye. Her tone only made matters worse as it was difficult to tell whether she was being genuinely sweet or deeply contemptuous. Either way, it made Avery tremendously uncomfortable.

How did this even happen, he wondered as he dropped to a crouch. How did they find him? How did they even get in here? He had locked the door, right? Yeah, definitely. It was, he recalled, one of the very first things he did upon entering this horrible place—that and wet his pants slightly though that's not terribly relevant at the moment. Besides, they were mostly dry now. At the moment.

"H-how?" Avery sputtered.

"Excuse me?" asked Pentas, kneeling down beside Avery.

A sense of panic began to bubble in Avery's chest, triggering a round of hoarse, painful coughing. "Locked," he wheezed.

"You are going to have to speak up."

"Door!" he cried out."Locked!"

Pentas looked up at her mother who gave a small shrug. "Sorry," she said, returning to Avery, "I do not quite understand what you are trying to say. What door?"

Having managed to get most of the coughing under control, Avery sat up and side-eyed Pentas. "I locked that door," he said pointing towards the wall of machinery. "There's no way you could have..."

"Locked the door?" the Mistress interrupted, looking behind her.

Avery nodded furiously.

"No you didn't."

284

"I did!"

"No. You didn't."

Yes. I totally did."

"You can deny it all you like…"

"I'm denying it a lot."

"…but the simple truth of the matter is that you did not. Otherwise I wouldn't be standing here having this inane argument with you." She looked behind her again and paused. "Ah," she said, turning to face Avery, "that would explain it."

Avery looked at her confused which was pretty much the only look he had ever given her so she didn't hesitate to explain the "it" in her previous statement.

"The regulator," she said. "I wonder…did you really not know what you were doing? It takes, dare I say, some level of skill to properly shut down."

Taking a cue from Avery's continued silence, she added: "The panel with all of the gears and levers that are very un-door-like—that's the regulator. That's what you "locked." To deactivate it by accident, even for you..."

"Look, I came through…there was this door with a billion locks on it. Then there was this hallway and...lots of doors."

"The maintenance entrance?"

"I don't know. Sure."

"It was destroyed."

"Right! So okay, I didn't lock it but," Avery paused for more than a moment as if attempting to solve a multi-step algebraic equation in his head. "But," he continued, "it was destroyed so that means...how did you get in here?"

"The front entrance." The Mistress's response was completely deadpan. "There," she added, pointing across the room towards Dahlia. Behind the inhuman torch stood a sort of gate that was significantly more door-like than anything else found along the circumference of the rotund butchery.

Inanimate Objects 2. Avery 0.

"It was dark," Avery said. Weakly.

"I can see just fine."

"Yeah, well, if my face was covered in a bunch of eyeballs I'm sure my vision would be great, too."

"Hey," Dahlia barked, her hearing keen as ever.

"That's enough, Dahlia," said the Mistress, followed by, "Pentas."

With a faint sigh Pentas stood up. "Of course, mother." And with that she rounded the planetarium-sized pit to help—supervise, really—her sister.

"Now then, Mister Hall," said the Mistress, "I think it's time we discussed your arm."

Avery, teasing his hair nervously, returned to his feet. "Really? What about..." he began, looking around the demolished room.

"You have caused me a great deal of distress, it's true, however..."

"*I* caused *you* distress?!" Avery snapped. "You stripped me naked down to my boots!"

"It wasn't exactly pleasant for me, either."

Avery ignored this. "And she put me in a giant cage with thorns and stuff," he said angrily, pointing a shaking finger at Pentas.

"And that one," he continued, now pointing at Dahlia, "that one hit me!"

"Wimp!" Dahlia yelled.

"And calls me names," Avery added, his voice cracking very slightly.

"I'm sorry to say that these misunderstandings have been their fault. It's an unfortunate truth but my daughters have a tendency to act impulsively."

"Much like yourself, it seems," she added quickly. "Look at this place..."

"About my arm..."

"I don't think you appreciate what you've managed to do here. Then again, maybe you do. I find it hard to believe that you don't know what this room is..."

In an effort to put together at least a semblance of an answer that didn't make him sound like an idiot, Avery looked very seriously to his left and then his right.

"Some kind of weird mailroom?" he replied, sounding like an idiot.

"This, Mister Hall, is...was...my masterpiece. Not that nonsense above us. Not the ridiculous resort, not the tree, and certainly not those accursed flowers. This. The Nest."

"Wait, I think I've heard this before."

"I designed it all myself," she said proudly. "It's a processing room." The Mistress's tone shifted suddenly from utter contempt to melancholic reflection. "How long has it been?"

"Look, I don't mean to be rude," Avery said insincerely, "but I really don't want to be here. I mean, I should probably leave. I'm sorry I turned off your regurgitator..."

"Regulator."

"Sure. But I almost died and no one seems to care about that but me."

"Don't you want to know why I built this place?" she asked. There was a hint of excitement in her voice now that made everyone else in the room panic slightly.

"Not particularly," he said, eyeing the gate across the room. "I just want to leave."

"And where would you go? You don't even know where you are now."

"The Nest. You just told me."

"Very good, but where is the Nest?"

"Moron."

"Excuse me?"

"It's on Moron, right? Moron Island?" he said, turning to Pentas. Pentas shook her head in gentle disagreement. "No?"

"I built Love's Lost," The Mistress began, rubbing her head furiously.

"On Moron island," Avery interrupted.

"I built Love's Lost," she said again, though with a heavy dose of curtness, "as a means to an end. I hadn't thought about it in such a long time...I suppose I had actually forgotten about it. Your arrival, however, jostled something deep within me."

Avery felt uneasy with the idea of jostling anything within the old woman and his face made this very clear. This hardly stopped the Mistress.

"Me. You. We're not so different."

"Oh yeah we are," Avery added.

"No, not really."

"Yes, really. You've got, like, twenty eyes and look like someone's mummified great, great grandmother. We're nothing alike. Sweet holy cripes, why would you even say that?"

The Mistress drew in closer and, as if on cue, the Nest began to rumble. Avery tried to look away but found himself both mesmerized and paralyzed by the Mistress's fascinatingly horrific facial features.

"Because I know," she said, her words aligning themselves perfectly with the movements of her mouth, "I know what you...what we both desire."

"I-I really don't think so."

The Mistress, quite expertly, maneuvered her lips to Avery's right ear and whispered something into it.

Avery, of course, found this to be awfully disturbing. What was even more disturbing, however, was that she had been right.

One of the smaller roots unfurled itself and rose high into the air. It was soon followed by a dozen others, each larger than the last. Lree stared blankly at the deadly armada of arbor threatening her from above. It was, she figured, too late to run. Fast as she was, nimble as she was, there was simply no way that she could dodge a small forest being thrown at her.

The first root struck hard, hitting the ground beyond Lree with a deafening blast. Earth, flatware, food, and guests—largely in pieces— filled the air, as did an enormous gust of wind that sent the girl tumbling closer to the tree. She had barely begun to pick herself up before she was hit by several more indirect blasts.

Fortune was definitely acting strange even for a twisted amalgamation of necrotic ent parts and malice brought to life by the heart of her mother's dead lover. She wasn't the target—that was clear enough seeing as how she wasn't staining the pavilion with her liquefied remains. This fact brought surprisingly little comfort, however, as she was still getting inadvertently pulverized by the tree's devastating tantrum.

While Lree attempted to dodge or at the very least brace herself against the oncoming barrage she noticed that a portion of Fortune's roots had pushed the Truth upright and had begun to wrap themselves around the giant column. She wasn't sure why, after laying waste to the pavilion, the tree was so determined to carry on with its festive duties but it did present her with an almost perfect opportunity. The strange sentience of Fortune's roots made it impossible to climb, however, the Truth was a different story. It was mantled in layer after layer of desiccated vines left over from innumerable Reconciliations. Better still, many of the vines featured large, conical thorns that made for ideal grips.

Fortune always rose the Truth high in the air. Higher than the plateau. If she could climb to the top of the column before Fortune released it, she thought, she could leap onto to the base of the tree that housed the heart.

Or she could do the sensible thing by returning to her cave to sleep. That's almost exactly what she thought as she lowered her goggles and scrambled over towards the column. Though the Truth wasn't quite airborne it soon would be, giving Lree all the motivation she needed to start climbing.

At this point, her mind had accepted that whatever it told her, no matter how safe or sensible such advice may be, it would be ignored. Which is a shame because it's absolutely worth reiterating that the afore mentioned fortuitous opportunity had been described as "almost perfect." That is to say imperfect. As Fortune's roots were still wrapping themselves around the Truth, it wasn't long before the two became intertwined.

"Don't touch that," said her brain, well aware that its warning came after she had grabbed a root instead of a vine. If it could grin it would be doing so right about now. The jerk.

Lree held onto Fortune's precarious bark with no small amount of care, resulting in a grip that was less suitable for climbing a tree than, say, transferring a fresh loaf of whole wheat from the shopping cart to the trunk without squishing it. The root bulged rather violently, though it wasn't clear whether this was due to Fortune lifting the column or Lree's presence. Not that it mattered much as she had already moved onto a series of vines several feet above.

As the Truth rose skyward Lree scurried upwards along with it. Fortune was relentless in its attack, throwing every root it could spare at the young girl while she navigated the hellish latticework of splintered wood and vicious thorns. Untethered by doubt and driven by a surge of near-lethal adrenaline she managed to dodge the onslaught with relative ease.

At last the column stopped, held aloft by some of Fortune's mightier and less violent roots. Knowing it could drop at any moment, Lree ceased her ascent and looked over her shoulder for the plateau. At first she had difficulty seeing much of anything as it was far darker in the sky than it was on the ground. Her confidence, which had been her trusted climbing partner up to this point, now betrayed her by leaping to its death and the realization that what she had done was not only foolish but almost certainly final festered in the pit of her stomach.

Before she could follow after her confidence she spotted the plateau—or a plateau—quite far away in the distance. It was small and otherwise empty save for some grass, moss, or some other form of greenish vegetation capable of carpeting the ground and lashing her feet. Now squinting, she spotted more landings scattered about the sky—a few lower and closer, most higher and much further away. They seemed to be congregated around one massive, floating island—a mountain suspended in the air by Fortune's penetrating roots.

Lree climbed down a bit to align herself with the nearest plateau which in retrospect turned out to be not particularly near but seeing as how she had already leapt from the Truth it didn't really matter. By her account she missed the plateau by a fingertip and though this is a gross understatement it doesn't change the fact that she had, indeed, missed her target. Fortune, however, had not. One of its roots launched itself at Lree, piercing the palm of her hand. She couldn't help but scream and, had the root not taken immediate action to rid itself of the doomed mountaineer we would have also experienced some more of Lree's excellent curses. Shooting skyward, the root made a sharp, snapping motion that flung its potty-mouthed victim onto (and partially into) the plateau she had originally been aiming for.

The impact of the landing, her perforated hand, her wrenched arm, her scorched ankle—it all hurt a great deal but it paled in comparison to the awful and, unfortunately, familiar taste of earth. She rose out of her little crater coughing and spitting out gooey gobs of grass and dirt. For a moment she seemed genuinely concerned that this was becoming a habit, however, the thought was quickly discarded when it became clear Fortune's attack wasn't over. Another root, thinner and tapered, struck the ground next to her like a maleficent lawn dart. It wasn't alone, a fact that sent Lree scrambling to the edge of the plateau.

Holding onto her injured arm tightly she peered over the edge of the landing. It and the other plateaus appeared to be held up by a complex network of roots quite unlike those bent on her demise. From what she could see—it was still quite dark, after all—these particular roots were lighter in color, lacked the offensive armor of her woody assailants, and led towards the top of the large, central island. They weren't moving, either, which Lree would have found exceptionally curious had she the time to ponder such things.

Suffice it to say, she did not. Several more roots struck the platform at once, ultimately destroying it. She dropped down onto one of the dormant roots and ran along it until she spotted another landing. This one was a short ways down but quite a bit larger so she knew that this time, for sure, she could jump over to it. And while her returned confidence resulted in success it's worth noting that she had only regained said confidence after she had made the jump.

Lree landed awkwardly, crumbling into a roll that took her just past the center of the floating island. She had a breath, maybe two, before she came under attack again, she figured. Before the first wave of deadly roots rose into view she was off the island and onto the next.

This pattern repeated itself a dozen or more times until she had reached a plateau just below the central island. Unfortunately, every leap, dash, and tumble exacted a penance on Lree's distressed body. She could feel her movements becoming increasingly constrained and her breathing had grown into a conscious challenge, as if she were attempting to breathe through a log. She was crouching with her hands clawing into her knees in order to remain standing or at the very least awake. And she was smiling.

"What will you do?" she asked herself.

Lree stood erect as best she could and shuffled over to the edge of the island. There, as suspected, she found an inert root. This root led to another root that led to another root that led to a root that rose along the wall of the floating mountain towards yet more roots that climbed higher still, eventually disappearing behind a precipice.

She took a slow step off the plateau and onto the first root. Having once again been abandoned by her traitorous confidence, she relied upon the old standbys of resentment, anger, and self-loathing to fuel the final stage of her journey. Determined but no less shaky she ventured onward—never once looking back, never once looking down.

If the roots were to set upon her, she figured, that would be the end of it. She simply hadn't the energy to do anything about an attack. Were it not for a single spark of something she wouldn't have been able to clamber over the rocky precipice and onto the mountain. That something was the feeling of hope and it had been stirred from the most unpleasant bowels of her being by a brief glimpse of the great tree, Fortune—the true Fortune, as she now understood it to be.

It was a proper tree, albeit one of immense size, with seemingly amicable roots that strangled much of the floating island. This made navigating the terrain tricky and she constantly lost her footing as she attempted to traverse Fortune's perimeter. Her eyes had become fixated on the tree's voluminous trunk. It appeared to be mostly bare save for a relatively small portion walled off by naturally interlocking roots. Beyond the wooden wall lay a cavity—a dark hollow maybe three times herself in size—that might as well have had a sign posted saying:

ENTRANCE TO THE HEART OF LOVE'S LOST
GENERAL ADMISSION: $12.50
CHILDREN UNDER 3: FREE

—

PLEASE, NO SMOKING, FLASH PHOTOGRAPHY, OR
WISHING FOR REFUNDS ON GENERAL ADMISSION

Lree crept closer to the wall, close enough peer into the hollow.
"Hello, Fortune," she sighed.
"Hello."

THIRTY
Leaf Blower

It had started off as another normal, boring day. Why is that, Avery thought. Why did they always start off as normal and boring? Why didn't these types of stories start with "Our hero got out of bed, grabbed his sword, and slew a gelatinous hydra featuring the heads of each member of New Kids on the Block?" What kind of sick thrill did authors get by taking perfectly ordinary, even dull protagonists out of their everyday lives and thrusting them into surprising and terrifying situations that end in being torn limb from limb by Joey and Donnie?

He—Avery—needed time to think. He needed to collect his thoughts without being harassed by the bride of Two-Face. Even if the Mistress hadn't been there this was hardly the environment for calm cogitation. It was, to put it bluntly, one of the most horrific places he'd ever been to outside of a bus station bathroom. Even more distressing was the fact that the only way out was on the opposite side of a gaping orange death hole flanked by a foot fetishist's greatest nightmare and a violently disgruntled chunk of animated granite under the misguided belief that it was a person.

Avery wanted to go home—to return to his life, normal and boring as it may have been. Or at least, that's what the Mistress told him he wanted. At the moment, he really had no reason to argue with her.

"Can you?" Avery asked, his voice low and cracking.

The Mistress backed away. "I could, yes," she said with an unsettling smile. "I am Mistress All, after all."

"So you can?"

"Could."

Avery stared at the least offense portion of the Mistress's face. "Can," he said.

"Could," All corrected him.

"I'm not sure we're talking about the same thing," he confessed.

"Allow me to be blunt. You are utterly ordinary in nearly every way. There's not a single thing about you that's special."

"Thanks."

"I mean it. I don't think I've ever met an individual so devoid of life. You're plain. Average."

"Okay, yeah."

"Dull. Tedious."

"Thank you, I get it."

"I don't think you do. As you've pointed out, being ordinary is, in itself, extraordinary."

Avery waited for the Mistress to explain what she had meant, only realizing after quite a while of silence that she required prompting. "Go on," he said, hoping she wouldn't pick up on the fact that he had already forgotten what exactly she was supposed to be going on about.

The Mistress drew in closely with a startling amount of speed. So startling that Avery fell onto his backside, dropping his satchel and spilling its contents in the process. Before he could retrieve his precious accessory, the voorn quickly slipped beneath the flap and back into the bag, narrowly avoiding Avery's hand as he swept the kind of gross but also magical bone comb into it. The orb was too close to the Mistress to retrieve casually, which was a shame because it was still kind of cool.

"You fascinate me, Avery, and it's been a very long time since I've been fascinated by anything."

"Uh-huh," he said, his eyes darting between the Mistress and the orb.

"I'd like to make you an offer," she said, moving away from the glass ball. This was his chance, he thought. He reached for the orb but quickly withdrew his arm as the Mistress retraced her steps. "Stay here at Love's Lost. Let me study you."

She moved away. "Study," Avery replied, once again reaching for the orb. "Sure thing."

"Splendid!" she exclaimed, kicking the orb away from Avery's grasp with a small amount of nonchalance and a whole lot of maliciousness. "I didn't think you'd…ah, I suppose it doesn't matter. The girls can handle things here. Come. We'll head back to the laboratory and get right to work. The arm will have to come off first, of course."

"Of course," Avery parroted, watching the orb ricochet off of fallen cages and busted machinery until finally settling near the far side of the pit. "Wait, my what will have to come off?"

"Your arm."

"Oh, right. I thought you said my arm."

"I did."

"Because that would be crazy."

"I did say your arm."

"But that's crazy!"

The Mistress forced out a heavy sigh. "Look," she said, "Avery, aesthetics aside you are a fine specimen."

"But that arm," she continued. "Something's wrong with it."

Had Avery been drinking he would have been forced to release whatever beverage had just passed by his lips outward in a conical spray and sputter, "What?!" As he had no beverage in hand, he settled for dry, incredulous sarcasm.

"I knew it. It's blue. Arms aren't supposed to be blue, right?"

"I hadn't noticed that before," All continued, unfazed by Avery's rare attempt at wit. She leaned down to look closely at his arm, poking at it a couple of times as she spoke softly to herself. "It's as if...as if it's not supposed to be here I wonder..."

"It's not," Avery interrupted, slapping her prodding finger away. "None of me is supposed to be here. Which is why I think I'll be leaving." He picked up his bag and started towards the orb. Avery had the advantage, or so he thought. True, he wasn't particularly adept at running—all of his previous attempts seemed to end up with him passing out, throwing up, or both—but in a footrace solely against a spider-faced crone the odds were strongly in his favor. She could never catch up to him.

"Dahlia," the Mistress called.

But, Avery quickly realized, the walking quarry could and, in fact, did catch up to him before he had even gotten halfway to the orb.

"I suppose it's not going to make you feel any better knowing that I don't particularly find any of this satisfying," said the Mistress, inching ever closer.

"No," he said without turning around. "No it really doesn't."

"That's fine—I'm actually lying."

"That doesn't make me feel better, either." Pinched between a literal rock and a hard place (and a gaping hole in the floor but that kind of ruins the idiom), Avery's exit strategy had been whittled down to a large mound of debris to his left. And Avery, being Avery, slowly braced himself for one of the shortest and least exciting escapes in literature.

"Don't do this," the Mistress said while he was deciding whether to start with a mad dash or a slow, steady stride. "It's just going to cause a big headache for everyone, for me. If you'd just come with voluntarily you'd save me a lot of time."

"I never realized what an inconvenience I was being," said Avery. Mad dash or steady stride? Why was this so hard?

"Obviously. Come along now," she said, turning around and

gesturing at Avery to follow her.

Mad dash. Without a word, Avery ran towards the mound as fast as his rubbery legs could take him which, by sheer coincidence, was about as fast as a steady stride.

"I swear," said the Mistress to herself under her breath. "Very well, then. Girls!"

While it might be much more thrilling to hear that Avery was caught just before he could climb to freedom this would require a gross exaggeration of Avery's athletic capabilities. We're talking about a young man who becomes light headed on lengthier elevator trips and will often select a single floor at a time to avoid passing out before reaching his destination. Avery had only made it to the base of the mound when Dahlia grabbed him.

The first thing Avery felt was a heavy tug on his shirt that definitely wasn't a dress. With an effortless motion, Dahlia flung him back into the outer wall of the pit. It was regrettable that Avery blacked out only after experiencing a brief but no less potent moment of excruciating pain.

There are worse ways to be awoken. The sound of your cat throwing up, for example. You're never quite sure where he is which means you're guaranteed to either step in his mess that morning or discover the remnants of it stained into your carpet or term paper a couple of days later. What's worse is that it always happens five minutes before your alarm is due to go off, giving you enough time to listen to the whole ordeal and no chance of going back to sleep. It's odd then that no one has replaced the piercing, oven timer beeps of your basic alarm clock with that of a hacking cat because the latter would be much more effective in waking you up and significantly less cruel.

All of this talk about alarm clocks is moot as such devices don't seem to exist in Love's Lost or, indeed, anywhere given that time is a null concept. And while this knowledge would bring Avery a tiny bit of comfort it didn't change the fact that something or someone was quite clearly attempting to rouse him from his slumber and he wanted none of it.

"Avery?" said Pentas as she slowly stroked her hand along his arching back. It wasn't an unpleasant feeling, however, the confusing mix of concern and antipathy in her voice did little to put him at ease. "Avery? Are you alright?"

He wasn't alright, of course, and not just because he had been thrown face first into a stone wall by a stone wall. Moving a bit like a tangled marionette, Avery righted himself enough to crawl away. Or at least try to.

"Will you not stay with us?" Pentas asked.

Scraping along the floor, Avery continued his pitiful and painful escape. Where, exactly, he was escaping to hadn't crossed his mind. He was far more concerned about where he was escaping from.

"With me?"

Scrape. Scrape scrape scrape scrape.

"Please?"

Avery froze mid-scrape. She said "please," didn't she? And not please like "please pass the butter" or "please stop going through my garbage or I'm really going to call the cops this time." This had been a genuine plea. A want. She wanted him to stay?

Unable and unwilling to stop himself, Avery turned his head so that he could look at Pentas. She was kneeling down which by sheer coincidence allowed the slit in her dress to cascade over her thigh. Yeah, she was pretty, he thought. Absurdly pretty, really. Her hair, her eyes, her lips, her...other areas. And she was reaching out for him, asking— no, begging—please. Please stay with me.

Avery stood up. Would it really be that bad? It's not like he had anywhere else to go and what was an arm, anyway? As fantastic as this world was he'd probably be able to replace it with something cooler, like a sword or a cannon or a leaf blower.

He took a step towards his potential future. Probably not a leaf blower. How would he plug it in? Or would it be gas powered? He'd need a backpack, then, and those looked heavy.

Another step. He could see Pentas quite clearly but everything else around her was losing focus.

Another step. What would he use a leaf blower for, he thought. Aside from blowing leaves. Sword, cannon, leaf blower. Huh. He had never even picked up a leaf blower before.

Pentas, arms held out before her, stood only a few steps away. Avery, staring at those warm, welcoming arms and thinking about leaf blowers, didn't notice the look of scorn that had befallen upon her face.

He also failed to notice the animated brick oven closing in behind him or the winged hand grenade climbing out of his satchel. Of these three individuals, one would set off a series of events that would result in a particularly nasty bruise, the death of a major character, a large explosion, and a torn tunic, though not necessarily in that order.

Avery shambled into Pentas's grasp with as much mission as a middle schooler that had been sent to the principal's office. With practiced finesse she set the trap, bringing her arms slowly to a close.

"What will you do?" she asked sweetly.

Avery rested his head against her shoulder and instinctively began to wrap his arms around her. He was safe, he thought, and happy? Maybe not happy. Maybe...blissfully ignorant. That was it; safe and blissfully ignorant which, coincidently, made him happy.

"I'll stay," he'd say. He'd then hug her tightly and add, "With you." Damn the consequences. The Mistress could chop his arm off and replace it with anything. Well, almost anything.

"Not a leaf blower," he said, squeezing Pentas and, unwittingly, crushing the voorn that had been caught between two wildly differing torsos during the initial embrace. She responded as one would be expected to having been caught in the same situation and that is by calmly making their presence known and politely excusing themselves.

Just kidding. She actually bit Avery in one of the fleshier parts of his stomach with her terrifying mandibles, the shock of which sent his body into a sudden, violent, and frankly hilarious spasm. His arms flailed about like that of a man who had walked into a hornet's nest, breaking him free from Pentas's tender incarceration. In a single swift, graceless movement he swatted the voorn away from his ample midsection, tearing his tunic and elbowing Dahlia hard in the chest. The combination of panic-induced strength and unusually pointy elbows allowed the surprise attack to crack the rocky shell that covered her right breast, resulting in a particularly nasty bruise.

As you might have assessed by now Avery was a magnet for embarrassing situations and as such had developed an involuntary response for every time he hugged someone instead of shaking their hand, sneezed on someone's newborn baby, or accidentally punched someone in the privates.

"Oh my god, I am so, so sorry," he said, spinning around to see Dahlia holding part of her chest. "I didn't mean to. I am so sorry. So sorry. So..."

Sensing a thought forming in the bottom of his befuddled brain,

Avery froze.

"What is wrong with him now?" the Mistress asked, cautiously approaching the inanimate young man.

"I don't...he's crazy, that's what's wrong with him," chided Dahlia.

"No," Avery snapped back, startling everyone. "I'm not crazy. You're crazy!" He then spun around clumsily and pointed furiously at Pentas. "And you're crazy!" he said as he launched into a final spin. "And you," he continued, stopping at the Mistress, "You...you're just scary."

The Mistress stared at Avery.

Pentas stared at Avery.

Dahlia stared at Avery.

Avery, feeling all eyes upon him, decided that now would be a good time for an awkward retreat."So, okay. Bye," he said and ran away from the forbidding troupe.

The Mistress quickly attached her nasal apparatus and gave pursuit, storming past Dahlia and nearly knocking Pentas over.

Pentas reached out. "Mother, please! Allow us."

"Yeah," added Dahlia as she wiped away both her bruise and the part of her body that simulated her breast, "I can do this."

"Clearly!" the Mistress bellowed. She stopped her pursuit, turned around to face her daughters, and continued bellowing. "Clearly, you cannot "do this," Dahlia. Clearly, I have misplaced my trust in you—both of you."

Dahlia couldn't bear to hear her mother talk down to her and chose to look away. She knew she couldn't justify her failure and apologizing would do nothing but make the situation worse than it already was. Pentas, on the other hand, appeared unfazed. She simply stared at the Mistress with an expressionless mask.

"Well?" the Mistress asked with a considerable amount of impatience. "Go get him. Urge him back into the lab. Unharmed, Dahlia."

Looking at the ground as she passed her mother, Dahlia replied with a soft, defeated, "Yes, mam."

"And Dahlia?"

"Yes, mam?"

"Cover up."

"Yes, mam."

Given the chaotic state of the room in addition to his own fitness-related shortcomings Avery made it to the front entrance in surprisingly good time. Unfortunately, the large, probably iron gate had been locked and remained steadfast in its apparent duty to keep Avery from escaping. There were no latches or handles or knobs and no amount of pushing or pulling or pleading could coax the gate open. This is why, once again, Avery found himself before a wall of buttons and levers, none of which seemed to do anything when flipped, turned, or switched. Slapping, slamming, and kicking them didn't seem to do anything either.

This was ridiculous, he thought, kicking a lever to break the cycle of doing everything in cubes. Even if he had been lucky enough to choose a section of the wall that could unlock the gate it's not like he knew how to actually operate any of this machinery.

He readied a lumpy fist, determined to spill his bountiful frustration upon the gadgetry that mocked him. What was almost assuredly to be an embarrassing display of witless ferocity was prevented at the last moment by a small, pitiable creature of gold and violet. The voorn pulled on Avery's leggings with what appeared to be purpose. Once she gained his attention she scrambled up his side and skittered along his arm to his fist which, against all reason, he opened to create a convenient platform.

At some point Avery began to suspect that the bug had been trying to communicate with him, however, he had tried to brush that idea aside as a coincidence or, at best, wishful thinking. It was like those people who credit their dog with alerting them to a fire or a well-bound child when, in fact, the dog simply wants to be let out.

The voorn, too, wanted to be let out but not for walkies or to bark at a particularly menacing shadow along the fence for the next three hours. She wanted to escape. More than that, she wanted to escape with Avery. Or so he had hoped.

"Do you know how to open the gate?" he whispered, having tremendous difficulty accepting what was actually happening.

To his surprise—and mild disappointment—the creature responded immediately by pointing to the consoles on the far side of the room.

Before Avery could ask, "Which one?" or even, "Why am I still holding this terrifying wasp-thing?" he was interrupted by the words, "When I find you." They were spoken in a low, angry hush and came from just beyond a large boulder that had not too long ago been part of the room's ceiling. In a flash the boulder flew aside, smashing into the adjacent wall. At its origin stood a familiar figure, seething with anger, bitterness, and lava.

"There you are," said Dahlia. "I hope you enjoy pain."

It doesn't necessarily need to be stated but just so we're all on the same page here Dahlia wasn't being sincere and Avery especially did not enjoy pain.

His options were becoming increasingly limited. He looked at Dahlia—glared at her—and saw the fire in her eyes.

"Mother wants me to bring you back. Personally, I think it'd be better if you disappeared," she said. Her tone wasn't threatening which frightened Avery even more.

He gritted his teeth. He was tired of running. He wanted to make a stand. He wanted to show Dahlia—no, to show everyone he could fight. He was strong and funky and more often than not confused lyrics from 80's pop music with his own thoughts.

"Beat it," he muttered.

"What was that?" Dahlia asked, stopping her approach.

Avery flipped his hand upward, snatching the voorn out of the air before she could flutter away. She tried desperately to bite him but he held her in such a way that prevented such an attack.

"Do you know what this is?" his voice cracked. "It's a...she's..."

Dahlia's eyes squinted. "She?"

"Yeah. And you...you know what she can do?"

"Tell me," she replied, continuing her approach as she was unable to hide her disinterest any longer.

"She's like a grenade." Avery shook the voorn violently, sending small showers of sparks every which way. It's important to note that hand grenades do not actually behave in this manner and if by chance they do it's too late to do anything about it.

"I-I've seen her kind punch holes through *stone* a whole lot thicker than you, sister." Avery grinned, impressed with how tough he sounded. That was a good threat, wasn't it? The way he emphasized "stone?" Brilliant. Oh, and ending with a casual "sister?" He never knew he could be such a badass though he suspected that this might have always been the case.

Dahlia stopped again. The boy was bluffing, of that she was certain. He was no more of a threat to her than a bee was to a ballista. He was holding an unclassified voorn, however, and that could very well be a problem. "Could" being crucial to that thought. There really was only one way to find out.

"Hey! Come on now," Avery barked. "I don't want to do this!"

"I know that, you simp."

Dahlia, still a few yards away, reached for Avery which was enough provocation necessary to send him into a panic. He leapt back, hastily readied his arm, and lurched his body into a hard pitch. The voorn screamed towards Dahlia for about a foot then slowed down into a gentle, upward flutter. Dahlia watched as the creature flew unsteadily towards the ceiling and then the far side of the room.

"You missed," she said, half looking back at Avery. "Want to try again? I'll..."

He wasn't there. She slowly scanned the area where she thought he had been.

"...get closer..."

He was nowhere. Mother would not be pleased.

"What the crap?" Avery cursed, evidently having run into something.

Dahlia spun around. Sure enough, there he was—the ugly little man ball cradling his knee like a child who had been pushed down onto a brick path because they were so slow and stupid and always liked best by mother. How had he slipped by her? And how had he managed to get so far away? He was practically at the center of the room already!

"H-hey!" she yelled. "Hold it!"

Avery flinched. "I'm good!" he called back. He then stood up and immediately ran into something else. Dahlia couldn't help but gawk as he continued his awkward escape, bouncing around the broken environment like a hamster ball in a clothes dryer. It was as fascinating as it was pathetic. Just what was this boy worth to mother?

While the definitive answer to that question would not be revealed any time soon, even a raging rock monster with a propensity for punching could ascertain that Avery was, at least at the moment, quite important to her mother as evidenced by the fact that she herself was trying to stop him. This only made Dahlia feel worse. Mother so rarely involved herself in her own orders and was now participating only because the head of security, her most trusted daughter, had failed her.

This wouldn't do.

Dahlia steadily marched towards the gathering at the center of the room. She was so focused on reaching her target (and regaining her mother's trust) that she failed to notice that Pentas was missing. Not that it would have mattered, really. Dahlia had learned long ago that it was safer to remain ignorant of her older sister's motivations and actions.

The boy's haphazard dance with debris brought him closer and closer to mother. Dahlia knew she had to act now to save face. Without even drawing a breath she took one, two, three, four steps, each faster than the one that came before, and launched herself into a low, long arc. As she descended, large portions of her body burst into bright yellow flames. Her fist, like a fiery meteor, made it clear that she was more interested in creating a large, flaming cavity in Avery's chest than she was capturing him without harm.

Avery, sensing the danger, shifted ever so slightly to the side. He caught Dahlia's arm as she sailed by and used her momentum to set both of them into a violent spin. Unable to hold onto her burning arm any longer, he released her and she rocketed over the Mistress and into the pit.

"Top that," he said brushing the ashes from his hands.

No no. Hang on.

"You spin me right round, baby," he said. "Like a record."

Eh. Oh! How about this?

"You try to take a bite out of me, sister, you'd better watch for the pit." Oh man, that one is awesome. Wait! Where are you going? I've got lots more—tons more! I...fine. Okay, look, none of that actually happened. I was just really excited at the prospect of writing a pun-soaked quip and it's not like I'm ever going to have the chance again with any of these losers, am I? The best I could possibly hope for would be a cheesy catchphrase like, "Did I do that?" or "Kiss my grits!" and even that's a stretch. It's not easy, you know? Telling this story. It's like, why did I even start this? When did I start this? I should lay down for a while.

THIRTY ONE
Keeping Promises

Lree was beset by dozens of furious roots from every direction. The first set came in hard from above, bringing her to her knees. The next, having tunneled through the mountainous plateau below, launched her battered body into the night sky. More roots appeared, each flailing about like a professional tennis player whose mid-set Gatorade had been spiked with mescaline. One of these new arrivals struck Lree on her way down, sending her over the edge of the island and plummeting towards a demise guaranteed to be both unpleasant and messy.

As fortune would have it the great tree chose this precise moment to release the Truth. The false roots that had held it in place withdrew one by one, creating a loose entanglement that more or less impeded Lree's descent. She smashed into the first root hard enough to knock loose one of her shark-like teeth. Rebounding into the second then third then fourth then fifth root resulted in more involuntary orthodontics among other injuries typically associated with being hit by a speeding truck.

Lree continued to bounce from one root to another like a fuzzy pachinko ball until, at last, there was nothing left to bounce off of. She would continue to fall until she hit the pavilion, creating a pathetic crater filled with gore and bitterness. Mother would probably turn it into some sort of attraction. No, she wouldn't do that. She'd plant some hedges around the rim and convert it into a classy refuse pit or lavatory. "I'll just be a moment, dear," some obese socialite would belch, "I've got to visit the Lree for a bit."

Her ire went beyond her mother. Soon it spilled over onto the great willow, her sisters, and Avery before puddling onto herself.

"It's all her fault." That phrase had been central to her very being. It was only now that Lree, soon to be smeared into a chunky dinner sauce at the center of the biggest party in the Chain, realized it wasn't "her." It was "my."

And, after an all too brief moment of self-reflection, Lree hit the ground with a terrible tremble. Hundreds of tiny, needling shockwaves reverberated throughout her body and then they were gone. She was gone. All that was left was a shattered shell of a girl and a whole lot of regret.

"Mrrrmf frrrrp ma," she said, which was a rather rude thing to say but given the circumstances not necessarily uncalled for.

Regret? Really? What was the whole point of dying, then? And where was she? It was dark and uncomfortable—wasn't she supposed to be bathed in sunlight or something? And the trumpets! Someone said there'd be trumpets. Death was turning out to be a real disappointment.

Wait, she was dead, wasn't she?

"Mrrrmf frrrrp ma," she said again, testing both her state of permanence and the boundaries of good taste.

From the viewpoint of the casual observer it was as it always had been: a spectacular sight. The Truth, resting snugly once more in its hold, was alight with flowers of every kind. Even with a pair of legs sticking out of its top like an unfortunate case of pili multigemini it was beautiful, inspiring, team building, and other words you'd expect to find on a motivational poster of a whale, forest, or mountain.

Hardly being the first time she had found herself stuck headfirst in a fruticose growth on the shaggy back of Mother Nature, Lree wiggled her way out of the braky trap with little difficulty. She was alive, she reminded herself, and after a cursory inspection of her surroundings she had a very good idea of where she was. The bright, glowing flowers, the thick layers of bramble, the previous paragraph—they all screamed the Truth. Still, she couldn't quite bring herself to believe it.

A sharp, burning odor drew Lree to the edge of the giant pillar. Below she saw the pavilion—or what was left of it, anyway—empty, smashed, and burning.

"Get down," she thought. This was, of course, excellent advice given that she was standing on what was essentially an enormous pile of kindling. She climbed over the edge and, unsteadily, began making her way down the Truth.

"Run," she thought. This, too, was good advice. Only, she hadn't quite reached the ground yet and even if she had, given her condition, running wasn't possible. It was nothing short of astonishing that she could even climb. Every movement, no matter how slight, reminded her that she had barely managed to escape death. Needless to say, the gaping hole in her hand wasn't making things any easier.

Her eyelids grew heavy. "Hide," she thought as she looked down at the burning pavilion. She was still so very high up and she was so very, very tired.

"Stay safe," she thought as she released her grip. That's all she really wanted, wasn't it? To hide away in her rocky home, safe from, well, everything?

Lree smiled, however, her expression quickly betrayed her by giving way to despair. She tried to cover her face but couldn't convince her arms to do anything but thrash wantonly in the wind as she tumbled towards the ground. She closed her eyes and, as she did, caught a glimpse of an enormous, bony hand—a hand large enough to throttle the Truth—emerging from the smoke towards her.

Terror overwhelmed her every sense. All she could do—all she wanted to do—was keep her eyes shut. Nothing else seem to matter—not regret, not despair, and not even the ground.

And nothing happened.

She waited.

Still, nothing happened.

She cursed. It took a great deal of effort to open her eyes—much more than she would ever care to admit and definitely much more than the reward warranted. The scenery was vague and murky, offering very few points of interest to focus on. This, of course, made the next event all the more startling.

"PROMISE," said a deep, disturbing voice. The dust in front of Lree's face swirled, giving way to a large, mostly skeletal face composed of poorly preserved bone, wood, and metal. For whatever reason, it was upside down.

"PROMISE," Jones repeated, the word seemingly spilling out of the creature's malformed skull.

As the dust began to settle Lree found herself in the familiar position of being held upside down by her ankle—the one that wasn't burned, surprisingly—before the image of Death. Jones looked worse than they ever had which was pretty impressive. Parts of their frame had been singed or burned away entirely while the rest of the monster seemed to have been gilded with what once was expensive and extraordinarily tacky jewelry.

"Yeah," she said without punching, kicking, or attacking Jones in any way. Once again, her expression betrayed her, turning from terror to twisted satisfaction.

First she swore at no one in particular. Then, simultaneously, she swore at Avery, the horrific trash elemental, and herself. Finally, she swore at Avery again. She did all of this while pacing in a very limited area, ultimately creating the world's smallest crop circle.

"Look," she said, stopping to point at the towering skeletal monstrosity beside Avery. If she had anything else to say she kept it to herself as she returned to her nervous pacing.

"You," she said, stopping once again to point at the towering and menacing trash golem beside Avery. She sighed heavily and dramatically. This was stupid. It was also reckless, drastic, and so terribly irrational. In summary, it was perfect.

"Ah need your help," she couldn't believe she heard herself say. "He's gonna die. Ah can't have that, right? And Ah can't carry his fat ass all the way back to the Garden—not before that happens."

The creature failed to respond outside of a whistling sound made by the wind blowing through their broken skull. Oh, how they repulsed her. Simply talking to them made her want to peel away her skin and burn it. She had to get this over with quickly—no more beating around the bush.

"Carry 'im," she quickly babbled, disregarding the area around said bush entirely and giving the bush itself a savage pummeling. "Do it and Ah'll do whatever you want. After we get to the Garden."

Had they understood her? Were they listening? Were they even capable of listening? She felt foolish and began to consider her lack of options when the terrible refuse giant pointed to something in their chest. It appeared to be an old, filthy kettle.

"Yer…hungry?" Lree asked with adequate nervousness. "Fer what? And where would it go?"

The horror tapped the kettle slowly, shaking their head as if to illustrate some sort of point. Each heavy tap resulted in a gong that traveled far into the distant valley.

"How'm Ah s'posed to get that thing out? How'd it even get in there to begin with?"

The creature lunged forward, taking Lree by surprise. Before she could fail to defend herself, they fell to the ground in a cloud of dust.

A weak "Hey!" is all she could manage before succumbing to a violent coughing fit. She had just regained the ability to breathe without hacking when the word "HEART" seemed to swarm around her. Soon the dust settled and the creature was kneeling before her, tapping their kettled chest like before.

"What did you jus'…?" Lree asked. It was hard to tell if she was shocked or angry.

The creature nodded.

"You c'n talk?! If you…all this…why?!" She was definitely angry.

Without turning their head, the creature pointed at the Avery-shaped man-ball behind them. They then picked up a fistful of dirt and shook it, beclouding the area in front of whatever was left of their face with dust. "IDIOT," Lree heard.

"Yeah," she said, her anger giving way to startling empathy. This, in turn, filled her with an overpowering sensation of fear and dread. "S-so what d'ya want?"

"HEART," it said after creating another small dust cloud. This was followed by more rhythmic kettle taps.

Lree thought for a moment. "Ah," she said. She then thought some more. "Ah don't have your heart."

The creature stood back up and pointed one of their decrepit fingers in a direction that surprised Lree less than it should have. It was towards the Garden. Towards Love's Lost.

"It's not real, you know," she said, stuttering. "The lost heart? It's not real—jus' made up."

With this came a sudden wind that blanketed the area in a thick, grimy haze. Having missed the opportunity to shield her eyes, Lree rubbed them furiously to counter (and, unintentionally, exacerbate) the stinging. As she did this, she heard the creature say "HEART," "HELP YOU," and, loaded with a significant amount of severity, "PROMISE."

"Fine," she blurted out, wiping a murky solution of dirt and tears from her face. "Ah promise. We'll go and Ah'll get you the heart or whatever. But only after the Garden, right? You gotta take him to the Garden before he dies."

The word "PROMISE" faded with the settling dust. After a long enough silence to make everyone uncomfortable—at least everyone who was conscious—the creature kneeled down beside Avery and hoisted him over their axe-less shoulder.

The heart. Of all the things the creature could have asked for they wanted the heart. While she had certainly come to question its very existence, deep down she still believed it was real. She had to believe it was real, otherwise she…everything up until this point…none of it would have mattered.

As her hope and enthusiasm abandoned her, she couldn't help focusing on the worst case scenario: what if there really wasn't a heart?

What would she do about the creature? In the off chance that there was an actual heart...well, what then? She couldn't hand it over to that monster. What would they do with it? This was the same monster that was shrouded in death and decay. The same monster that threatened both her sanity and existence. The same monster that was currently running away very, very fast.

Lree said nothing. She thought nothing. Instead, she did what she always did when considering the consequences of her own actions: she ran.

"PROMISE."

Lree turned her head in order to barely side eye Jones. "Shut it," she snapped, "Jus shut..."

Jones stood motionless which wasn't at all an uncommon thing for them to do. Indeed, it was one of the things they excelled at and, coincidentally, one of the many, many things that Lree found so unsettling about the skeletal menace.

"Shut whatever your noise comes from," she continued. "Ah'm thinking of a plan."

This wasn't entirely true. Lree had already conceived of a plan to retrieve the heart. It was a well thought out plan—at least by her standards—and it seemed highly likely that she would succeed. Unfortunately, it involved one of the other many, many things that Lree found so unsettling about the skeletal creature.

She scratched her head, loosening a bushel of crunchy strands from the hair Pentas had so carefully tied up for her. "What will you do?" she thought.

"Certainly not what you are thinking about doing," her mind answered in its best impersonation of Pentas. "That thing will never comply and even if they did..."

"Jones!" Lree yelled, cutting her thoughts off. "Ah'm gonna need that."

Her eldritch acquaintance reacted about as quickly as she had expected them to. Slowly, oh so slowly, they pointed at their plaque.

"Why would Ah...? No. Ah need a hand. Your hand. Your...actual hand."

Jones awkwardly extended their hand towards Lree. She reached out for it then stopped upon realizing that it looked as if it had been the failed result of an experimental bone enema.

"Okay maybe not your hand," she said withdrawing her own. "Somethin' else. Somethin' less horrible."

The creature took a step back and seemed to look themselves over. They then pointed at their jaw which received immediate disapproval from the young girl. This continued for a bit; Jones pointing at increasingly inappropriate areas of their malformed frame and Lree rejecting each proposition promptly. Too promptly, as Lree's rejections seemed to outnumber the creature's propositions. In a rare display of something that could almost be described as emotion, Jones suddenly grabbed their right femur and yanked it loose, sending the creature crumbling to the ground.

Needless to say this hasty, rather violent act of personal disassembly gave Lree a bit of a start. "Why'd you do somethin' like that for?" is what she would have asked were she not busy cursing at the creature. From their awkward position on the ground, Jones tossed the peculiarly stained bone to the ill-tempered young girl.

"This," she said, snatching the bone out of the air. She then touched the opposite end of the bone to the ground and watched as the grass shriveled up and turned to ash. "Right, this'll work."

Jones, still in a pile on the ground, raised a hand and gave a thumbs up.

"Don't give me that," Lree berated the mound of monster pieces. "What are you gonna do if Fortune loses it again?"

"Why, I'll be smashed to teeny tiny bits!" her mind answered for the mildly conscious junk heap.

Right, that'll work, too.

Lree, battered, bloodied, and running almost entirely on frantic exasperation, turned around and slowly marched towards Fortune. Everything from her tired posture to her heavy pace revealed her resignation and yet onward she went. Past the broken tables, the shattered chairs, and the spoilt meals. Past the neglected fires, the broken brickwork, and the last lamp post curiously left standing in the pavilion. Past everything until she reached Fortune's restless base of destructive wooden tentacles.

She looked over at the Truth. The arms of the false trunk had long since released the column and had been retracted back into Fortune's twisted base. It wasn't going anywhere.

This left Fortune's base itself. Lree's body, realizing the futility of the situation, took several large steps back. Still, she was not dissuaded. She'd climb the base or die trying. And die trying, sorry. Fortune's true trunk was set on a boulder floating thousands of feet in the air. Even ignoring her exhaustion, her injuries, and her innate ability to rile Mother Nature, there was no chance she'd be able to reach Fortune—the true Fortune—simply by climbing.

She knew this, of course, which is why she had already committed herself to going through with it. The reason she hadn't, however, was because her mind was inexplicably filled with thoughts of the sad pile of skeleton she had left behind.

Slowly, reluctantly, Lree looked over her shoulder and was rather surprised to find that Jones was barreling towards her on all fours minus one of the afore mentioned fours. Paralyzed by a combination of fear and bewilderment, Lree could only watch as Jones raced on like a three-legged puppy at dinnertime. Past the broken tables, the shattered chairs, and the spoilt meals. Past the neglected fires, the broken brickwork, and the last lamppost curiously left standing in the pavilion—the last landmark of which they caught from behind, sending the creature into a dizzying spin. As Jones came around a second time they reached out their free arm, snagging the back of Lree's patchwork disguise and, consequently, Lree herself.

Only slightly heavier than a throw pillow and always under constant threat of being stepped on, Lree instantly fell victim to the powerful centrifugal force created by the creature's terrifying pole dance. The odd duo spun around and around, gaining speed instead of losing it. Had this not caused Lree to black out she might have noticed that she was also being spun at a pretty high angle. Without warning, Jones released their grip on the girl, rocketing her skyward nearly parallel to the great tree. Lree was moving through the night air at such speed that Fortune's false roots had only begun to unfurl themselves after she had long since passed them.

When she came to she found herself laying safely upon Fortune's landing, which isn't even remotely true and I apologize for getting your hopes up. Instead, she awoke to discover the mountainous underside of Fortune's landing coming right towards her. Instinctively—because she had no idea what was going on and clearly didn't have the time to ponder on such matters—she flung her hands in front of her face and closed her eyes.

When she opened her eyes again she found herself laying in the remains of a violet bonfire quickly burning out atop Fortune's landing, which, this time, *is* true.

THIRTY TWO
All That Is Lost

Enough. The Mistress adjusted her bizarre breathing apparatus and inhaled deeply, assaulting the remnants of her lungs with a colorful miasma of enchanted roach remains. The figurative threads that bound each and every soul to the world were now literal. Literal and, more importantly, tangible.

The boy had somehow loosed himself from such threads and was lumbering towards her. She reached out for him, bringing her hand to a close. There was, to her dull surprise, no effect. She couldn't even ensnare his clothing anymore.

Again she reached out, but this time she swiped her hand through the air. This placed a portion of the fallen ceiling almost directly in the boy's path which did have an effect and a significant one at that.

Avery bounced off the debris just as Dahlia—or more precisely Dahlia's fist—came crashing down behind him. The floor, taking the full force of Dahlia's magmatic rage, didn't simply shatter—it exploded. Avery's less-than-nimble body was sent tumbling through the air towards the Mistress like a toad strapped haphazardly to a dozen bottle rockets.

It should be noted that while the Mistress may look like she's a single misstep away from total hip arthroplasty she is quite agile. She hopped out of the way of the doughy missile with a surprising amount of grace, making it all that much more unfortunate that her nearly poetic performance was botched by Avery's lost wish. The glass orb shattered beneath the force of her landing but not before it twisted her ankle and sent her stumbling precariously close to the edge of the pit.

Dahlia wrenched her hand free of the shattered brickwork and started after Avery, stopping almost instantly when she saw her mother, the Mistress of Love's Lost, tumble backwards over the side of the evidently short wall that surrounded the central pit.

There was a scream, a splash, and a thud. Dahlia said nothing. She did nothing.

"Stop the boy!" the Mistress yelled from the pit.

"R-right," she said and continued after Avery. The boy was already at the far side of the room frantically flipping switches and pulling levers on one of the numerous control panels grafted to the wall.

"And get me out of here!" the Mistress added.

"Right!" Dahlia said again, ending her pursuit and turning towards the pit. She peered over the side cautiously and saw her mother laying on her back in a shallow pool of glowing orange goo. She didn't look hurt, which was a relief, but she did look very, very angry. The angriest Dahlia had ever seen her mother, in fact, and it paralyzed her.

A loud clinking sound caused her to pause. The clinking was followed by an even louder clanking and eventually a not-quite-as-loud but significantly more concerning humming. The inappropriately named wooden tendrils that had only just recently been calmed began once again to writhe about in an appropriately inappropriate fashion. Finally, a hard ker-chunk echoed from the main gate.

"Yes!" Avery yelled, stopping just short of high-fiving no one.

"What are you doing, you dolt?!" the Mistress bellowed. "Stop him! And get me out of here right now!"

Dahlia was understandably confused. "I," she stammered, "But what...who should I...?"

Oh for the love of...why did she think she could depend on Dahlia? Or on anyone for that matter? All propped herself up out of the radiant muck using her elbows, readying herself to exit the pit on her own accord. In actuality, she remained flat on her back. The fall—well, the landing—was much worse than she would ever admit. She could move her fingers and even her hands to an extent but this hardly improved her situation or her mood.

This is the point at which a normal person—even a person with a half-dozen extra eyes and nearly translucent, olive-colored skin—would begin to panic. This was, without any hyperbole, a dire situation. Only an individual of remarkable bravery and fortitude would remain calm in such a terrible spot.

The Mistress wasn't normal, nor was she particularly strong minded. She was, however, utterly blameless. Once she was out of the pit she'd catch Avery, obviously, then have a few words with her daughters. The chaos wrought by their ineptitude had initially served as an amusing distraction, however, they had clearly allowed things to go unchecked for too long. This was all their fault.

"Dahlia!" she called, though it wasn't so much as a beckon as it was an accusation.

Dahlia had never been a difficult person to read as she only seemed to have a handful of basic moods that left no room for ambivalence. So, for example, if she was happy but suddenly encountered something unpleasant she would pause for a moment as if first having to shut down her joyous feelings before cold booting her anger. This is precisely what happened when she heard her mother call her.

"Dahlia!"

Her body jerked, successfully making the transition from confusion to determination. "I'm going!" she yelled, turning to face the open gate. "I'll get him back!"

A sudden, violent wind spun her back around. The pit had vanished, the bright orange light was snuffed out by a great brown blur. The Truth had returned.

The Mistress, too, witnessed this peculiar happenstance. However, seeing as how she was on the receiving end of the Truth she had little time to fully appreciate what was happening. She closed her eyes, took a deep breath, and disappeared.

The Truth landed with all the grace, elegance, and precision one would expect from a failed rocket launch. The earth shook, rattling chains and sending cages and dumpy protagonists crashing to the floor.

Soon the shaking degraded into a rumble and finally a gentle tremble as the Truth settled against the pit's upper walls. All was quiet, save for the sound of hooves slowly tapping against crumbling brickwork. The sound grew almost unbearably loud and then faded entirely. All was quiet once more.

"What am I supposed to do now?" Dahlia asked, fully expecting a response. When none came, she asked again. And again. And again. She continued to ask the same question, her desperation rapidly forming a bubble of frustration that burst into elated revelation.

"You can't stop me," she said first as a question and then as a declaration. As if on cue, the Truth shifted within the pit. It was a slight shift, however, given that the Truth was essentially a skyscraper that fell victim to a mad eco urban experiment even the slightest movement meant an unsettling amount of rumbling and shaking. Dahlia, unfazed, waited for the brambly tower to settle before quietly adding, "She's dead."

Lree arose from the grassy floor startled, confused, and tingling ever so slightly. Her eyes were fixated on whatever her head had pointed them towards. After a moment she began to pat herself down from the top of her head to the tops of her toes.

She was fine. Her wrenched arm, her stinging hand hole, her crisped ankle—all fine.

This was of course very curious but, at the moment, Lree didn't care. She quickly determined that she was alive enough and as no one was around to dispute her diagnosis or at least offer a second opinion she could get on with her business.

Business, she thought. Right. The bone and the…wait. Where was the bone? A panic unlike any other seized Lree but, just as quickly as it had come on, the discovery of the large bit of Jones beside her quelled that particular sense of unease instantly. This was good as it made room for an entirely different sense of unease—one that hung heavily around Fortune.

She stood up, lowered her goggles, and began walking towards the base of the great tree. So determined was Lree that she didn't bother to dust herself off or even realize that there was next to nothing on her person that needed to be dusted. Even the tingling sensation fell to the wayside or would have had she not already forgotten all about it. Her focus—her drive—was on Fortune. Specifically, what laid within.

As she had done before Lree maneuvered her way around the massive trunk climbing over and sometimes under its docile roots. When she reached the gated hollow she readied her leg. Jones's leg. She readied the leg that belonged to Jones but was currently in her possession. Happy now? This is a big, dramatic moment leading up to a particularly wild action scene and you completely ruin the mood with your pedantic quibbling.

No, you know what? I'm not going to do it. I'm not going to tell you about the half-dozen roots that burst through the ground and lunge towards Lree. The ensuing battle—Lree fending off these monstrous roots using Jones's leg—will be left to your imagination. It was really brilliant, too. There was this one bit where she swings the femur like a baseball bat, repelling and eventually disintegrating a number of roots attacking her from opposing directions. There were acrobatics and crazy swordplay, err, boneplay and a big explosion at the end—it was all immensely satisfying. But you missed it because you just couldn't quiet your inner-editor for one second and not because I'm so damned tired and want to go to bed at a normal time for once. This is all on you.

Wiping sweat and shrapnel from her brow after such an exciting action sequence, Lree turned to the gated hollow once more. There was no pause for reflection, no moment of doubt, no conflicted hesitation for dramatic effect. Using what little strength she had left, she hefted the oversized femur above her head with both hands and brought it down upon the rooted gate. Like the assaultive roots before, the wooden latticework cracked and crumbled into dust. With a few more heavy strikes the gate was open and the dark hollow was now assailable. Lree lifted her cracked goggles onto her forehead and stepped into the cavity.

The very first thing she encountered was a wall. This was quickly followed by feelings of disappointment and frustration, neither of which she felt obligated to keep to herself. Hurtful words like "damn," "stupid," and "liar" echoed throughout the hollow accompanied by the thumping of a tiny but exceptionally angry fist against the wooden wall.

She lied. Mother lied. Of course she did. No doubt she was looking down from her study and laughing.

"Stupid," she said rather weakly. She was so, so stupid. Her mother was stupid. Her dream was stupid. Everything. Everything was stupid. A sudden sting upon her cheeks suggested that she might have been crying.

"Hello?" asked a deeply aphonic voice.

Lree's gentle sobs came to an abrupt end. Quickly, she wiped the tears from her cheeks and snot from her nose using virtually every part of her arm. She hadn't imagined it. Someone *had* called out to her, just as they were calling out to her now.

"Hello?" she said first in a uncertain whisper and then again with a bit more aggression. Her call was answered by a faint light cast deep from within the darkness. Lree placed her free hand upon the wall and slowly, steadily, made her way towards the light, wherever it might have been coming from. As she advanced deeper and deeper into the wooden burrow she realized that she was being led along a wide spiral, the end of which was imbued in an unsettling, emerald glow. Bunches of luminescent mushrooms of all different sizes littered the floor, leading the young girl down another path and into the heart of the great tree.

She wasn't entirely prepared for what she might encounter around the final corner of the winding passageway but, in all fairness, she wasn't entirely prepared for pretty much every encounter she's ever had so she entered the brightly lit chamber with an expression that said "I really don't care." This was to change rather quickly.

There, in a recess at the end of the tiny chamber, was a most peculiar relief carved from the tree itself. It was a woman—or part of one, it seemed—resting against what appeared to be another, much smaller trunk. There didn't seem to be much consistency in its detail, though. For example, one of her arms was immaculately sculpted from her shoulder down to her elbow, featuring a dark wood so finely polished that it could easily be mistaken for flesh. Beyond that, however, lay a gnarled, vaguely arm-shaped root with no hand or fingers to speak of. Much of her lower half was the same, with legs that faded in and out of the surrounding wood. It was as if the woman hadn't been sculpted from the tree but had been consumed by it.

A torrent of discomfort overtook Lree, causing her to drop Jone's femur and, as a result, significantly darken the chamber by snuffing out a large patch of luminous fungi. It was hot—and getting hotter still—yet she couldn't stop shivering. She shut her eyes hard and turned her head hoping that when she were to look upon the relief again that it would be gone.

Lree opened her eyes and, to her surprise, saw nothing. It was darker now, the atmosphere having been altered from eerie to downright frightful, so it took a moment for her vision to adjust. The sculpture of the ensnared woman was different. Smaller. The image seemed to have been replaced with that of a young girl. A young girl with one and a half ears and deeply dark ochre skin marred by countless cuts, scrapes, and bruises.

Again, Lree shut her eyes. After a much longer wait she reopened them to the sight of the original relief. And despite her mind pleading with her to turn and run away she found herself inexplicably walking towards the tormented and tormenting sculpture.

Even in such poor lighting it was impossible to find the detail of the relief anything but exquisite. The artist had managed to express so much through the woman's body language. Her head hung low as if she had just fallen asleep, her long hair flowing over her face and onto her chest where the sculpture took on a particularly disturbing tone.

Lree caught a gleam cast from the shadows that had overtaken the piece. She crept in closer still to discover the gleam's source: a hilt from a small sword or unnecessarily large dagger. The fact that it was made of steel and not wood was almost as strange as the fact that it was jutting out from the woman's left breast.

"The heart," Lree whispered.

"Was it you?" asked the relief of the woman, raising her head. This action was accompanied by a small symphony of ear-splitting creaks and squeals. Lree didn't respond. Not to the horrific sounds nor to the question from the equally horrific sculpture.

"There was," the woman began, only to trail off into an endless repetition of "Is someone theres?", "Please, say somethings," and "Why have you comes?"

"Shut it," Lree said, backing up from the relief slightly. "Please. You're as bad as that idiot. All you do is ask and ask and..." Slowly the realization that she was talking to a relief—or indeed that a relief was talking to her—diminished her annoyance enough to allow astonishment to properly take over. "What are you?" she asked.

"I am..." said the relief, pausing momentarily to look over at her arms and down at her legs, as if assessing her condition. With every movement came a pained expression from both the relief and Lree. "I am not sure. What do you think I am? Why...why have you come? Please. Please, why..."

"A-Ah don't know," Lree stammered. "Ah do know. Ah mean, Ah'm here to make a wish."

"A...wish?"

"With the heart of the tree. Fortune's heart."

The woman's eyes grew wide as she cocked her head at an unimaginably uncomfortable angle. "Fortune's...heart. Fortune. Of course. Fortune."

"Yes," Lree said, wishing the woman would return her head to a more natural position for a head to be. "Fortune's heart. You see Ah need the heart to make my wish."

"I had forgotten," said the woman, possibly ignoring but definitely annoying Lree. "That was...she...my name is Fortune. I am Fortune."

Uncertain and exhausted, Lree simply replied with, "Hello."

"Hello."

The two stared at one another well beyond the amount of time necessary to become awkward, at least for Lree. And it's not that Fortune hadn't noticed. She was becoming more and more aware with each passing breath.

"You said a wish? Tell me, child, what is it that you wish for?" she finally said.

Lree was so shocked by the clarity and bluntness of the question that she momentarily forgot the answer. "Ah wish," she said, looking at the ground for inspiration or at the very least a clue. Surprisingly, she found both.

"Dirt and dust," she said. "Ah want it gone. All gone. Ah want this place turned to dirt and dust. Ah want to end it. It has to end."

Fortune rolled her head in order to look Lree in the eyes. "And why would you say that?" she asked. "Why must it end?"

"Because," Lree said, offended and not afraid to show it, "this place is a cage! Ah escape and come back, escape and come back."

"You escape?"

"Yeah."

"And then come back?"

"Yeah, look, is there anyone else Ah can talk to?"

"No. If you can escape, child, why would you come back?"

Lree sighed heavily. "You don't know what it's like out there. Here it's…it's not much better but Ah know how to take care of myself. Ah know where to hide. Ah know that mother…"

"Mother?"

"Mother," continued Lree, slowly, "will protect me."

"In your cage, yes?"

"In my cage."

There was another round of silence, though this time significantly less awkward. It was more of a sad, thoughtful silence that suggested empathy instead of uncertainty. Eventually, Fortune asked, "What is your name, child?"

"What? Lree."

A small but no less notable wooden tumor formed around the bottom of Fortune's left eye, stretching itself thin along her cheek until reaching the corner of her very large smile. "You're right, Lree," she said, "this has to end."

THIRTY THREE
Heartbroken

"This a trick?" Lree asked, leaning over to grasp the hilt that protruded from Fortune's chest. The young girl had positioned herself somewhat above the tragic relief using what was left of her arms as footing.

Fortune looked up at Lree with a disarmingly genuine smile. "It's not a trick, child," she said, then quickly added, "But I'm not sure what will happen afterwards."

Lree straightened herself up. "What do you mean you're not sure? You said you were going to grant me my wish."

"How long has it been, child?" asked Fortune, her tone shifting suddenly to something more akin to fear than curiosity. "How many have come? How many…"

Not this again. "Fortune!" Lree barked, seemingly snapping the wooden sculpture out of her trance.

"Yes," she said. "I will. Yours and mine. Are you prepared?"

Lree nodded though the question wasn't entirely directed towards her. This familiar, dark-skinned girl—bold, brave, and belligerent—was offering her finality. Finality or perhaps something more.

Fortune could feel her mind returning to her, expanding her rationale and memory exponentially with every beat of her burdened heart. The perilous pits of La'lapu La'fala, the perplexing pillar peculiarly positioned in the piazza, the petulant person who had pinned her to the prideful pendula—it was as if an aggressively alliterative wind had blown through her hoary hollow, hewing a hole through the haze that hung like a hood over her head for so, so long. She was cognizant—and there was much to do.

"How?" was an obvious question. There was no denying that she hadn't been feeling altogether well as of late, what with her turning into a tree and all. While she couldn't exactly get up and leave this very instant it wouldn't be completely irrational to think that, eventually, she might. With Avery's help.

Oh, Avery. She seemed so hurt. That's okay, she thought, she would make it up to her somehow. Some flowers or maybe a book—she was very easy to please. Yes, that would do. Everything was going to be fine.

"I've decided…"

"Donk," said Lree as she yanked hard on the hilt. The blade came out about an inch before getting caught on something within Fortune's chest. Fortune said something along the lines of "HURK!" or "HARG!"

Lree pulled on the silvery hilt again and again, a loud cracking sound following every attempt. Finally, Fortune's wooden chest splintered to reveal a deeply violet mass stuck to the end of the long blade. Lree pulled once more, ripping the sickening wad of decayed muscle and rotten wood—the heart—from Fortune's newly hollowed chest.

Still, the prize was not quite hers. Dozens of tiny tendrils held onto the still-beating heart and actually seemed to be drawing it back. No matter how hard Lree pulled she couldn't quite free the sinewy muscle of the nasty little roots. She dropped to the ground and began walking backwards, stretching the tendrils beyond their limits until they either slipped out of the heart or snapped.

A number of alarming things began to happen in rather quick succession once the final tendril was severed. The heart stopped beating and, almost immediately afterwards, Fortune appeared to wither. This was followed by a cacophonic bombardment of creaks and cracks loud enough to rattle the remaining of Lree's viciously pointed teeth. This clamorous assault was accompanied by a quake that leveled the majority of Fortune's niche, otherwise trapping Lree were it not for the fact that she had already fled from the alcove with the heart before it had been completely severed.

Lree dashed out of the hollow and into a blinding beam of light. Unable to reduce her momentum, she crashed into the frame of the broken gate and fell onto her side. The heart, cradled in her arms, remained undamaged.

The blazing light beam moved on but was succeeded by dozens more, blinking in and out of existence like a strobe light in a trailer full of angry wildebeests. Lree lifted her goggles and, through a pained squint, looked skyward. The extraordinarily dense, nigh-impenetrable dome of branches that kept Love's Lost in iniquitous darkness was failing. Fortune, it seemed, was dying and it was the most beautiful thing Lree had ever seen.

As moving as this moment was she was hardly in a position to reflect on her accomplishment or even pat herself on the back for a job well done. Fortune, as previously stated, was dying and the young girl was still hundreds of feet up in the air. All congratulatory back patting would have to wait until she had safely returned to the ground.

She could, she thought, allow the whole problem of getting safely out of the tree work itself out by losing consciousness again. There was no denying just how terrifically successful that strategy had been. She was almost fortuitous in her rotten luck.

Lree watched on as one of the monstrously large branches above her snapped, hurtling a particularly long leafy outgrowth towards the resort's lavish hospitality district. In mere moments, high-priced hotels, over-priced bodegas, and irresponsibly-priced brothels were flattened like a dairy cow that had slipped through the fencing and wandered onto a neutron star.

The rumbling beneath her was intensifying and she was pretty sure the ground—the mountain that held Fortune aloft—was disintegrating. Unknown to Lree, matters were worsening as the colony of regrettably named wooden tendrils that held the mountain on which Fortune stood was also disintegrating. This caused the gigantic rock to teeter slightly, sending Lree rolling into Fortune's rapidly crumbling roots. It soon became clear that the problem of returning safely to the ground had grown tired of her indecision and, indeed, worked itself out.

If she was going to do something, she thought as she picked herself up, it would have to be done now. She gave her predicament a quick look. Fortune's branches continued to fall, basking Love's Lost in a horrific mix of bright light and calamitous destruction. They fell every which way; some descending straight down at sharp angles, others swinging about wildly as they caught themselves on neighboring branches, and a very select few were falling broadside to Fortune's base. It was on one such branch that Lree suddenly found herself riding down.

The mountain split with an ear-piercing crack, exposing much of Fortune's complex root system while consequently sending an assortment of boulders hurtling towards the pavilion below. Lree failed to notice as her attention had been focused not on what was happening or what had just happened but what might happen. She didn't think or plan, she simply acted.

As the branch began to lurch to one side she righted her position by scrambling to the other. When it became impossible to maintain her footing any longer she leapt into the shattered sky and onto a flailing root. The root hardly had enough time to notice Lree's presence as the young girl had almost immediately leapt onto a passing branch. And as this branch was falling towards the ground at a much more rapid pace it wasn't long before she leapt off of it and onto something equally precarious and only barely safe.

There wasn't much logic to Lree's actions. She had managed to escape Fortune's plateau but she was still falling at a disconcerting speed. Her movements were largely lateral, leading her further and further away from Fortune. Not that she had noticed this, of course. Driven solely by instinct, she would continue to jump from limb to limb until she and the clutched heart reached solid ground. The thought that her means to reach solid ground would almost assuredly result in a gruesome death hadn't occurred to her.

And so she continued to aimlessly bound from one falling branch to another. Lree's mind, which had deliberately gone comatose in a desperate attempt to protect the girl's sanity, was jarred awake by a terribly rough landing. As it fell back into a comforting, ignorant haze it noticed something that could possibly get both it and Lree safely out of this disaster.

"Truth!" it yelled. It then fell silent.

This brief mental outburst stopped her from leaping onto yet another precarious branch. Unfortunately, it also left her clinging onto a precarious branch that had just been knocked into a rapid spin. She held on tightly with her free hand but the increasing momentum proved too much for her exhausted body. Her grip failed and Lree was flung from the branch and into a wall of hard, familiar, and inert brambles.

Without pause, Lree made her way down the barbed lattice that enveloped the Truth. Occasionally a branch or rock or gigantic boulder would bounce off of the column but these occurrences went largely unnoticed by the young girl. The only thing that seemed to matter was moving her body down. She didn't think about why she needed do this or even how much longer she would be able to do this which, by pure coincidence, would be until about now—just a few feet above the ground.

Lree landed on her back with a muffled thud. Planted firmly in a shallow hole of loose dirt and rubble, all she could do was stare up at the chaotic scene unfolding above her. None of it seemed to make any sort of sense despite being precisely what she had wanted. She felt tired. Tired and aching. Tired, aching, and utterly satisfied with herself. She had Fortune's heart, Love's Lost was in ruin (or at least in the process of being ruined), and great swaths of sunlight were busy eating away at the darkness that had both protected and persecuted her for so very long.

She had gotten her wish and it felt good. Or it didn't. It didn't feel good at all. It didn't feel bad, either. It felt...hollow. Whatever satisfaction she had experienced had quickly dissipated, leaving behind an almost overwhelming sense of emptiness.

"Right," she muttered. "What now?"

An answer, though not necessarily her answer, came in the form of heavy footsteps, creaking joints, and an inexplicable feeling of terror and disgust. Slowly, painfully, Lree rose to her feet, turning to face the gargantuan creature that had inexplicably helped grant her wish. Jones had replaced their missing femur with the remains of a lamp post, allowing them once again to stand in that unsettling way that made it seem as if they were busy falling onto you. This would be bad enough were Jones not a heaping pile of refuse and horror. Being as such, however, encouraged most people to grant the monster an enormously wide girth. Say, twenty or thirty miles.

Suffice to say, Lree was not most people. She raised her goggles with one hand and held up the oozing heart with the other. "Here," she said. "Ah got it. It's yours."

Without hesitation, Jones snatched the heart from the girl's hand and lifted it to eye-level. For a moment—despite the symphony of panic and destruction that surrounded them—all was silent.

"So," Lree began as she stood up.

Jones tightened their grip into a fist, squeezing the heart until it popped like a balloon filled with chunky tomato soup long past its expiration date. If you happen to enjoy chunky tomato soup I apologize since you will no longer be able to eat it without thinking about violet chunks of fetid organic matter dripping off near-fossilized bone. Oh, and the sound—bursting like a basketball-sized pustule pinched between the skin folds of a man made entirely of mayonnaise.

Try not to think about it.

Lree tried to wipe the gooey remnants of the heart off of her face and chest. "What?" she said, clearly surprised.

"What?!" she said again, clearly more agitated than surprised. "Do 'ya know what Ah went through to get that hunk of meat for ya?!"

Jones loosened their grip to allow the silver dagger and the sticky remnants of Fortune's heart to slowly slurp towards the ground, eventually landing with a series of sickening splats. They then turned around and began walking away, pausing briefly to wipe their hand clean against a fallen branch. Said branch turned to ash as a result.

"Y-you," Lree called. "You can't just—Ah—get back here!"

Jones did no such thing.

"Here! Right now!" she added, raising her voice as if scolding a child that had just made away with an ill-gotten treat from the cookie jar. In the child's defense, it is a stunningly arrogant move on the parent's part for placing a playfully sculpted jar full of seductive, sugary snacks in plain sight and expect the child—the same little proletariat you routinely force broccoli, carrots, and other inedible forms of vegetation upon—to have the willpower necessary to not steal a tiny taste of the bourgeoisie in the form of peanut butter chocolate chip.

Lree stared at Jones for a moment before continuing her angry diatribe. "Go! Go on!" she yelled, changing her message. "Yeah, that's right, go!" This was followed by an assortment of muttered words describing her displeasure with the creature, including "stupid," "selfish," "useless," and something that sounded a lot like "brass pole?"

She shut her eyes and took in a deep breath through her bloodied and potentially broken nose. This resulted in a fair amount of pain—and oh, had the pain returned. She released her breath quickly and violently. It took longer than it should have to regulate her breathing but eventually she devised a short, shallow rhythm that wasn't entirely unbearable.

She stood there—in the remains of the pavilion—barely breathing. And watching—watching her world literally and figuratively fall apart. The shell that had once protected her, imprisoned her, had been cracked and its cold, familiar darkness had been nearly obliterated.

A warm light fell onto Lree's face and she smiled. It was a weak smile—perhaps a bit more of a pained grimace, really—but a positive sign nonetheless. "Ah should be going," she said to anyone who might have been listening.

Unfortunately, there was someone listening and they disagreed not so much in words but rather by throwing a fist-shaped boulder into her face. If her nose hadn't been broken before, it most assuredly was now.

Strangely enough, Lree's smile remained even as her limp body spun helplessly into the ground. Her expression only seemed to change when she heard Dahlia say, "Like I've told you before, little flower: you're going to die here."

THIRTY FOUR
Loose Threads

Avery trotted through the crumbling corridor with less enthusiasm and purpose than he had the previous crumbling corridor and significantly less than the crumbling corridor before that, now not so much crumbling but adequately crumbled. He had finally managed to open the abattoir's gate and where did it lead? To confusion and resentment, that's where.

Let's say, for fun, that the next dilapidating hallway actually led to an exit. A real exit, one beyond the hedge maze and outside of Love's Lost. Then what? Go hang out with Khauphase or Lupus back in the Garden? And damn it, why could he remember their names? He couldn't remember a single one of his professors and more often than not what classes they were teaching but the name of that jiggling blob that set him on fire? That guy in the booth that voluntarily sung a song about himself? Yeah, those are things worth remembering as they will certainly serve some grander purpose later in life.

Now almost completely absorbed with the idea of getting a sweet-smelling garbage shack with Khauphase—and how that really didn't sound all the bad—Avery failed to notice the legion of diminutive, dour-faced creatures rapidly approaching him from the other side of the corridor. As they were quite adept at navigating around lumbering louts, oafs, lummoxes, and buffoons, they slipped by Avery with ease. All but one.

Everyone had agreed that while fleeing in terror as the complex fell around them was absolutely essential to their continued survival so was securing a steady flow of lucre. The labs below Love's Lost presented the means to such security.

They had all drawn straws to see who would be the one to carry all of the ill-gotten goods out of Love's Lost and he happened to draw the shortest. At least, that's what everyone told him. They hadn't actually shown him their straws or anything. Well, whatever. They were a swell bunch of guys and no doubt would be grateful for his hard work. They'd probably buy him a drink or surprise him with a gift basket. Wouldn't that be nice. A gift basket. Maybe with some gourmet chocolate or a body scrub or yeah, something like that. Coupons.

Coupons would be fine, too. If you're gonna spend the lucre you might as well be smart about it, right?

Confidence sufficiently renewed, the creature upped his pace from drunken snail to headless chicken. He held no less than half a dozen bags—each nearly as tall as he—in front of him. They were heavy and awkward, wantonly stuffed with possibly essential and definitely profitable laboratory equipment, chemicals, and who knows what else.

It was inevitable that these two forces—Avery and the overburdened shy guy—would meet in a spectacular collision. Silvery metal instruments clanged, delicate glass tubes shattered, and caustic chemicals splashed onto the brickwork of the narrow hallway. Scores of syringes, charged with glowing green liquid, blanketed the area like a New Jersey beach. Neither Avery or the little gray ghost were injured beyond a couple of scraped knees and a torn sheet.

He wasn't exactly sure who or what he had run into but felt it necessary to apologize regardless. Still on the ground with his head down, Avery clumsily turned around and said, "Sorry," to a pair of cloven hooves. A soft hand gently cupped his chin, lifting his head until he came eye to eye with Pentas.

"Hello, Avery," she said.

Avery wanted more than anything to run away. Almost more than anything. If we're being honest he wanted to stay more than anything. I suppose I should have lead in with that instead.

"Sorry," he said again. Pentas's lack of immediate response sent Avery into a panic. Did she hear him? Oh no, what if she misunderstood him?

"I was thinking about shooting a text to a guy called Cowface," he explained as calmly as a knife-wielding man discovered at a murder scene would. "Did I...did I tell you about him? He doesn't really have a cow face, that's just what he calls himself. The thing is I never got his number. Not that I have my phone on me. Even if I did, I doubt I'd have service wherever this is so—hey, you've got a big ass needle there."

Pentas looked down and discovered that, as Avery had pointed out, she was holding a needle. Unfortunately her inexperience with Avery's colorful vernacular made it difficult to determine whether or not it was, indeed, big ass. She didn't remember picking it up which was certainly enough to spark a raging wildfire of concern had she any interest in doing so.

"What will you do?" she asked plainly, ignoring the big ass needle in her hand.

"Nothing, I guess. Just like always."

With a fair amount of struggle Avery brought himself to his feet only to step back onto one of the many, many syringes that littered the room. He returned to the cold, cobblestone floor with a thunk, a crack, and a brief but no less significant burst of discomfort.

"Damn it," he hissed, cradling his head. He continued to whisper curses and hold his oft-abused skull. The pain had faded yet the tears wouldn't stop. "I tried, you know. I really, really did. Or, I mean, I was...going to."

Avery, face red, wet, and filthy, looked up at Pentas. "I wanted to."

"What did you want to do?"

"I don't know," he sighed, his eyes returning to the floor. "Go out, make friends, find a, uh, someone. A life, you know? A new one. One that I liked."

Pentas, who was now examining the syringe with an unsettling amount of interest, smiled. Barely. "A new life," she said. "Curious. What would you do with the old one?"

"That's kind of a weird question," Avery thought aloud. Realizing this he apologized and added, "Forget it, erase it. Whatever."

"Do you think you could?"

"What?"

"Forget it. Your old life, as you put it. Could you forget it?"

"Sure," Avery said. The conversation—the act of having an actual conversation with another person, that is—emboldened him to the point of being able to stand once more. "Well, maybe not completely," he continued, "but if my new life was awesome enough then I'd forget all about the bad stuff, right?"

Pentas drew in closer—not so much as to be intimate but certainly more than enough to make Avery feel less emboldened. "But how would you know that the life you were to live would be better if you could not remember the poorer life that you had lived?"

Avery took a careful step backwards, unintentionally placing his back flatly against the wall. Pentas pursued with near fevered concern. "I," he began. He repeated it a few more times until Pentas backed off slightly.

"Would you know?" she asked with what could easily be mistaken as anxiousness.

"I don't...I...would it matter? Look, I'm...okay, I should probably tell you something. I may have overstated, uh, myself."

Avery rubbed his temple and sighed heavily. "I've got nothing," he said, "and I mean nothing really going for me other than my great hair and good looks. My life is, like, bottom of the barrel. Anything different would have to be better. You know, by default."

"Even if anything meant nothing?" It's important to note that this was said after Pentas raised the syringe to her face and rested her cheek upon the terrifying instrument.

Whatever the future may hold for Avery it would invariably be marred by his response. In dreams yet to be and moments of quiet reflection he would recall this specific scene beneath Love's Lost with fear, loathing, and deep, deep regret.

"Probably," he said, shifting slightly to the side in what he thought was a subtle move to place a greater distance between himself and the lovely yet still needle-wielding woman before him.

Pentas reacted instantly, pinning the boy to the wall with her free hand and extraordinary presence. "The irony," she almost laughed, "is that *you* have given me everything I have ever wanted."

"I don't really see the irony in that," Avery replied, unable to keep his eyes off the needle growing ever closer to his pillowy body.

"I tried to kill you before, did you know that? Twice. When I realized I could not I provoked my sisters into doing it for me."

For Avery, this revelation was a bit shocking but mostly disappointing. After all, were he to die right here with a big ass needle sticking out of his forehead he couldn't do so while taking solace in the fact that his life was so boring it wasn't even worth ending. The best he could hope for now was that at least it wasn't worth ending thrice but even this was questionable.

"I was almost relieved when that plan had also failed."

"Right?" Avery said, shrugging his shoulders. He wasn't exactly sure how he was expected to respond to someone proclaiming relief to not having him murdered but "being in agreement with" was probably wrong.

Pentas stared hard at the blubbery blubbering mess before her. It was true, wasn't it? After all, it was she who placed Avery in a cage with a creature capable of breaking it open. And it was she who allowed Avery to unlock the main gate to the Nest and escape.

"Right," she said. In one swift motion she raised the syringe into the air and brought it down hard, jabbing the needle into her thigh. She released her grip on Avery and struggled to depress the plunger. The pleasant expression that masked her face shattered into one of anguish. Teeth clenched, she hissed violently as she tried to catch her breath.

It was she who placed Avery in a cage with a creature that should have killed him. And it was she who allowed Avery to believe he had unlocked the main gate to the Nest.

"I never," she tried to say, only to succumb to a sudden wave of immense pain. "I...don't like you," she managed to say.

Avery didn't ask why she didn't like him or why she had done this terrible thing to herself. He also failed to ask if she was okay or if it hurt at all, which were the sort of thoughtless questions we'd expect Avery to ask in such a situation.

Expectations, however, are not guaranteed.

Avery found himself unable to do anything other than try to catch Pentas as she collapsed. She was, in fact, quite heavy and fell fast, dragging Avery along with her. Her legs—those weird, weird legs—coalesced into a mass of grass and dirt. Her arms grew thinner and greener until they, too, began to break down into sod and a soil.

She had seen an opportunity—*the* opportunity—and seized it. She had unlocked the gate for Avery, but only after she let him unwittingly activate the Reconciliation.

Pentas looked up at the strange boy from the mysterious land of Pataskala and frowned. There had been so many schemes, so many lies, so many betrayals. All to rid herself of that which she had become: the Mistress of Love's Lost.

"When you see...," she breathed. "...see...s-say hello..."

She closed her eyes and seemed to smile just as a batch of pointed flowers began to overtake her face. What remained of her body was quickly replaced by a myriad of rich crimson and violet flora.

Avery, covered in dirt and flower petals, sitting in a dungeon filled with needles and broken glass, said the only thing he could possibly think of to say.

Fortunately, no one was around to hear him say it.

It had become a familiar feeling—laying face-first deep within the grass, dirt, and debris of what was once a quite lively party—but it should come as no great surprise that this brought Lree no sense of relief or comfort. Nor did the presence of her older and significantly more violent sister, now looming over her like a volcano with a grudge.

"You really are stupid," Dahlia growled, lifting Lree partially up off the ground by the arm. Lree didn't move. More accurately, she couldn't move. This somehow angered Dahlia further.

"Stupid," she repeated, yanking Lree into the air in order to stare her down. "And predictable. You could have run, you know."

Lree could hear her sister speak but she couldn't understand what she was saying. Not that it mattered, really. Given her current position and the fact that her sister was on fire made it pretty clear that she was upset and therefore anything she had to say was more than likely unpleasant.

"But like the coward you are...the frightened little...coward...you're still here. You're still hiding here."

"Look!" she yelled, thrusting Lree skyward to help illustrate her point. "There's nothing left! You destroyed it all! My home, mother—all gone!"

"Ah...I...Ah didn't," Lree said. Her words seemed to fall out of her mouth on their own. What was that about mother?

A large portion of Dahlia's arm cracked, releasing a stream of molten rock down onto her upper body. "Say it!" she hissed. "Oh, I want you to say it. Say you didn't do it."

Lree had only two choices. She could do as Dahlia asked and say that she didn't do it which would almost definitely result in being thrown across the pavilion. Alternatively, she could say that she did do it which would almost definitely result in being thrown across the pavilion. At this point it didn't really matter that she didn't know what she was supposed to have or have not done. She was going to be thrown across the pavilion regardless.

"Ah," Lree began.

"Shut it!" her sister screamed. Then she threw Lree across the pavilion. The force of the throw combined with Lree's own waifish physique might have actually allowed her to continue sailing beyond the grounds of the gala and into the remains of the Mall had she not collided with one of Fortune's many fallen branches.

Displeased with having to walk all the way across the pavilion in order to torment her sister, Dahlia released a disgruntled "Tch!" Still, it had felt pretty good flinging her like that. It probably hurt, too. Not just the collision with the branch, but simply being held—her hands were red hot, after all—should have caused her a considerable amount of pain. That made Dahlia smile or at least manipulate her rocky facial structure to approximate an expression that could be interpreted as either personal satisfaction or having just soiled oneself. Or possibly both.

Dahlia would have been perturbed—that is to say incensed to the point of murder—to discover that Lree wasn't in pain. She was obviously injured, however, she seemed almost ignorant of the cumulative abuse her lithe body had incurred. This was made abundantly clear when she quickly popped up from the ground to face her blazing sister.

"You're better off dead!" Lree thought she heard her sister yell. The continued aerial deconstruction of Love's Lost made it terribly difficult to hear much of anything aside from crunches, bangs, and kabooms and from this distance all she could see was a bright yellow ball of light.

Lree unsheathed her curiously enchanted dagger from wherever it had been sheathed, confident that her sister really meant to kill her. She quickly spun the handle so that the blade was facing the bright yellow ball of light, now significantly brighter, bigger, and most likely angrier. Of course, she knew it wouldn't matter. No blade could penetrate whatever the hell passed for Dahlia's skin. And truth be told the sight of her waving the pert dagger around menacingly would probably amuse Dahlia more so than it would threaten her.

Lree tightened her grip on her strange, glowing weapon and trained it on what she assumed to be her sister. The faint, violet flame that had always enveloped the blade seemed to react to its target, igniting into a raging inferno. Lree dropped the dagger, shut her eyes, and threw her arms in front of her face in a flash.

Perhaps if we knew the details surrounding Lree's mysterious knife we'd understand why it suddenly exploded. Perhaps we'd also understand why, despite her arms being covered in flames from the afore mentioned explosion, Lree was largely unharmed. If it's any consolation, Lree, too, lacks such understanding which is why it's even more baffling that right now—exhausted, battered, and aflame—she believed that she could defeat her sister.

"Do you really believe you have any chance of defeating me?" asked Dahlia, clearly having skipped over the previous paragraph. "Look at you—you're a mess. Do you even realize you're on fire?"

"Ah dunno," said Lree trying very, very hard to focus on her sister, "Do you?"

"Is that it? Is that the best comeback you've got?"

Lree smiled. "Good enough for you."

This brought Dahlia's slow but threatening approach to a brief halt. "Mother's dead," she said coolly.

"Yeah?"

"Yeah."

"She can't protect you anymore."

"Ah never needed her protection."

A large portion of Dahlia's chest cracked and crumbled to the ground, releasing a mass of molten flesh and tendrils. Lree was unfazed.

"Yeah, you think that but you have. You did."

"From me," she added.

Lree was now a little less unfazed than she had been.

"Pentas won't..."

"Pentas won't know. Do you feel her? Do you hear her? She's not here. Face it, little flower, you're alone," Dahlia said, charging her sister once more, "and now you're dead."

Fear, despair, regret—something gripped Lree deep inside, paralyzing her. Dahlia was still a distance away yet it was as if she were right on top of her, crushing her.

"No!" she screamed, her curious flames now dancing all around her. And with that, she ran towards her sister. Dahlia leapt high in the air, poised to run her volcanic fist through Lree's tiny, fragile skull. Lree, in turn, leapt into Dahlia, despite knowing full well it would be like trying to use a spitball to stop a fat man from cannonballing into the shallow end of a public swimming pool. Fortunate for Lree, she didn't know what any of that meant.

The two sisters clashed. There was a sound—a terrible, unsettling sound like that of tearing flesh—and Lree pushed her sister to the ground.

"I'll kill you!" Dahlia cried, thrashing about. Lree, straddling her sister, pinning her to the pavilion, raised her fist and did nothing.

"Dahlia?" she whispered.

"Get off of me!" Dahlia—or someone who sort of looked like Dahlia—screamed. It was Dahlia, wasn't it? Her body was less bulky and completely devoid of its terrifying geological properties. Her face was smooth, almost unnaturally so, with many features flattened like those of a dragon's. She still had her horns, however, they were now perfectly symmetrical.

She was also on fire, which for Dahlia wasn't out of character. It was, however, a cool, violet fire that didn't so much burn as it did radiate.

Lree looked behind her and, despite seeing exactly what she thought she might see, twitched. There, crouching just a couple of yards away, was Dahlia. Or, more precisely, Dahlia's body.

"Ah," Lree began, quickly turning her attention back to the increasingly translucent person beneath her. "Ah'm..."

"What...what did you do to me?!" Dahlia yelled. She had managed to loosen one of her arms and took a swing at her sister, only to have her fist pass through Lree and then dissolve.

"Ah, Ah didn't! Ah don't," Lree stammered.

Dahlia was now almost completely transparent.

"Dammit!" she said.

"...you..." she said.

"Damn," she said.

The ghostly flames that had enveloped her flickered and then faded into nothing. Dahlia was gone.

Lree stood up and brushed herself off. There were questions—many of which would prove to cause Lree a great deal of angst once answered—but they would have to wait. She was still in Love's Lost which was more dangerous than it ever had been, what with the raging wild fires and gigantic falling branches.

"Ah've gotta go," she probably said to Dahlia's rocky body. As she refused to face the lifeless statue it was difficult to say. Even Lree was uncertain, though this didn't stop her from walking out of the pavilion along a narrow path of decayed earth.

THIRTY FIVE
Daybreak

The laughter and chatter and music had vanished. Curiously, so too had the buildings and that awful, awful hedge maze—all presumably buried beneath a fiery mountain of leaves, limbs, and bramble.

It was a strange scene—certainly well within the top five of the ten strangest things Avery had encountered since waking up in this world—but he couldn't seem to muster up the enthusiasm required to give a care, a crap, a damn, a wing-dang-doodle, or anything else that one might feel inclined to impart when presented with such a spectacular sight. He had been up—more or less—all night. This was not especially odd behavior for Avery, of course, but that was typically done of his own volition. Rarely was it because he was being chased by strange women all with a deep desire to bring harm to his personal being. Oh sure, it sounds quite exciting but from a practical standpoint? Naw.

Morning had come, or so the sunlight led him to believe, and the party was over. Somehow he had managed to navigate the labyrinth of corridors below ground to emerge from a sort of manhole in the middle of a cobblestone pathway a good distance from the burning remains of the resort town. Turning around, half-heartedly, he realized that the path on which he stood lead to a pair of broken gates and beyond that? Who knew.

Avery took a heavy step towards who knew, burdened by thoughts of what he could have done with his life. He asked all kinds of questions, to himself, but never found the answers. He could cry at the top of his voice but no one would listen.

"'Cause you're boring," said a voice from behind.

Avery didn't bother to turn around. The near-crippling sense of despair borne from the remark made it all too obvious who had said it.

"I was trying to be deep, sprout," he grumbled.

"Deep what?" Lree darted around Avery to block his path. "You look terrible," she said with a toothless smile.

"Me? Jesus, have you looked in a mirror? You look like...like you've been crapped out of a shark! What the hell happened to you?"

"Wait," he quickly added, "You know, shut up. Never mind. I don't care just...go. Away."

With what could be mistaken as a thoughtful look, Lree somewhat obliged by moving alongside the one-man pity party. "We're leavin' this place," she said.

Avery resumed his slow shamble. "Good for you."

"Ah'm done with it."

"Uh-huh." He stopped for a moment. "When you say we...?"

"Jones."

"Ah, right," he grunted, resuming his snail-paced escape. Lree, walking sideways, followed along beside him. "Of course they'd be alive. Or...dead but not dead dead. Or whatever."

"Don't you wanna know where Jones is?"

"Not particularly, no."

"Look," she said, pointing far beyond Avery.

Always the first one to drop out of a game of Simon Says, Avery instinctively obeyed Lree's order, turning his head to come face to fleshless face with the forgotten fifth horseman of the apocalypse.

Imagine a banshee singing karaoke through a megaphone while slowly being fed into an industrial mulcher. That is the sound Avery made as he leapt behind Lree who, consequently, found all of this very amusing.

"That was very amusing," she might have said were she an entirely different character. Instead she nearly threw up laughing.

"W-what is wrong with you?!" Avery yelled. "Both of you! That wasn't...that's not..."

"Oh yeah it was," Lree gasped. She took a moment to catch her breath, waving her hand in front of Avery in an effort to delay his response. "That was great. Ah needed that. Oh, Ah needed that so much."

Avery glared at the waifish sprite, reducing her to a red hot pile of goo with his laser vision which he didn't actually have.

"What?" she said. It shouldn't come as a surprise that this was asked rather innocuously.

"If you jerks are done, I've got places to go."

"No you don't," Lree replied curtly.

This was true and everyone knew it. Well, everyone except you, Miss Cindy-Skips-to-the-Last-Chapter. I mean, why? What's the point? Do you walk into a movie five minutes before the credits? What happens if you like what you see? Do you hide under the seats until the next showing begins? Have you ever actually looked at a theater floor? I mean *really* looked at it? It's like a separate plane of existence composed almost entirely of mucilaginous filth and what I hope to god are just Raisinets.

Avery looked away. "S-shut up."

Taking a heavy breath, Lree simply said, "Alright," and beckoned Jones. Together, the odd pair walked away from the flustered young man and towards the broken gate. They had nearly reached the exit when Lree came to a sudden stop.

Just a few more steps, she thought, and she'd be through with this place. She'd be free. Really, really free.

Just a few more steps, she thought, and she could begin her new life—whatever it may be.

First came misery. Misery was followed by discomfort. Discomfort preceded resentment and misery, discomfort, and resentment led to terrifying rage.

She turned to look at her newly gilded companion only to discover that the creature had already passed through the gates. More specifically, they had knocked down and trod over the remainder of the gates. She then turned the other way to look at Avery—with his blue arm, sad face, and oversized man bag—confusing the lyrics of *In Too Deep* with *Another Day in Paradise*. Of course, she didn't actually know that this is what he was doing but even if she had it wouldn't have changed anything.

Probably.

"Hey," she tried to stop herself from calling back. "You coming or what?"

Avery flinched. He then stared back at Lree as if she had just said, "You coming or what?"

"Why?" he asked earnestly.

It was an excellent question and one that she did not have an answer for. At least, an answer that made any sense at that precise moment. "If you wanna stay," she said, "then that's on you. We're gettin' out of here."

Avery looked back at the devastated resort town. He had actually made a decision but it was precisely this decision that made him so disconcerted. He knew that it was the worst decision he would probably ever make. He also knew that it was the right decision.

"This is a load of crap," he said, defeated.

Lree, either satisfied or deeply angered, continued towards the exit without saying a word. Avery, too, was silent as he followed, an unusually dark shadow beneath him, an air of uncertainty about him, and a faint yet familiar sound of fluttering wings behind him.

Begin.

About the Author

In addition to be being a talented and handsome writer, Jason is a world-class coupon clipper, guy who initiates awkward conversations with you while you wash your hands in public restrooms, and sworn enemy of secret Santas everywhere.

He's also terrible at writing personal bios.

—

First paperback edition November 2020

Cover Artwork & Book Design by Jason A. Plott

ISBN 978-0-578-79189-0 (paperback)
ISBN 978-0-578-79188-3 (ebook)

https://fb.me/vestigialdreams